The *Philadelphia In...*
to watch and savor for...
Coeur says she is "one...
of mainstream c...

MARIAH STEWART
THE CHESAPEAKE DIARIES

"The town and townspeople of St. Dennis, Maryland, come vividly to life under Stewart's skillful hands. The pace is gentle, but the emotions are complex."
—*RT Book Reviews*

"If a book is by Mariah Stewart, it has a subliminal message of 'wonderful' stamped on every page."
—*Reader to Reader Reviews*

"The characters seem like they could be a neighbor or friend or even co-worker, and it is because of that and Mariah Stewart's writing that I keep returning again and again to this series."
—*Heroes and Heartbreakers*

"Every book in this series is a gem."
—*The Best Reviews*

"Captivating and heartwarming."
—*Fresh Fiction*

A DIFFERENT LIGHT
"Warm, compassionate, and fulfilling. Great reading."
—*RT Book Reviews*

"This is an absolutely delicious book to curl up with . . . scrumptious . . . delightful."
—*Philadelphia Inquirer*

PRICELESS

"The very talented Ms. Stewart is rapidly building an enviable reputation for providing readers with outstanding stories and characters that are exciting, distinctive, and highly entertaining."

—*RT Book Reviews* (4½ stars)

"Stewart weaves a powerful romance with suspense for a very compelling read."

—*Under the Covers Reviews*

MOON DANCE

"Enchanting . . . a story filled with surprises!"

—*Philadelphia Inquirer*

"An enjoyable tale . . . packed with emotion."

—*Literary Times*

"Stewart hits a home run out of the ball park . . . a delightful contemporary romance."

—*The Romance Reader*

WONDERFUL YOU

"*Wonderful You* is delightful—romance, laughter, suspense! Totally charming and enchanting."

—*Philadelphia Inquirer*

"Vastly entertaining . . . you can't help but be caught up in all the sorrows, joys, and passion of this unforgettable family."

—*RT Book Reviews*

Pocket Books
An Imprint of Simon & Schuster, Inc.
1230 Avenue of the Americas
New York, NY 10020

First Pocket Books paperback edition July 2015

POCKET and colophon are registered trademarks of Simon & Schuster, Inc.

For information about special discounts for bulk purchases, please contact Simon & Schuster Special Sales at 1-866-506-1949 or business@simonandschuster.com.

The Simon & Schuster Speakers Bureau can bring authors to your live event. For more information or to book an event, contact the Simon & Schuster Speakers Bureau at 1-866-248-3049 or visit our website at www.simonspeakers.com.

Manufactured in the United States of America

10 9 8 7 6 5 4 3 2 1

ISBN 978-1-4767-9257-6
ISBN 978-1-4767-9258-3 (ebook)

DEVLIN'S LIGHT

"A magnificent story of mystery, love, and an enchanting town. Splendid!"

—*Bell, Book and Candle*

"With her special brand of rich emotional content and compelling drama, Mariah Stewart is certain to delight readers everywhere."

—*RT Book Reviews*

CAROLINA MIST

"Ms. Stewart has written a touching and compassionate story of life and love that wrapped around me like a cozy quilt."

—*Old Book Barn Gazette*

"A wonderful, tender novel."

—*Rendezvous*

MOMENTS IN TIME

"Intense and unforgettable . . . a truly engrossing read."

—*RT Book Reviews*

"Cleverly and excellently done—Ms. Stewart is an author to watch."

—*Rendezvous*

MARIAH STEWART

That
Chesapeake
Summer

POCKET BOOKS

New York   London   Toronto   Sydney   New Delhi

For Christina and Patrick

Acknowledgments

~~~~~

THERE are so many people to thank for putting this book together that I hardly know where to begin, and I know I'm leaving out a bunch, but let's start with my editor, Lauren McKenna, who was a total rock star when it came to making this book as good as it could possibly be. She is the absolute best, and I'm so fortunate to be working with her. I can't thank her enough for all the time she spent whipping this manuscript into shape! Thanks also to Elana Cohen for her help smoothing out the bumps during my transition from one publisher to Pocket, and for always being there when I have questions. Thanks to the art department for the eye-catching cover. I love it!

Closer to home, I must thank my team of personal cheerleaders who help keep me going—Jo Ellen Grossman, my BFF since kindergarten (and no, I'm not telling you how many years ago that was!); Helen Egner, who read the first draft of my very first book over twenty years ago and insisted that I keep writing; and Chery Griffin, who shares the trenches and who understands that the difference between a good day and a bad day is a blank page. I'm eternally grateful for your friendship.

I had to be led kicking and screaming to join Facebook, but I've come to realize that it has replaced the office watercooler when it comes to gathering to chat with friends during the day. It's so fun to stop in from time to time to see what's on everyone's mind. We talk about books and families and television shows and all manner of things (and we have occasional book giveaways). I've met some of the nicest people on my FB page! If you'd like to be one of them, join us at Facebook.com/Author Mariah Stewart. And if you'd like to check out my website, go to www.mariahstewart.com.

Last, but never least, I need to send love to my family: Bill, Becca, Katie, Mike, and the most adorable little guys in the world, Cole and Jack. Thanks for being the biggest and best part of my life. You are everything to me.

That
Chesapeake
Summer

Diary~

What a lovely time we had last night at the fund-raiser for the new art center! Since being in a wheelchair does hamper my comings and goings, I so appreciated having the festivities right here in the inn's ballroom. So nice to see so many old friends again! Yes, of course, people have dropped in to see me since my accident, but it's not the same as being at a party, however much I did occasionally have the feeling that there were some who just wanted to see if I had survived that fall down the main stairwell last year. After all, I haven't been seen in public in months, so I guess a bit of speculation is to be expected. Having had a second surgery on that pesky fractured leg has set back my summer plans, but it is what it is, and the doctors assure me that I'll be as good as new once the break heals completely. I've been assured that soon this cast and the past months will be nothing more than a sorry memory. Ha! Fat chance . . .

Speaking of which—things in the past, that is—I've been having the oddest dreams these past few weeks, and I have a strange feeling that something big is about to come our way. The odd thing is, it's good _and_ it's not so good, both positive _and_ negative. There's a swirl of energy that I see, but I can't quite make out where it will land. I sense something that's been hidden for a long time about to resurface, something lost but found, if you follow my drift. And it's going to affect several of us in different ways. That's the confusing aspect—that sense of positive and negative energy converging. I'm not sure how to interpret all this, and not sure how I feel about it, because the overwhelming sense I have is that in the end, it's going to be a good thing for everyone involved.

And all that having been said—I couldn't be more confused. I think it's time to dig the Ouija out of the closet and see if any of my friends on the other side can shed some light on the situation. Surely, Alice, you have something to say!

Grace

Chapter 1

~~~~

JAMIE Valentine lifted the last leggy geranium from the flat that had been sitting in the backyard of her family home for the past four weeks. Her mother, Lainey, had picked up six flats of annuals and had planted almost half of them before suffering the heart attack that took her life on a late-April morning. Jamie had kept the flowers watered and had all intentions of planting them sooner, but things had gotten in the way. Like shock, and grief, and pain. Finishing the job her mother had started seemed to Jamie like she'd accepted that her mother was really gone. Acceptance wasn't part of Jamie's process just yet. She was still in the wishing-it-weren't-so phase of denial. Tending to this task for her mother would go a long way to move past that phase, but the grief was still fresh.

She knelt at the edge of the bed and stabbed the earth with the old trowel she'd found on her mother's potting bench. The handle was bent, some of the red paint worn off, the point perhaps not as sharp as it once was, but it was the one her mother preferred, so it was the one Jamie had selected from the assortment on the bench. She'd planted almost two entire flats before resting back on her heels and draining the bottle of water she'd brought with her. It was closing in on noon, and the sun had been beating down on her back for a good two hours. She wished she'd pulled her hair into a higher ponytail instead of letting it rest on her back, but when she tried to redo it, she ended up with gritty soil on her neck, despite the fact that she'd wiped her hands on her jeans.

"There's some of that chicken salad you like in the fridge." Jamie's aunt's voice called from ten feet away.

"Hey, Aunt Sis. When did you get here? I didn't hear you come up." Jamie looked over her shoulder and found her mother's sister—christened Evelyn but known to all as Sis—sitting on the bottom step of the back porch.

"About five minutes ago. I put some things in the fridge for you." Sis paused. "You should have worn a hat."

"Thanks. You know I love your chicken salad. You did put walnuts and grapes and pineapples . . ."

Sis nodded.

"Bless you. And as for the hat, I didn't remember that it got this hot in May in Caryville."

"Welcome to spring in central Pennsylvania. The weather's unpredictable." Sis stretched her legs out in front of her. "Want some help?"

"No, thanks. I've got this." Jamie resumed planting. "Hope I'm doing this right. I never had much interest in gardening."

Sis got up and walked over to inspect Jamie's work.

She pointed to some flowers Jamie had already planted and said, "The begonias need shade. They're going to fry out here in the direct sun."

Jamie scanned the flower bed. "Which ones are begonias?"

Sis pointed to the row of small pink flowers.

"If they need shade, why did Mom buy them?" Jamie looked up at her aunt.

"She bought those for the planters on the front porch. Planted the same flowers every year in the same urns."

"No one can say Mom wasn't a creature of habit," Jamie murmured.

"The urns belonged to your grandmother, and that's what she planted on the front porch of the house we grew up in. I think Lainey planted them for Mom." Sis smiled. "Nice to carry on the tradition."

Jamie nodded and turned back to the flower bed. "What should I do about the begonias I already planted?"

"Just pull them out and stick them back in the trays that you took them out of."

"Won't that kill them? Damage their roots?"

"They've survived in those trays with only sporadic waterings for the past month. I think they'll be fine for a little while, but I wouldn't wait too long to replant them. They haven't been in the ground that long this morning, and the soil is soft."

"Okay." Jamie tugged gently on the plants that were to be moved and placed them in the flats.

"Nice," Sis said as she returned to the porch step. "Your mother would be proud of you."

The lump that had become part of Jamie's anatomy since the day she'd gotten Sis's frantic call— "Jamie, come home. Your mother . . ."—rose in her throat.

Sis blew her nose quietly. "It was all so sudden. I'd just been over that morning to return that digger." She pointed to the trowel in Jamie's hand. "I'd borrowed it a few days before and pretty much forgot about it."

Jamie prepared herself to patiently listen to her aunt's recitation as if she hadn't heard it at least a dozen times already. She knew that it helped Sis to talk about it, and she didn't mind listening.

"Lainey wanted to set out her annuals in those back flower beds and had about driven herself crazy looking for that little trowel before remembering that I still had it." Sis teared up at the memory. "She called to ask me about it, and I said I'd drive it right over. We sat out back in those old lawn chairs she swore every year she'd get rid of, and we drank iced tea. The mint was just coming into leaf, and she'd put some into the pitcher with the tea bags." She blew her nose again into a tissue. "We had such a warm spring. I said I thought it was too hot to be planting and maybe she should wait until later in the afternoon, when it was cooler and the sun was behind the trees, but you know your mother. She was going to do what she set out to do when she felt like doing it."

Jamie nodded. That pretty much summed up Lainey Valentine.

"I keep thinking maybe if I'd tried harder to convince her to wait, maybe she—"

"Don't, Aunt Sis. Don't blame yourself." Jamie

swallowed hard. "I spoke with her doctor. He assured me that this could have happened at any time. Of course, she never shared with me that she was having problems with her heart."

"Nor with me. I had no idea. I knew she was taking a handful of pills every day, but I figured they were just her vitamins and the usual stuff they start pumping into you when you get into your sixties. You know, cholesterol, blood pressure. She never let on that there was something serious going on."

"So let's just say that she was doing what she loved best until the end, all right?" Jamie smiled gently at her aunt. "I think if she'd been given the choice, that's how she would have wanted to go out."

"Except she wouldn't have chosen to be alone."

"Maybe, maybe not. I've thought about that, about the fact that she was alone at the end. On the one hand, I wish I'd been with her, because she must have been so frightened." Jamie felt her throat tighten and her eyes begin to burn. "On the other hand, I wonder if things hadn't gone just the way she wanted them to."

"You mean to spare you, or me, or anyone else she cared for, from having to watch her pass?" Sis's voice was almost a whisper.

Jamie nodded.

"The thought did cross my mind. Lainey always wanted to shield everyone she cared about from anything unpleasant or painful. Even when we were kids, she tried to protect me from anything that might hurt. She took that whole big-sister thing very seriously. Just as she took her responsibilities as a mother seriously. She never wanted you to have to deal with anything that might upset you."

"That wasn't very realistic," Jamie noted.

"True enough, but that's how she was. You and I both know that your mother always got what she wanted." Sis sighed deeply. "And I think she would have wanted you to stay with me during this time instead of staying alone in this big old house. At the very least, she'd have wanted me to help you get things in order here."

"When I get to the point where I need help—and eventually, I will need help deciding what to do with some of the furniture and other things in the house—I promise you will be the only person I call."

"I had better be."

"You can count on it. Besides, I know there are some things of Mom's that you'd like to have."

"Now, you don't need to be doing everything this trip."

"I know. But I did want to pack up a few things to take back with me, and there are some others that I'll ship home to Princeton. Frankly, I could use a break . . ." Jamie looked around the yard, then back up at the house. "You know, we had a great life here. We really were a happy family. After I grew up, there wasn't much for me in a small town like this one, out in the middle of nowhere. But I always loved coming back, being here. Now . . . I don't know how I feel about being here without Mom. It was always *us*. Now it's only me. Pretty soon I'll run out of things to keep my mind occupied, so it's probably time to get back out there. I don't really know how much time I'll have once I start back on my book tour. My publisher has arranged a lot of TV appearances. They told me to take all the time I need, but I have things pretty well organized here for now, and like I said, I could use a break."

"I understand your needing a little space, and I guess traveling and meeting your readers and fans will be good for you. You know, I sometimes forget you're a big media star these days. Your mom and I especially liked that time you were on *The View* and got into a bit of a tussle with—"

Jamie laughed. "Mom said afterward that she wished she'd taped it so she could watch it again and again."

Sis nodded. "It was one for the books, that's for sure. But listen, honey, why don't you think about staying with me for a few days? Or if you'd rather, I could bunk here with you for a day or two. I hate the thought of you rambling around this old place alone."

Jamie got up and walked over to hug her aunt and place a kiss on her cheek. "I'm fine here alone. Thank you for everything you've already done. I would have been lost without you, Aunt Sis. I wouldn't have known who to contact or where to start. I sure wouldn't have known to call all those people who showed up for Mom's funeral. I didn't recognize even half of them."

"Your mother lived in this town for thirty-six years. She was well known and well loved. I expected a crowd at the church, but I have to admit even I was impressed by the number of people who went to the cemetery in such a storm."

"Mom loved a good storm."

"She sure as heck did." Sis blew her nose again, then cleared her throat. "So if you're sure I can't talk you into having company . . ."

"I'm positive. But thanks again."

"By the way, how's the new book coming along?" Sis stood, preparing to leave.

"About the same."

"That bad, eh?"

Jamie nodded.

"What page are you on?"

"Thirty-two."

"That's not too bad."

"It wouldn't be if they weren't all blank."

"Oh."

"You know, I never believed in writer's block. I always thought you could write through anything. But these past few weeks . . ." She held up her hands. "I got nothing, Aunt Sis."

"Well, no wonder. Off on that book tour, you get a call out of the blue that your mother just keeled over in her backyard while she was gardening. It's been a tough blow. I think about her every day, I miss her every day. I remember the good times we had growing up in that house over on Mercer Street. The fun your uncle George and I had with your parents after they moved here to Caryville. The way she held me up after George died, and the times I held her hand after your dad passed away." Sis glanced back over her shoulder. "This place holds a lot of memories for both of us. I'd hate to see it go, but it may be best in the long run to sell it rather than have it sit empty for too long."

"I've been thinking that, too. That's just one decision on a long list, but certainly the most important. Fortunately, I don't have to make that one immediately, but I know it's not far down the road. I don't get back here that often, and I don't know if it should still be empty come winter."

"You'll know when the time is right," Sis assured her. "In the meantime, you let me know what your plans are, and remember to tell me what I can do to help you. I'd stay for the afternoon and give you a hand with those planters out front, but today's my day to volunteer at the animal shelter." Sis smiled. "I don't want a dog in the house, but I sure do love the time I get to spend with them each week."

"You don't want to be late, then." Still carrying the trowel, Jamie took Sis by the arm and walked her out front to the aged sedan that she'd parked at the curb.

"You probably need to buy some potting soil for those urns," Sis said as she got in the driver's seat. "Cameron's Hardware in town has it on sale this week."

"I'll stop there today. I have a few other errands in town." Jamie closed the car door.

Sis turned on the ignition and rolled down the window. "Let me know if you're going to take any of your china with you, and I'll help you pack up."

"Will do." Jamie stepped back from the car as her aunt pulled away, one arm out the window flapping a wave. Jamie waved back and watched until Sis made a right at the corner.

She stepped onto the sidewalk and took a good

long look at her family home. Three stories, a large American four-square with an addition on the back that served as a library and her father's office. The first floor was of stone, and weathered brown cedar shingles covered the second floor. Crisp white curtains hung in all the windows; the trim was white, including the porch railings, the paint having been refreshed two years ago. On a whim, Lainey had the porch ceiling painted a robin's-egg blue, telling Jamie at the time, "One of your father's favorite old songs was 'Blue Skies.' I think of him every time I open the front door and look out. Even on the stormiest day, your dad has his blue sky."

And as everyone knows, you loved nothing better than a good rousing downpour, best when served up with an ample amount of lightning and really loud booms.

It had rained like a son of a gun the day Lainey was buried. Everyone said it was the worst April rainstorm they could remember.

"I knew you'd have insisted on a banging storm. I'm glad you got your wish, Mom." Jamie had said aloud after returning to the house following the funeral luncheon. She'd stood at the kitchen window and watched the wind-driven rain whip across the backyard. *Come look, Jamie,* she could almost hear her mother calling. *This storm's a doozy!*

"It sure is, Mom." Jamie had turned away from the window and wondered what to do with herself.

In the days and weeks that followed, Jamie discovered there was much to do.

Each room was filled with so many memories,

thirty-six years of her family's life beneath this roof to be gone through, decisions on which furniture and knickknacks to keep, which to be sold or donated, papers to be sorted and saved or shredded. Common sense told her that the job would be massive. It had taken thirty-six years for the family to accumulate a houseful of possessions. It would take time to figure out what to do with it all.

Jamie unlocked the front door and went into the kitchen and poured herself a glass of water. She drank half of it, then wandered into the dining room, where her grandmother's best china filled the built-in cupboard. From there she went into the living room, with its furnishings that Jamie always thought too formal to be welcoming or comfortable. On the coffee table, her mother had loosely stacked a copy of each book Jamie had written: *The Honest Life, The Honest Parent, The Honest Marriage, The Honest Family.* The latest, *The Honest Relationship,* lay atop the wrappings it had come in. Her mother must have received it shortly before her death.

Jamie sat on the edge of the sofa and picked up the first book on the stack and read the dedication: *To my parents, who taught me everything I know about life, and everything I will ever need to know about living it honestly.*

Funny, Jamie thought as she closed the cover and replaced the book on the table, *I never saw my mother read a book. Any book. Even mine.* Lainey had subscribed to and read a dozen monthly magazines and devotedly read the newspaper from front to back first thing every morning, but she never read an entire book that Jamie was aware of. The irony wasn't lost on her that the person who'd inspired the books that had made Jamie a fortune and a talk-show favorite often said her favorite part of the book was the dedication. She always *meant* to read them from cover to cover but admitted that she just hadn't gotten around to it, though she did assure Jamie that she'd read "bits and pieces" of each one. Had Jamie not known her mother so well, she might have been offended. But truth be told, Lainey was always buzzing and couldn't sit still long enough to read a book. She defended her preference for magazines by saying they were her quick fix. She could read an article in less than fifteen minutes before being called away by something else.

Jamie's dad was the reader in the family, and it was from him that Jamie had learned to love books. Beyond the living room was his study. She pushed open the door and leaned against the jamb, picturing him seated at that big oak desk, a lit cigar in the green glass ashtray, papers in piles as he made his way through one legal file or another, writing a brief or an appeal or preparing for a trial. A mug proclaiming *Small-town Lawyer* held an assortment of his pens mixed haphazardly with the mechanical pencils her mother favored. In one corner stood the child's rocking chair Jamie's father bought for her when she was five so she could join him for a little while after dinner each night. There she would read one of her many books, her father glancing at the newspaper before turning his attention to the work he'd brought home. Jamie knew her time was up when he stubbed out his cigar, folded the newspaper, and dropped it on the floor. She'd close her book and go around the desk for a good-night kiss, then leave the room, quietly closing the door behind her.

On the wall, Jamie's law diploma from Dickinson Law School hung next to his, although it hadn't taken her long to realize she was ill suited for the profession. Her first—and last—job as an attorney had been with a firm specializing in divorces, which she had found depressing, frustrating, and dull. She'd feared her father's reaction when she told him that the law wasn't for her—he'd been so pleased when she told him she was applying to law school—but he'd merely grunted and said something along the lines of "I was wondering when you'd figure that out." Jamie had spent the next year writing her first book, inspired by the sorry state of relationships between the parties she'd represented.

Why don't you just tell him—or her—the truth? she had often asked her clients. *Why not say how you really feel, or admit what you did and apologize, or say what you really mean?*

Fortunately for Jamie, that book had started a dialogue on talk shows and in magazines and newspaper articles, and had launched her career.

Her stomach reminded her that she'd had an early breakfast, and that Sis's wonderful homemade chicken salad was waiting for her in the fridge. She closed the office door and went into the kitchen, where she made a sandwich and ate standing near the back window. The view of the garden was a familiar one, and Sis had been right. You couldn't tell which flowers Lainey had planted and which had been placed in the beds that morning by Jamie. Unless you got close enough to see that Jamie's spacing was a bit uneven, and Lainey's plants, having been in the ground a full four weeks longer than Jamie's, looked stronger and happier—not a leggy geranium or verbena in sight. While she'd never claim to have had a green thumb, she was well satisfied with the job she'd done that morning.

But the job, she reminded herself, wasn't finished. There were those begonias to plant in the porch urns out front. She finished her lunch and washed her hands, considered running upstairs for a quick shower, but rejected the idea; she'd already scrubbed her nails to get the soil out. She dabbed at the back of her neck with a wet paper towel to remove the grit, putting off the shower till after planting. She did stop to brush her hair and redo the ponytail, but other than that, Caryville would just have to suck it up and take her as she was.

She slipped into sandals and grabbed the list she'd made over breakfast, her keys, and her bag, then went out through the back door, sneaking one last peek at the garden while she started the car and backed out of the driveway. She decided to hit Cameron's for potting soil first, then the drugstore for a few items, and she'd finish up at the supermarket.

"Food shopping always last" had been one of Lainey's mottos, because "you never knew when you'd spy that yummy new flavor of ice cream you've been dying to try but the store hasn't had in until today."

The Valentine house was four blocks from the small shopping district. There were the usual storefronts—a deli, a flower shop, several restaurants, a coffee shop, and a hardware store that stocked just about anything you would need for your home or garden.

The sign over Cameron's Hardware advertised exactly that: "Every Thing for Your Home and Garden." Jamie parked in the small side lot and went inside. Three checkout counters were set up on the left, and to the right was the hunting and fishing counter, where most of the hunters in the area bought their firearms and ammunition, and the fishermen picked out their rods and lines and lures. Most afternoons, there'd be a gathering of hunters or fishers, depending on the season, who'd come to pass the time and talk about the one that got away—or the one they'd bagged.

Jamie knew from countless trips with her mother that all the gardening supplies were located in the back of the store, mostly on the right. She found the bags of potting soil, which were, as Sis had suspected, specially priced that day. She was looking over the selection of sizes when she heard footsteps pause at the end of the aisle.

"I thought that was you, Jamie." Ben Cameron, founder of the store fifty years ago, approached her with a smile, a smile that faded when he recalled her recent loss. "Real sorry about your mother, Jamie."

"Thank you, Mr. Cameron. We appreciated you and your wife coming to the funeral, and I know that Mom would have, too. You know how she loved her gardens."

The elderly man nodded. "I could always count on Lainey to be the first one in the door come spring. She'd have a list with her as long as your arm. What pots she wanted for which plants, how much potting soil, and if I had any tubers or bulbs in, she'd go through them and see if there was anything she didn't already have. Loved her dahlias. Faithfully dug them up and stored them away every year before the first frost." He paused. "I suppose they're still in the garage over there at the house."

Jamie shrugged. "I don't know. I don't know what they look like."

"Be a box with some dirt and some hard tubers wrapped in newspapers. Yup, she really prized her dahlias."

"I'll look for them. Thanks."

"You won't be planting them for a while. At least until after the last frost."

"When's that?"

"Depends on who you ask, but we look to around Mother's Day. Just to be on the safe side. I know Lainey always waited till mid-May to bring them back out."

"I'll make a note of that. Thanks, Mr. Cameron."

"Sure thing, honey. Now, were you looking for anything in particular today? I see you eyeing up those bags of potting soil."

Jamie nodded. "I need to plant something in a couple of urns my mother had, but I don't know what to buy or how much."

"Those front-porch urns on either side of the door? The ones she planted begonias in every year?"

Jamie smiled. She'd almost forgotten what small towns were like. Of course he knew the house, the urns, where they were placed on the porch, and what Lainey planted in them. "Those would be the ones."

Mr. Cameron reached past her—"'Scuse me"—and grabbed a bag off the shelf. "This is what she bought."

"Great. Thank you." Jamie held her hands out for the bag.

"I'll just carry this up front for you, and you can check out when you're ready."

"I think I'm ready now."

"Right this way, then."

Jamie was greeted by the cashier with more condolences and paid for the bag of soil. Over her protests, Mr. Cameron insisted on carrying her purchase to her car.

"I thought Mom said you retired," Jamie said as he placed the bag in the trunk of her car.

"Not exactly. Turned the business over to my son—Ben Junior, I think he was in your class back in grade school—and he lets me come in and play shopkeeper when the spirit moves me." He slammed the trunk lid. "Glad I was here when you stopped by, Jamie. Like I said, your mom was a friend and one of our favorite customers. She will be missed."

"That's so sweet of you, Mr. Cameron. Thank you for saying that."

He nodded his white-haired head and walked her to her car door. "Don't be a stranger, now. Stop in from time to time."

"Will do that. Tell Ben I said hi."

He nodded again and waved before heading back into the store.

Her next planned stop was at the pharmacy, but she took her time driving the two blocks. Seeing her mother through an old friend's eyes had opened up the wound that was barely starting to heal. She hoped to get in and out of the drugstore without seeing anyone she knew.

Cunningham's Pharmacy had been a mainstay of the town for over a hundred years. It had managed to outlast the chain store in the strip mall outside of town by reason of its loyal customers. Tall, lanky Mr. Cunningham knew everyone in town, the names of their kids, who suffered with what chronic disease, and who was having problems at home. He knew which shade of lipstick would be the first to sell out over at the cosmetic counter, which of the ladies in town dyed their hair, and which brand and color they preferred. He'd played poker with Jamie's dad every other Wednesday night from the year the Valentines moved to Caryville until Herb's death. He had served as one of her father's pallbearers and, four weeks ago, had done the same for her mother. Jamie wasn't sure she could handle an encounter with him on the heels of her chat with Mr. Cameron.

But she needn't have worried. Her parents' old friend was in semi-retirement and now worked only three days a week. Had she known this? She wasn't sure. She'd spoken with him at length at her mother's funeral luncheon, but the whole experience had been so surreal that she barely recalled the conversation. She found the items she needed and paid for them at the front register. She placed her purchases in the car and walked two doors down to what passed for a supermarket in Caryville.

She had a list, and she stuck to it and considered herself fortunate to make it in and out with just a few encounters with well-meaning friends of her mothers, some she'd first met at the funeral—fortunate because not knowing them meant she had no personal memories of them with her mother, so there were no shared experiences to recall.

Returning to the house, she unloaded the car, put away her groceries, and proceeded to plant the begonias before she forgot about them. In this, she couldn't bear to let her mother down.

By the time she'd finished planting and stepped back to admire her work—the urns *did* look pretty damned good—she was past being ready for a shower, some dinner, and one more night of her first round of cleaning out the house. She'd tried to spend a day or two in each room and had already gone through the guest room, the living room, and the dining room, trying to decide what to keep and what to part with when the time came, though she hadn't decided when that time might be.

Tonight her father's study was on the schedule. From a quick glance, she knew the filing cabinets were filled with items like old bank statements and tax returns that would need to be shredded but would not require a lot of emotional investment. After the day she'd had—planting the last of her mother's garden and following in Lainey's footsteps around Caryville—mindlessly shredding paper and giving her poor heart a temporary respite was just what she needed. She could watch a movie on her iPad while she worked, and that, too, would distract her from the reality of the finality of her task.

It promised to be a good night.

Chapter 2

———

IN addition to the delicious chicken salad Sis had left for her, Jamie found a bowl of spaghetti and meatballs—long a comfort-food favorite—and a meat loaf wrapped in foil. She called Sis to say thanks while she heated the spaghetti, her mouth watering at the thought of her aunt's tomato sauce. Sis and Lainey had a firm date to make sauce together on the Sunday of Labor Day weekend, and they'd never missed a year. Jamie sat at the kitchen table and savored every bite as she watched the evening news on the wall-mounted TV that Lainey had sworn she could not live without.

After dinner, Jamie went into her father's study and turned on the overhead light and the desk lamp and promptly forgot about her plan to spend the night shredding. Her attention was drawn to the bookshelves, and almost without thinking, she began to sort through them. Those volumes that had been treasured by her as a child went into one box. Her father's favorite detective novels went into another. Those she would ship to herself before she left Caryville. The remaining books would be donated to the local library. Other items—her father's collection of bronze bookends, the photographs, the ashtray shaped and painted like a turtle's shell that she'd made for him one year at summer camp—would go home with her.

She groaned aloud when she opened the drawers of the five filing cabinets and found they were stuffed with endless folders of canceled checks, bank statements, paid bills, and tax returns. The task was more involved than she'd assumed. She closed the open drawers, turned off the shredder, and turned her attention to her father's desk, which she'd planned on saving for last, but surely it would take less time than the filing cabinets. She could do them tomorrow.

In the years since his death, Lainey had used the desk for writing checks and letters. Jamie found the shiny white pen with "Lainey" written in script; she'd given it to her mother for her birthday a few years ago. She set it aside to take with her when she left. On the corner of the desk stood a green vase holding a handful of dried hydrangeas next to a stack of unpaid bills and Lainey's checkbook.

Clearly, Lainey had moved into the space, though she'd kept her husband's personal items intact. His favorite pen and the money clip shaped like a feather, both gold and bearing his initials, were in the top drawer, along with a pile of paper clips, some rubber bands, and a box of staples. Several sheets of stamps and a stack of note cards, a worn leather address book, and lead refills for her mother's mechanical pencils were in the second drawer.

The next drawer held her mother's stationery, some envelopes, some postage stamps, and a fat file containing warranties for appliances that had long since been replaced. Jamie dumped the contents of the drawer into the recycling bin after confirming that none contained identifying information.

The bottom drawer was a file drawer. Jamie's eyes filled with tears when she found that each folder held mementoes from each of her school years, from her first attempts to make *J*s in kindergarten to several papers she'd written in high school that had earned her *A*s. There were school pictures from first grade (*I remember that dress! I LOVED that dress! Drove Mom nuts that I wanted to wear it every single day*) to fifth grade (*Oh my God, Mom, who thought it was a good idea for you to cut my bangs?*) through senior year (*I can't believe I dressed like that. Did I really think that was cool?*). There were photos and programs from dance recitals alongside prom pictures, dried flowers, and birthday cards. She was pretty sure she could have accurately dated each year by the style of her hair, from its untamed state in grade school to the sleek ponytails of her senior year. And there was a folder containing her old artwork. Inside were her early drawings of houses and people, most notably of Rosalia, her imaginary friend, who had aged along with Jamie. The drawings stopped when Jamie was ten or so, but until then, every time Jamie had a school photo taken, she'd drawn a picture of Rosalia wearing the same clothes.

She put the drawings back in the folder and left it on the desktop. She wanted to ship her school records to her house. She had no idea what she'd do with them once they arrived, but it somehow seemed sacrilegious to dump them here, after her mother had taken such pains to preserve every moment of her childhood.

She pushed the drawer, but it stopped midway and refused to close. Jamie leaned over to try to force it, but it was stuck. "Must be off the track," she murmured as she pulled the drawer out halfway, then tried once more to close it. The drawer remained stuck.

She leaned closer and saw a file wedged into the very back of the drawer. She stuck her hand inside and removed it. The date written on the file was October 12, 1979. Her birthday. Jamie smiled and opened the folder.

Inside was an envelope addressed to her parents, Mr. and Mrs. Herbert James Valentine. The return address was a law firm in St. Dennis, Maryland.

Curious, Jamie peered into the envelope and saw that it contained several sheets of paper. She pulled them out and began to read.

For a long moment, she could not breathe.

She read and reread the first page, but no matter how many times she saw the words, they bounced around inside her brain, a jumble that refused to make sense. She lowered herself onto the chair, her heart pounding in her chest, her mind buzzing wildly.

"There must be some mistake." Jamie shook her head as if to clear it. "This can't be true. It can't be real."

Dated January 28, 1980, the letter read:

Dear Mr. and Mrs. Valentine:

Our sincerest congratulations on the adoption of your baby girl!

Please be advised that all legal issues have been resolved as per our discussion. The birth mother, who wishes to remain anonymous, has signed the final agreement and requested the adoption records to be sealed. Please note that she has legally relinquished any and all rights she may have to the child. Rest assured there will be no change of mind or heart. The enclosed birth certificate has been duly revised as per our conversation of November 1, 1979.

A copy of the social worker's report and recommendations are also enclosed. You will receive a copy of the appropriate court documents directly from the law offices of Scott C. Parsons, Esquire, who represented your interests in the Lehigh County Court of Common Pleas.

Please do not hesitate to contact me or my staff if you have any further questions or require additional services in the future. On a personal note, I wish you and your daughter all the very best.

Very truly yours,
Curtis
CURTIS L. ENRIGHT, ESQUIRE

Mr. and Mrs. Valentine were crossed out and *Herb and Elaine* written in pen. Below his name, the lawyer had handwritten, *Delighted to have assisted you in this happy matter! Herb, I'm looking forward to seeing you at the next reunion. ~C.*

Jamie had no idea how long she sat and stared at the letter in her hand.

Had her parents adopted a child who died? Surely her parents would have told her if she'd had a sister who died. And wouldn't there have been photographs?

But if not a sibling, then who?

She tried to convince herself that the baby girl referred to in the letter could be anyone but her.

Hadn't she'd seen pictures of her happy parents standing outside the hospital where she was born? She'd been wrapped in a pink and white blanket, wearing a tiny pink bonnet edged in white eyelet, and cradled in the arms of her beaming mother. She'd seen one of the photos just two days ago, when she removed it from her mother's dresser and wrapped it carefully in tissue and tucked it into the box of photos and albums that even now sat on the dining room table, waiting to be mailed to her home.

She removed the other documents in the envelope and almost wished she hadn't. The birth certificate that bore the name of Jamie Louisa Valentine was dated October 12, 1979. There was the social worker's report, assuring the state that the Valentines more than met the criteria for adoptive parents—had exceeded them, actually, on every count. It was her recommendation that the adoption of the baby girl born on October 12, 1979, be finalized at the earliest possible time.

All the air went out of the room, and for what

seemed like an eternity, Jamie sat frozen on the edge of the chair. Then she rose, grabbed the file, and went into the kitchen, where she snatched her bag from the table. She removed the key from the hook near the back door and walked on legs she could not feel to the car parked in the driveway. Jamie jammed the key into the ignition and backed the car onto the street.

She drove in a daze to the bungalow three blocks away and parked at the end of the driveway. She forced herself to walk, rather than run, to the front door and opened it, entering the home without knocking, something she had never done before.

"Who . . . ? Oh, Jamie. I was just about to call you to see if you'd like to . . ." Sis stood in the hall outside the kitchen doorway. She paused, studying her niece's demeanor. "Sweetie, are you all right? You look so pale. Come in and—"

"You knew, didn't you?" Jamie thrust the file at Sis. "All this time you knew, and you never told me."

A long stream of air escaped Sis's lungs, as if she'd been holding a breath for the past thirty-six years and was grateful to let it out. It seemed like forever before she found her voice.

"It wasn't my place to tell you." Sis's eyes brimmed with tears. "I told Lainey and told her: 'You have to let Jamie know.' The last time we had that conversation was a week before she passed. I'd yelled at her when she admitted you still didn't know and she promised she'd tell you when you and she went to Rehoboth next month."

"Yeah, well, that's not going to happen," Jamie snapped. "Why didn't they tell me?"

"She and Herb had agreed they'd tell you when you were six. But that was the year my mother passed away, remember? Lainey said she just couldn't deal with anything else then."

"That was thirty years ago," Jamie reminded her. "Surely at some point during those thirty years she could have 'dealt' with it."

"She certainly should have. But she and Herb . . ." Sis shook her head and walked into the living room and lowered herself into a wing chair near the front window. "There was always an excuse. You were going to camp that summer, and they didn't want you to think they were sending you away because they'd changed their mind and didn't want you anymore. When you changed schools, the excuse was that you were having a hard enough time making the transition without adding to your stress."

Sis motioned to the chair opposite hers and Jamie sat. "Lainey was so afraid you'd be upset, that you'd run away and look for your birth mother. She loved you with all her heart and soul. Herb did, too, but he didn't have the same fears that Lainey had. He was against keeping it from you, several times threatened to tell you himself." Sis's voice lowered. "I think Lainey couldn't bear the thought that you'd reject her as your mother."

"That's crazy." Jamie dismissed the idea.

"Is it?" Sis reached out and touched Jamie's knee. "For a woman who'd longed for a baby, who'd had miscarriage after miscarriage after miscarriage, to finally have the child she'd so desperately wanted— whether she'd given birth to that child or not—can you try to understand the devastation she felt at the thought of losing you?"

"She never would have lost me. She was the best mother in the world. I was so lucky to have her. I loved her and my dad more than anything."

"And they both adored you. Imagine how she'd have felt to lose that love."

"But she wouldn't have."

"She never got over that fear."

"I had no idea she was so insecure. She was always such a *force*."

"Underneath it all, Lainey was always a little insecure."

Jamie leaned forward, her head in her hands. "I don't know what to think about all this."

"Try not to judge them too harshly. They both wanted what was best for you, always. Yes, they should have told you, unquestionably, and yes, there'd been ample time to do that. But after your dad died, it became harder and harder for your mother to even talk about the fact that you were adopted." Sis sighed heavily. "Frankly, I think she wanted so badly to believe she *was* your mother—your only mother— that she was beginning to believe it herself."

"She was—*is*—my only mother." Fat hot tears rolled down Jamie's cheeks. "I wish I'd had the opportunity to tell her. I wish she'd have given me the chance. I wish she'd have trusted me that much."

Sis gently took Jamie's hands. "I do, too, sweetheart. And I'm so sorry you had to find out this way."

"Aunt Sis, if I hadn't found the file . . . if I hadn't

read the letter from the attorney . . . would you have told me?"

"I don't know. I've been wrestling with this since the day your mother died. Should I tell you? Did I have the right to tell you?" Sis shrugged. "Would you have believed me if I had?"

"You wouldn't have made up something like that." Jamie softened. "It's such a hard thing to get my mind around. There'd never been a hint, you know? Not one thing. I never suspected . . ."

"I'm so sorry, sweetie. I'm sorry your parents didn't tell you when your dad was alive, and I'm sorry that I didn't push my sister harder to tell you. And God knows I'm sorry you found out the way you did."

"Did they know her . . . my birth mother?" Jamie asked.

Sis shook her head. "The lawyer—the one who wrote that letter—he arranged everything. He and your dad went to law school together and were friends up until your father's death. They got together every year at their law school reunion. Herb told his friend how the doctors had cautioned Lainey against getting pregnant again—she'd had so many miscarriages, I think there'd been three or four—and they were thinking about adopting a child. Some months later—gosh, it must have been at least a year later—this attorney called Herb and asked if he and Lainey were still interested in adopting. They'd already gone through home studies with the agency they were working with . . ."

"He knew someone," Jamie said softly. "Dad's

friend knew someone who was having a baby she didn't want."

"I'm not so sure it was a matter of not wanting . . ." Sis paused.

Jamie's head shot up. "It's okay. You can say it. A lot of babies are unwanted. At least she—my birth mother—didn't abort me or leave me in the ladies' room at some turnpike rest stop."

"I think it was a matter of the girl being very young—your mother said the lawyer told them she was only sixteen—and having come from a family that was unsympathetic to her situation."

"You mean her parents forced her to give me away?"

"That's the impression I got from Lainey. After the attorney called Herb, he and your mother talked about it for all of about ten minutes before they made a beeline to Maryland to talk it over with the lawyer. From everything Lainey told me, it all went very smoothly."

"So just like that . . ." Jamie snapped her fingers.

"Just like that." Sis nodded. "The attorney had it all worked out before your parents even arrived at the hospital after you were born."

"Did they meet her?"

"No, no. No one wanted that, not your parents, not the girl or her family. No, the attorney was there, and the social worker, and your parents. You were turned over to your parents, and they left the hospital with you." Sis smiled. "I know you've seen the photographs a million times of the three of you the day they brought you home."

Jamie nodded. "At least a million times. Mom always said that was the happiest day of their lives."

"Oh, it was." Sis hesitated, then said, "You know they brought you here, right?"

"Here? What here?" Jamie frowned.

"They were living outside of Pittsburgh when they got that first call telling them there would be a baby. Once things got under way, they decided to buy a house here, move to Caryville, so they could raise you where there was family."

"And where no one would know that I was adopted?" Jamie asked. "Where no one would know she hadn't been pregnant?"

"I do think that played in to her decision, I'm not going to lie, Jamie. But she also wanted to be near me and our mother. We were all Lainey had, you know, and it was important to her—and to your father— that you grow up among family."

"I always wondered why my dad left that big-city firm to become a small-town lawyer, as he liked to describe himself. I always thought he sounded a little wistful."

"There may have been a touch of that. Your dad was a partner in a large, prominent firm out there. I'm sure more than one person wondered why he'd give up the one for the other."

"Was he happy with that choice?" Jamie asked. "Do you think he regretted it?"

"Not for a minute. He loved his life—his family and his work. He wouldn't have changed a thing. Herb was very happy with his choices and with his life. He never looked back."

Jamie nodded, then rose to leave.

"Stay. Please." Sis stood and took Jamie's hand. "You really shouldn't go back to the house now."

"I appreciate your concern, I really do, and I know that this has been hard on you, too. I'm sorry that you've been left to deal with it. But I need to be alone for a while and process this. I don't even know how I feel. I was so angry when I realized what those papers meant. I'm still angry." Jamie held up a hand as if to ward off any protests her aunt was about to launch. "Yes, I understand everything you told me. I understand how depressed my mother must have been after so many miscarriages. I can even understand her wanting to believe that I wasn't adopted, that I'd been hers all along. But what I don't understand is how she could have let me believe a lie my entire life. It's all such a shock. Something inside me doesn't want to believe it. But I have to make peace with the truth, and I have to do that without her, without my dad. This would have been a lot easier if I'd heard this from them when I was younger."

"I'm sure that's true." Sis followed Jamie to the front door. "But you know that your mother could be . . . well, I suppose 'self-centered' might serve as well as any other word. This wasn't about you and how you felt, honey. For Lainey, it was about her and how *she* felt. I'm sorry, but that's as much truth as anything else."

"Truth," Jamie repeated. "Mom always told me that the truth was what mattered. That even if it was hard, you always had to tell the truth. I guess this was a case of 'Do as I say, not as I do.'" Jamie opened the front door and took a step out onto the porch, and Sis followed. "Ironic, isn't it, that I've built my career based on *truth*—truth at any cost—and it turns out that my whole life has been a lie." Halfway to the car, she turned and asked, "Did she ever look for me? My birth mother? Did she ever contact them?"

Sis shook her head. "I don't know. Lainey never told me if she had."

Jamie acknowledged the response with a nod. She followed the walkway to the car and got in. She wanted to sit there for a while and try to think it all through, but she knew her aunt would be worried if she sat for too much longer. She started the engine, turned around in the driveway, and waved to Sis as she drove off.

She returned to the house she'd grown up in and studied it as if she'd never seen it before. "House of secrets," she whispered. "House of lies."

She unlocked the back door and went inside. She tossed her bag on the kitchen table and went into the front hall. "Okay, you two. I know," she said aloud to the empty house. "I know now. So we don't have to pretend anymore, all right?"

Her hands on her hips, she tried to call up her parents. "You should have told me, okay? It might have hurt—it would have hurt like hell—but at least I'd have been able to talk to you about it. This way— your way—you left me with so many questions I'll never get to ask and you'll never be able to answer. What am I supposed to do?"

She started up the stairs to the second floor, still talking. "You were right to want to tell me, Dad. I wish you'd just gone ahead and done it. And Mom, you didn't do me a favor by not telling me. You might have protected yourself, but you did me a terrible disservice."

In her parents' bedroom, she sat on the side of the bed. "Did you know anything about her, this girl who gave birth to me? What about her family medical history? Did you wonder how she felt about giving away her baby?"

Jamie waited in the quiet room, her head tilted, almost as if expecting a voice from beyond that would reassure her and answer all her questions. But after a moment she rose and went into her room across the hall. She sat at her old desk and opened her laptop, turned it on, went to her favorite search engine, and began to type:

Curtis L. Enright, Attorney-at-Law, St. Dennis, Maryland.

Chapter 3

JAMIE sat up half the night making a written list of all the reasons she should not place the call, a list she tore up and tossed into the trash over coffee in the morning. Even as she touched the keypad on her phone, she was questioning the wisdom of ignoring her own good advice to sleep on it a few more days.

"Enright and Enright. How may I help you?"

"I was . . . ah . . . wondering if I might speak with Mr. Enright." Jamie forced the words. "Mr. Curtis Enright."

There was a pause before the woman responded. "I'm sorry, but Curtis Enright is retired. Would you care to speak with either Jesse Enright or Sophia Enright?"

"Ah . . . no. No, thank you. I was hoping . . ." Jamie bit her bottom lip. Just what *had* she been hoping?

"May I ask what this is in reference to?" the woman on the other end of the line asked gently.

"I was hoping to . . . to touch base with him. He

was a friend of my father's—he went to law school with my dad—and I just thought . . ." Jamie heard her own voice begin to fade away. She should have thought this out more clearly before making the call.

"Oh?"

"Yes, and my mother passed away recently, and I thought perhaps he'd like to know that." There. That sounded reasonable enough.

"And your father was . . . ?"

"Herb Valentine."

Another pause, almost imperceptible. "Oh, of course. I recognize the name. Your father passed some time ago, if I recall correctly?"

"Yes, it's been almost ten years."

"Why not leave your number, and I'll contact Mr. Enright and give him the message. He may wish to personally offer his condolences."

Jamie repeated the number of her cell twice.

"I'll be sure to pass this along as soon as I speak with him," the woman assured her. "In the meantime, please accept the firm's sympathy."

"Thank you, and—"

The call disconnected before she could finish her thought.

Jamie wondered when or if Curtis Enright would return her call, and if he did, what exactly would she say to him? She figured she had plenty of time to think of something while she packed up kitchen items to be donated to a thrift shop that supported a local shelter for battered women. She had just finished wrapping a shelf full of unmatched glasses when her phone rang. Expecting Sis to be calling right about then to check on her state of mind, Jamie tucked the phone under her chin and reached for paper to wrap around a blender she'd found in a bottom cupboard. "Hello?"

"This is Curtis Enright." The man sounded old and just a little gruff. "I was returning a call from Jamie Valentine."

"Oh. Mr. Enright. This is Jamie Valentine." She set the blender on the table. "Thank you for returning my call."

"Do I understand correctly that your mother recently passed away?"

"Yes. Four weeks ago." Her heart began to pound.

"I'm sorry to hear that." His tone softened. "I was fond of Lainey. She was a lovely woman."

"Yes, she was. Thank you." Jamie paused, wondering how to keep the conversation going long enough to find an opening to ask the questions that were on the tip of her tongue and fighting to tumble out.

"Had she been ill?"

"No. It was very sudden, very unexpected. She had a heart attack."

"May I offer my condolences? I knew your father for many years. He was a good man."

"Yes, thank you. He was. And I was aware of your friendship, Mr. Enright. I called because I thought perhaps you'd like to know . . ."

"Thank you. I appreciate your thoughtfulness."

Jamie took a deep breath before adding: ". . . and because I found a letter that you'd written to them."

"A letter? From me?"

"A letter you wrote many years ago. Thirty-six years ago, actually."

The silence that followed was so long and so complete, Jamie thought he'd hung up.

Finally, he said, "Ah, so that's what this is really about."

"Yes, sir."

Another silence.

"There's nothing I can tell you that your parents haven't already."

"That's the thing, Mr. Enright. My parents never told me anything."

"Excuse me?"

"I said, they never told me anything."

And yet another silence.

"Mr. Enright?" Jamie wondered if the man was still on the line.

"Yes, yes. I'm here. I just . . ." He cleared his throat. "I'm . . . well, surprised, certainly. Beyond that, I hardly know what to say."

"Neither did my aunt when I showed her the letter you sent them after my adoption was finalized."

"Jamie, I'm very sorry, I truly am, but if you're calling to ask me any questions about your birth parents . . ."

"Actually, yes, I was."

"Then I'm afraid you're going to be disappointed. I have an obligation of confidentiality to my client not to reveal the details of your birth, and I am bound by that."

"Your client being my birth mother?"

"That's correct."

"I respect your position, Mr. Enright. But surely you can understand that there is certain information I should be privy to. Medical history, for example."

"I do understand your concern, but I'm sorry. There is nothing I can tell you."

"So I have no way of knowing if I carry the gene for heart disease or cancer or—"

"Well, I suppose it wouldn't hurt for me to tell you that I know of no such illnesses in the family. And I believe that in Pennsylvania, the law does permit adopted persons access to their medical history as long as any confidential information is redacted, so you could find out that sort of information on your own."

"So you did know her family? My birth mother . . ."

Curtis Enright sighed heavily.

"Yes. I know the family. And I know her. St. Dennis is a very small town, Miss Valentine." The switch from the more familiar Jamie wasn't lost on her. Nor was the fact that he used the present tense rather than the past. *I know her.*

"Your letter mentioned an attorney named Parsons . . ."

"Scott, yes."

"May I ask who he is and what his involvement was?" she pressed.

"Scott Parsons was the attorney who handled the paperwork at the local level."

"I don't understand."

"The adoption was finalized in Pennsylvania. I'm not a member of the bar in that state."

"So he was the attorney who actually handled the legal proceedings."

"Yes."

"Was he also a friend of my father's from law school?"

"Yes, he was."

"Was?"

"Scott passed away about eight years ago."

Jamie made a mental note to see if the firm was still in existence. "The birth certificate said Lehigh County," she said.

"Correct."

"So this was a private adoption?"

"Yes."

"I'm not sure I understand what your involvement was, Mr. Enright."

"I've represented the birth mother's family on many occasions over the years. This was one of them. As much as I'd like to help you, I'm afraid I can't give you any information other than that which we've already discussed, and all of that is public record except for the fact that I facilitated the adoption. I knew the expectant mother, I knew your parents wanted to adopt an infant, both Herb and I knew Scott. It was a matter of putting the pieces together."

"I understand the position I've put you in, Mr. Enright, and I apologize, but please try to understand my shock at learning that I am not Herb and Lainey's natural child. When I discovered that letter last night—"

"You just found out *yesterday*?"

"Yes." Unwanted tears formed in the corners of

her eyes, and her voice tightened. "My aunt said that my father wanted to tell me long ago, but my mother always had a reason why the time wasn't right. I was very close to my parents, Mr. Enright, so I'm sure you can appreciate how devastating this news has been."

"Please don't think I'm not sympathetic to your situation, but I can't give you what you're looking for." His voice dropped slightly, and his sincerity was evident. "I truly am sorry."

"If I could just ask you one more question . . ."

"I'll answer if I can."

"Has my birth mother ever expressed any interest in finding me? Has she ever asked about me?"

"Actually, Miss Valentine, she's never in all these years mentioned you at all."

"And my birth father?"

"I know nothing about him. He wasn't involved in any way."

"Thank you for your time, Mr. Enright."

"I'm sorry I wasn't able to be of any more assistance," he said. "Thank you for letting me know about your mother's passing. Again, you have my condolences."

Jamie held on to the phone long after the connection had been broken, trying to process the information. Finally, she hit "end" and put the phone down on the table in front of her. What had she learned from her conversation with Curtis Enright? Other than the fact that he was a man who valued his commitments.

I know the family. And I know her.

Not *I knew her* but *I know her*. To Jamie's mind, that suggested that she was most likely in or around St. Dennis.

Actually, Miss Valentine, she's never in all these years mentioned you at all.

Not *I wouldn't know* but *she's never in all these years mentioned you at all*. Didn't that seem to imply that Curtis Enright had seen her and spoken with her, though never about the baby she'd given up? Again, the woman was likely to live in close proximity to St. Dennis.

And she'd learned that her birth father was unknown even to the man who helped to arrange her adoption.

Jamie tapped her pen on the notebook. To her mind, the chances that her birth mother was alive and living in St. Dennis seemed pretty good.

Jamie couldn't help but think about the sixteen-year-old girl who'd given birth to her, the girl who'd had choices made for her that she may or may not have made for herself. Choices that changed the course of both their lives forever. *Did she ever think of me, worry about what kind of home I was raised in, what my parents were like? Did she wonder about what kind of life I had and whether or not I was alive? Healthy? Happy? Where I live or who I am? What kind of person I grew up to be?*

Jamie couldn't help think the fact that she'd never mentioned her baby to her parents' lawyer—the same lawyer who had facilitated the adoption—didn't necessarily mean that she never thought about her lost child.

And what kind of life did she have? What kind of person did she grow up to be? Was she happy? Did she marry? Have other children? The thought that Jamie might have siblings somewhere out there in the world—even half siblings—stopped her in her tracks. If so, did they know about her, or was she someone's deepest, darkest secret?

Jamie knew in her heart that she'd ended up where and who she was supposed to be: Herb and Lainey Valentine's daughter. The shock of the truth had caused deep anger, but her love for her parents trumped every other emotion. She might still be angry at having the truth withheld from her for so long, and she'd always wish she'd had a chance to discuss it with her parents, but she never doubted their love for her or her for them. Nothing could ever change that. No one would ever take their places. But the truth had opened a tiny hole inside her, and as much as she loved Lainey, she could not ignore that there was a piece of her that was unknown, a piece of herself missing from her life. The decision to find that missing piece was easy after that.

THE EVENING AIR had the sweet smell of late spring easing into early summer. Jamie sat on the back porch, her iPad in her hand. She'd found sites on the Internet where birth parents searching for their lost children could go to reconnect, sites where adoptees such as herself could go to search for their birth parents. She'd checked out several as she scrolled from page to page. This was a whole new world to her, so much to learn. She wanted to proceed one step at a time, because she knew that starting on this journey, she would follow through to the end, wherever that might lead her, even if the end were to be a dead one.

She was born in Pennsylvania, that much she knew. Was Pennsylvania a state that permitted access to adoption records? Hadn't Curtis Enright mentioned that her records had been sealed? She knew from online conversations she'd been reading that the laws in several states had changed, in some cases opening all previously closed records. Had the law in Pennsylvania been modified since her birth thirty-six years ago?

Though Jamie had graduated from law school, she knew nothing about the adoption laws in her home state, so she had to do an online search of the commonwealth's statutes. She was more than a little disappointed to learn that the law, while under discussion, had remained the same: Her records were still sealed. They could be accessed only if her birth parents had signed a form consenting to the release of identifying information. Had such a consent form been signed by either or both of her birth parents? If that were the case, would Curtis Enright have told her?

She visited a few more sites before turning off the device. Unless she was prepared for the consequences, she dared not proceed beyond clicking on the link that led to the Orphans' Court Division of the Lehigh County Court of Common Pleas and its adoption registry.

Adoption records are sealed by statute, and the

contents thereof cannot be released without a court order.

Let it be, she could imagine her mother saying. Like the song. Just let it be. But unlike the song, there would be no answers unless Jamie pursued them.

Even if she could somehow unseal her records and locate the woman who had given birth to her, there was no reason to think she'd want to see Jamie. She had read enough of the Pennsylvania statute to know that sealed records could be available only if the birth parent consented, but there was no guarantee that this unknown woman would agree. Jamie wasn't sure she could handle further rejection on the heels of discovering that her parents had kept this secret all her life.

She's never in all these years mentioned you at all.

Had this woman tried to forget Jamie's very existence? Had she blocked out the fact that she once gave birth to a daughter and handed over that baby to strangers to raise as their own?

And should Jamie somehow manage to learn her identity, what next? Should she try to find the woman? How would she react if Jamie contacted her? Would she welcome her long-lost daughter with tears and open arms, or would she accuse Jamie of trying to ruin her life? Certainly there was much more to consider than what Jamie wanted.

Then there was the matter of her birth father. Curtis Enright had said he wasn't involved in the proceedings, but what did that really mean? Had he died? Deserted her mother when he found out she was pregnant? Maybe her birth father hadn't known about her. Aunt Sis had said that her birth mother was very young and that her parents had arranged everything. Curtis may have confided those details to Jamie's parents, and Jamie's mother must have passed the information on to Aunt Sis.

Darkness crept around her while she was staring at her feet, deliberating her options. Nothing could—nothing *should*—be decided on a whim. While she knew this was a matter she wanted to pursue to find that missing piece of herself, she had to proceed cautiously for the sake of the woman whose identity she sought. If her birth mother had put the matter of Jamie's birth behind her, as the attorney intimated, what right did Jamie have to remind her?

Even if she chose to pursue the truth, she still had obligations in Caryville. After much soul-searching, she came to two realizations: She would sell the family home once she'd finished with the task of sorting through it and cleaning it out. The second thing she realized was that the matter of sorting could not be done in one visit; nor did it have to be completed immediately. It had taken her family many years to accumulate the contents: It wasn't practical or logical that she could make so many decisions in this one visit. But holding on to an older home indefinitely wasn't practical, either, especially one so far from her own home in Princeton. There were the issues of maintenance through the seasons—lawn and garden care in the spring, summer, and fall, snow removal in the winter. Someone would have to check on a regular basis for water leaks, roof damage, vandalism, and break-ins, and after speaking with her parents' homeowners' insurance company, she learned that, after a year of vacancy, the only insurance coverage would be for fire damage. That pretty much sealed the deal. Then, too, was the matter of keeping the house heated in the winter and all the utilities turned on.

Unless she planned to live there or rent out the house—which she would never do—it would be best to make a plan to sell while she had time to make the right decisions.

It seemed that everything she touched had a dear memory attached, from the furniture that had been passed down from family members to the Christmas ornaments she found in boxes in the attic to the little gifts Jamie had bought for her mother over the years. The inexpensive ceramic baby animals Jamie had loved had been treated by her mother with as much care as the Lladró figurines of dancing ladies in their flowing dresses purchased by Jamie's father.

"Mom, you can put away those little baby lambs and fawns and puppies," Jamie once said. "I know they're not fine china."

"Bite your tongue." Her mother had grinned. "My baby girl bought those for me with money she saved from her allowance. I cherish every one."

Jamie's throat constricted at the memory.

The new plan was to tag all the furniture—yellow tags for the eventual estate sale, blue tags for the pieces that would go into storage until she was ready to take them, green for the pieces that Sis had expressed an interest in. Next up: Box household items that neither she nor Sis wanted or needed, some things to be sold, others with more sentimental value to be shipped to her home. She'd been surprised to find that so much of her father's clothing had remained in the house, as if her mother had been preparing for the possibility that at some point Herb would be back and looking for his favorite blue-and-white-striped sweater or his slippers.

Donate clothing to thrift shop made it onto her list at number four.

By the end of the week, she'd moved through most of the first floor, making what she considered were the best decisions, reminding herself that there wasn't room in her home—or her life—for everything. It made more sense to pick out the items she loved best. She'd find room in her house for those that made the cut and would make arrangements for the rest. Having made a firm game plan, Jamie felt a weight lift from her shoulders. She had headier matters to deal with than what to do with a cabinet filled with unmatched dishes, old appliances, and several years' worth of bath towels and bedsheets.

She'd work one more week here, then she'd focus on the other task she'd set herself.

She called her literary agent, Lynne Manning, to say she'd finish that last week of her tour, but after that she'd need more time to recover from her mother's death. Another month might be better, she told the woman. She was even thinking about taking a vacation.

"Of course I understand," her agent sympathetically replied. "I think a vacation is absolutely in order right about now. Go someplace where you can relax, let go of the stress, enjoy yourself."

"That's exactly what I was thinking. Some time off where I can relax."

"Take all the time you need." After a brief pause, she added, "Maybe you'll come back with an exciting idea for that new book that's been giving you so much trouble."

"That's part of the plan," Jamie assured her.

Her laptop sat on her dad's desk, open to the page she'd bookmarked earlier. She read through the avenues for information available to adoptees:

There are procedures whereby an adult adoptee (age 18 or older), or the parents of a minor adoptee, can petition the Orphans' Court Division for access to either non-identifying or identifying information from their adoption files. The latter information can only be released if the Court successfully locates a birth parent and obtains his or her consent thereto. If the court determines that the birth parent is deceased, the name of the deceased birth parent can be released to the adoptee.

Jamie was sure that her birth mother was alive, since Curtis had spoken of her in the present tense. Non-identifying information would not answer any of her questions, so she scanned several pages for instructions on how to access identifying information.

The path to the truth was clear. All Jamie had to do was to send a written request for her birth mother's identifying information. The court would have thirty days to notify Jamie if an authorization form was on file. If her birth mother had signed a consent form authorizing release of her information, the court would have 120 days to send Jamie a copy of the record or to "use reasonable efforts" to locate Jamie's birth mother and try to obtain written authorization, if none existed in the file.

Jamie was pretty sure the latter would be the tricky part. Assuming that she chose to request the information—and assuming that reasonable efforts resulted in locating her birth mother. If she were the person doing the search, she knew where she'd begin.

She clicked on the link to the website extolling the wonders of St. Dennis, Maryland. Scenic views of the Chesapeake, beautifully preserved historic buildings, an active arts community, fine dining at world-class restaurants, etc, etc, etc. The list of B and B's was extensive, and someone had taken the time to describe each in great detail, from history to amenities. Some of the smaller establishments oozed charm, but the beautiful Inn at Sinclair's Point was more her style. If she were ever to go to St. Dennis, that was where she'd stay.

She found herself scrolling from page to page on the town's website, reading about the historic sights and following the links to several of the restaurants. When she realized that her casual wanderings had left her wondering if her birth mother dined out in St. Dennis and, if so, whether she preferred the elegant Lola's Café to the more casual dining ascribed to Captain Walt's, Jamie turned off her laptop and closed it. There was no point in thinking along those lines if she wasn't going to follow up.

It could take the court all of the allotted time to complete reasonable efforts to locate her birth mother, but Jamie knew exactly where she'd begin her own search. Her decision made and her path no longer in doubt, she picked up the phone and entered the number for the Inn at Sinclair's Point.

"Yes," she replied when her call was answered. "I'd like to make a reservation . . ."

Chapter 4

DANIEL Sinclair stopped in the kitchen of the still-slumbering Inn at Sinclair's Point and poured himself the first of several cups of coffee he savored every morning. There were few times of the day he enjoyed more than that first hour before the guests made their way into the dining room and the stately, historical inn began to come alive.

He wandered out onto the lawn, looking the part of a man of leisure, though he was anything but. As the owner and proprietor of the current most-talked-about place to stay on Maryland's Eastern Shore, he took his responsibilities very seriously. He used that early-morning walkabout time to check on the exterior maintenance—no faded paint or overgrown shrubs permitted, thank you very much—as well as the weather and the condition of the outside activity areas, the children's playground, and the tennis courts. Later in the morning, if he had time, he'd check with the crew building the putting green on the far side of the inn. Back inside, there would be other issues to deal with, like making sure there was enough house-keeping for the sold-out week ahead and checking on the event schedule for the weekend. His sister, Lucy, was in charge of event planning, and he knew there were two weddings coming up. He'd been meaning to call her to confirm that all the arrangements had been made and the required staff was on board and there were no last-minute glitches. Not that he needed to check up on her—no one was better at the whole wedding thing than Lucy—but he felt compelled to keep his finger on every pulse. He knew it drove her crazy, but he couldn't help himself.

He walked down to the dock and stood at the end, admiring the peace of the morning. The water of the Chesapeake lapped gently against the shore, and the rising sun shed a sweet glow over the place to which he'd devoted the last eighteen years of his life. Having picked up the reins for the family business following the death of his father when Dan was newly gradu-ated from college, he'd taken the rundown, rambling old building that had fallen into the red, and through sheer hard work, smart planning, and extraordinary vision, turned it into a premier destination. He was justifiably proud of his accomplishments, though as the widowed father of two teenagers, he rarely had time to pat himself on the back.

Next on the tour was the front of the inn. He circled around the building from the bay side and crossed the macadam driveway—would it need coat-ing before the summer got into full swing? should they think about widening it?—and held one hand over his eyes to shield them from the rising sun while he inspected the facade. Built in the Federal style with three stories of white clapboard and pillars that extended upward to form a balcony that served the second-floor rooms, it had a welcoming veranda that led to the front entry. Huge urns, painted black and filled with tall dark green ferns, stood on either side of the double doors. A row of black and white rocking chairs lined the porch, and here and there, planters bursting with bright petunias and trailing lime-green vines hung over the railing. All in all, the inn appeared to be exactly what it was: a gracious historical home that promised rest, restoration, and relaxation to its fortunate guests.

He inspected a few suspect leaves on a rosebush near the front walk, making a mental note to ask the landscaper to check it out soon, before making his way to the back of the inn. There, the tiny guesthouses reserved for summer interns stood in a row reaching down toward the water. Staff parking was nearby, and the large lot for guests led to the rear entrance to the building and the double doors into the lobby. His morning stroll complete, his mental checklist in order, Dan went into his office and dove into the day's emails.

His phone alerted him to an incoming text. The front desk was letting him know that the large party they'd been awaiting had arrived. He'd be there to greet them, of course he would. It was part of the ritual his father had established long ago with certain guests who for years had been planning vacations around their time at the inn, some for generations. Honoring those families was a way of honoring his father, a sacred trust, and in all the years Dan had been running the inn, a trust he'd never broken. There were things that mattered to him more than anything else. The Sinclairs considered some of the old-timers part of their extended family, and he knew that at this very moment his mother, temporarily wheelchair-bound following a fall some months earlier, was headed toward the freight elevator so she could be at the reception desk before the Marshalls had finished checking in. One of the things he loved most about this place was the continuity, the predictability, down to knowing that certain guests would return again and again, at the same time every year, requesting the same rooms each time.

After his family, the inn meant more to Dan than anything else on the planet. It had been his for as long as he could remember; he had always known that he would be the keeper of the Inn at Sinclair's Point someday. It had never occurred to him that the title would pass to him when he was barely twenty-two years old. It had been a tremendous undertaking for a man so young, but he'd taken on the responsibility of keeping the inn afloat without hesitation. Over the years, his careful management had allowed them to grow the business, to upgrade the guest rooms and baths, eventually adding a few luxury suites in the east wing. The dining room was completely redone, then the lobby and the exterior. Before long, Dan had started looking into adding other attractions that would bring in new customers. The old tennis courts were unearthed and restored, the pool area renovated, and a new kiddie play yard constructed. The old boathouse was rebuilt, and new kayaks, canoes, and rowboats were purchased. Over an almost twenty-year period, Dan had taken the inn from a slightly shabby Eastern Shore hotel to a fabled resort that his father would have been proud of.

"Your vision far exceeds anything your dad and I would have thought of," Grace had said to him while the new playground was being completed. "We never thought to add something like this."

"I don't know. Dad was pretty smart. I think if he'd watched how other places were evolving, he would have done much the same."

"I doubt it," Grace had disagreed. "Your father was content with keeping things the way they were. He'd have been of the mind that the old girl had held up just fine for well over a hundred years, so she'd be good for a few hundred more. He wouldn't have spent the money on the upgrades or on the construction of the new suites. It never would have occurred to him that things could be done better or different. He might have had a coat of paint slapped on from time to time before he headed out fishing, but that's about it."

"He might have surprised you, Mom."

"Dear, in twenty-seven years of marriage, your father never surprised me, not once. He was as predictable as the day is long." Grace had smiled. "We understood each other perfectly."

Dan had smiled then, and he smiled now as he made his way to the lobby to greet their guests, wondering how his creature-of-habit father had won the heart of his freethinking, open-to-anything mother.

Four hours later, the Marshalls having been duly greeted, their newest grandchild fussed over, and bags efficiently delivered to the guests' respective rooms, Dan stood at the top of the main stairwell and watched the steady flow of people pass through the double doors that opened from the parking lot.

"Not bad for a Tuesday morning in June." Grace joined him on the landing, a newspaper tucked under her arm.

"Not totally unexpected, though," he noted with satisfaction. "Not after that article in last month's issue of *Your Chesapeake Destination* declared the Inn at Sinclair's Point the 'crown jewel of the Eastern Shore.'"

"Your father would have loved that." Grace chuckled. "He definitely would have been proud of all you've done here."

"Just doing my job, Mom." His phone buzzed. He checked the number, saw that it was his sister, and realized he was late for a meeting with her and one of her bridal clients, who wanted them to move the gazebo to the water's edge for her big day. It would be up to him to be the heavy and explain to the woman and her parents why it couldn't be done. Lucy—as the feel-good wedding planner—always got to play good cop.

The lobby doors opened again and a woman dressed in black leggings, a pale blue tunic, and thong sandals came into the lobby dragging what might have been the biggest suitcase Dan had ever seen. Her ash-blond hair was pulled back in a ponytail that draped over one shoulder, and huge dark glasses covered half her face.

"Well, Lucy's waiting for me to—" He moved toward the top step, but his mother grabbed his arm.

"Dan, one of our guests appears to need help with her luggage," Grace said. "Go give her a hand."

"Where are all the busboys?" Dan frowned and scanned the lobby.

"Helping other guests, one likes to think." She tapped him impatiently with the newspaper, which she'd rolled up. "Go. She shouldn't have to be struggling so."

"Aaron should be coming back this way any second. Send him down." Dan looked at his watch. "I'm late for—"

"Lucy can wait," his mother insisted. "That poor young woman cannot."

Dan sighed and jogged down the steps.

". . . on *Good Morning America* week before last," Karen, the receptionist, was saying as Dan approached. "I ran right out and bought your book. It's wonderful. Really a whole new way of looking at relationships."

"Thank you," black leggings/blue tunic replied. "But I think you're giving me too much credit."

"Oh, no, I totally agree that we don't seem to place as much emphasis on honesty anymore, and I . . ." Karen looked up as Dan lifted the guest's suitcase. "We were just waiting for a bellhop."

"I've got this one," Dan told her. "Room number?" He held his hand out for the key.

"Miss Valentine is in Captain Tom's suite," Karen told him.

Dan frowned. "I thought that was already occupied."

"The previous guests had a family emergency and canceled the remainder of their stay. Miss Valentine just happened to call shortly after the room was vacated."

"Great. This way, please." Dan hoisted the bag—which was heavier than it appeared, if that were possible—and gestured for "Miss Valentine" to follow him. As they crossed the lobby to the wide stairwell, in an effort to be cordial, he said, "So you're a writer." That much of the conversation he'd heard.

"Yes." She matched him stride for stride, as if she couldn't get to her room fast enough and had no desire for conversation.

"What do you write?" He wrestled the heavy suitcase up to the landing.

"Nonfiction." While she climbed the steps, she made a show of looking through her bag.

"History? Biography?" He went right to the top of the stairs, and she followed.

"Self-help."

"Oh? In what area?" No wonder she'd had trouble with her bag. Damn, but it really did weigh a ton.

"Relationships." Her eyes remained focused straight ahead.

"How many books have you written?"

"Five."

"Feels like you brought them all with you," he muttered.

"Excuse me?" Behind him, her footsteps appeared to pause.

"Your bag feels like it's filled with bricks." They'd turned onto a short stretch of hallway, and at the last room, he paused and opened the door, which he held aside for her to enter.

"Might not have been as bad if we'd taken the elevator," she replied coolly.

"Guess the inn's architect forgot to pencil one in." He could have mentioned there was a freight elevator that was added in the 1960s, but it wasn't for guests, so he didn't bother. "Okay, so. We call this room Captain Tom's suite because that's him, hanging over the fireplace," Dan recited. He set the suitcase down behind a small sofa that faced a brick fireplace and nodded at the portrait over the mantel. "He was a sea captain, lived here at the inn. Rumored to have spied for the Union during the Civil War. Smuggled slaves up north in his spare time. Spent his last days here."

She paused partway into the room to glance at the painting. "Handsome devil." She dropped her shoulder bag on the sofa and removed her large, round dark glasses.

"So it's been said." Dan stood with his hands on his hips, watching her. Her eyes, up until now hidden, were the truest electric-frosty-blue he'd ever seen. Well worth a double take. If his phone hadn't started buzzing—Lucy no doubt texting him to *Hurry up, dammit!*—he would have taken that second look. "Some think he's still around. We've had reports of cold spots from time to time."

"I don't believe in ghosts, but I suppose that's a good marketing ploy."

"The inn doesn't need marketing ploys to keep the rooms filled." There was that insistent buzz again.

"Where would you like your bag? That's the bedroom through there, bath is the second door. And there's a balcony off to—"

"Thanks," she interrupted. "I think I can take it from here and find my way around."

"Right. If you do need anything, the front desk is zero-one on the phone, room service is zero-four." Buzz. Buzz.

"Got it." She paused at the sofa and reached for her bag and took out her wallet. She reached around him to open the door leading out of the suite, making it clear that he was being dismissed. Once he was in the hallway, she held out manicured fingers holding a folded bill. "Here you go. Thanks," she said before closing the door in his face.

His phone buzzed again, and he pulled it from his pocket. "What, Lucy? You're being a pain. I know, but for some reason Mom got a sudden bug about me playing bellhop and . . . Oh, never mind. I'm on my way."

He absently stuck the bill in his pants pocket and put the pretty blond writer with the extraordinary eyes out of his head. Right now he had a fire to put out.

JAMIE CLOSED THE door, hoping that the rest of the staff lived up to the Inn's reputation of "gracious and accommodating" better than the bellhop. When was the last time she'd had a bellhop comment on the weight of her luggage? This was the first. The fact that he'd been really good-looking didn't make up for his lack of manners.

She opened the French doors to the balcony, stepped outside, and took her first long, deep breath of the Chesapeake. *Lovely,* she thought as she exhaled. Just what she needed. A nice change of scenery and a welcome change of pace after the past few emotional months. Two days ago, she'd driven from Caryville to her Princeton home, the car loaded with some of the precious things from her family home that she couldn't bear to leave behind, like her grandmother's wedding china and books from her father's study. She'd given herself a full day to put things away before packing for a month away.

Jamie had deliberated long and hard before making up her mind to take even the first step on this journey, but in the end, she had sent her request to the orphans' court for a copy of her adoption file. Part of her felt painfully disloyal to the people who'd loved and raised her; she couldn't help but wonder what her parents would think if they knew. On the other hand, if she'd been told the truth years ago, the search she was embarking on might have been unnecessary. Still, the conflict—the feeling that she was betraying Lainey by searching for her birth mother—was alive and well within her. Every night since making her decision had been a sleepless one.

From her conversation with Curtis Enright, she knew that the records were sealed, but she wanted to follow protocol. The court's response—that no signed authorization existed—had been received in under the allotted thirty days. Before she lost her nerve, Jamie had immediately followed up with the request that the record be unsealed. Though Jamie suspected that her birth mother might decline, there was always the chance that she would—

Would what? Jamie had asked herself that same question a thousand times since discovering she'd been adopted.

Over the past several weeks, Jamie had spent hours searching websites devoted to helping adoptees reunite with one or both of their birth parents. On one of the sites, there was a page where either birth parents or adoptees could post birthday messages anonymously. Jamie had skimmed the postings much as she had skimmed over other websites, but almost as if drawn directly to one particular post, her eyes had settled on the greeting from "Maryland Mommy" posted on October 12 of the previous year: *Wishing my birthday girl only happiness and joy, wherever you are. Always.*

A search for Maryland Mommy found the same message repeated every year since the website was founded.

Of course, there could be dozens of Maryland mommies who posted birthday greetings to their lost children on this same website, children who were born on the same day as she. And surely Jamie's birth mother wasn't the only woman in Maryland whose October 12 baby had been adopted. There was absolutely no reason to think that the messages were intended for her, but something drew Jamie back to the site over and over again.

She knew that her birth mother had never made any attempt to find her (*She's never in all these years mentioned you at all*). But maybe somewhere deep inside, the woman remembered the baby born on October 12, whom she'd allowed to be placed in the hands of strangers thirty-six years ago. Maybe if she knew Jamie was looking for her . . .

Maybe, maybe, maybe.

Regardless of whether her search ended in a dead end or a reunion, once she'd decided to contact the state, Jamie made up her mind. She was committed to pursuing the truth wherever it might lead.

In the interim, she'd resumed her book tour, but she'd felt like a total fraud for the past week, talking about how important truth was in establishing solid relationships, how nothing of lasting value could be built without total honesty. There were times when she could barely respond to readers who came to book signings, eager to tell her how important her books had been in their lives. From city to city, talk show to talk show, she'd felt as if she were playing a role. All the joy she'd once experienced when meeting readers and talking about her books was gone. It had been increasingly difficult to get through the tour, but it was at a library discussion in Maine—her last stop of the tour—that she realized she couldn't pretend any longer. Once the tour was over, she promised herself, she'd find the truth, no matter how long it took or what she might find at the end of her search. The truth, as *The X-Files* promised, was out there.

The irony that she might be led to that truth by the lie that had been her life was not lost on her.

When the week was over, Jamie reminded both her agent and her publisher that she was taking time off. She had already studied the website for St. Dennis, and after looking over the selection of places to stay, decided on the Inn at Sinclair's Point. The reviews and the photographs showed a charming, sprawling historical building with its own dining facilities as well as room service, and when she called to ask about available suites, she found that a two-room suite with a fireplace and a waterfront balcony had just become available. She booked it for a month, promising herself that if she were no closer to finding answers in that time, she'd leave St. Dennis and not look back.

But now that she was here, the enormity of what she was undertaking settled in. Jamie had to face the reality that if she succeeded, she'd learn the identity of the woman who gave birth to her. If she failed, she'd be no more in the dark than she already was. Either way, her life would never be the same.

Jamie leaned on the railing and watched a group of teenagers heading to the tennis courts, rackets over their shoulders or swinging from one hand, chatting and laughing. She'd been young and carefree like that once, when summers seemed made for friendships and boyfriends and days in the sun. But that was a long time ago, back in the days when she knew who she was, when it never occurred to her to question her place in the world or to whom she belonged. Back in the days when she was Herb and Lainey Valentine's daughter.

On her way out of Caryville, she'd stopped at the cemetery where her parents and many members of her mother's family had been laid to rest. She'd carried the last of her mother's prized peonies wrapped with the honeysuckle vines her father had favored, and sat in the space between the two graves, the makeshift bouquet in her hands.

"I hope you understand," she'd said softly. "I love you both more than anything, and I don't want you ever to doubt that. But now that the cat is out of the bag, so to speak, I have to chase it. I need to do this for myself. I need to know. I don't know what I'll find—if anything—but I need to look." Leaving the flowers on the ground, she'd blown them a kiss and whispered, "Wish me luck."

She'd left Caryville at peace with her parents and herself. Aunt Sis was a different story. Jamie had taken her out to dinner to tell her she'd be vacationing in St. Dennis.

"Oh, honey," Sis had said, sighing. "Do you think that's wise? What if you can't find her?"

"Then I go home, no worse off than I am now, and I go back to the business of writing my book. At least I'll know I made the effort."

"But what if you do find her? What if she's . . ." Sis had lowered her voice. "You know, not a *nice person*. Or in prison for selling drugs or something?"

"Being forced to give up your baby when you're sixteen years old could do all sorts of things to a young girl's mind, so I suppose anything is possible. But we're going to take the high road here, Aunt Sis, and we're going to assume that she's an upstanding citizen and a perfectly nice person. Until proven otherwise, anyway."

"I just don't know how Lainey and Herb would feel about all this. Don't you worry they might be upset that you're tracking this person down?"

"'This person' gave birth to me. I'm pretty sure that if I could have more than a one-sided conversation with them, they'd understand."

"Well, it sounds like you've made up your mind," Sis had said, obviously still uneasy with Jamie's decision.

"I have, Aunt Sis. And it's going to be fine." Jamie had hugged Sis to reassure her. "I promise I'll keep in touch and will let you know what, if anything, I find."

The trip to St. Dennis now a reality, Jamie had arrived at her destination exhausted. Leaving the balcony doors open, she went into the bedroom, slipped off her shoes, and lay across the quilt. Pulling a pillow under her head, she hoped that her parents, in whatever dimension they might be, would understand and approve of her journey. She fell asleep wondering where she might have been at that very moment had she never found the envelope hidden in her father's desk, and whether or not ignorance, in the long run, truly was bliss.

IT WAS LATE afternoon when Jamie awoke, shadows from the large pines outside her window blocking the afternoon sun. Jamie stretched, realized where she was, and checked her phone for the time. Her stomach reminded her that she'd slept through lunch and was only an hour or so away from a very early dinner. She'd planned on making her first foray into the center of town first thing to get a preliminary lay of the land. If she hurried, she could still grab a late lunch on Charles Street at one of the restaurants touted by the town's website and still have lots of daylight left to explore the town.

She splashed water on her face, refreshed her makeup and her ponytail, then changed into black capris and a sleeveless black-and-white button-down shirt. She grabbed her bag on the way out of the room and closed the door softly behind her. She smiled at the young family she passed in the hall and made her way down the wide stairway; the lobby was busy with people coming and going. She headed through the back doors and into the parking lot. Her car was exactly where the valet had told her he'd left it. She started the ignition, waited for a trio of young teen boys to pass, then headed for the exit and the main street.

The only stoplight on Charles Street was smack in the center of town. Jamie had studied the online maps of St. Dennis and knew where the cross streets were and where to find each of the shops she'd read about. On the corner of Charles Street and Kelly's Point Road was the flower shop, Petals and Posies, where red and purple and pink flowers overflowed the pots that neatly lined the steps. Next door was Cuppachino, the coffee shop that bragged it served the best coffee on the Eastern Shore. Next came Lola's Café—"fine dining with a local touch"—declared an absolute must by a number of restaurant reviewers.

Directly across the street was Bling, a high-end women's clothing and accessory shop that boasted a string of five-star reviews on their website and had a gloriously decorated storefront window. It was nestled between Book 'Em—she'd definitely have to check out the bookstore—and Sips, a small storefront that served take-out beverages. The bookstore was followed by an antique shop and a small supermarket. The main shopping district appeared to end with a bakery—Cupcake—the sign for which was, aptly, a large pink-frosted cupcake.

The streetscape was all Jamie expected, with large planters filled with flowers lining the sidewalks on either side, and window boxes on every building overflowing with vinca vines and bright geraniums. People strolled along in small groups and in couples, many of them tourists, she guessed, judging from the cameras hanging around their necks. The total effect was utterly charming, the perfect picture of upscale summer leisure and small-bay-town chic. Jamie couldn't wait to see more.

She drove slowly up one street and down the next, trying to get a feel for the town. The historic homes—from white clapboard colonials to fancier Victorians—were marked with black lawn signs and brass numbers stating the year they were built. Scattered here and there were a few bungalows, and she discovered a section of new townhouses with views of the river. All in all, St. Dennis was a pretty place, exactly as its website had promised. There were worst places her quest could have taken her.

She followed River Road to its end, past Blossoms, the breakfast-and-lunch spot that had closed at two, and past the new film production facilities owned and operated by Dallas MacGregor, the A-list movie star who'd moved to St. Dennis to marry her high school sweetheart and establish her own studio. The town's website proudly noted that the first feature film would be ready for distribution by the end of the year, and that the studio—Lavender Lady Productions—had just bought the rights to another book and would be naming the cast soon.

Jamie sighed. She'd been a fan of Dallas's forever and knew that her roots went deep into St. Dennis's past. She amused herself momentarily by thinking how cool it would be if she and Dallas turned out to be related. Still smiling at the thought, she drove to the end of River Road, past huge summer cottages and smaller, more humble residences.

At the corner of Old St. Mary's Church Road, she followed the signs for the historical district. Though she'd initially planned on just a drive around town today and a stop for a bite to eat, she parked her car on a side street and walked to the square, where the tiny brick church—the original St. Mary's Church—still stood. The front door was locked, but a sign on the lawn noted that the building had served the earliest settlers as their house of worship, and that visiting hours were on Tuesday and Thursday mornings. Had Jamie's St. Dennis family been among those early settlers? she wondered. If they had, how might she find out?

With her phone, she snapped a picture of the church and made a mental note to stop back later in the week, when she could go inside.

Halfway down the block was the white clapboard house where the St. Dennis Historical Society made its home. It, too, was locked but offered the same visiting hours as the church. Across the street stood the sprawling brick library. It had obviously been added on to time and again. While not reflecting the historic nature of the neighborhood, it wasn't totally without charm, surrounded by a courtyard and tall trees. Jamie snapped a few photos and looked around to get her bearings.

On the opposite corner stood yet another redbrick building. Jamie crossed the street to read the sign, and her breath caught in her throat.

Enright and Enright, Attorneys-at-Law.

Jamie stood frozen to the spot for a very long moment. She leaned against a nearby magnolia and stared as if seeing a vision or watching a video of her parents arriving that day so long ago. Her father parking his big white Oldsmobile out front, getting out of the car to open her mother's door, and taking her arm. Jamie could almost sense their excitement, their anticipation, their anxiety, as they walked to the door and opened it. Later, they'd have left hand in hand, their steps buoyant, wondering if they dared believe this wonderful thing—this promise of a baby they'd wanted for so long—could actually come true.

She blinked and the vision was gone, but she was pretty sure that was the way it would have gone. They'd been to this very place, arranging to take her as their child. That she stood here now raised goose bumps on her arms. For a moment, she felt them here, too, and then the moment passed and they were gone.

Funny, she thought as she walked back to her car, *the last place I expected to find my parents was here, in St. Dennis.*

Jamie couldn't help feeling that she just might have their blessing after all.

SHE RETURNED TO the inn armed with a mental list of things to do and several photos on her phone. She opted for dinner in her room and a leisurely stroll on the grounds at dusk. The bay was quiet and deep blue, and from the end of the main dock, she watched several sailboats glide into their berths. She heard music drifting from somewhere—one of the boats at anchor on the water, maybe?—and saw lightning bugs dance across the darkening landscape. When her stroll found her at the front of the inn, she took a seat in one of the comfy-looking rocking chairs and sat back with a contented sigh. Her eyes closed—the chair's movement gentle and rhythmic—she embraced the solitude and the peace of the moment. It was, she realized, the most relaxed she'd felt in . . . She couldn't remember the last time she felt so weightless. After the emotional drain of the past couple of months, such moments were bliss. She easily could have fallen asleep right there.

The sound of a man and a woman arguing beyond the nearby hedge brought her back to reality. "You didn't have to be such a heavy, Dan. A simple 'Sorry, but I can't do that' would probably have sufficed," the woman said.

"Do you really think that was a practical request?" The man's voice drifted across the veranda.

"I think you could have at least pretended to give consideration to it. I think you could listen more and talk less. You know, sometimes you can come across as a real knucklehead."

"Knucklehead? Really, Luce? That's the best you can come up with?" He snorted.

"Shut. Up."

"There was—is—no point in discussing it. It's out of the question."

"Could you at least apologize for your attitude?"

"What's wrong with my attitude?"

"I can't believe you actually asked me that." The woman reached the walk leading to the veranda, muttering something about "Mr. Crankypants."

In the porch light, Jamie could see that the woman was petite and had long, light auburn hair trailing down her back. She was followed by a tall man with a nice set of shoulders. Jamie couldn't see his face, but she recognized the walk. She'd followed him from the lobby to her room earlier that day.

Looks like the bellboy has a real way with the ladies, Jamie thought dryly. *Color me surprised.*

The petite woman opened the front door and went inside, slamming the door in his face. He swore softly under his breath before following.

Some guys got it, Jamie mused, *some guys wish they had.*

Minutes later, the tranquil spell having been broken, she walked through the lobby to the stairwell, and there *he* was again, outside the dining room doors, this time in conversation with a pretty dark-haired girl in her mid-teens. Whatever he was saying made the girl roll her eyes and walk away with a toss of her hair.

I feel your pain, Jamie could have told the girl as she walked past.

But halfway up the stairs, Jamie glanced back over her shoulder and took a second look. He was standing in the same place, his hands on his hips, watching the young girl disappear through the double doors, a somewhat confused look on his face. Instead of the polo and khaki shorts he'd worn earlier, he was dressed in a gray suit with a white shirt open at the collar where a tie draped and hung untied.

What a shame, she thought. *He really looks pretty hot in a suit.*

She'd gone back to her room and hunkered down for the rest of the night, mapping out her game plan. Tomorrow she'd stop at the library and do some research on the early days of St. Dennis. She didn't expect to have any epiphanies, but she did want to get the lay of the historical land. She wasn't sure what she was looking for, but it was a starting place. The library might have a copy of the phone or property directory from 1979, and that could help her get a feel for the population, for who lived here back then. Sometimes phone directories listed the children's phone numbers separately, so that information could be useful as well. If her birth mother had been sixteen in 1979, was there a chance that she had her own phone line? Again, a long shot, but the entire trip was about long shots.

She tapped her pen on the desktop. Didn't some libraries keep high school yearbooks? That, too, was worth checking into. The woman she sought most likely graduated in 1980 or '81. Assuming she attended the local schools, her name and photo could be there. If Jamie made a list of the girls who graduated in those years, she might somehow, eventually, be able to narrow down the list to a few likely suspects. Of course, the woman could have attended a different school, and by now she could have married and changed her name, or she could have moved to one of the nearby small towns.

Jamie knew the odds were very slim that any of her maybes would lead her to the eureka moment she was hoping for, but as her father always liked to say, every journey begins with a single step. Tomorrow she would take that first step. Time alone would tell where it might lead.

Chapter 5

J<small>AMIE'S</small> first full day in St. Dennis began with breakfast on the terrace overlooking the inn's tennis courts. The only sound was that of a ball being lobbed back and forth by a couple of early-morning players. The air was scented by a nearby flower bed, and the sailboats heading out onto the bay on the easy breeze made the perfect picture of a June morning on the Chesapeake. Jamie sighed, content to be where she was at that moment. It hadn't taken much to convince her to sit just a little longer and enjoy a second cup of coffee before signing her name and room number on the check and heading out into her day.

Her first stop was the library, where, after a chat with the librarian, she discovered there was in fact a directory on the shelves for each year since there'd been phone service in town. She located the one for 1979 and eagerly took a seat at one of the tables and opened it, but it was impossible to sort through all the names and businesses. There'd been far more residents than she'd assumed back then, and the book covered not only St. Dennis but several nearby towns as well. She skimmed from page to page before having to concede that the exercise was a waste of time. She returned the directory to the front desk and inquired about school yearbooks.

"From which school?" the librarian asked.

"The local high school," Jamie replied.

"There are two," the woman said. "Bayside Regional High School and St. Dennis Academy." She paused. "Before the regional school was built, there was St. Dennis High."

"What year would that have been? I'm looking for 1979 and 1980."

"The new school was built in the 1990s, so you want the old high school and the academy."

"Right."

"You'll find them in the local history section." The woman pointed off to the left.

"Thanks."

Jamie located the section and pulled the respective years—1979 and 1980—for both schools. She carried the four yearbooks back to her table and took a deep breath before opening the first one. The class of 1979 of St. Dennis Academy consisted of forty-two students, not all of whom, she discovered, lived in St. Dennis. She turned the pages carefully, studying the face of each girl before writing down the name. She scrutinized each one for some similarity to her own features that could possibly hint at a relationship—a hairline, the shape of the eyes, the nose, the smile. But there was nothing that stood out, nothing that made her place a star next to a girl's name. It took several hours, and when Jamie closed the last of the four yearbooks, she had almost one hundred names.

Ridiculous, she thought as she returned the yearbooks to their respective shelves. *How in the world am I going to pare that down?*

She thanked the librarian and went outside to sit in the shaded courtyard, where she looked over the pages she'd filled in her notebook. Any one of the girls could turn out to be her birth mother. She softly read aloud several of the names, hoping to feel something stir inside her at the sound; again, nothing. But far from being discouraged, she got off the bench and walked down the street to the building that housed the historical society.

A minivan was parked in front of the lovely Victorian building—surely once the home of someone prominent—and three boys in their early teens were carrying boxes from the van to the front porch.

"That looks heavy," Jamie remarked as she passed by.

"Nah, we're good." The boy—tall and skinny, all arms and legs, his dark auburn hair falling over his freckled forehead—transferred the box to his right arm, then made a show of his virtually nonexistent bicep with his left. He exchanged a grin with Jamie— *Yeah, I'm a ham*—and stood back to let her pass.

Jamie was still smiling when she went up the path to the porch. A plaque reading *1877* hung next to the front door. The earliest she'd seen thus far had been 1718, but there could be some even older. She stepped inside the building, wondering exactly when the first settlers arrived, when the town was established, and which home was the oldest. Perhaps she'd find the answers here. She might not learn anything about her birth mother, but a little local history could be interesting, if not potentially useful, depending on what else she discovered during her stay in St. Dennis.

"Hello?" Jamie called from the foyer, assuming that since the building was open, there would be someone there, a docent or a member of the organization, but no one responded to her call.

Her freckle-faced friend came into the hall from somewhere back in the house. When he saw her, he said, "I think they might be opening a little late today. Mrs. Ferguson—today's her usual day—hasn't gotten here yet."

"Oh. I saw the door open and you and the others coming in and out, and I just thought . . ." Her voice trailed away.

"We're just here 'cause my gramma asked us to bring some stuff over for her. Stuff she was sort of archiving and is finished with." He leaned against the newel post.

"Is your grandmother the local historian?"

"Not officially, but I don't think anyone knows more about St. Dennis than she does. She knows everything that ever happened in St. Dennis and everyone it happened to."

"She sounds like someone I'd like to know."

"She's pretty old, but she's pretty cool." He sat on the bottom step. "You can probably wait here till Mrs. Ferguson gets in."

Jamie looked through a wide doorway into the next room. "I'd like that."

"I don't think you should be wandering around, though." The boy was obviously having second thoughts.

"Maybe I could just wait out on the front porch," Jamie said.

"That might be . . ." He looked beyond Jamie. "Oh, there's Mrs. Ferguson."

A woman in her late sixties came through the door carrying a grocery bag. The boy jumped up and held out his arms. "I can take that for you," he told her.

"Oh, thank you, D.J. You can put it in the kitchen next to—" The woman noticed Jamie and frowned. "I'm afraid we're not quite ready for visitors. I apologize for running late. If you wouldn't mind waiting outside for ten minutes or so . . ."

"I was just about to do exactly that." Jamie flashed her friendliest smile.

"I let her in, Mrs. Ferguson," the boy said over his shoulder on his way out of the room. Mrs. Ferguson was still frowning.

"Really, I just thought the building was already open. I haven't gone beyond the foyer," Jamie explained.

"I suppose it's all right," the woman said. "It is my fault that we didn't open on time."

"We all have those mornings when, no matter what we do, we run a little late."

"Yes, well. Thank you for understanding. Now, was there something in particular you wanted to see?"

"I was hoping to find some information on the early settlement of the town." Jamie added as if an afterthought, "And maybe something about the early families." *Might as well start at the beginning.*

"Oh, there's lots of information about the First Families. That's what we in town call the early folks who settled and stayed. We have a big event every year to honor them."

"When is that?"

"The second Sunday in November." Mrs. Ferguson was clearly beginning to warm to Jamie.

"What kind of things do you do?"

"Well, the usual, you know. Speeches down the street at the square, and they do some sort of reenactment, which is fun."

"Reenactment?"

"Important events in the town's past. Like the time the British tried to shell us during the War of 1812. Or the pirate invasions."

"Pirates invaded St. Dennis?"

"Oh, yes. For years starting in the 1700s and lasting for over a hundred years. Because we're right on the bay, you see. We were an easy mark. Mostly, a bunch of them would pile into a boat, row to shore—our harbor's too shallow for those big ships, you know—grab a few residents, and hold them for ransom. Once they got paid, they'd leave. No one ever got hurt."

"The pirates traded their hostages for money?"

Mrs. Ferguson nodded. "Exactly."

"They ever take anyone with them?"

The woman shook her head. "No. Although I

have heard tales of the occasional sailor falling under the spell of a hostage and deciding to stay on in St. Dennis."

"That's a romantic thought."

"You've no idea how many people in St. Dennis claim to have pirate blood," Mrs. Ferguson confided. Jamie wondered if she might be one of them. "After the reenactment, we have a ham supper at the Grange Hall. Same dinner every year, but everyone in town goes, and it's always fun."

"Sorry I won't be here for it," Jamie said.

"You're visiting?"

"Just for a few weeks."

"Vacation?"

Jamie nodded.

"Well, we welcome you to St. Dennis. Now, would you like a tour?"

"I would love one, thank you."

The tour lasted exactly twenty minutes, and if Jamie hadn't asked so many questions, it would have gone half as long.

She spent another hour going through the records of the early days and was making a list of the First Families when she sensed someone in the doorway. She looked up to find her young friend watching her.

"Hi," she said.

"Are you, like, a teacher or something?" he asked.

"No. Why?"

"Because mostly only teachers spend so much time with those." He pointed to the books.

"Oh. Well, I'm only in town for a little while, but I always like to know the stories about the places where I stay." Jamie held up the book where the names of the early settlers had been written down. "I was just wondering if the descendants of any of these folks were still around town."

He came closer to look at the title. "Oh, yeah. The First Families. Sure. Lots of them. And there's a book here somewhere that has maps that show where all the houses were back in the early days. It's pretty cool."

"You seem to know a lot about the town."

"My dad's family is in that book." He pointed to the one she was holding.

"Oh? What's the name?"

"Sinclair."

"As in the inn?"

He nodded. "My great-great-great . . . I forget how many greats . . . grandfather built it. It's a famous place."

"It sure is. I'm staying there."

"You are?" He smiled. "Cool. It's the coolest place in St. Dennis. We have—"

"D.J., come on." One of his friends appeared in the doorway. "My mom is waiting for us, and she said we're already late."

"Okay." He turned back to Jamie. "Nice talking to you. See you around the inn, maybe."

The two boys disappeared, their footsteps heavy on the porch. Moments later, Mrs. Ferguson reappeared. "Those are such interesting tales, aren't they?" she asked.

"They are. I was wondering, does the historical society sell copies, by any chance?"

"No, but we've been asked to have some made. I think the board of directors is considering doing something like that for a fund-raiser next year. If you'd like to check back . . ."

"Is there a mailing list?"

"No, but we can start one." She searched her pockets for a small notebook, opened it, and looked for a blank page. She handed it to Jamie, saying, "I'm afraid I don't have a pen handy."

"I have one, thanks." Jamie wrote her name and address, then handed the notebook back. "Do I understand there's a book that shows where all the First Families made their homes?"

"Oh, yes. It's right on that shelf behind you. It's locked, though. If you'd like to see it . . ."

"I would."

"I'll get the key."

Jamie read for another few hours, making notes on things that may or may not prove to have some relevance but for now were interesting all the same. While she doubted anything she'd found would help in her personal search, she learned a lot about the town and its settlers. The more she read, the more she admired those early folks who had to ward off the native tribes as well as pirates and, from time to time, the British. She learned that the first Sinclair was an entrepreneur who made his money in ships and rails and lumber. He built the inn for his son, Daniel, and Daniel's beautiful English bride, Cordelia, whose portrait hung in the inn's Blue Room. Jamie made a note to check that out. There was no mention of Captain Tom, she noticed, and wondered if that story had been made up to tantalize the guests who stayed there. She wondered if the inn charged extra for the legend.

By the time she'd finished, she had pages and pages of notes listing names and dates and pages relating incidents and anecdotes. Jamie rose and stretched, gathered up her things, and went off in search of Mrs. Ferguson, whom she found in the front hall.

"Thank you so much for sharing your journals with me." Jamie handed her the books that had been behind locked glass. "They were most interesting."

"Were you looking for anything in particular?"

"Not really. Just trying to get a feel for the town."

"And did you?"

"I believe I did."

"Stop back anytime."

"Thanks. I might do that."

The temperature had been rising steadily all morning. In the car, Jamie rolled the windows down and turned on the air conditioner, which blasted her with hot air. *Your impatience isn't going to make the air cool down any faster, you know,* her father used to tell her. *You just have to be patient. Give it a minute or two to get the job done.*

Jamie smiled at the memory. Her seeming inability to wait for anything had driven him crazy. "Sorry, Dad, but it's hot as blazes in here." She kicked the fan up as high as it would go and drove away from the curb.

It was a little after one; she was hungry and wanted a quiet place to sit and read over her notes and have something delicious to eat. She recalled the restaurant she'd passed on River Road yesterday—Blossoms—and headed there. The reviews on the town's website were great, and the description of the decor intrigued her. In under five minutes, she was parking her car in the lot and heading into the café.

There was a vacant table near the side window, and as Jamie found her way to it, the waitress waved and assured her she'd be right over. Jamie took a seat and glanced over the menu under the table's glass top. There were a few specials, a soup of the day, and several salads and sandwiches. The desserts of the day were displayed under glass on the counters.

The waitress arrived with a small bowl of something that looked like chickpeas.

"What are those?" Jamie asked.

"Roasted garbanzo beans," the waitress replied. "Chickpeas."

Jamie popped one in her mouth. It was spicy and had more than a subtle kick. *Not bad,* she thought.

She ordered a crab cake and a side salad, and munched on the roasted beans and sipped iced tea while she waited for her food. After a few minutes—that matter of impatience again—Jamie got up and strolled around the near-empty restaurant. She stopped and stared at the wall next to the kitchen door.

"So cool, right?" the other lone patron said. "All those photos are pictures of old St. Dennis, the buildings, the people." The woman got up and walked over, then pointed to a photo of a lighthouse. "That used to stand down near the end of Bay View Road. Got blown over in a storm. The stone base is still there, but the rest of it is gone. The lens from the lighthouse was saved. It's in the carriage house at the historical society." She pointed to a couple in full wedding garb. The bride wore a long white mantilla over her dark hair. "This is my husband's aunt Gloria and uncle Frank on their wedding day. And over there"—she reached past Jamie—"is my husband as a baby on his grandparents' porch." Smiling, she turned to Jamie. "I think it's the most clever thing ever, this photo wall. People from all over town brought in vintage photos so they could be copied and framed and displayed."

"So you're from St. Dennis?" Jamie asked.

"No, I'm from Baltimore. My husband's from St. Dennis."

"You live here now?"

The woman shook her head. "Ballard. I just come here because Sophie makes the best crab cakes on the Eastern Shore." She grinned. "Besides, I'm a big celebrity watcher. Dallas MacGregor opened that film studio down the road, and she eats here all the time, so you never know who you're going to see here." She lowered her voice. "Last week Laura Fielding sat right at the table I'm sitting at now."

"Wow," Jamie said because she knew she was expected to be impressed. She'd heard the name but couldn't place a face.

"I know, right?" The woman nodded. "Plus, the owner—that's Sophie Enright—makes everything from scratch. Which is why the menu is so limited."

Jamie heard little after "Sophie Enright." Surely a relation to Curtis. She remembered calling the law office and the receptionist asking if another attorney could help her, saying there were other Enrights, but she honestly couldn't remember the first names. So she asked, just in case the chatty customer knew. "Sophie Enright. Name's familiar. Is she related to the lawyers?"

"She's one of them. She and her brother, Jesse, took over when their grandfather retired and their uncle moved to Florida." The woman lowered her voice to a whisper. "Her father—Sophie's father— was the black sheep of the family. Disbarred lawyer. Married like a dozen times. My in-laws know the family. They've lived here for, like, forever."

The waitress came out of the kitchen and glanced at the two women. "Angie, I have your check ready."

"Oh, great." Jamie's new friend held her hand out for the check. "Nice talking to you," she told Jamie, who turned her attention back to the wall of photos. She studied the faces, thinking she could be looking at an ancestor she'd never known and couldn't recognize. When the waitress brought her order, she returned to her table. "Thanks," Jamie told her.

"You're welcome." The waitress started to walk away, then turned back and whispered, "I think it was only four."

"Four what?" a puzzled Jamie asked.

"Four times that Sophie's father was married."

"Oh." Jamie smiled. "Not that I was wondering."

The waitress smiled and went into the kitchen.

The crab cake lived up to its reputation, and the salad was fresh and the dressing delicious. Everything was so tasty that Jamie could not resist the dessert special: lemon merengue pie.

"What do you think?" the waitress asked after Jamie had taken her first bite.

"I think I might be back for breakfast if this is on the menu," Jamie told her.

"I doubt there will be any left by then—it's the owner's fiancé's favorite. But stop back any day. There's always something delectable on the menu."

"I will definitely do that. Everything was amazing."

"I'll pass that on to the kitchen."

Jamie finished her lunch, paid the check, and walked into the hot June sun. On her way back into the center of town, she debated what to do next. She'd done her research for the day, sampled one of the restaurants on her list of places to go, and thought she should give herself the afternoon off to do something fun. After all, this was her vacation.

The light at Charles Street and Kelly's Point Road was red, and being the fourth car in line gave her a moment to look around at the shops lining Charles. That was all it took for her to make her decision. She made a left onto Cherry Street and parked the car, then walked back to the main street. The front window of Bling showcased summer fashions, and the sundress on the mannequin screamed Jamie's name. She stood out front, admiring the pretty white dress, before going into the shop.

"Hi," the woman behind the counter greeted her. "Can I help you?"

"I need to try on that sundress in the window," Jamie replied.

"The white one with the little red cherries?" the woman asked.

Jamie nodded.

"It's darling, isn't it? What size do you need?"

Jamie told her, and the woman went to a rack and pulled out the size and handed it to her. "The dressing rooms are in the back, but I think they're both occupied."

"I don't mind waiting. I can browse."

"Please. Be my guest."

Jamie's browsing led her to a pair of sandals and a bag she couldn't resist. She took both to the counter and handed them to the woman and asked her to hold them.

"Of course," the woman said. "Those sandals are too cute with the dress. You really want to try them on together."

Jamie reached for them just as a young girl stepped out from the back of the store. "Vanessa," the girl called to the shopkeeper. "What do you think?" The girl twirled around twice, the pale pink dress swirling around her tanned legs.

"I love it. You look adorable," Vanessa told her. "It's perfect on you." She turned to Jamie. "Agreed? Isn't it darling on her?"

"Absolutely." Jamie smiled at the girl, who smiled back. Was there something familiar about her? "I'm guessing you're . . . what . . . seventeen?"

"I'll be sixteen soon." The girl grinned. What teenage girl didn't like to look older than she was?

"The color is perfect on you, and the dress is totally age-appropriate. Not revealing but still . . ."

"Just the tiniest bit sexy," Vanessa whispered. "Just the teeniest, tiniest bit."

"Oh my God, don't let my father hear you say

that." The girl rolled her eyes, and Jamie recalled where she'd seen her: speaking to the rude but hot guy at the inn.

Vanessa laughed out loud. "I can take care of your father."

"I really want it, but since it's over my budget, I have to come back with my dad and have him okay it." Another roll of the eyes. "You'd think I was twelve or something."

"I'll be more than happy to hold it for you, Diana. You tell your dad I have it tucked away for you."

"Thanks, Vanessa. You're the best."

Vanessa smiled and watched the girl return to the dressing room. When she came back out a few minutes later, she handed the dress to Vanessa. "I'll see how soon I can get my dad to come in."

"You tell him I said not to drag his feet. The party is in four weeks, and everything fancy I have is flying out the door."

"I'll let him know. Thanks again, Ness."

"Anytime, sweetie." Vanessa hung the dress on a hanger and took it to the back of the store, telling Jamie, "You can use the dressing room on the right now."

Jamie tried on the dress and was surprised to find it just enough too small that she couldn't zip it. She took it off, dressed, and returned to the front of the store. "I'm afraid I need the next size up," she told Vanessa. "Funny how a few pounds here and a few pounds there . . ."

"Tell me about it." Vanessa took the dress. "I'm afraid this is the only one I have right now. I'm expecting a shipment really soon, though, maybe even tomorrow. If you're going to be in town . . ."

"I am. I can stop back."

"Staying locally?"

"The Inn at Sinclair's Point."

"The best. If you give me a number, I can call or send a text when it comes in."

"I'd appreciate that."

Vanessa handed Jamie a slip of paper, and Jamie wrote down her information.

"In the meantime, I am taking the sandals and the bag," Jamie told her.

"Terrific. The bag is brand-new, and I could only get three of them. I sold one this morning." She reached for Jamie's credit card. "I put the third one aside for my best friend's birthday. I can't wait to give it to her."

"She's going to love it." Jamie paid for her purchases and left the shop. She paused out front and debated her options. Across the street was Cuppachino, where she was sure she'd get iced coffee that would take the edge off the heat. But next door to Bling was Book 'Em, and books always trumped everything else. It had occurred to her that a book signing in St. Dennis might bring out a lot of the locals. Maybe even the local she was here to find.

The window of the bookstore displayed a wide variety of reading options, from children's books to bestselling novels to Jamie's own latest work: *The Honest Relationship*. Her stomach turned at the thought of facing a group of her readers after discovering what she had about her own life. She pushed the thought from her mind. Time enough to angst over that.

She went inside, appreciating the cool of the air-conditioning as well as the placement of the book near the front of the store. Another display near the cash register held a copy of each of her other titles. The young cashier—could she have been over twenty?—was busy with customers, so Jamie wandered around the store, picking up a few titles she'd read about, or books written by authors she'd met in her travels. When she realized she had a stack and that the cashier was free, she went to the counter and put down her selections.

"Is the owner around?" Jamie asked the girl.

"She's out for a while," the girl told her. "Is there something I can help you with?"

"I wanted to talk to her about a book signing." Jamie opened her wallet for her credit card.

The girl frowned. "I don't think there are any book signings scheduled until the guy who wrote the kids'—I mean, the children's—book about the rabbits on the submarine. That's in July." She handed Jamie a flyer.

"Thanks. Do you know when the owner will be back?"

"Sometime this afternoon. She didn't really say. But I'm only here till five, so I hope it's by then." She proceeded to ring up Jamie's purchases.

Jamie signed the slip for her books and took the bag, along with the one from Bling, and walked outside. She paused on the sidewalk. She really wanted ice cream, and she knew from her Internet reading that One Scoop or Two was at the end of Kelly's Point Road. But it was too hot for a walk, so she retrieved her car and drove the distance. She parked in the crowded municipal lot and still had a ways to walk to get to her destination. By the time she arrived at the shop, she was sweating. A bell rang over the door as she opened it, and she stepped inside to find several small round tables and chairs, all occupied, and one glass-fronted freezer case in which eight flavors were displayed. There were six customers ahead of her, so Jamie joined the line and read the day's specials on the blackboard that hung behind the counter. When she finally drew close enough to the freezer to see the containers, Jamie scanned the offerings, unable to choose. Every flavor sounded delicious, from Cool Mint Jubilee to Berry Bliss to Chocolate Thunder Road. She was still debating with herself when she realized it was her turn to give her order.

"Ummm. Maybe—"

"Hey, you're the lady from Bling."

Jamie looked up to see the girl who'd been trying on dresses before her. "And you're the girl who looked so cute in that darling pink dress." Jamie smiled at her.

"I sure hope my dad thinks so. He can be such a pain sometimes."

"I think it's in their job description," Jamie said, wondering why it was all about the dad. Where was the girl's mother?

"Totally." The girl nodded. "So what can I get for you?"

"Maybe a scoop of Cool Mint Jubilee," Jamie

said, then immediately changed her mind. "Or maybe the chocolate."

"How 'bout a scoop of each?" the girl suggested.

"I already had pie today, so I should go easy this time around. Maybe just the mint."

"Sure thing. Cone or dish?"

"A dish, please."

"I'll meet you at the cash register," the girl said as she grabbed a dish from behind the counter. She was at the register in a flash, and Jamie traded a few bills for her ice cream.

"Good luck with your dad," Jamie told her as she tucked her wallet back into her bag. "I hope you get your dress."

"Thanks," the girl said before going on to the next customer. "I hope so, too."

Jamie strolled along the wooden boardwalk that ran along the bay from the ice cream shop to the marina. There were benches here and there, and when she found one shaded by a maple tree, she sat and watched the sailboats out on the bay. In the distance, a fast-moving motorboat skimmed the water, heading south and leaving a rolling wake behind. She polished off the ice cream and tried to remember the last time she'd eaten so much in so short a period of time. "It's my vacation, damn it," she grumbled to herself as she headed back to the car. "If you can't eat crab cakes and ice cream on your vacation, when can you?"

And lemon merengue pie, she reminded herself when she got to the car. "Okay, and pie," she muttered as she opened the car door. "So I'll skip dessert tonight."

kick

" Sis

She returned to the inn and went straight to her room, bags in tow. It had been a good day, in her estimation—any day that found her crossing off a few things on her to-do list and buying some pretty things and a few good books was a good day in her book. *Not to mention superb ice cream and that incredible pie.*

A nap would be nice, she thought as she slipped off her sandals. Later, she'd look over her notes from the day, but right now she wanted nothing more than to stretch out on that sofa and close her eyes. She opened the bag from Book 'Em and spread her new books out on the table. "Here's one you might enjoy," she said, addressing the portrait of the old sea captain. "*A Comprehensive History of Maryland's Eastern Shore.* If you find a mention of yourself, mark the page, okay? I'll just be catching a little nap here." She rested back against a throw pillow, her eyes closing, and added, "I sure hope you don't read out loud . . ."

Chapter 6

~~~

J AMIE had been shocked when she awoke and realized how long she'd been asleep. She'd been planning a trip to the dining room for dinner but opted for a shower and a room-service order of Caesar salad with shrimp. As she ate, she went over her notes from that day and mapped out tomorrow's game plan. Finding out which of the girls from the yearbooks still lived in St. Dennis was critical to her search, but she had no idea how to go about doing that. She could look through the most recent directory at the library, but she knew that many of the girls would have married, and others might not have landlines. Still, it was one more step, and the only one that occurred to her at that moment. In the meantime, she'd curl up with a good book and enjoy her second evening in St. Dennis.

And she had done exactly that after she'd checked in with her aunt.

"So what's it like there in St. Dennis?" Sis wanted to know.

The town itself is charming. There's a real historical vibe here, and I like that. There are some beautiful old homes and pretty streets. The inn is right on the bay, so there are water views from just about everywhere on the grounds, at least the parts of the grounds I've seen. All in all, it's a pretty cool place. I'd be happy to be here even if I wasn't on a mission."

"And how's that going?"

"I've only been here two days, so I can't say I've learned anything." Jamie told her aunt about the previous day's search at the library and the historical society.

"Doesn't sound like you've found anything useful."

"Maybe not immediately, but I'm looking at this as a big puzzle. I think I'll have to gather a lot of pieces before any of them begin to make sense," Jamie told her. "Besides, I've just started. I think if I find the right piece, I may actually solve it."

"You mean find that woman."

"I mean discover the identity of my birth mother." Jamie decided it was best to ignore Sis's negativity.

"Same thing."

"Not necessarily. I may find out who she is and choose not to 'find' her. There may be other factors to consider. We'll see what's what as this thing progresses."

"Maybe you won't figure out who she is, and this whole trip will have been for nothing."

"You're right, Aunt Sis. There's a very good chance that I will never learn her identity. I'm prepared for that. But at least I'll know I gave it my best.

And besides, I like it here. It's a great place to back and relax. You'd really like it."

"You promised to let me know what happens, reminded her.

"And I will. It may take a while, though."

It may take the entire month I'm here, Jamie reminded herself after she hung up. *I could leave here no closer to the truth than I was when I arrived.*

She knew the odds and was okay with them. "Nothing ventured, nothing gained" were the words of the day.

Jamie thought that her next step might be to figure out which of the women on her list of graduates would have been sixteen in 1979, when she was born, which would make her birth mother fifty-two today. Sometimes yearbooks gave birthdays next to the photos. Had Jamie overlooked something that important at the library? She thought she would have noticed, but there was always that chance. She'd return this morning to check.

And was there some sort of record of births in the town? If so, where would she find such a thing? While she didn't expect her own birth to have been announced, was there a chance that her mother's might have been? Her mother's and those of how many other girls born in 1963, which would have been the year of her birth.

Jamie made a trip back to the library after breakfast and started again. But the yearbooks did not have birth dates under the photos of the graduates, and there didn't seem to be any sort of record of births in St. Dennis from any year.

She stopped back at the librarian's desk. "Is there any sort of publication that would have announced things like births, deaths, marriages, that sort of thing?" Jamie asked.

The librarian shook her head. "Not that I know of."

"Thanks." Jamie turned to walk away.

"Unless maybe the town's newspaper."

"There's a town newspaper?" Jamie brightened. "Like a local press?"

"The *St. Dennis Gazette*, yes. It only reports on local happenings, no hard news."

"That's exactly what I'm looking for. How long has the paper been in operation?"

"Oh, forever," the librarian told her. "I'd guess something like a hundred years or so."

"Perfect. And you have old copies available?"

"No, I'm sorry. I don't think anyone thought it was important enough to archive the old issues." The librarian paused. "Though I did hear that the owner was going to do that. I don't know if she actually started, though."

"Who's the owner?" Jamie's mind went racing. If she could locate the owner, she could see how far back the archiving had gone. Maybe as far back as the sixties or the seventies.

"Grace Sinclair."

"The same family that owns the inn?"

The woman nodded. "Yes. Same family."

"Where is the paper's office located?"

"On Charles Street. It's the building right next to the bakery, Cupcake. Or maybe it's two buildings away . . ."

"I'll find it. Thanks for the information." Jamie went back to her table and started to pack up her notebook, which she had opened on the table in anticipation of finding some new facts. She'd just picked up her bag when her phone alerted her to an incoming text. She opened the phone and read, *Dress is in! Another customer asked for same size but will hold till 5 for you if you're still interested. Vanessa/Bling*

Jamie texted back, *On my way! Thanks!*

No way was she going to lose out on that dress. After she hit Bling, she could walk up to the newspaper building and ask about the availability of back issues. Her spirits lifted all the way around, Jamie headed for Charles Street.

She found a parking spot across the street and crossed at the light. Vanessa was at the counter helping another customer, but when she saw Jamie, she grinned.

"That was fast." Vanessa laughed and pointed to a rack behind her. "It's right here."

"Thank you so much. I can't wait to try it on." Jamie took the dress from the rack and headed for the dressing rooms.

"Good luck. I hope it fits."

"So do I."

Jamie had just undressed when she heard someone enter the other dressing room. She slipped the sundress over her head and zipped the back as far as she could reach, then turned to look at her reflection in the mirror. Was it a little lower in the front than she liked? She stepped outside the dressing room and walked to the counter.

"Oh, wow. Look at you," Vanessa said. "That dress is perfect on you."

"You don't think it's too low in the front?" Jamie tugged at the V between her breasts.

"Are you kidding? I'd kill for cleavage like yours." Vanessa turned her around and finished zipping the dress. "And I have the perfect necklace to wear with this. Come over to the counter and I'll show you."

Jamie followed Vanessa to the jewelry display, and it was then she noticed the man watching her from his seat on the upholstered chair near the door. He caught her eye at the same time she saw him. He nodded to Jamie as acknowledgment, but didn't speak. She nodded back.

Vanessa wasn't oblivious to the cool exchange. "Oh, right. You're staying at the inn," she said to Jamie.

Jamie nodded and tugged self-consciously at the top of her dress. What was he doing there, anyway? Not that she cared. She turned her attention to the jewelry counter.

"So Dad." She heard a girl's voice coming from the dressing room. "What do you think?"

Jamie turned and saw the girl from the inn and the ice cream shop. She was wearing the pink dress again and twirled in front of the man, who Jamie realized was the girl's father. Jamie should have figured that out from the way the girl had been rolling her eyes at him the first time she saw them together.

Before the dad could respond, Vanessa stepped in and said, "Don't you love it, Dan? It's perfect on her."

"It's too short," the girl's father replied.

"It's not too short," Vanessa scoffed. "What century are you living in, anyway?"

"She doesn't need to show off her thighs."

"It's barely above her knees, old man," Vanessa chided.

"She's only fifteen," he protested.

"She's almost sixteen, if I recall. Old enough to have a job," Vanessa countered.

"Can I say something, please?" The girl was close to tears.

"Of course, sweetie." Vanessa's voice was soothing. Jamie marveled at the way she was trying to ease the situation in favor of the girl.

"I love this dress, Dad. I love the way I look in it. It makes me feel pretty."

"Of course you're pretty. You always look pretty." He sounded exasperated. "Pretty is not the issue."

"Pretty *is* the issue," both the girl and Vanessa said at the same time.

"Really, Ness? Do you want to make a sale that badly?"

"Really, Dan? You don't know me better than that?" she snapped.

"Sorry. Sorry. That was uncalled for." He ran a hand through his hair. "Diana, let's finish this conversation at home."

"Can I have the dress? Please?"

"I think it's a little old for you," he said softly.

"Old? It's . . . it's *age-appropriate*." Diana had noticed Jamie standing at the counter. "Isn't that what you said yesterday?"

Jamie was reluctant to be drawn into a family

argument, but she couldn't resist the girl's plea for backup, and she couldn't deny having said what she'd said. Jamie nodded. "I did."

"And you said it was perfect on me, right?"

"It is perfect on you. I love the color."

"See, Daddy? Everyone thinks it's perfect. Please, Dad? I really love it, and Dallas's party is going to be so fabulous, with all those beautiful Hollywood people. Don't make me dress like a dorky twelve-year-old." She lowered her voice to a whisper. "Please?"

Her father was wise enough to recognize defeat when he saw it. "All right. We'll take the dress, and you can try it on for your grandmother. If she thinks it's okay . . ."

"Thanks, Dad." The girl threw her arms around her father's neck. "Yay! I love my new dress!" She danced toward the dressing room.

"I said we'll see what your grandmother says," he called after her.

"Gram will love it." She paused outside the dressing room door. "You know she always says you're an old fuddy-duddy."

"Don't push your luck," he grumbled.

"Fuddy-duddy." Vanessa grinned. "I couldn't have said it better myself. Really, Dan, you need to ease up on her."

"And you need to mind your own business." He paused, then muttered, "Like that's going to happen, since it would be a first."

"Well, since we're talking age-appropriate dressing," Vanessa said, "what do you think about Jamie's dress? Think that's too short, too?"

"What?" He blushed to the roots of every hair on his head. "No. I wasn't looking. I didn't notice."

But you did. Jamie stifled a grin. Ignoring his obvious discomfort, she turned to Vanessa and said, "I think I'm good with jewelry for now. I'll just go change." She returned to the dressing room, grateful to be out of the drama zone.

She and Diana exited the dressing rooms at the same time, both carrying their dresses.

"Thank you," Diana whispered.

"You're welcome. And have a great time at the party. You're going to knock 'em dead."

"You really think so?"

"Absolutely," Jamie assured her.

As she approached the counter, she realized that Diana's father was glaring at her. She met his gaze head-on, unapologetic, and then, choosing to ignore him, she handed her credit card to Vanessa.

"I loved this on you," Vanessa said as she slipped a dress bag over the hanger. "It's fabulous with your figure."

"Thanks."

"Try it on with those sandals you bought yesterday and see what you think." Vanessa swiped the card and handed it back to Jamie.

"As soon as I get back to the inn," Jamie told her.

"Oh, that's right. You're staying at the inn." Vanessa's smile was pure mischief. "Then you must know Dan."

"We met briefly." Jamie put her card in her wallet and her wallet in her bag, then picked up the dress from the counter. "Thanks again for letting me know when the dress came in."

"Anytime. Come back and see me again."

"I definitely will do that." Jamie turned and winked at Diana, then left the shop, making a mental note to avoid Diana's father for the rest of her stay at the inn. The look he'd flashed at her as she left was far from friendly. Obviously he didn't care for strangers tossing their two cents into a conversation between him and his daughter.

Jamie made another stop at the bookstore, hoping to catch the owner, but she was out of luck once again. The same young woman was at the counter and had as much information as she'd had the day before.

"Sorry, I'm not sure when she'll be back. Do you want to leave a note?"

"I'll try another time," Jamie told her. "By the way, do you know where the newspaper building is located?"

"You mean the *Gazette*?"

Jamie nodded.

"It's on the other side of Cupcake."

"Thanks." Jamie left Book 'Em and passed the antique shop, the grocery store, and finally, the bakery. The building next door had a sign in a second-floor window that read THE ST. DENNIS GAZETTE. The door for the paper was on the side of the building, but when Jamie tried it, she found it locked. There was no *Out to Lunch* sign, nor anything to indicate the hours of operation. *Strange way to run a business,* a disappointed Jamie thought as she walked back to the corner. Maybe she should get a number for the paper and try to call.

The light was green for crossing, and Jamie followed the crowd to the other side. She followed several into Cuppachino, where she stood in line to order an iced coffee. She sipped the drink as she walked back to her car. It was cool and refreshing, and she was sorry that she hadn't ordered the larger size. The cup was empty by the time she got back to the inn, and she tossed it toward a trash can at the edge of the parking lot after she parked and locked the car. She missed the can by about a foot and was walking over to pick it up when she heard footsteps behind her.

"Not only can she not mind her own business, she can't shoot, either." Dan reached the trash can before Jamie did and picked up the cup.

"I was going to do that," Jamie told him.

"Of course you were." He flipped the cup one-handed into the can and continued on his way, his long legs carrying him to the double doors, through which he disappeared.

Jamie followed, cursing under her breath. He was starting to bring out the worst in her, and that wasn't her nature.

Determined to put him out of her mind, she went straight to her room and hung up her dress, then went to the balcony to read her email on her phone. An hour later, her stomach growling, she went downstairs for lunch in the dining room. After a walk around the grounds, she went back to her room and googled the *St. Dennis Gazette*. She was disappointed to find an *Under Construction—Stop Back Again Soon!* notice on the website. There was a phone number, but when she dialed it, she got voicemail. She hung up, then debated whether she should have left a message. She called back and left her name and number and hoped that someone would actually listen to it.

She listened to her own voicemail and returned a call to her agent, who wanted to talk about foreign rights and to check in on the status of the book Jamie was supposed to be writing.

"It's coming along," Jamie told her.

"Great. If you want to send me a chunk, or if you want to talk about it . . ."

"No, I'm good for now," Jamie assured her.

She hung up feeling guilty for having told a bald-faced lie. She had no clue what she was going to write. She'd always believed in what she wrote. An honest life was a life worth living, her parents had told her, and she had believed it. She believed in honesty in her relationships and had tried to put her words into action in her own life. And yet here she was, lying through her teeth to someone who was always on her side, someone who would help her if only she asked for it.

Finding out that your entire life has been a lie puts a whole new spin on that whole honesty thing, she thought wryly.

She turned on her laptop and opened the file where she'd made notes about a possible theme for the new book, and for the rest of the afternoon, she played around with a few of the ideas. By the end of the day, she'd deleted everything she'd written and was back where she'd begun, at a blank page. It was tough to write about honesty when you felt like a fraud. She turned off the computer and decided to go downstairs for dinner, then come back up and try again.

She walked into the dining room, requested a table by a window overlooking the bay, and was shown to the perfect spot for watching the boats as they returned to the marina. She was scanning the evening's menu when she looked up and saw a woman in a wheelchair approaching the table. The woman looked to be in her seventies and was tiny, almost birdlike, her white hair pulled back in a loose bun; her left leg was wrapped in a cast that probably weighed more than she did.

"J. L. Valentine?" the woman said as she drew up to the table.

"Yes."

"I'm Grace Sinclair. Would you mind if I joined you for a moment?"

Ah, the owner of the inn. Jamie recalled having seen her name on the inn's website.

And, more important, the owner of the *St. Dennis Gazette*.

"Please." Jamie rose and moved a chair to make room for the wheelchair at the table. "I'd love to have you join me."

"Thank you," Grace said. "I can't wait to get rid of this damned thing."

"How did you . . ."

"Fell down the steps out there in the lobby. All the years I've lived here, I've never so much as tripped. And yet there I was, tumbling from the top to the bottom. Fortunately, I don't recall any of it, though I understand I gave my kids heart attacks."

"How long . . ."

"Another month or so in the cast. We thought it was healing well, but it was a little crooked. So they rebroke it, put some pins in, and recasted. I should be set now." Grace smiled as she positioned herself at the table. "I better be. They're not breaking it again."

"I'm so sorry. I hope it heals well and quickly."

Grace waved a hand as if to dismiss the thought. "I'd rather hear about you. When I saw your name on the list of upcoming guests, I was so tickled. We get our fair share of celebrities here at the inn, but not so many famous authors. And just between us, while we have movie people from time to time—a goodly number reserved for next week, I understand—I prefer a good book to most films." Grace leaned closer and lowered her voice, her brown eyes twinkling. "Delia Enright always makes it a point to stay here when she's in town."

"Delia Enright the mystery writer?"

Grace nodded. "The same."

"I'm such a huge fan of hers," Jamie said. Could the writer be related to Curtis Enright? She mentally added that thought to her list of things to find out.

"Who isn't?" Grace beamed and signaled for a waiter, who appeared instantly. "We'd like menus and a glass of that red wine I'm so partial to. I can't remember what it's called, but Hugo will know it."

"Yes, Mrs. Sinclair." The waiter turned to go, but Grace grabbed his arm and turned to Jamie. "Would you like a glass of wine, J.L.?"

"I'll have whatever you're having."

"Make that two of the red," Grace told the waiter.

"And it's Jamie, Mrs. Sinclair," Jamie told her. "I only use *J.L.* for the books."

"Then I am 'Grace.' *J.L.* does sound very professional and no-nonsense," Grace noted. "Much like the author of serious nonfiction should sound. Tell me, dear, were you a psychology major?"

"Actually, yes, I was. How did you know?"

"Just a good guess. Have you practiced?"

"Law, for all of about three months. My dad was a lawyer."

"You followed in his footsteps?"

"Tried to. I hated it."

"Well, good for you that you found something you really enjoyed doing, something you're very good at." Grace tapped the menu with her index finger. "Now, take a look at tonight's specials, and let's get our order in."

"What do you recommend?" Jamie asked.

"Everything. We have a wonderful chef, Gavin Kennedy. We stole him from a very famous restaurant in D.C."

"What are you having?"

"I'm going with the sea scallops tonight. He serves them with an orange sauce that is simply delicious."

"Great." Jamie put aside her menu. "I'm in."

Grace gestured for their waiter. "Two of the scallops, please, Andrew." She turned back to Jamie. "Now, tell me. What brings you to St. Dennis?"

"Vacation, mostly." The wine was served, and Grace tilted her glass to touch the rim of Jamie's before taking a sip. "My mother passed away in April, and I needed to go someplace."

Jamie realized it was true as soon as the words left her mouth, though she hadn't thought of it before. She did need a change of scenery while she healed from her loss. She took a sip of her wine. "It's delicious. Thanks for the suggestion."

"Of course." Grace placed a hand on Jamie's arm, and Jamie felt a zing race up to her shoulder. "Please accept my condolences on the loss of your mother. Were you very close?"

Static electricity? Jamie wondered. Grace seemed not to have noticed.

"Thank you," Jamie said. "Yes, very close."

"I hope that you find some peace here in our little town for as long as you stay." Grace took another sip of wine.

"Thank you, Grace. I appreciate that."

"How long were you planning on staying with us?"

"I'm not quite sure." Jamie averted her eyes and added the excuse she'd decided on for coming to St. Dennis, should anyone ask. "I'm hoping to get a head start on my next book, so we'll have to wait and see how that goes."

"I hope you'll find your suite conducive to working. I believe there's an adequate desk in there, and there's Wi-Fi throughout the inn, but if there's anything we can do to make things easier for you, please let us know."

"Thank you, I think I have everything I need for now. I am looking forward to taking some time off and just enjoying St. Dennis before I get back to the business of writing."

"This is truly a wonderful place to visit. An even nicer place to live. Is there anything in particular you'd like to see?"

"Some of the historical buildings, for a start. I'm intrigued by the history of the town. I stopped at the library and the historical society yesterday, just to get a bit of local history. One interesting thing I learned is that many of the current residents are descendants of early settlers."

"Oh my, yes." Grace nodded. "My husband's family was one of them. And while not a First Family—we celebrate the early settlers with an entire weekend in the fall—my mother's people arrived shortly after the War of 1812."

"So you grew up here?" Jamie asked, a thought beginning to float in her mind.

"Lived here my entire life," Grace told her.

"You must know everyone in town."

"And the closets where their skeletons are hidden." Grace's eyes danced merrily, and while Jamie could tell the woman was kidding, she suspected there was more than an ounce of truth to her words.

Their dinners arrived, effectively ending that conversation, but Jamie could hardly believe her luck. Grace admittedly knew everyone in town, and she owned the town's only newspaper. Jamie recognized a gold mine when she saw one.

They chatted over dinner, and Jamie found she really enjoyed the older woman's company. It was on the tip of her tongue to ask about the newspaper's archives, but something told her to hold back on that score.

"How was your dinner, dear?" Grace asked when they'd finished.

"Terrible. Horrible. You can see how much I hated it by looking at my plate."

Grace laughed. Neither she nor Jamie had left so much as a scrap on their plates. "Now, tell me what it's like to be a famous author."

Jamie shrugged. "It's a job, mostly. People think it's somehow glamorous, but the truth is, it's hard. Every writer I know works every day, or close to it. You're alone most of the time, in your own little world, just plugging away."

"When you say it like that, it doesn't sound glamorous at all."

"So, tell me what it's like to run an inn," Jamie said.

"Oh, I don't run the inn. My oldest, Dan, runs the inn. It's really his baby. He's totally devoted to it, maybe a little too much. Never takes time off, never does much for himself." Grace looked out the window. "He's raising two kids on his own—both teenagers now. His wife died about eight years ago. I kept hoping he'd . . . Well, that's neither here nor there. Suffice it to say he spends far too much time here. Works from sunup to sundown, and when you live where you work . . ."

"You live here, at the inn?" Jamie asked.

"We do. At one time, this was a private home. When it was converted to an inn some years ago, family living quarters took over most of the east wing. My husband grew up here, as did his father. I raised my three children here, and my son is raising his here as well."

"It's a beautiful place to live," Jamie said. She lived where she worked, too, but wasn't sure she'd like living in such a huge place, separate quarters or not.

"Enough about us. Is there anything you're looking forward to doing while you're here?" Grace asked.

"I really wanted to meet the bookseller in town," Jamie said, "but both times I stopped in, she was out. I was hoping to do a book signing while I'm here."

"Oh, what a great idea. Of course you should do a book signing." Grace's eyes lit up, and Jamie assumed it was because she was so enthusiastic about the idea of a book signing. "I know the owner, and I'm sure she'd love to have you at her store. As a matter of fact, I'm going to have—Over here, son." Grace waved to someone behind Jamie. "Jamie, I want you to meet my son." Grace beckoned him closer. "Dan, this is Jamie, my new friend. She's a guest here at the inn . . ."

Jamie and Grace's son stared at each other for a long moment.

"We've met," Dan Sinclair said flatly.

". . . and she was just telling me that she wants to meet Barbara down at the bookstore but hasn't been able to catch up with her. So I want you to take her down to the store right now—you know Barb is always there in the evening—and I want you to introduce them. Jamie would like to do a book signing at the store, and that should be arranged as soon as possible." Grace paused. "Daniel, have you heard anything I said?"

"I did, Mom, and I'm sorry, but I have a staff

meeting in . . ." He made a show of looking at his watch. "Ten minutes."

"Nonsense. That meeting is for the housekeeping staff, and Mrs. Bennett is more than capable of handling it."

"Really, Grace, it's nice of you to offer to have your son make the introduction, but if the owner is there now, I'm sure I can—"

"Don't be silly." Grace looked up into her son's face. "It won't take you more than a half hour. Surely you can spare so little time."

He sighed heavily and glared at Jamie. "All right. Let's go."

"Oh dear, one would think I was sending you to the guillotine," Grace said.

"I hate to leave you here by yourself, after you've been such good company," Jamie said. The last thing she wanted to do was go somewhere—anywhere— with the grumpy guy.

"Not to worry, dear. The second shift has just arrived." Grace waved toward the door, and Jamie looked over her shoulder as a dark-haired man and a lovely blond woman approached the table. "My son Ford and his girlfriend, Carly."

The couple arrived at the table, and Grace's son leaned down to plant a kiss on her cheek. "Glad to see you made it downstairs, Mom." He turned to Jamie and introduced himself. "Ford Sinclair." He put a hand on the shoulder of his companion. "Carly Summit."

"Jamie Valentine. I'm happy to meet you both." Jamie turned in her chair to face them and repeated thoughtfully, "Carly Summit. There's an art gallery in New York . . ."

"Yes, that would be me." The woman extended a hand and Jamie took it. "Have you been?"

"On several occasions. I saw an exhibit you had last year. Elvira Chesko was the artist. Glorious watercolors."

"Oh, you liked her work?" Carly's eyes sparkled.

Jamie nodded. "Very much so."

"Jamie is our newest celebrity guest." Grace gestured in Jamie's direction. "J. L. Valentine."

"Oh, I'm reading your new book now," Carly told her. "I was going to recommend it to my mother."

"Thanks. I hope she enjoys it."

"I'm sure she will."

"Well, the two of you had best get going." Grace looked from Dan to Jamie and back to her son. "Give Barb my regards."

"Where are you off to?" Ford asked Dan.

"Mom wants me to take Jamie down to Book 'Em so she can meet Barbara," Dan said between clenched teeth.

"It's poker night," Ford said. "What was with all the big talk about winning back that twenty you lost last time?"

"I will be back in time for the game, and I will win back that twenty," Dan told him.

"Really, Grace, it's not necessary for Dan to take me," Jamie protested. "I can—"

"It's the least he can do for one of our guests and one of my favorite authors." Grace patted Jamie's arm again, and again, that zing.

"Oh. Then thank you for joining me. I hope I see you again soon."

"Absolutely you will. And I'm hoping you'll let Ford interview you for the *St. Dennis Gazette*." Grace tapped her younger son on the arm.

"I was just about to suggest that," Ford said. "Could I talk you into sitting down with me for an hour or so?"

"Of course. Just let me know when," Jamie replied.

"How about Monday morning around ten?" Ford suggested. "I can meet you in the lobby."

"Perfect." Jamie stepped away from her chair and bumped into Dan, who'd been standing closer to her than she'd realized. "Sorry," she muttered as she felt a flush rise to her cheeks.

He took a step to the left, then pushed in the chair she'd vacated. "See you guys later."

Jamie had to practically run to keep up with Dan, who couldn't seem to get out of the inn fast enough.

"Look," she said as they went through the double doors in the lobby, "you don't have to go with me. Your mother will never know."

"Of course she'll know. She knows everything. For some reason, she thinks you need an escort to the bookstore. So I'll escort you because it seems to be important to her, though God knows why it should be." They were halfway across the parking lot and headed around the back of the building. "I will drive you down there, and I will take you inside. I will introduce you to Barbara, and I will give you five minutes to do whatever it is you want to do. Then I'm leaving, got it? You want more than five minutes, you walk back to the inn." He pointed to the car in front of him. "This is my Jeep. Get in."

Jamie got into the passenger seat and strapped herself in.

"So what do you do besides write books and interfere with the way people raise their kids?"

"I wasn't trying to interfere, I just—"

"Put your two cents in where they weren't wanted."

"Your daughter asked me for my opinion, and I gave it to her."

"That age-appropriate crap. That was you, wasn't it?"

"Yes. The dress *is* appropriate for a girl her age."

"How many girls her age have you raised?"

"None, but—"

"So you admit you have no experience."

"I may not have raised any fifteen-year-old girls, but I have been one. I know what it's like to have parents who don't want you to grow up."

"You know nothing about the situation."

"No, I don't, but . . ." Jamie paused. "Did you give Vanessa this much of a hard time because she thought the dress looked great on your daughter?"

"I've known Vanessa as long as she's been in St. Dennis. Her brother is one of my oldest friends. She knows exactly how I feel. And being a friend of the family gives her privileges that don't extend to strangers."

"I see."

"Good. I hope you do." He pulled over to the side of the road and parked the car. "We're here.

Remember, I introduce you to Barb, you have five minutes. I'm not missing my poker game."

"All right, all right. I got it." Jamie got out of the car in a far fouler mood than when she'd gotten into it. She stood on the sidewalk and took several long, deep breaths to calm herself. "All right," she said. "Let's do this."

"Hey, Dan." Barbara glanced up from a customer to greet him. "Don't tell me your mother has finished reading that pile of books I dropped off for her on Sunday."

"I don't know how many she's read," he told her.

"Oh? Could it be that you're here to pick up something for yourself?" The shopkeeper looked up again. "You might actually sit still long enough to read an entire book?"

"It could happen," he said. "But what I really wanted to do was—"

"Hold that thought," Barbara said as she stepped away to assist a woman who was looking for a book with a blue cover. "Fiction or nonfiction?"

"I'm not sure. I only know it's blue and that everyone's reading it," the customer replied. "Oh, and the writing on the cover was white. Does that help?"

Barbara finished up with the customer and walked over to Dan, who was standing next to the new-release table, flipping through first one book, then another. "You know, I've known you all your life, and I don't think I've ever seen you with a book in your hands after the age of, oh, I don't know, ten, maybe? I don't even know what you like to read or who your favorite authors are."

"You know how it is when tourist season hits, Barb."

She nodded. "I sure do." Lowering her voice, she leaned over and added, "I still find time to read just about every title I bring into the shop, though."

"Listen, the reason I stopped down tonight—my mother wanted you to meet one of the guests staying at the inn."

Barbara looked around and appeared to notice Jamie, who stood quietly off to one side observing the conversation, for the first time. Her eyes lit with recognition, and she snapped her fingers. "J. L. Valentine." She extended a hand to Jamie.

"Jamie Valentine, but yes. I can't believe you recognized me. Most people don't know what authors look like."

Barbara reached behind Jamie and picked up a book and held it up for her to see. It was *The Honest Relationship*. "I see your face every day." Barbara smiled. "I've been selling this book since the day it was released. Can't keep it in the shop. Are you visiting? Vacationing?" She poked Dan in the side. "Or slumming around with this guy?"

"I'm staying at the inn," Jamie told her. "Dan was kind enough to bring me in to meet you. I was hoping maybe I could—"

"You have to do a signing while you're in town. And soon. Would you be willing?"

"That's actually what I came in to ask about."

"Tuesday of next week would be perfect. Does Tuesday work for you? Maybe around one?"

"You know your clientele. If you think Tuesday at one is good, that's fine with me."

"Excellent. I'll order the books first thing in the morning. In the meantime, could I ask you to sign the ones that are in stock?"

"Of course. I'd love to." Jamie reached into her bag for a pen, but Barbara had one at the ready. "Thanks." She signed her name in the seven copies that were on the table. All the while, Dan stood behind her, counting down the time by keeping his eyes on his watch.

"Thank you so much, Jamie." Barbara smiled. "These will be sold before noon tomorrow. Stop back anytime. You don't have to wait until Tuesday."

"Four minutes thirty seconds," Dan whispered in Jamie's ear.

"Great meeting you, Barbara. I'll see you on Tuesday."

"Right. Looking forward to it. See you, Dan," Barbara called as he headed for the door. He waved without turning around. At the risk of being left in town to walk home, Jamie followed him out the door.

"How'd I do?" she asked when they got into the car.

"Fine. Lucky you get to ride back to the inn."

They rode in silence, and when Dan made the turn onto the inn's drive, Jamie said, "Look, I'm sorry if you think I overstepped some boundary. You need to understand the circumstances."

"You need to understand when to butt out of other people's conversations."

"I was asked for my opinion."

"You didn't have to give it. Or be so enthusiastic about it."

"What did you expect me to say? Your daughter looked beautiful. She was absolutely beaming in that dress."

"She should have picked something else."

"Maybe something with a turtleneck that hit her around the ankles?"

"Do they make dresses like that?"

Was he serious? He sounded serious.

"Only for the Amish." Jamie paused. "Except for the turtleneck. Look—"

"No, you look." He stopped, then blew out a breath. "Never mind." He parked in the same spot behind the inn.

"Look, I'm sorry."

"No, you're not." He got out of the car and waited for her to get out before locking it and heading for the inn at a quick pace.

"Thanks for the ride." She didn't bother trying to catch up to him.

"I'd say anytime, but I wouldn't mean it." He went into the inn, leaving her behind, wondering just what his problem was, and how a warm, friendly woman like Grace Sinclair could have raised such a grumpy son.

Chapter 7

JAMIE pulled the summer-weight blanket under her chin and stared at the ceiling. She'd forgotten to close the drapes over the French doors leading to the balcony before she went to bed, so she'd woken up with the early-morning light shining, annoyingly, smack in the middle of her face. She twisted and turned first in one direction, then another, but there was no way to avoid the glare. She flung back the covers and headed for the shower, stopping only to call room service with a request for coffee to be delivered in twenty-five minutes. In precisely twenty-three minutes, she was wrapping her hair in a towel and tying the belt of her fuzzy white robe when her order was delivered.

She poured a mug of steaming coffee from the covered pot and stepped out onto the balcony. She lowered herself into one of the comfy chairs and sat back to enjoy the scenery. She'd found that she enjoyed the first quiet early moments, when the rest of the world was just starting to wake up, here on the banks of the bay. On the grounds below, a man, a woman, and a child walked through light fog toward the water. In the hush, she heard the squeal of hinges and the sound of a heavy door being pushed open, then moments later, a splash. Jamie leaned closer to the railing for a better look, just in time to see the woman and child climb into a kayak and, after a minute or two, the craft slide across the water and disappear into the fog that cloaked the tranquil bay. The man who'd accompanied them turned and walked back to the inn, his stride and his profile familiar.

She rested her arms on the rail to get a better view as Dan Sinclair paused to pick up a piece of litter from the ground before resuming his trek to the building. She watched until he disappeared beneath the roofline. There were worse ways to start a new day than watching a good-looking man in cargo shorts and a tight T-shirt go about his business, even if that man brought a new meaning to the word "grouchy." She couldn't help marveling once again that a woman like Grace had produced such a child. Maybe he'd been dropped on his head a few times as an infant, Jamie mused. Something must have happened to make him so miserable. Was it possible to be born with such a disposition? Jamie thought not.

Grace, on the other hand, was so pleasant. Jamie paused to wonder how nice Grace might be if she knew that Jamie's real reason for coming to St. Dennis was to ferret out a woman who'd kept a very personal secret for thirty-six years. Odds were better than good that Grace knew the woman in question—a family friend, maybe even a relative—though she might not know her secret. How would she feel when—if—Jamie turned that woman's world inside out?

Jamie sipped her coffee and reflected back over the last two days in St. Dennis. Everywhere she'd gone, from the parking lot to the library to Bling and the bookstore and Scoop, she'd been mindful of the women around her, wondering always if this one might be *her,* or be related to *her,* or might know *her.* Jamie recognized it as a foolish, pointless exercise, but she seemed helpless to stop. She'd come to St. Dennis with one goal, and she understood enough to know that she needed to be careful, lest her quest turn into an obsession. She was aware that she was already skirting the line a little too closely.

Not for the first time, she asked herself if she really wanted to go down this path, if she should pursue this search for someone who likely did not want to be found.

Searching didn't necessarily mean *finding, and finding* didn't necessarily mean *confronting.* The best thing to do—the wisest thing—was to go one step at a time, she thought. It was very possible that she'd never identify this woman she sought, so no harm, no foul. Jamie was well aware that it would take a miracle of coincidences to find someone who truly was the proverbial needle in a haystack. What Jamie needed was a clearer plan and a reasonable deadline to complete that plan. She needed to decide what her next steps would be.

She'd work under the assumption that the notice she'd receive from Pennsylvania would indicate that her birth mother declined to open her records. If she got good news from that quarter, so much the better, but in the meantime, she'd given herself one month— four weeks—to determine if her birth mother did in fact reside in St. Dennis, and if so, to discover her identity. Not much time, considering that right now she had nothing to go on, but if she were no further along in her quest in four more weeks, she would go back to Princeton while she awaited notification from the state and return to her work. Work that had centered around one theme: honesty. Her stomach churned at the thought.

How could she continue to write such books after finding out that she'd spent her entire life living a lie? Wouldn't that make her the world's biggest hypocrite? And if she couldn't write, what would she do? Writing had been her life, honesty had been her platform, and the two books that remained on her contract haunted her. How could she possibly fulfill that obligation when the concept of honesty no longer held meaning for her? Even the thought of going on another book tour made her ill. Just thinking about facing a room filled with people who quoted her well-known lines—"Relationships with those you love are sacred trusts in which deception of any kind has no place"—made her flinch.

Well, when she'd written it, she'd believed it. Now not so much. Her career—which would most likely sink like a stone once her publisher realized she couldn't produce what she'd promised—had been put on hold. She needed to focus on her reason for being in St. Dennis. It was time to decide on her next steps.

Everyone in St. Dennis seemed to know everyone else, so it followed that someone knew her birth mother and knew there was a secret in her past. To meet as many people as possible, she'd have to go where the residents went. That they seemed to congregate in any number of places left her undaunted. She wrote down the names of the local businesses on her pad.

She paused with the pen in her hand, then wrote one name: Grace Sinclair. She circled it.

By her own admission, Grace knew everything about everyone—she'd lived in St. Dennis for all of her seventy-some years, and she owned the newspaper that for years had chronicled the comings and goings of the people who lived there.

Jamie chewed on the end of the pen. Grace, it would appear, could very well be the key to learning all she could in the shortest amount of time. How Jamie could pick the woman's brain without appearing to be doing so, that could be tricky. It was a fortunate coincidence that she'd been able to make the acquaintance of the one person she felt sure would know who the likeliest suspects might be. Jamie couldn't ask her outright—tempted though she might be to do exactly that—but there was a good possibility that Grace knew more than she realized about the matter. How to get the woman to not only unlock her memories but share them? Jamie would have to trust her own instincts, and right now her instincts were telling her that Grace was her starting point.

Her conscience tugged at her. Cozying up to Grace to tap into the well of information about the residents of St. Dennis—didn't that smack of using the woman? But Jamie really had liked the woman the moment she'd met her; there was no pretense there. Still, she'd have to be mindful where Grace was concerned.

Draining her mug, Jamie stood and stretched before going into her room to dress for the day. She'd try to catch up with Grace downstairs—in the dining room, maybe, or in the lobby. Jamie would see if she could track Grace down for a friendly chat and take it from there.

And to that little twinge of guilt she felt for plotting to use the woman's warm and friendly manner to further her own ends, Jamie silently apologized in advance.

GRACE WAS NOT in the lobby, nor was she in the dining room. Jamie ate breakfast alone at a table overlooking the beautifully maintained grounds. She crunched the last of her English muffin and signed her room number on the check before walking back through the main part of the dining room. She'd just stepped through the double doors when she saw Dan and his daughter in discussion. Diana waved and called out to her, "Jamie, wait." She said something else to her father before tossing her head and walking in Jamie's direction.

"Hi, Diana," Jamie said, well aware that Diana's father was standing thirty feet away, hands on his hips, watching his daughter.

"I tried my dress on for Gram last night and she loved it. She said the same thing you and Vanessa said, that it was just right for me." Diana smiled smugly. "Dad has to come around. Even Gram told him he was being silly."

"I'm sure your father only wants what's best for you," Jamie said.

"He wants me to stay, like, ten years old so that he can always tell me what to do." Diana made a face.

"It's hard for fathers to let go of their daughters sometimes."

"Did your father treat you like you were a little kid even after you were, like, a teenager?"

Jamie nodded. "He did. And we had our arguments over clothes and boys and where I could go and . . . well, the stuff that all girls and their dads argue over. It gets better." She smiled in spite of the fact that she knew Dan was watching. "It will. It always does."

"Boy, I sure hope you're right. I'd hate to have him following me around when I get to college."

"I'm pretty sure he'll come around long before that."

"That's what my gram said."

"Speaking of your grandmother, I was hoping to catch up with her this morning. Any idea where I might find her?"

"I saw her at breakfast. She said she was going to her office for a while."

"Where's her office?"

Diana pointed to a hallway to the left of the lobby. "The second door on the right."

"Do you think it would be all right if I stopped in to say good morning?"

"I think she'd love it. She doesn't get around the way she used to, and I know it drives her crazy when she doesn't have anyone to talk to. Go on over, tap on the door."

"If she's in the middle of something, I'd hate to disturb her."

"Don't worry, if she's in the middle of something, she'll let you know."

"Thanks, Diana."

"Oh, there's my friend Paige." Diana waved to a tall pretty girl who just entered the lobby and had stopped to say something to Dan. "We're both working at Scoop this morning. Dad's driving us."

"I won't keep you, then. I'll see you later."

"Sure." Diana turned and hurried across the lobby.

Jamie headed for the hallway and Grace's office. She could see a light shining under the second door, which was unmarked except for a numeral two painted by a precise hand in purple. She rapped softly with her knuckles, and before she could knock a second time, the voice behind the door called, "Come in."

Jamie poked her head through the doorway. "Good morning, Grace."

"Oh, Jamie. How nice to see you. Please, come in." Grace beckoned, a broad smile on her face.

"Are you busy? I could come back." Jamie hesitated.

"Not at all. Come, take a seat and tell me what you thought of our bookstore." Grace pointed to a chair opposite her desk.

Jamie lowered herself into the cushioned chair. "It's a great little shop, busy as all heck. Dan introduced me to Barbara, and she was really nice. She has a lot of my books in stock. I was just about to ask if I might do a signing there when she suggested it herself."

"Barbara's had some very memorable book signings at her store. She'll have lots of locals there as well as the tourists. You will sell a lot of books."

"Great. That's the idea." *Well, that and seeing how many fifty-two-year-old local women I can meet.*

"What have you seen so far in St. Dennis?"

"The library, the historical society—I like to read about the places I visit."

Grace nodded. "Very good."

"I had lunch at Blossoms yesterday."

"One of my favorite places." Grace sighed.

"I bought a dress and some sandals and a bag at Bling, and I'm thinking about going back for some shorts. I didn't bring many pairs with me."

"A favorite place to shop, even for an old girl like me." Grace nodded. "Vanessa carries lovely things. Where else?"

"That's about it. Oh, wait, I did stop at the coffee shop for an iced coffee."

"With whipped cream?"

Jamie shook her head. "I passed. I'd just had lemon meringue pie at Blossoms and ice cream at Scoop. Whipped cream in my coffee would have been overkill."

"Cuppachino. How I miss that place."

"Oh? A favorite haunt?"

"My very favorite." Grace nodded. "Met my friends there almost every morning since it opened about six years ago, at least until I broke my leg. A lot of the local businesspeople gather there for coffee early every morning. Coffee and gossip. Is there a better way to start off your day?"

"Sounds good to me. Maybe I'll stop there this morning. I wanted to explore a little more."

"What I wouldn't give to go with you."

"Is there any way we could make that happen?"

Grace stared at her for a long moment. "I suppose if we could get someone to help me into the car . . . but no, no. That would be too much to ask of you."

"Not at all. I'd love your company. And I bet I could manage." Jamie stood. "I drive a big car, and the front seat can be moved back so you could stretch out your leg. It might take us a few minutes to get you in, but I'm game if you are."

"I can wheel my chair out through the lobby and down the ramp if you pull your car up close." Grace's eyes lit as she spoke. "It might be tough getting me into the car, but maybe . . . What the heck, Jamie. Let's give it a try." She wheeled around the side of her desk, grabbing her purse from the corner and pointing to the door. "Let's do this."

Jamie grinned and held the door open for Grace. "I'll bring the car around."

Grace followed Jamie across the lobby, pausing only to tell the startled receptionist, "If anyone's looking for me, I'll be at Cuppachino."

Jamie waited for Grace to catch up and, once outside, watched the wheelchair glide down the ramp.

"Oh my, it's going to be a hot one today." Grace looked pleased in spite of her forecast.

"You wait right here. I'll be right back." Jamie

took off for the parking lot. Minutes later, she pulled up in front of the lobby doors and got out of the car. She opened the front passenger door and moved the seat back as far as it would go. "Okay, Grace, let's see if we can figure out how to do this."

Jamie wheeled the chair as close to the car as possible and, after several attempts, got Grace standing on her good leg, the one in the cast resting gently on the ground.

"What the hell are you doing?" Dan's voice broke Jamie's concentration.

"What does it look like we're doing?" Grace snapped.

"It looks like you're about thirty seconds from breaking the other leg." He turned to Jamie. "Want to tell me what's going on?"

Before she could reply, Grace smacked her son on the arm. "Don't talk past me as if I'm not here, and don't speak to me or to Jamie in that tone. We're going to Cuppachino for coffee. You're welcome to join us if your attitude makes a speedy adjustment."

"Mom—" Dan protested.

"Don't 'Mom' me. I've been stuck here forever, and I'm going stir-crazy. Jamie's going to the coffee shop, and I want to go." Her eyes were glassy with tears. "I am *going* to go."

"If you wanted to go to Cuppachino, why didn't you tell me, or Ford, or Lucy?" Dan's tone softened.

"Because you all have so much to do. You're always so busy in the morning, and that's when all my friends are there. That's when I want to go. Jamie was kind enough to offer to take me, and I accepted."

"All right." Dan sighed. "Let's see if we can get you into the car without doing further damage."

"That's my boy." Grace smiled up at her son, and Jamie took a step back.

With little fuss and great care, Dan lifted his mother and got her settled in the front seat, then folded the wheelchair.

"Here, I'll take that," Jamie told him. "I'll put it behind my seat."

He ignored her outstretched hand and carried the chair around to the driver's side. Before Jamie could open the door, he caught her arm. "Next time you decide to take my mother somewhere, I'd appreciate it if you discussed it with me first."

"Your mother was the one who decided she wanted to come with me," Jamie replied, "and I think she's capable of making decisions for herself."

"What if I hadn't come along? What if you'd dropped her while you were trying to get her into the car?"

"I'm a lot stronger than I look, thank you very much, but if I'd found I wasn't able to safely move her, I would have called the trip off or found someone to give me a hand."

"And once you get in town, how are you going to get her out and into the chair?" He leaned the chair against the side of the car. "And how are you going to get her back in to come home?"

"Oh, knock it off, Dan," Grace called from the front seat. "You know as well as I do that there will be someone at Cuppachino to give us a hand if we need one. It didn't seem like such a big deal for you to get me in here. It won't be a big deal to get me out. I'm sure I can find someone to give us a hand, even if I have to ask Carlo to come out and hoist me up." She took a breath, then added, "And stop treating me like I'm a five-year-old. I am perfectly capable of deciding when I can and when I can't do something."

"All righty, then." Dan slid the wheelchair into the backseat and slammed the door. "I guess she told me."

"Thanks for helping." Jamie smirked and got behind the wheel. "We'll see you later."

"Take good care." Dan leaned close to Jamie's open window. His voice was cordial, but the fire was still in his eyes.

"As if she were my own," Jamie told him.

"Oh, for crying out loud," Grace grumbled. "You'd think we were going all the way to Baltimore."

Dan stood back while Jamie drove past him onto the long driveway that led to Charles Street.

"Honestly, you'd think I was on my last leg." When Grace realized what she'd said, she laughed. "Well, I suppose, in a way, I am. But we'll manage."

"He's just worried about you. I'm sure the fact that I'm pretty much a stranger has him wondering if I can be trusted."

"Funny, but I don't feel as if you're a stranger at all," Grace said solemnly. "I feel as if I've always known you." She paused. "Are you sure you've never been in St. Dennis before?"

"I'm positive," Jamie assured her.

"There's something about you that's so familiar," Grace continued. "I'm not sure what it is, but it will come to me."

Jamie's heart skipped a beat. "When it does, I hope you'll share the revelation with me."

"Of course, dear."

Jamie made the turn onto Charles Street and headed toward the center of town.

"You know, I think it's that you remind me of someone," Grace continued. "I can't quite figure out who, but sooner or later, I will remember."

And that, Jamie thought as she stopped at the red light, *is exactly what I'm counting on.*

ONE WOULD HAVE thought that no one in St. Dennis had seen Grace in months by the way she was greeted when Jamie wheeled her into the coffee shop. Apparently not willing to take any chances, Dan had called ahead and asked if there was anyone who could assist his mother out of the car, and Carlo, the owner, had volunteered immediately. There were happy cries and even a bit of applause as they made their way to the front table where the locals gathered every morning before opening their businesses for the day. As the one responsible for Grace's reunion with the group, Jamie was welcomed into the fold with open arms.

"We've missed you so much," Nita Perry, the fifty-something owner of the antique shop across the street, assured Grace.

"Now, Nita, we see each other at least once a week, when you have dinner at the inn with your niece," Grace reminded her.

"That's not the same, and you know it. Can't very well bitch about my sister with her daughter sitting right there," Nita told them.

"You know you love Nancy like a . . . I'd say 'like a sister,' but I suppose that goes without saying." Grace patted Nita's hand, then turned to the woman seated across the table from her. "Eleanor, I've been dying to know how things are going at the flower shop."

"Here's your order," Carlo said as he approached the table with two mugs, a plate of scones, and a small pitcher of cream. "Special delivery."

"I'll say it's special." Barbara leaned back in her chair. To Jamie, she said, "The routine here is, you order at the counter and wait for your coffee or whatever, then you go to that station over there"—she pointed to a table on the other side of the room—"get your sugar, creamer, et cetera, then you find a table. It appears Princess Grace here is getting special treatment."

"Of course," Carlo said. "Why not? We've all missed her. We're happy to have her back." He dried his hands on his white apron, then patted Jamie on the back as he passed on his way to the counter. "You let me know when you're ready to leave, and we'll give you a hand getting her into the car."

Jamie nodded. "Thanks. Will do."

She sat back and listened to the chatter, trying to absorb as much as she could about the women at the table. The chance that the person she sought was actually *at the table* was pretty slim, Jamie knew that. But she paid attention all the same. Wasn't it maddening that all three of the women were *all* in their early fifties and *all* had lived all their lives in St. Dennis—like her birth mother? Jamie wondered how many more women in town fit that description. Her heart sank just a little more. Her plan was looking more hopeless with every passing minute. For the next half hour, at least a dozen women in their early fifties—St. Dennis residents one and all—stopped by to chat with Grace. Jamie studied each one, making note of their names on her phone and trying to commit their faces to memory, but she gave up after Lisa, who waitressed at a restaurant outside of town, and Joanna, the assistant librarian, joined the group.

"I'm sure the book club that meets at the library every other Thursday night would love to discuss your book with you," Joanna gushed. "That is, if you're willing and still here the week after next."

"I'd love to," Jamie told her.

"Oh, that will be fun." Grace was beaming. "It's such a fun group. Mostly women of a certain age, you know, but they're all fun."

Jamie smiled. The more events she attended, the more people she'd meet, and who knew whose path she might cross?

"Isn't that terrific, Jamie?"

At the sound of her name, Jamie tuned back in.

"I'm sorry, what did you ask?" Embarrassed, she felt a flush from her chest to her hairline.

"I said, since putting the sign in the store window last night about the book signing, I've already had forty people leave messages on my voicemail to confirm that they would be there," Barbara told her.

"Wow. Word travels fast around here," Jamie said.

"Indeed it does. We'll have a packed house," Barbara said. "I left a message for my distributor, but I think I may need to up the number of copies of your new book." She took a sip of tea, then added thoughtfully, "Maybe we should bring in extra copies of your last one as well."

"Whatever you think," Jamie told her.

"Jamie, I'm embarrassed to say I'm not familiar with your books." The woman Grace had introduced as Eleanor from the flower shop leaned forward slightly to make eye contact with her. "What can you tell me about them?"

The unexpected question caught Jamie off guard, and for a moment, that deer-in-the-headlights look was hers, and she knew it. "Ah well, mostly, I write about relationships and how it's important to try to . . . ah . . . relate to one another openly."

"She's being modest," Grace told Eleanor. "Her books are blueprints for establishing honest communication between spouses, siblings, parents and their children, friends . . . anyone with whom you're in a committed relationship." Grace beamed. "I have to say that I own all of Jamie's books, and I've bought copies for all three of my children."

"Did they actually read them?" Nita asked.

"They did." Grace nodded vigorously. "I know for a fact they did, because we've discussed them over dinner several times. Why, last winter, I had my grandkids read that chapter from *The Honest Family,* and we talked about how parents need to set the example for their children and how kids need to know that their honesty will always be respected." She turned to Jamie. "The kids seemed to understand the concepts. I've no doubt your books have opened doors to discussions for many other families as well."

"Thank you, Grace. That's nice of you to say."

"Well, we can continue this conversation at the book signing on Tuesday." Barbara stood and gathered her mug and a plate holding half a croissant. "Right now I need to get my guy on the phone and make sure he got the message about the books."

"I should go, too." Nita balled up a paper napkin in her hand. "I have someone coming in this morning to look at some Foo dogs I picked up at a house sale last week, and I know that somewhere in that back room of mine, there's a ginger jar that would be perfect with those puppies." She slid the strap of her bag over her shoulder and turned to Jamie. "It was nice to meet you. I'll see if I can get someone to cover for me at the shop so I can stop over to your signing."

"If not, let me know. I can put a copy aside, and I'm sure Jamie would sign it for you," Barbara said.

"Of course." Jamie smiled.

"That would be great, thanks." Nita returned the smile.

"Wait and I'll walk out with you." Eleanor, too, stood. "Nice meeting you, Jamie. I hope we'll see you around. Other than at your book signing, that is."

"I'll be around for a while," Jamie told her.

"I'll see you on Tuesday." Barbara tapped her on the shoulder. "Gracie, so good to see you back where you belong."

"There was a song that went something like that." Nita paused behind Grace's chair.

"That was the Dolly song," Grace told her.

"Whatever." Barbara walked to the counter and deposited her mug and plate, the others following right behind.

"Are you in a hurry, dear?" Grace asked Jamie when her friends had departed.

"Not really."

"How about we get Carlo to give us a hand and we take a little drive around town? Would you mind a little detour on the way home?"

"Of course not. I'd love it." Jamie rose. "I'll see if I can get Carlo's attention."

It took under a minute for Jamie to catch Carlo's eye. As promised, he dropped what he was doing and came around the counter and met Grace at the door.

"I hope this means we can expect to see more of you, Grace," he said as he carefully eased her into the front seat of Jamie's car.

"Since I'm relying on the kindness of others, I'd have to say I hope so, too," Grace replied.

"Anytime, Grace," Jamie assured her. "As long as I'm here, I'm available whenever you want."

Both women thanked Carlo for his assistance, and Jamie prepared to pull away from the curb. "Which way, Grace?"

"Go up to the light, then take the first right."

The light was green, so Jamie made the turn.

"That's Vanessa's place there on the left." Grace pointed to a picturesque bungalow that had an abundance of roses overflowing an arbor that marked the front gate.

Jamie slowed as she passed the house. "It looks like something out of a magazine."

"She and Grady, her husband, have done a lot of work on the place. It had been neglected for a long time." Grace added quietly, "My old friend Alice Ridgeway grew up there, lived there all her life. Rarely ever left it, died in there as well." She smiled, her eyes twinkling. "Vanessa says that she still stops by from time to time."

"What do you mean?" Jamie paused. "You don't mean, like, her ghost is there?"

"'Ghost' is such a silly word. It conjures up thoughts of small children running amok on Halloween night wearing white bedsheets with holes cut out for their eyes," Grace said dryly. "I prefer 'spirit,' actually."

Jamie stopped at the corner and studied Grace from the corner of her eye. "You don't really believe in ghosts—er, spirits—do you? I mean, not really?"

"Who's to say what dimension we go to when we leave this one, or how one's spirit might communicate with those left behind?"

"I guess." Jamie continued to watch Grace, who was looking straight ahead and smiling.

"Make a left at the stop sign, dear."

Jamie did as she was told.

"That little house there—the third from the corner. Barbara Noonan owns that, inherited from her brother, Colin. Ford and Carly are renting it until they settle on the house they bought over on Grove Street. I daresay a wedding will follow in the spring."

"Oh, they're engaged?" Jamie slowed as they passed the two-story house.

"Not yet. But they will be." Grace's smug smile

held a touch of mystery. "Now, down at the end of this street is the old Enright mansion. Family owned the house for over a hundred years, but last year Curtis Enright—he was the owner—signed it over to the town to use as a cultural and art center."

Grace pointed straight ahead, so Jamie continued to the last stop sign, her heart beating a little faster at the mention of the attorney's name, her interest definitely piqued. "That's the Enright place?" Jamie leaned on the steering wheel and tried to take in the property.

Grace nodded. "Since the 1860s. Enrights have been handling legal issues for most St. Dennis residents since that time. If you lived in St. Dennis and had a legal problem, you stopped in at Enright and Enright—the office is up the street there, on the square—and you saw Curtis or, before him, his father and uncle. Before them, another generation or two, I forget how many."

"Is the art center where Carly works in the mansion?"

"No, it's that building at the end of the driveway. The old carriage house. It was renovated last year. Carly's doing a fine job of putting St. Dennis on the art world's map. Right now she's lining up an exhibit of works by Josette Taliferio."

A horn blasting behind them urged Jamie to move on. At Grace's request, she made a left onto Old St. Mary's Church Road. Along the way, Grace chattered about who had lived in which house, who had been born where, and who had recently purchased which property. The recital ran together in Jamie's head.

"Barbara lives in that yellow clapboard place there on the right. Nita—you met her, owns the antique shop—bought that little Victorian across the street about three years ago . . . My uncle James used to live there . . ."

On and on throughout the town. It seemed almost everyone had an ancestral home that had remained in the family over the years. Thinking about all those fifty-some-year-old St. Dennis women who'd been born and raised here gave Jamie a massive headache. Any one of them could be the woman she was looking for; any house, the one her birth mother grew up in.

"Are you all right, dear?" Grace touched Jamie's arm, and again she felt that odd tingle all the way to her shoulder. "You're looking a bit tense."

The tingle snapped Jamie out of her funk. "I'm fine. As long as you're not getting tired."

"I think maybe we've both had enough drifting around town for one morning."

"If you're sure . . ."

"I'm positive."

"Only if you promise to give me the rest of the tour some other day."

"I'd love to." Grace settled back into her seat with a grateful smile. "I can't thank you enough for indulging me, Jamie. I'm so used to driving myself around, coming and going whenever I please—I just can't stand being dependent. On anyone. For anything."

"I understand. I do," Jamie assured her. "I've done for myself for years, and I can't imagine what it would be like if I had to wait for others to take me places. Believe me, I'm more than happy to take you wherever you'd like to go as long as I'm in St. Dennis." When it appeared that Grace was about to protest, Jamie added, "Really. It's my pleasure. So don't hesitate to ask if there's something you want to do or somewhere you'd like to go."

"Thank you. You're a lovely young woman, Jamie. I'm sure your parents were very proud of you," Grace said softly.

"I hope they were. My dad's been gone for a long time. Ten years. I often wonder what he might have thought about my writing career." Jamie turned the car around and headed back to the inn.

"I'm sure he would have been pleased as punch." Grace reached a hand across the console, her fingers resting on Jamie's forearm. "Do you have siblings?"

None that I know of was on the tip of Jamie's tongue. Instead, she merely shook her head.

"You know, St. Dennis is the perfect place for you right now. The bay is almost magical early in the morning, restorative. You might consider asking Dan for a kayak to take out."

"I've never been in a kayak. I wouldn't know what to do in one."

"There's a brief learning curve. Talk to Dan when we get back. Start on the river if you don't feel comfortable taking on the bay."

"To tell you the truth, I've never been completely comfortable on the water. I'm more of your classic landlubber, I'm afraid."

"Well, then, take one of the bikes."

"That could be fun." Jamie considered. The

thought of biking around this lovely town did have appeal. "I haven't been on a bike in . . . I don't remember the last time."

"You know what they say about riding a bike."

"I do." Jamie nodded. "I think I'll take your suggestion and go for a spin tomorrow."

"You can talk to whoever is at the front desk to make sure a bike is available. It's become a very popular early-morning activity, and there are only so many bikes, so if you don't have one reserved, you could find yourself out of luck." Grace paused. "I suppose we should see about investing in some new ones."

"I'll do that as soon as we get back." She stopped the car near the back door and turned to Grace. "I'm going to run in and see if I can find someone to give you a hand."

"Don't bother, dear." Grace pointed toward the parking lot. "There's one of our waiters. Looks like he's a little early for his shift." She rolled down her window. "Donald, if I could ask you for a favor . . ."

The young man was more than happy to help Grace out of the car and into the wheelchair once Jamie had it in position, and he offered to wheel her into the lobby.

"See how easy this was, Jamie?" Grace was all smiles. "No fuss, no muss." Jamie laughed. "I can't thank you enough for taking me with you this morning. It meant a great deal to me," Grace told her.

"It was my pleasure, Grace." Jamie opened the driver's-side door. "I enjoyed meeting your friends and seeing a little bit of the town."

"Next time we'll finish that tour," Grace promised, then turned to Donald. "All right, then. Let's head on inside."

"I'll see you later, Grace," Jamie called before getting into the car and driving into the parking lot.

On her way through the lobby, Jamie stopped and requested a bike for the following morning.

"I'm sorry, but all our bikes have been booked."

"How 'bout the next day?" Jamie asked.

The receptionist scanned the computer screen. "Nothing until Tuesday morning."

"Fine. I'll reserve one for Tuesday."

"What time would you like?" the receptionist asked.

"Early," Jamie replied.

"Earliest is six a.m.," the young woman told her.

"Fine. Six, then. Thanks." Jamie crossed the lobby, climbed the steps, and went to her room.

The suite was quiet and felt oddly empty. Jamie checked the time and was surprised to find that less than two hours had passed since she'd gone down to breakfast. She picked up the copy of the *St. Dennis Gazette* that room service had brought with her coffee and skimmed each page. There was little news but several interesting, well-written features and a lot of advertisements. She read the piece on the historical society's plans for a new museum, and one on Dallas MacGregor, the A-list actress who made her home in St. Dennis with her young son and her new husband, Grant Wyler. According to the article, Dallas had renovated several old warehouses and started her own film production company and studio in St. Dennis. In the accompanying photo, the smiling star stood outside one of the warehouses holding a copy of *The Autumn of My Dreams,* the book she'd recently announced would be the second film her new company would produce. Jamie finished reading the article, then folded the paper and dropped it on the coffee table, but not before noticing the byline, Ford Sinclair, whom Jamie had agreed to meet on Monday. Who knew what could come out of the interview? Everything she did in St. Dennis, everyone she met, could eventually prove to hold a clue.

While the tour of the town with Grace had been interesting, it had left Jamie feeling restless and out of sorts. Was it her imagination, or did everyone in town have roots that went back to the beginning of time, complete with ancestral home and pedigree? Was one of those pedigrees hers? Were some of her roots here in this bayside town?

Jamie sat at the desk and opened her laptop and logged on. She still had a book to write and needed to spend more quality time trying to come up with the opening chapter. Her hands rested on the keyboard, waiting for a signal from her brain, but her mind was blank. The premise her agent had suggested in the email Jamie had read last night—"Inherent Truths: Honesty in Our Everyday Lives"—was good, but Jamie couldn't come up with an opening line.

After an hour, it became abundantly clear that as hard as it had been for her to talk about honesty to the crowd who'd gathered for her last book signing, writing about it was proving to be impossible. She closed the file and opened the one containing the names of girls who had graduated from local schools in '79 and '80. To the list, she added the names she'd jotted down earlier in Cuppachino. There was always the chance—remote thought it might be—that one of them might prove to be the one she was looking for.

Chapter 8

DAN paused in the doorway of the family's living quarters and watched his mother scan the latest issue of her newspaper. "Mom, I'm sorry about this morning."

"Apology accepted." Grace peered over the top of the page. "I hope you apologized to Jamie as well."

"Not yet." He avoided his mother's eyes.

"You were very rude to her, and I didn't appreciate it," Grace said from behind the paper. "She was doing a favor for me."

"I'll run into her at some point, I'm sure."

"Or you could make it a point to see her and admit that you're a jerk sometimes."

"Did my mother just call me a jerk?"

"Yes, she did."

"Swell."

The last thing Dan felt like doing was apologizing to Jamie Valentine. Jamie the busybody who couldn't seem to help herself when it came to interfering with other people's lives.

"I have to pick up Diana and Paige at Scoop and drop them off at Ellie's. Gabby is having a sleepover, and they were both invited. Dallas did the driving the last time, so . . ."

"So it's your turn tonight. It's only fair to take turns." Grace smiled before going back to her reading.

"Right. I'll see you later."

"Give Ellie and Cameron my love."

"Will do."

Dan started down the steps, then slowed as the busybody in question came through the lobby doors. If he didn't meet up with her, he could honestly say he hadn't had an opportunity to apologize. His eyes narrowed when he saw her pause near the dining room doors, where his son stood talking with his friend Hunter. She and D.J. acted like they knew each other. What was that all about?

Jamie disappeared into the dining room, and Dan hurried down the rest of the steps and caught up with D.J. before he could leave the building.

"Hey, that woman you were just talking to . . ." Dan grabbed his son by the arm.

"She's hot, right?" D.J. grinned.

Dan was this close to rolling his eyes à la Diana. Instead, he said, "How do you know her?"

"I met her at the historical society the other day."

"The historical society?" Dan frowned. What would she have been doing there?

"Yeah. When we were dropping off those boxes for Gramma. She was waiting for Mrs. Ferguson to get there and open up. Mrs. Ferguson was late, so I talked with her—with Jamie—for a while. She said she always liked to learn stuff about places she visited."

"Stuff like what, did she say?"

"Stuff about families who'd been in St. Dennis for a long time. So I told her about the First Families. She seemed real interested in that."

"That's all?"

"All that I know." D.J. shrugged.

"That's the same lady I saw at the library the other day," Hunter said.

"It's summer. What were you doing at the library?" Dan asked.

"I had to stop to see my mom. She's the librarian," Hunter explained.

"And Jamie was in the library?"

"Yeah. She was looking through a bunch of old yearbooks. She had a stack of them on the table."

"Yearbooks? Did you notice where they were from?"

"The one on top of the stack said *St. Dennis High School*."

"What year, did you notice?"

"Nope."

"Thanks, guys." Dan patted his son on the back and walked away. What would Jamie want with a bunch of old yearbooks? Maybe she was looking up a relative. St. Dennis High had been closed for as long as he could remember.

For the rest of the day, his curiosity nagged him. What was Jamie Valentine looking for in a bunch of old yearbooks?

He'd promised his mother he'd apologize to

Jamie, and he would, though he wished he'd kept his big mouth shut earlier in the day, wished he hadn't said a damn word other than "Thank you for making my mother happy." He did owe Jamie an apology for being an ass, and he owed her gratitude for showing such kindness to Grace, whose mood had improved greatly since her morning outing. He was kicking himself in the butt for not having thought to do what this relative stranger had done. Which made him more of an ass and maybe even a little more resentful of Jamie.

If he were honest with himself—which he wasn't really in the mood to be—he'd admit that Jamie had caught his eye the minute she first walked into the lobby. He might have been interested if his mother hadn't tried to play matchmaker; she wasn't fooling anyone when she goaded him into helping Jamie with her bag. Or worse, when she twisted his arm into taking Jamie to Book 'Em. There were times when Grace was anything but subtle. He could tell she really liked Jamie, and she wanted Dan to like her as well.

He kicked a stone from fifteen feet away into one of the Jeep's back tires. He knew his mother had his best interests at heart, and only wanted what she thought was best for him. He was well aware that she wanted nothing more than for him to find someone to fill his life.

Not that he hadn't had his share of female companionship these past few years, mostly with women he'd known for years, women who understood their relationships to be mutually beneficial and without expectations beyond spending an occasional night

together. Dee Baldwin, his last such friend with benefits, had recently announced her engagement to a
broker from New Jersey, and no one had been happier
for her than Dan had been. Well, maybe Dee's mother,
but that was to be expected. But as for a true romantic
relationship, there'd been no such thing since his wife,
Doreen, died eight years ago.

The truth was, for a long time Dan just hadn't
been ready to think about sharing much of anything
with another woman. Doreen's death had been sudden and traumatic, and even now he got a lump in
his throat if he thought too much about her drown-
ing, alone, in the bay. That maybe she'd brought on
a bit of her own bad luck by going out too far on a
day when a storm was brewing only factored into the
pain he and the kids had felt. Her bad judgment had
left him angry and confused for a long time, and the
bombshell she'd dropped in his lap that very morning had only made the situation more difficult to deal
with.

How could anyone keep a secret like the one she'd
kept for as long as she had kept it? How had he never
suspected? Was he so thick-skulled, so dense, that
he'd never caught on? Or had he been so wrapped up
with running the inn that he'd been oblivious to the
fact that she wasn't happy—hadn't been happy for a
very long time and wanted out of their marriage. That
she was leaving to go back to California where her
family lived and it was always warm.

"Look, I know it sounds harsh," she'd said, "but
I've had about all I can take of being the innkeeper's
wife."

"Doreen, you can't take the kids to California" was the first thing Dan had said.

She had shaken her head. "Who said anything about taking them?"

"You'd leave your kids?" He'd been stunned.

"Only because I agree they belong here. They're happy, they're doing well in school, they adore your mother, and they both love living in the inn. They love St. Dennis."

"I thought you liked St. Dennis."

"I did. For a while. For the first couple of years, it was okay. But for someone who grew up in the sun, who swam and surfed every day growing up—the Chesapeake just doesn't cut it, Dan. I can't do this anymore."

"Diana . . . D.J. . . ."

"I love them, I really do. Look, they'll be fine. They have you and they have Grace and they can spend their summers in California." Doreen actually patted him on the back. "You'll all be fine, but if I stay any longer, I'll be even more miserable than I am."

"I had no idea," he'd mumbled.

"Of course you didn't." She'd stood and walked toward the inn. "You're busy doing what you love."

The anger he'd felt with her that morning had been all-consuming for a long time even after her death. There was also a touch of guilt at the undeniable relief he'd felt when he realized that he wouldn't have to explain to his kids why she'd left them. He hadn't been sure which pain would have been greater—that of her death or that of knowing she was leaving them.

It was only after he realized how his anger was affecting his son and daughter that he knew he'd have to let it go and concentrate more on helping them cope with the realities of being without their mother than on whatever issues he might have. After all, he was the grown-up; they were kids who needed their father to be strong and focused. For the most part, Dan had been. He was there for almost all their activities—D.J.'s softball and football games and sailing competitions, Diana's dance recitals and lacrosse and field hockey games. He made it a point to have at least one meal with them every day, and he tried to have one dinner every week with everyone at the table.

And he never, never told anyone that Doreen had planned to leave them—all of them—and that she hadn't wanted to take her children with her.

Thank God for his mother. When Dan was falling apart, Grace had held him together. If he'd grown stronger over the years, it was because she had strength enough to share. He could never thank her enough for all the ways she helped them to be a family. Having Lucy come back to St. Dennis and marry her childhood sweetheart, and having Ford—finally—come home and find his place had made his mother beyond happy. All she'd wanted was to have her family together again. But once she had that, she'd gotten it into her head that she had to find someone for Dan, since he hadn't found someone on his own. He knew from past experience how futile it was to try to talk his mother out of anything once she got hold of an idea.

He blew out a long breath as he started the engine and backed out of the parking spot. The trip to Scoop took less than five minutes; he had another fifteen minutes' wait once he got there for the girls to finish their shift. The usual Friday-night crowd packed the small shop, so Dan waved to Diana to let her know he was there, then gestured to the door to let her know he'd be waiting outside. The bell over the door rang, and he stepped aside to let a few more customers enter, then slipped out behind them and headed for one of the benches on the nearby wooden walkway.

It was quiet by the water, the silence broken only by the occasional banging of the door at Scoop, or the chatter of this group or that coming from Captain Walt's on the other side of the marina. It was so still, Dan could hear the lapping of the water against the sides of the boats that were tied up twenty-five feet away. The heat of the day had not left with the setting sun, and in the halo of the glow from one of the light poles, moths fluttered and burned themselves out on the hot bulbs. The scent of diesel fuel hung over the marina and reminded Dan of a small outboard his dad had owned when Dan was about ten. They'd take it out to Goat Island and spend the afternoon crabbing in the narrow inlet and soaking up a little too much sun on their arms and backs, and Grace would scold them both when they got back to the inn. Dan had brought up that boat with Ford one night, and his brother had drawn a total blank. He didn't recall ever having been on it. What he did remember was the Bay Rider he and their dad used to take all the way down the bay to watch the Bay Bridge–Tunnel being constructed. Conversely, Dan hadn't spent much time on the Bay Rider.

"Your father had his special places and times for each of you," Grace had told them. "It was his way of spending a little bit of individual time with you."

"Hmmmm . . ." Lucy had pondered. "I never got to go to Goat Island to crab, and Dad never took me down to the edge of the bay. But I do remember getting that pretty blue two-wheeler for my birthday when I was eight, and getting up early in the morning to bike-ride around town with Dad. We'd go as far as River Road, then turn around and come back before breakfast."

"Like I said." Grace nodded. "Your father wanted special time with each of you."

Dan couldn't deny he'd lucked out as far as his parents were concerned. He hoped that one day his own kids would feel the same way about him.

He looked up now to see Jamie walking along the boardwalk. "Hey, Jamie." He stood.

"Dan." She acknowledged him but kept walking.

"Listen, could I, um, have a word with you?"

"Why?"

"Because I owe you an apology."

"Yes, you do. Are you apologizing now?"

"Well, yeah. I'm trying to."

"Apology accepted." She resumed walking.

"Wait. Jamie."

She stopped and turned halfway around.

"Look, I was a colossal ass this morning." He ran a hand through his hair, but it immediately flopped back onto his forehead.

"You were," she readily agreed.

"I think . . . that is, I know . . . I wasn't as angry with you as I was with myself for not realizing how much Mom missed getting together in the mornings with her friends." He was almost surprised to hear the truth slip from his lips; he hadn't been planning on that. "You taking her made me realize how little thought I'd given to her situation and what a rotten son I am. I shouldn't have taken it out on you. I'm really sorry."

"I didn't mind taking your mother out for coffee, and I seriously doubt that you're a rotten son. I got to meet some of her friends, and she got to catch up on some gossip. I like your mother. A lot. She's a terrific lady. I was glad to do something for her that made her happy. The fact that I did it and not you does not make you a rotten son. It doesn't matter who took her where she wanted to go. What matters is that she went."

"Look, would you mind sitting for just a few? I'm waiting for my daughter and her friend. They have a sleepover at another friend's house tonight, and I'm the designated parental driver." He gestured for Jamie to sit first. This might be his chance to find out what she was looking for in those old yearbooks.

She looked at him warily, then took a seat at the end of the bench.

"And I suppose I should apologize for . . . you know, Diana. The dress. It's tough being a single parent. Diana's at the age when she needs her mother." All true.

"We always need our mothers," Jamie said. "I lost

mine in April, and I'm still coming to terms with the loss."

"Had she been ill?"

"It came completely out of the blue. She had some heart issues that she hadn't bothered to share with either me or my aunt. We were totally blindsided by her death."

"I'm really sorry." He really *was* sorry. "I guess you and she were very close?"

"I thought we were." Her face turned away.

"Your dad?"

"Passed away about ten years ago."

"I'm sorry," he repeated. This conversation wasn't going anywhere near the way he'd planned.

"Anyway, not to burden you with all that . . ." She looked uncomfortable now that she'd made the admission.

"So you came to St. Dennis to . . . what? Just take a little time off? A breather?"

"More or less, yes."

"Ever been here before?"

"No."

"Why'd you decide on St. Dennis?"

She turned and stared at him. Finally, she said, "I liked what I saw on the website. Why?"

"Just wondering if maybe you had family here."

"No. It just looked like a place I'd like."

"Have you had time to sightsee at all since you arrived?"

"Just a little this morning with your mother. We went for a little ride around town, and she pointed out some historic houses, that sort of thing."

"Did she tell you we have a historical society?"

"No. I suppose in a town as old as St. Dennis, that's a good thing."

"I'm surprised you didn't pass it."

"If we did, I didn't notice."

The door to Scoop banged open, the bell clanging, and Diana and her friend Paige Wyler spilled out, laughing hysterically, their heads close together.

"Oh my God, did you see . . . ?" Paige sputtered.

"How cra' was that?" Diana tripped over a small rock on the walkway, and the two laughed even harder.

"*Totally* cra'."

"There they are." Dan stood. "Over here, girls."

Still laughing, Diana and Paige drew closer. When Diana saw Jamie, her pace slowed. "Jamie?"

"Hi, Diana."

"Hi." Diana looked from Jamie to her father and back. "What are you guys doing?"

"I was waiting for you, and Jamie happened to be passing by, so we've just been talking."

"About what?" Diana eyed her father suspiciously.

"Nothing in particular." Dan looked to Jamie, who nodded and confirmed, "Just chatting."

"Diana, introduce Jamie to Paige," Dan told her.

"Oh, we've met," Paige said. "Sorta. At Scoop."

"That's right, we did." Jamie smiled. "So is Scoop closed now? I was hoping to pick up some more of that amazing ice cream I had the other day. I don't remember what it was, but it was delicious."

"You had Cool Mint Jubilee," Diana told her. "I remember. Steffie won't close for at least another ten minutes. I think she's all out of Cool Mint, though."

"Sounds like I have just enough time to get in and try to choose a flavor." Jamie stood, then glanced over her shoulder at the bench as she began to walk to Scoop. "See you, Dan. Have fun tonight, girls."

"Let's get you two over to Gabby's before she's calling your cell phones to find out where you are."

"She already called. I told her we'd be there in five minutes. What were you and Jamie talking about?"

"Mostly about your grandmother. She's been missing seeing her friends at Cuppachino in the mornings, so Jamie drove her there this morning."

"She did?" Diana paused for a moment midstep. "That was nice of her."

"It was. It made your grandma very happy."

"Jamie's awesome," Diana said as she climbed into the backseat of the Jeep after Paige. "I'm so glad she came to St. Dennis."

Dan turned the key in the Jeep's ignition and watched Jamie disappear through the doorway into Scoop. He wasn't psychic, but he was pretty sure she was hiding something. She definitely wasn't telling the truth about the historical society. D.J. had seen her there, spoken with her. Why, when she had the opportunity, wasn't she forthcoming about having been there? And what—or whom—had she been looking for in those old high school yearbooks?

Yeah, she was hiding something, all right, and one way or another, Dan—never one to ignore a challenge—was going to find out what it was.

Diary~

I knew if I could be patient (always a stretch for me!) and focused, and paid attention to what was going on around me, I would be able to see more clearly what was afoot. I believe my patience has paid off. With dear Alice's help, I've seen through that swirl and the vision was nothing like I've had before. While the confusion of <u>what</u> has been lifted, how to deal with this knowledge has kept me awake for the past two nights. Leave it to Alice to disappear without offering a solution!

But here's what I know for certain:

That swirl of energy? Simply put, Jamie Valentine. I felt it the moment I first saw her in the lobby the night she arrived. She is both the force and the source of the unrest. The woman is on a search—it's clear to me that it was no accident that she chose our inn to begin her quest.

And—I know what she is searching for.

My dilemma lies in whether or not to share what I

know—after all, lives will be changed forever. I don't often find myself in the position to make such a difference—okay, maybe that teensy little spell a few years ago that I put on . . . really, that wasn't much of a spell—barely a muttering—and the outcome would have been the same without it, or so I believe, but that's not the point. That was a very small bit of meddling—but this, <u>this</u> thing, is life-changing. If I speak up—how to explain how I know what I know? And if I do nothing . . . the outcome could be a heartbreak that will last through all eternity and cause never-ending torment for all involved.

Which matters most, the truth or the lie?

All I know is that the heart of a dear friend has been in pain for a very long time, and I may have a way to help her start to heal. But is it my place to tilt fate one way or the other?

If I do nothing, will the outcome result in a lifetime of loss?

My instincts all tell me that I cannot ignore what I know. Perhaps the question really is, how to help Jamie see through that swirl of misting energy that surrounds her to find what she's looking for without appearing to do so. Oh, sometimes it's such a curse to feel, to sense, to know. And once knowing, choices must be made.

I do not wish this "knowing" on anyone I love.

Grace

Chapter 9

J AMIE!" Grace waved from across the lobby as Jamie came through the back doors from an afternoon walk around the inn's grounds.

"Hi, Grace."

"I was just going in for tea. Would you like to join me?"

"I would, thank you." Jamie walked next to Grace's wheelchair.

"We could go into the dining room or on the terrace, or . . ." Grace's attention was drawn to the door, where Ford was wheeling a freight dolly loaded with banker's boxes into the lobby. "Oh, for heaven's sake, I didn't think they'd get here until tomorrow." She tried to get her son's attention but failed. "I'm sorry, Jamie, but I'm afraid I have to postpone our tea. I'll have to unlock my office and make sure Ford puts all those boxes where I want them."

"What's in them, if I may ask?"

"Several years' worth of back issues of the *St. Dennis Gazette*."

"Oh?" Jamie's heart skipped a beat. "Which years?"

"I have no idea. That's the problem." Grace started to roll her chair in the direction of her office, and Jamie followed. "I've been wanting to archive all the past issues, starting with the very first, put them in chronological order, you know. Right now they're scattered here, there, and everywhere around the newspaper office. I started the project before I fell, and it's been making me crazy that I haven't been able to get to the Charles Street office. It's on the second floor, and there's no elevator. The other night it occurred to me that there was no reason why the papers couldn't be brought to me. I can organize them here and send them back when I'm finished."

"Great idea." Jamie moved ahead of the chair to open the office door and hold it while Grace wheeled herself inside.

"So what have we here, son?" Grace asked.

"You tell me. I just picked up ten of the boxes, as you requested, and delivered them, as you instructed." Ford lifted the last box and set it on a table next to the others. "What else can I do for you, Mom?"

"I think this should keep me busy for a while, dear. Thank you." She reached up to pat her son's cheek as she rolled past.

"Let me know when you want me to pick up and bring over the next batch," he said.

"I will do that." Grace was lifting the cardboard lids of the boxes so she could peek inside. "This is insane: 1943, 1968, 1972, all in the same box." She shook her head. "This is going to take forever. I hope I live long enough to finish it."

"Maybe I could help," Jamie offered.

"Oh, no, dear. You have a book to write . . ."

"The book is just not happening, Grace. I can't even decide what to write about."

"Oh?" Grace tuned back in. "Want to talk about it? Bounce a few ideas off me?"

"The truth is, I don't have any ideas. At least right now I don't. So it's frustrating, you know, because I have the time now and really nothing to do. You plan on doing something, and then something happens that stops you in your tracks." Jamie shrugged.

"Tell me about it," Grace said. "Still, I would never impose."

"It's no imposition. You'd be doing me a favor, giving me something useful to do. And besides, who knows, maybe something in one of those back issues will inspire me."

"Well, if you're sure . . ." Grace smiled.

For a second, Jamie wondered if Grace knew her secret. The older woman's smile was just this side of sly. Jamie dismissed the thought. How could Grace possibly know?

"So. I say we have our tea brought to us, and we'll do a preliminary check of these boxes, then maybe start in earnest tomorrow," Grace suggested.

Jamie nodded. "Sounds like a plan."

Tea was requested and delivered, and while they sipped from mugs bearing the *Discover St. Dennis* slogan, Grace told Jamie how the newspaper had come down through her father's family to her older brother, who'd flat-out rejected it.

"Just wasn't his cup of tea." She held up her mug.

"Pun intended. He wanted nothing to do with it. All he wanted was to join the navy, which is what he did. Retired after many years and went to Florida with his third wife. The paper came into my hands by default. But I've loved it all these years, and I still love it. Killed me to turn over so much of the day-to-day to Ford after my accident, but in the long run, it worked out just fine. Maybe the way it was supposed to."

"What do you mean?" Jamie asked.

"If I hadn't had to talk Ford into running the paper for me after I was injured, I doubt he would have stayed around St. Dennis. He wouldn't have met Carly, and he wouldn't have discovered that running a small-town newspaper is exactly what he was meant to do. So, win-win."

"Except for the fact that you're still in the wheel-chair."

"There is that." Grace signed. "It was worth the trade-off."

"Almost sounds like magic."

"Almost, yes. Yes, it does." Grace set her mug down on her desk and clapped her hands. "So. Shall we begin?"

"Oh, wow. Check out the dates on these boxes. All the way back to the 1930s." Jamie pointed to one of the boxes near the bottom of the pile.

"My grandfather was still at the helm then." Grace was clearly in heaven.

The boxes were dusty, so Jamie dusted them off and set them side by side on the long table.

"I'm so excited, I can hardly stand it," Grace declared. "Jamie, go ahead and pull a box. Let's see what we find in that first one there." Jamie set a box on the end of the desk, unpacked the contents, and stacked the old newspapers in front of Grace.

Grace scanned the front page above the fold. "Goodness, Pearl Harbor." She shook her head. "This must have been one of my dad's first assignments."

"So we'll start a pile for 1941 issues." Jamie waited patiently while Grace skimmed the issue and oohed and ahhed at everything from the social notes to the advertisements. When Grace was finished, Jamie put the December issue on the corner of the desk. "Let's see what's next."

"This one is from . . ." Grace squinted. "April 1952." She glanced up at Jamie. "Really. Where else can you skip ahead by eleven years?"

They spent most of the afternoon sorting through boxes, with Grace reading snippets aloud, commenting on the local events that had appeared on the social page, and Jamie making piles by decade by year. She'd clearly underestimated the project. There must be thousands of newspapers to go through. She wondered if the clues she was looking for would be found hidden in one of the boxes, or if this would prove to be an exercise in futility. Maybe there was no reported social event that would tip her off, or maybe the issue that reported it was missing somehow. Even if that tidbit was sprinkled somewhere between the pages of an old paper, would she recognize it if she saw it?

Still, Jamie scanned each paper carefully, hoping to find at least one issue from 1979, something that would tell her she was getting close.

Jamie couldn't help but feed off Grace's enthusiasm. The woman was having such a great time, reliving so many memories, good and bad. The death of friends and family members brought a veil of sadness to her face, and the happy moments, the weddings, the graduations, the cheery reporting of remembered parties and holiday events, brought smiles. It wasn't hard to get into the spirit of Grace's discoveries.

But by seven o'clock, Jamie felt as if her eyes were crossing and her mind was starting to spin, though Grace seemed to be totally unaffected. Jamie had stood and gone through the piles again to make sure she hadn't misplaced anything when she felt she was being watched. She turned and found Dan in the doorway, a curious expression on his face.

"Hi," she said.

"Hey," he returned the greeting.

"Dan, you won't believe what this wonderful girl is doing for me." Grace all but chortled.

"I heard all about it from Ford." His eyes were on Jamie. "Nice of you to help Mom out. It's something she's been talking about for a long time. Must be boring as hell for you, though. All those old papers filled with stories about people you don't know." He picked up one from the pile, turned a few pages, then read, "'Mrs. Alexander Finnegan had as a houseguest her sister, Miss Emily Jessen, from Trenton, New Jersey. Miss Jessen is pursuing her education as a high school Latin teacher.'" He put the paper back on the pile and, still looking at Jamie, said, "Fascinating."

"Well, it does give a little snapshot of who lived here and what was going on back then," Jamie said casually.

"Oh, and this one: 'Mr. Peter Coughlin is the proud owner of a new Chevrolet coupe. The car—a two-toned cream and brown beauty—was delivered by the dealer, Calvin Espy, and brought all the way from Baltimore to St. Dennis. Mr. Coughlin has been seen driving his wife and children to the market and to school, respectively.'" He turned to Jamie. "Now, I ask you, is this exciting real-life drama or what?"

"You best stop making fun of my newspaper, Daniel Sinclair, or you will be wishing you had." Grace glared at her son.

"Sorry, Mom. I wasn't really poking fun as much as . . ." He paused.

"As much as what?" Grace was waiting.

"As much as teasing Jamie about her interest in days gone by, St. Dennis–style."

"Same as any place else, I imagine." Grace's tone was still a tad frosty.

"You never know what you might learn." Jamie maintained her casual stance.

"Guess that depends on what you're looking for."

"Don't you have a wedding to attend to?" Grace fixed a stare on her son.

"I do." He smiled at his mother. "Get it? Wedding? I do?"

Grace rolled her eyes and pointed to the door. "Please."

Dan grinned, gave Jamie one last look, then closed the door behind him.

"Sometimes that boy of mine gives me a headache," Grace muttered.

I feel your pain, Jamie could have told her. There

was something in the way Dan had been looking at her, as if he knew her decision to help Grace was based less on her desire to help and more on something else. Though he might have his suspicions, there was no way he could know the truth of the matter.

But hadn't the conversation last night sounded like an interrogation? Was it her imagination, or had he seemed to be fishing for something? She wished she'd said flat-out that she'd been to the historical society, because after she'd denied knowing about it, he'd brought it up again, as if he knew. But it had caught her off guard, and her first instinct had been to shrug off his interest.

It was clear to her that she'd done nothing but fan any interest he might have had.

. . . *teasing Jamie about her interest in days gone by, St. Dennis–style.*

. . . *depends on what you're looking for.*

How could he possibly know?

He doesn't, she told herself. *He just thinks he's clever, that's all.* He thought she'd been a little shady in her response to some of his questions about where she'd been and what she'd been doing since she arrived in St. Dennis. *Best to ignore him. Let him have his suspicions, but don't feed in to them.*

". . . wrap up here for the day and pick up in the morning where we left off." Grace tucked her glasses into their case and put them into her bag. "I do want to be able to peek into the ballroom later to catch a glimpse of tonight's bride. Lucy's been telling me all week that this wedding is going to be spectacular."

"What time would you want to start tomorrow?" Jamie asked.

"Oh, please don't feel that you have to come back."

"I want to. I think it's fascinating. I love looking at the pictures of old St. Dennis and seeing what folks were up to back then."

"It is interesting, isn't it?" Grace wheeled out from behind her desk. "Now, only if you're sure . . ."

"I'm sure."

"In that case, I usually have breakfast early—before seven—so I should be here around seven-thirty."

"I'll see you then." Jamie followed Grace out of the office, pausing at the door to turn off the lights. At the stairwell, Grace went to the dining room, and Jamie climbed the steps to the second floor. When she got to her room, she went straight to the desk and opened the laptop and read through the names of graduates to refresh her memory. She was halfway through the list when she recognized several of the names—Nita Etheridge must be Nita Perry. The first name wasn't that common, and Perry would be her married name. Eleanor Borden—that could be Eleanor Cash who owns the flower shop. Barbara Noonan—the owner of the bookstore—either never married or kept her maiden name. Jamie had also met Lisa, a waitress, and Joanna, the assistant librarian, but neither name was on the list, so either they hadn't lived here then or weren't in the 1979 or 1980 graduating class.

And there were so many names of women Jamie hadn't met yet. Discouraged, she closed the laptop.

Whatever had made her think that *seeking* would translate into *finding*? She was no closer to identifying her birth mother now than she had been when she was in Caryville.

Patience.

She could almost hear her father whisper in her ear, and the thought made her smile. She reminded herself that she'd been in St. Dennis only a few days, and in that time she had managed to make friends with the one person in town who might lead her to the truth. Surely a truth that had been hidden for thirty-six years would not be found out over so short a period of time.

Patience.

She sighed and wished she'd been blessed with the virtue.

". . . SO I TOLD Tom—he's the Realtor I think we should list the house with when we're ready—I said that we decided to hold off putting the house on the market. He thought we were missing a good opportunity to sell because sales are high right now, but I said no, we wanted to wait a bit." The words poured out of Sis's mouth almost the minute Jamie answered the phone. "Unless you've changed your mind about waiting . . ."

"No, I'm not quite ready."

"That's perfectly fine, honey. I told him I'd check with you and get back to him."

"Thanks, Aunt Sis."

"Now, did you make any decision on that lawn furniture we found in the garage?"

"I haven't thought about it," Jamie told her.

"That's okay. It's been sitting in there for the past, I don't know, six, seven years now. A little longer isn't going to hurt. Lainey picked it up at a house sale and thought she'd repaint it and get new cushions for it. You know how she loved doing that sort of thing."

"Right."

"Jamie?" Sis asked tentatively. "Is everything all right there?"

"Things are fine."

"You sound like you're thinking."

Jamie laughed. "You say it as if it's a bad thing."

"You know what I mean. Thinking about . . . things."

"You mean my birth mother."

"Well, yes. I know you're tied up in knots over that whole business."

"That 'whole business' is my life, Aunt Sis," Jamie reminded her.

"Of course it is. I just worry that things aren't going to go well for you, and you'll come home even more confused and sad than when you went down there."

"I'm still confused and sad. I probably always will be, to some extent. I'll never have the opportunity to talk to Mom about how she felt and how I felt. That's a conversation that needed to be had, and it never will be."

"I'm so sorry, honey."

"Not your fault, Aunt Sis."

"Maybe if I'd nagged Lainey, if I'd—"

Jamie snorted. "You know that nagging was never

effective where Mom was concerned. And there's nothing you could have done. She did what she wanted to do, in this and everything else in her life. I don't want you to stress over this anymore. I will make my peace with the situation regardless of what happens here in St. Dennis. It may take a while," she acknowledged, "but I will make peace with it all."

"I believe you will, Jamie. Speaking of St. Dennis, what *is* happening there?"

"I've met a number of women who are around the right age, but I can't say I met anyone who reminds me of myself."

"Maybe she's not there," Sis said softly. "Maybe she left town and hasn't come back."

"There's that possibility, but little things the lawyer said made me think she might still be around."

"Maybe you've already met her and didn't know it."

"I guess that's possible, but you'd think we'd know each other, wouldn't you?"

"You were three days old when you were handed over to Lainey and Herb, so there's no way you'd recognize each other. I don't know that I believe you'd instinctively *know*. I think that's the romanticized version of how those things go."

"Maybe." Jamie sighed. "I guess I thought I'd look enough like someone in her family that she'd wonder . . . Oh, I don't know what I thought."

"I wish you luck, babe. I really do." It was Sis's turn to sigh. "Now tell me how you're spending your time."

"Funny you should ask. I've met this remarkable woman—Grace Sinclair is her name, she's the mother of the guy who runs the inn. She's also the owner of the newspaper that's been published in St. Dennis for . . . I don't know exactly how many years, but I would guess it's close to one hundred. It's been in her family since it was founded. She's just started this project, archiving all the old issues because they're in no order whatsoever. The paper has a social column that reported on all the local events from week to week, like who got married and who died."

"We used to call that the gossip column here in Caryville. We had the old *Banner* that came out once a week."

"It's like that, yes. Anyway, I offered to help Grace go through the old newspapers, and she's letting me work on the project with her. It's interesting and it's fun, actually."

"You're spending your vacation helping someone organize a collection of old newspapers? Doesn't sound like fun to me."

"Oh, but it is. I really think that somewhere in those stacks, I'm going to find a clue to my birth mother's identity."

"How do you suppose that's going to happen?"

"I don't know. It's my only option right now, but I think it's going to lead me in the right direction."

"I suppose something could come of that," Sis said. "By the way, have you gone to see the attorney yet?"

"You mean Curtis Enright? No. I haven't decided how best to approach him. Knowing he doesn't want to be involved with me, I don't want to alienate him by ringing his doorbell. I'm sure he'll be easy enough to find."

Sis changed the subject, chatting on about how her friend Kathleen's son Andrew was back in town and how she, Kathleen, and Lainey had always thought that Andrew and Jamie were perfect for each other. Jamie strolled to the balcony and watched some little ones line up for the sliding board on the playground, tossing out the occasional "ah-huh" or "hmmm."

Directly below her balcony, a Jeep drove up and parked at an awkward angle to the building. Jamie watched as Dan got out and walked to the edge of the parking lot, where he was joined by his sister, who was wearing a navy blue chiffon dress that floated around her knees. They stood and talked for a minute before he took her arm and helped her navigate the stone-filled parking lot in her mile-high heels. Jamie couldn't deny that he definitely did justice to a tux, from what she could see. Damn.

"Aunt Sis, I'm going to run. I want to get down to the dining room while they're still serving. I'll give you a call in a few days and let you know if I learn anything. Love you."

She disconnected the call and went into the bathroom, where she took a quick shower and blow-dried her hair. It was Friday night, and she wasn't sure how dressed up other guests got on the weekend. Through the window, she could hear what she assumed was the wedding band tuning up, and the music made her feel like dancing. She pulled a dress from the closet— a basic tank style in teal—and draped a light scarf around her neck. She searched through the few pieces of jewelry she'd brought and snapped wide hoops of hammered silver into her ears. She slipped her bag over her arm and her feet into sandals and headed downstairs.

The dining room wasn't as crowded as she'd thought it might be, so she was able to get a table near the windows, where she watched the children on the playground while she drank a glass of wine. She was starving, so she ordered a steak and a salad and a second glass of wine, then tiramisu and coffee to finish off the meal.

Grace was right, Jamie thought as she strolled back into the lobby. *The chef here is amazing.* Everything she'd ordered had been delicious, but she felt she needed to walk it off. She went outside and down to the edge of the bay and watched geese land feet-first, honking loudly, by the last light of day. She followed the paver path around the inn to the front of the building, hoping to sit for a while in one of the rocking chairs, but was disappointed to find that other guests had the same idea. She went in through the front door and paused in the foyer.

Music was coming from behind a pair of double doors on the right. The wedding Dan and Grace had spoken of—the one he'd donned a tux for—must be behind those doors, she thought. What harm would there be if she took a quick peek? Didn't Grace mention that Lucy had said it would be spectacular? What did a spectacular wedding look like, anyway?

Jamie couldn't resist the opportunity to find out.

She opened the door just a sliver, enough to slip through. Some of the guests were seated and some were milling around the bar; despite the music, the dance floor was empty. Though Jamie didn't know what the ballroom looked like on an average day, tonight it looked like a lush summer garden. There were white birch trees in shiny silver pots and white twinkling lights everywhere. The tables were set with silvery cloths over white, and the centerpieces were silver vases overflowing with lavender and white flowers, some of which Jamie didn't recognize. She stepped closer to the table nearest the door to get a better look. There were roses in both colors and some sort of silvery green vine that trailed onto the tabletops, but everything else looked exotic and unfamiliar. She had just leaned closer when she felt someone behind her. "May I see your invitation?"

She knew the voice. She opened her purse and peered inside, then patted her hips where pockets would be—if the dress had pockets—and shrugged. "I must have left it in my room," she told Dan.

"Then I guess I have to ask you to leave," Dan said solemnly.

"Not until I find out what those purply-silver things are. They sort of look like thistle."

"That's because they are thistle."

"Trying to impress me with your horticultural knowledge?"

"Did it work?"

"Maybe." She looked around the ballroom. "Your mother wasn't kidding when she said this place would look spectacular."

"That's Lucy. She really is a wizard at putting these things together. I honestly don't know where she gets her ideas from."

As if on cue, Dan's sister hurried over, looking flushed. "Dan, no one's dancing," she told him.

"It's still early," he told her. "Lucy, I don't think you met Jamie. She's—"

"J. L. Valentine. Mom told me. Thanks for helping her out with her project. She's so excited to finally be getting through those old newspapers."

"I'm enjoying it," Jamie replied.

"Not to be rude, but Dan, no one is dancing, and Franklin—that's the guy playing the piano—is threatening to stop playing."

"What difference does it make to him who dances and who doesn't? He gets paid whether people dance or not, right?"

"That's not the point. At least it isn't to him. He thinks it looks bad for the band, like no one likes what they're playing."

"What *are* they playing?" He frowned.

Lucy smacked him on the arm but tilted her head to listen. "I think that's a really slowed-down instrumental version of 'Can't Take My Eyes Off of You.'" She looked from Dan to Jamie and back. "Go dance." She gave her brother a little shove. "You and Jamie. Go. Maybe others will follow."

"Lucy . . ."

"Pleeeease, Danny?" Lucy put her hands together. "My favorite brother? Pleeeease . . ."

Dan covered his ears. "Lucy, don't whine." He took Jamie by the hand. "Will you? If only to make her stop? I hate it when she does that."

Jamie laughed good-naturedly and followed Dan onto the dance floor. He put one arm around her and, with the other, held her hand. He pulled her close so that the top of her head was just under his chin. "I didn't realize you were so tiny," he said.

"I didn't realize you were so tall," she replied.

He hummed along with the music for a minute. "Lucy wasn't kidding when she said this was a slowed-down version. Maybe that's why no one else is dancing."

"But someone else is," she told him, and turned them around to face the opposite side of the dance floor, where another couple had begun to sway to the music. "See? Lucy was right. I guess no one likes to be the first on the dance floor."

"Actually, it wasn't bothering me." He leaned back and looked into her eyes. "You?"

"Not really."

"Good." He pulled her close again, and they swayed to the music.

When the song ended, they continued to slow-dance for a moment longer before Dan dropped her hand and said, "Hey, thanks for helping to keep the peace." He looked around the dance floor at the number of couples who had joined them, then looked down into her eyes. "Looks like that did the trick."

"Looks like," she agreed.

Just for a moment, his face was so close to hers that she thought he was about to kiss her. They stared at each other for a heartbeat, and the moment was gone.

Dan cleared his throat, and his grip on her waist eased. "So," he said. "Shall we leave the dance floor to the guests?"

"Good idea."

Dan walked her back to where he'd found her, and they were both surprised to find Grace sitting there watching them, a slight smile on her lips. "The band is quite good, don't you agree?" she said.

"Very good." Jamie took a step away from Dan, and he dropped his hand. "Well, thanks for letting me crash the party." She turned to Grace. "I'll see you in the morning."

Grace nodded. "Bright and early."

Jamie smiled a goodbye to Dan and went to the door. He followed and pushed it open for her. "Good night," he said. "Thanks for the dance."

"You're welcome." She walked across the foyer and into the main lobby, knowing that his eyes followed her every step of the way. Something had changed between them, and she wasn't sure if that was a good thing or a bad thing. She tried pushing him from her mind, telling herself that the last thing she needed right now was a distraction of any kind, particularly the kind that Dan could be. But when she fell asleep later that night, she dreamed of dancing on a cloud with a man whose eyes were almost as blue as her own, and arms strong enough to catch her if she fell.

Chapter 10

‸

DAN stood at the railing that wrapped around the crow's nest, his private sanctuary at the very top of the inn, and watched the moon spread pale light across the bay. It was a perfect night, a perfectly beautiful and romantic night, and yet here he stood alone, an unopened bottle of beer in his hand from MadMac, the craft brewery owned by his brother-in-law Clay Madison and Clay's partner, Wade MacGregor. He was thinking about Jamie and how good it had felt to hold her while they danced. But something about her was off. She was hiding something, and the last thing he needed in his life was another woman who kept secrets.

He couldn't figure out why his mother, who was normally so astute about such things, didn't seem to see it at all. Why, she and Jamie were as chummy as could be. Not only were they suddenly BFFs, Jamie was working with Grace on that pet project of hers. So what exactly was making Dan suspicious?

For starters, who in her right mind would

volunteer to spend hours going through dusty old newspapers if she wasn't hoping to find something, some bit of information that would lead . . . where?

Then there was that business of her pretending not to know anything about the historical society when he knew for a fact that she'd been there. Why do that?

And what was she looking for in old high school yearbooks? Four of them, Hunter had said. The kid was goofy, but he wasn't blind, and he could read.

It all added up to her looking for something—or someone—in St. Dennis. So her story about finding St. Dennis randomly and thinking it looked like a nice place for a vacation, or whatever it was she claimed, clearly was a crock.

If he were to be honest with himself, he'd admit it was eating at him that he liked her in spite of it all.

As for tonight, he couldn't explain the way he'd felt when he held her, or that urge to kiss her. Lucky he backed away when he did. Who knew where that could have led?

And then there was his mother, sitting there with that enigmatic smile on her face, the smile he'd seen many times before. That look that said she knew things other mere mortals didn't.

So why was she so blind to the fact that Jamie was, if not actually up to something, hiding something? Unless, of course, Grace wasn't blind at all. Unless Grace, too, was hiding something.

He tucked the bottle under his arm and headed for the deck chair overlooking the inn's grounds, where he'd drink a beer or two and try to forget what it had felt like to look into those electric blue eyes and to hold that perfect body in his arms.

JAMIE ARRIVED AT Grace's office minutes after Grace.

"Lovely wedding last night," Grace said.

"It was. The room looked beautiful."

"Lucy has always loved parties with themes. I suppose that's what makes her so good at what she does." Grace took a sip of tea from her mug. "So. Let's get started, shall we?" She opened the first of the boxes with a flourish. "I think we should keep an eye on the social columns from now on."

Jamie stared at Grace. Had she been reading Jamie's mind?

"I think we'll find some interesting tidbits in these issues," Grace went on.

"Oh?"

"My parents were married during this time, and all of my siblings and I were born in the forties. I'm sure there are announcements of all those events." She opened the box. "Not that I believe the boxes contain all the issues between those years. It would be too much to ask that someone was that well organized, ever. I know my father was not." Grace handed Jamie a stack of papers. "The social pages used to be ten through twelve, depending on how much news there was that week. Let me know if you find anything interesting."

"Hi, Gram." Diana peered around the doorjamb. "Hi, Jamie."

"Well, good morning, sunshine." Grace positively beamed at the sight of her only granddaughter. "What brings you down here so early?"

"I heard Dad get up, then you, then D.J. got up, so I thought maybe I should get up, too. Dad said you guys were working on a project." She boosted herself up to sit on the long table. "What are you guys doing?"

"We're going through old issues of the newspaper, trying to put them in chronological order," Grace told her.

"Why?"

"For one thing, they should be in order, at least by year, because the issues go back a long way. And once they're in order by date, you can see everything that happened in St. Dennis over the past hundred and some years, just by looking at the *Gazette*."

"Everything, Gram?" Diana teased.

"Everything that mattered to the people who lived here."

Diana pulled a folded paper from the open box. "Let's see. This one is from . . . 1956." She glanced through it. "Oh, the interview is with Miss Berry." Diana told Jamie, "She was a famous movie star. I knew about her because she's Dallas's aunt, and Dallas is Paige's stepmom, and 'cause Gram knows her." She held up the paper. "Look, Gram, how pretty she was."

"Oh, I remember how pretty she was. St. Dennis was very proud of her," Grace said.

Diana passed Jamie the paper. "Beryl Townsend was her movie-star name. Everyone in St. Dennis calls her Miss Berry or Miz Eberle."

"I've seen some of her films," Jamie told them. "She was quite the comedic actress in her day."

"I believe Berry prefers to think of herself as a

great dramatic actor," Grace said. "Though you are right, of course. She could do it all."

"What else?" Diana dove into another box. "1993." She read through the first few pages. "Nothing really interesting . . . Oh, is this Uncle Cliff?" She held up a picture for Grace, then turned it so Jamie could see.

"Yes, it is. My older brother," Grace told Jamie. "He built boats—skipjacks—in an old building that used to stand where the new boat shop is. Cliff passed away a few years ago." She smiled. "He was quite the character. Never married, but he was real good to all the nephews and nieces. Took my sister Carol's boy under his wing when she and her husband died in that car crash." Grace shook her head, obviously saddened by the memory.

"Let's see what else we can find." Diana's enthusiasm was growing.

"Somewhere in those newspapers, you'll find my birth announcement, as well as those of all my siblings. Wedding announcements, graduations . . . Our family history played out in that newspaper." Grace added, "And the histories of every other family in town."

Jamie had the feeling Grace was speaking directly to her. But how would she know that Jamie was looking for family milestones of her own?

Eventually, they were successful in finding not only Grace's birth announcement and those of her siblings but her parents' wedding photos as well.

"Oh my, Mother was so young here." Grace's smile was touched with nostalgia. "And so pretty."

"Let me see," Jamie said. She and Diana both looked over Grace's shoulder.

"She was beautiful, Gram. Aunt Lucy looks like her."

"She does. Everyone always said so." Grace sighed. "I imagine if we go back far enough, we'll find my grandparents in one of those papers as well. How about you put aside any issues that have photos in the social columns? It might be fun to have an exhibit someday. Old St. Dennis brides, maybe." She looked dreamily into space for a moment. "Maybe we could frame them and show them at the gallery . . . Or Sophie might want them to display."

"Sophie?" Jamie asked.

"Sophie Enright. She owns Blossoms," Diana said.

"The restaurant on River Road?"

"That's right," Grace told her.

"I had lunch there the other day."

"Sophie's relatively new in town, though her family has been here for a very long time. You might have seen the family law firm in your travels. It's over near the square. Enright and Enright, there's a big sign out front," Grace continued.

Jamie nodded. "I think I may have seen it."

"Sophie's grandfather is Curtis Enright, who donated their family home for the new art gallery. Remember, Jamie, we drove past there and I pointed it out?"

"I do, yes. It's a beautiful property."

"The Enright place was the only true mansion ever built in St. Dennis." Grace paused as if something had just occurred to her. "Oh, Jamie, there's going to be an exhibit at the gallery tonight. Why not plan on going? Everyone in town will be there."

"I think I might do that. Thank you for letting me know." As if it just occurred to her, she added, "Now that I think about it, my dad went to law school with a Curtis Enright. I'm pretty sure he was from Maryland."

"I'm sure it must be the same person. Fancy that," Grace said. "I will have to make sure you meet him at the gallery."

"I'm looking forward to it." Her heart pounding at the thought of meeting the man who held the key to her quest, Jamie turned her attention back to the stack of papers and went directly to page ten. "Oh, look. Here's a picture of someone named Elizabeth Sommerville, whose engagement to Clark Westfield was being announced."

"Oh, let me see." Grace held out her hand for the paper. "That's my Great Aunt Lizzie. Diana, come see."

There was more of the same, engagement and wedding pictures of noted residents; the day was broken up only by the delivery of a delicious lunch that Grace ordered from the kitchen because she, Diana, and Jamie were far too absorbed in what they were doing to leave the office to eat.

"Look, Gram." Diana held up an issue from 1990. "Here's a picture of Grampa crabbing out on the bay."

"Let me see that." Grinning, Grace reached for the paper. "He really did love to go out there with his net, late afternoons. He'd crab until he filled up a bucket, then he'd come back in and hand over his catch to

Mrs. Ewing—she was our cook back then—and she'd make the most delicious crab cakes."

"I like to crab with a net, too," Diana said. "And I'm pretty good at it."

"Yes, you are, dear." Grace passed the paper back to her granddaughter.

"Have you ever caught crabs with a net?" Diana asked Jamie.

"No. I thought crabs were caught in traps," Jamie said.

"Only by commercial trappers. They use traps 'cause they want to catch a lot of crabs at one time. When you use a net, you catch one—maybe if you're real lucky, two—at a time. It takes more skill." Diana smiled at Jamie. "I'll teach you sometime, if you want."

"Well, crabbing wasn't on my bucket list, but it sounds like fun, so sure. Thank you. I'm game," Jamie said.

"I think that's an excellent idea," Grace told Jamie. "You're here on vacation, and you've barely been outside. I think some time crabbing is just what you need. Put some color in your cheeks."

"It's supposed to rain in the morning, but maybe tomorrow afternoon, if you don't have anything else planned," Diana suggested.

"No plans at all, thanks." Jamie turned her attention back to the stacks of papers. She firmly believed that while she didn't know what she was looking for, she would know it when she saw it. Though she found some photos Grace enjoyed seeing, the subjects were all older than her birth mother would be.

She needed to get her hands on those boxes from the early 1960s, specifically 1962 and 1963, since she figured the woman she was looking for was born somewhere around that time. But they emptied the boxes Ford had brought over, and none of them was from the right time period. *Perhaps in the next group,* Jamie told herself. Sooner or later, those years had to turn up.

Diana made piles on the table by decade, the thought being that they could break those down by year as they added more issues.

"I think we should close up shop for today," Grace told them at four. "The reception at the gallery begins at six, and I promised Carly we'd all be there." She turned to Jamie. "Please plan to come for that. Just tell them at the door that you're with our party, and you should have no trouble getting in. The regular gallery showing opens at seven, but Carly always plans a lovely VIP reception. I think you'll enjoy it."

"I'm sure I will. I'll see you there."

Grace wheeled herself to the door, and Jamie waited while she locked the door behind them. To Diana, she said, "Are you going, too?"

"I have to work tonight at Scoop, so I'm going to miss it. But maybe you can stop by for ice cream after and tell me all about it."

"I'll do that. Grace, thank you again for telling me about the reception. I'll definitely go," Jamie said as they entered the lobby. Grace headed for the freight elevator—her only means of moving between floors—and Diana accompanied her.

"Thank you again for all your time today." Grace

turned in her chair as Jamie started up the steps. "I can't tell you how much I appreciate having help. I'm afraid, on my own, I'd never be able to get through all those newspapers. Who knows what important bit of news we might have missed?"

Jamie began taking the steps. Really, it was almost as if Grace knew.

AT 6:55, JAMIE was crossing the lobby when Dan stepped out of the dining room.

"Hey," he called to her, and she slowed her pace so he could catch up. She'd been trying to avoid thinking about him after last night. So far today, she'd done pretty well. But now, with him walking toward her, so handsome in his light blue suit that matched his eyes, she felt her pulse quicken.

"Hi" was all she trusted herself to say.

"You look nice," he told her.

"So do you."

"Off for the evening?" They walked together through the lobby doors.

"The gallery reception," she said. "Your mother invited me."

"Me, too." He paused at the railing. "So. Would you want to ride over with me? I mean, since we're both going to the same place."

"Oh. Okay. Thanks."

"You can wait here and I'll pick you up." He looked down at her high-heeled sandals. "Might pick up a few stones in those shoes. Probably wouldn't feel too good."

"Thanks." Jamie waited on the walkway near the

back porch, occasionally stepping out of the way of the other guests coming and going. She'd been trying to keep her nerves under control, knowing she would most likely meet Curtis Enright face-to-face, wondering what he would say to her when they were introduced. She'd even picked her clothes with him in mind, choosing the black mandarin-collared dress over the sundress she'd picked up at Bling, which showed more skin. She had considered wearing it with a shrug, but the weather was hot, so she thought the black dress would be more appropriate. It was one of her favorites, and judging by Dan's reaction, it had been the right choice.

He pulled up to the walk, and she opened the car door and got in.

"Who are the artists being shown tonight, do you know?" she asked, to make conversation. "I meant to ask your mother, but I forgot."

Dan shrugged. "I don't know. Some local people. Carly just said, 'I want you all to be there,' so we're all going."

He fiddled absentmindedly with the radio until they were on Charles Street.

"Is something wrong?" she asked.

"What? No. Why?"

"Because you seem really distracted."

"Sorry. Our best sous chef handed in her notice, and we have to replace her ASAP. We got a great response to the ads, and I was going over the résumés."

"Isn't that something the head chef would do?" she asked. "I mean, he has to work with everyone in the kitchen. Doesn't he get to choose?"

"My inn, my responsibility," he told her. "I'll weed

out those I don't think would work, and we'll bring in the ones who make the cut for an interview."

"My, you really are hands-on, aren't you?"

He glared at her across the console. "Like I said, my inn, my responsibility."

They arrived at the gallery in minutes, but due to the heavy volume of cars parked along Old St. Mary's Church Road, they had to drive several streets over to park.

"Looks like they drew a crowd," she observed as they walked the two short blocks to the gallery.

"I'm sure local artists bring people in. I guess friends and relatives show up."

"I wonder if any of them are really good."

"I guess we'll find out."

"The house is just magnificent." Jamie paused on the sidewalk and nodded in the direction of the house that stood off to their left. "Nice that it was donated to the town. Nicer still that it's being used for the benefit of the community."

"And nice for my brother," Dan said, "because it brought the love of his life to St. Dennis. Never thought Ford would settle down, but I guess miracles do happen."

There was a line to get into the carriage house, which served as the exhibition site. Jamie assumed that the space was very small, since it seemed that so many people had to exit before an equal number of people could enter. Once inside, however, she found that while space was limited, it was far from small. She and Dan followed the direction of the framed paintings from one wall to the next.

"Whoever this artist is," Jamie said, leaning closer to read the name on the wall, "this Shirley Hinson, she's done some lovely work."

"Shirley Hinson Wyler. Steffie's mother," he told her. "Steffie owns Scoop."

"Ah, the ice cream maker."

Dan nodded and turned her toward the far wall. "Stef's over there, with her mother and her twins."

Jamie craned her neck to see the babies, who were being held, one by a tall dark-haired man and the other by a woman with the palest blond hair. When the woman turned slightly to one side, Jamie recognized her profile. "Oh my God, that's Dallas Mac-Gregor." She grabbed Dan's arm.

"Sure. She's Stef's sister-in-law."

"Be still my heart." Jamie's fingers fluttered at her chest. "I've seen every movie she's made." She tried not to stare. "Who's the guy?"

"Steffie's husband, Wade. Dallas's brother," he told her. "He's my brother-in-law's partner in MadMac Brews. *Mad* for Clay Madison, *Mac* for Wade Mac-Gregor."

"And the older woman there . . . the one in the beaded caftan." Jamie's eyes narrowed. "Is that . . . Beryl Townsend?"

"Right. Dallas and Wade's great-aunt."

"She's a legend." Jamie couldn't keep from staring. "An absolute legend. One of the biggest stars ever. We were looking at a picture of her this afternoon. Diana found it in one of the old newspapers."

"Diana was in the office with you and Mom today?"

"Yes, she was a big help." Jamie smiled. "And she really seemed to enjoy going through the papers once she got into it. She got a kick out of seeing pictures of your mother when she was young; an uncle; and some other members of your family that I don't remember."

"What about you?" he asked casually. "Any relatives of yours?"

"I told you, I don't have family here."

A passing server offered hors d'oeuvres, and Jamie took advantage of the distraction to select a pastry filled with something that smelled delicious. "Oh, yum." She took a bite, ignoring the look Dan had given her. Clearly, he wasn't buying her story, but she wasn't sure why and wasn't about to ask. Best to ignore it completely, which she did. "I don't know what that was, but I want another."

She caught the eye of the server, and when he arrived, he suggested they each take several of the small bites. "The caterer is getting backed up in the kitchen, and I'm not sure when I'll be back out with something."

"You don't need to tell me twice," Jamie said. She placed several bits of puff pastry on a napkin. Dan followed suit, and they nibbled as they strolled through the gallery.

When they reached the reception area where the artist stood, Dan introduced Jamie. "Shirley Hinson—Shirley Wyler—meet Jamie Valentine," he said.

The artist regarded Jamie for a moment, then smiled. "You're J. L. Valentine. I saw your picture in the window at Book 'Em. I plan on coming to your signing."

"Thank you. I'll be happy to sign a book for you. I'm an instant fan of your work. I love watercolors, and I love the garden scenes you've displayed here. Are any for sale?"

"They all are, except for the large water lilies." Shirley put a hand over her heart. "J. L. Valentine likes my work."

"Jamie Valentine loves your work," Jamie corrected.

"Jamie, this is my daughter, Steffie, her husband, Wade, and my grand-darlings." Shirley made the introductions.

"You're the ice cream maker." Jamie shook Steffie's hand. "I've been haunting your shop since I arrived in St. Dennis, and I will be making a stop there before I go back to the inn tonight."

"Oh, wow. A famous writer likes my ice cream." Steffie beamed.

Wade and Dan stepped off to the side to chat with Ford and another man whom Jamie didn't recognize.

"From the reviews I've read online, I'd say everyone loves your ice cream. It's certainly the best I've ever had," Jamie told her.

"Stef, you'll have to name an ice cream flavor for Jamie," her mother told her. "Something like Honestly Fudge."

"A great idea. I'll do it." Steffie grinned. "What's your favorite, Jamie?"

"Chocolate, anything with mint, berries, nuts, just about everything, I think. But you don't have to—"

"It's a great idea. I'll see if I can come up with something in time for your book signing."

"That's really nice of you." Then, to deflect the attention from herself, Jamie asked, "Now, who are these two cherubs?"

"This would be Miss Daisy Wyler MacGregor and Master Ned Callahan MacGregor. Meet Miss Jamie." Steffie lowered her voice and whispered to the babies, "She's famous."

"They're adorable, but I'm hardly the household name that these ladies are." Jamie nodded in the direction of Dallas and Berry. Stef made the introductions, and Jamie gushed appropriately.

Carly joined the group, clearly pleased to see three high-profile ladies in attendance. "We'll be moving to the mansion in about an hour for a small invitation-only after-party. I hope you'll all be able to stay."

"I thought that's what this was supposed to be," Shirley said.

"It started out that way, but because all the artists are local, word got around. The next thing I knew, I was tripling the number of hors d'oeuvres and bottles of wine." She tapped Wade on the back. "And beer. Can't have a party in St. Dennis without a little Mad-Mac."

"I'd love to, but I have to get these little ones to bed," Steffie said, clearly disappointed.

"I'll take them back," Wade offered.

While they discussed the logistics, Jamie complimented Carly on the exhibit's success.

"Shirley's work is exceptional, isn't it? I was blown away when she brought in a few pieces to see if I'd consider them for the exhibit." Carly leaned closer to Jamie and whispered, "I'm taking her show to New

York next month, though she doesn't know it yet. Don't spill the beans."

"My lips are sealed," Jamie promised.

"You'll stay, won't you, for the reception?" Carly asked.

"I'd like to, yes. Thank you. I would." Jamie still hadn't met Curtis Enright, and while she'd been sure he would attend, she didn't see anyone who looked old enough to be the elderly attorney.

Dan stepped back into the conversation and asked Carly, "Is Mom here yet?"

"She's been here, gone through the exhibit, chatted with everyone, and left. She and Ford are already over at the reception. Feel free to join them," Carly said.

"Thanks. Maybe we'll just see what's on that far wall first." Dan pointed to one area they'd missed.

"I'll see you later." Carly turned back to Steffie and her family to assure them that the babies were welcome. "After all, we are honoring their grandmother's work tonight." Shirley, clearly unaccustomed to the spotlight, blushed.

"I can't get over the crowd here," Jamie said as she and Dan walked next door to the mansion, following a brick path.

"Shirley's well known and well liked," he told her. "I think most of the crowd is here to support her. One of the benefits of small-town living is having the whole town back your efforts."

The Enright mansion lived up to its website hype. It was sprawling and spacious and elegantly furnished. The reception was in a room at the back of the house on the first floor, in what must have been a ballroom at one time.

"Can you imagine just giving this place away?" Dan shook his head.

"No, frankly, I cannot. I wonder what prompted Mr. Enright's philanthropy," Jamie replied.

"I'm not so sure it was philanthropy as much as a desire to control the property's future," he said. "At least that's what my mother suspects. None of his grandchildren wanted it, and his son—the one he speaks to, anyway—is living in Florida."

"The one he speaks to?" Jamie raised an eyebrow. "That would imply there's a son he doesn't speak to." She recalled the comment made by the woman in Blossoms. "Oh, wait. I heard something about a black sheep . . ."

"Curtis's younger son—father of Jesse and Sophie, I don't know if you've met either of them—is the family black sheep. They've been estranged for, I don't know, twenty, thirty years or more."

"What's his problem?"

"Just general ass-hattery, I guess. Always in trouble as a kid and apparently never did clean up his act. Married three . . . no, maybe it's four times. Kids for every marriage, never bothers with them."

"Sounds like a charming fellow."

"Speaking of charming fellows, there's the old man himself." Dan nodded in the direction of an elderly man with white hair holding an ebony cane and chatting with Grace. "Here, let me introduce you."

Jamie's heart began to pound again as they approached the small group: Grace, Ford, several women

Jamie didn't recognize, and in the middle of them all, Curtis Enright.

Dan made the introductions. "Mr. Enright, this is a friend of ours, Jamie Valentine."

Jamie watched the old man's face as her name registered. "Jamie . . ." he said.

"Yes. Jamie Valentine. It's nice to meet you, Mr. Enright."

"Jamie is actually J. L. Valentine, the writer. Isn't it exciting that she's chosen St. Dennis for her vacation?" Grace said.

"Yes. Exciting." The unsmiling man seemed to step back from the others.

"She's been staying at the inn, and she's been so helpful to me with my archiving project." Grace went on about her desire to put all the back issues of the paper in chronological order, and to eventually display certain issues, but Jamie only half heard what was being said. Curtis Enright's eyes burned into hers.

"It really is nice to meet you, Mr. Enright," Jamie said very softly. She stepped away from the group and pretended to admire a floral arrangement on the mantel.

"I know what you're up to," the old man came up behind her and whispered in her ear. "I wish you'd leave this thing alone and go back where you came from."

"I can't do that, sir." Jamie turned to face him. "At least not yet."

"You're wasting your time here," he continued. "No one is going to tell you what you want to know."

"I don't expect anyone to 'tell' me," she said. "But

I do expect to know more when I leave than when I got here."

"Your parents must be turning over in their graves," he said stiffly. "Poor Herb . . . if he were alive today . . ."

"If he were alive today, this trip wouldn't have been necessary. If he were alive, I believe he'd have told me the truth before now. But since he did not, I have to find out on my own. And I will find out, Mr. Enright." She stared at him for a long moment, then added, "I will."

"God help us all," he muttered, and walked away.

Jamie watched him go, then realized that the exchange had been witnessed by at least one person. Dan was openly staring at her, his eyes questioning. She wondered what, if anything, he'd heard.

The rest of the evening passed pleasantly enough. Dan and Grace both made it a point to introduce her to everyone who crossed their path, so that by the time the evening was over, Jamie figured she'd met most of the people in attendance.

"I'm getting ready to leave if you are," Dan told her as the crowd began to thin.

"I am, thank you. I appreciate the ride."

Jamie made small talk as they walked to the car, hoping to avoid any questions he might be thinking about asking, particularly about Curtis Enright. She kept it up, chatting about the evening, Carly's successful showing, Shirley Hinson Wyler's talent, the history of the Enright property. Once seated in the car, Dan asked, "Want to stop somewhere for a bite?"

"Truthfully, I ate so many of those little puffy

things, and so many shrimp and crab claws, I don't think I could deal with anything else. Oh, but I did tell Diana I'd stop at Scoop on my way home from the gallery."

"Okay. Scoop it is." He turned the key in the ignition and headed for the center of town. "They'll be closing soon. I can give her a ride home."

He parked the Jeep in the municipal lot, and they strolled toward the dock and the ice cream shop. They were almost to the door when Dan's phone buzzed.

"Excuse me for a second," he said as he read the text. "Damn." He dialed a number, and Jamie walked over to a nearby bench and sat.

The call lasted for several minutes, and when he finished, he joined Jamie on the bench. "I'm sorry. I really am, but . . ."

"I know." She forced a smile. Couldn't he ditch that darned phone for ten minutes? "Something going on at the inn?"

"It can wait."

"Really?"

"At least until we get our ice cream and head back." He stood with his hands in his pockets.

They got as far as the door to Scoop when his phone buzzed again. Jamie asked, "Do you ever think of turning that thing off?"

"What?" He looked puzzled.

"Your phone."

He read the text while he opened the door for her and she stepped inside. "What if something happened?" he asked as they approached the counter.

"Something like what?"

"Something that had to be taken care of."

"You do have employees, right?"

He ignored her comment and asked, "What are you in the mood for?"

"I think I'll try the Peachy Mango Salsa," she said. "One scoop in a dish."

He'd turned to place their order when his daughter came up to the counter from the back room. "Dad. Hi. I thought you were at the gallery thing with Gramma." Diana looked surprised to see him. Her eyes darted to a table at one side of the room, where three boys and one girl sat talking quietly.

"We were. And now we're here." He glanced at his watch. "You must be almost done. We can wait and give you a ride home."

"No. I mean, I'm going to Paige's, remember? We talked about it yesterday." Diana's voice lowered, and she moved to the left of the counter. Paige stepped up to the counter to take Jamie's order.

"How are you getting there?" Dan asked Diana.

"Ummm, I think Dallas is going to pick us up on her way back to the house."

"You think?" he asked, clearly not buying it.

It took Jamie about thirty seconds to read the situation. It took all her willpower not to tell Dan to stop embarrassing his daughter. The group in the corner was listening to every word. Finally, one of the boys got up and walked to the counter. "Mr. Sinclair?" he said, his hand outstretched.

Dan turned and nodded.

"I'm Kevin Stiller. I'm a classmate of Diana's. It's good to meet you."

Clearly puzzled, Dan reacted on autopilot and took the hand that the boy offered. Diana looked trapped.

None of your business, Jamie told herself. *Keep your mouth* . . . "And I'm Jamie," she told the boy. "I'm a friend of Mr. Sinclair's. It's nice to meet you, Kevin." Taken off guard, the boy offered a smile and a hand, which she took. "Are you all together?" Jamie gestured toward the other two boys and the girl who remained at the table.

"Um . . . yes." Kevin nodded.

On their way in, she'd noticed a car parked close to the back of the shop. "Is that your car out back, the blue SUV?" she asked.

"Yes."

Jamie turned to Dan. "I'll bet Kevin wouldn't mind dropping Diana and Paige off."

"I'd be happy to do that, sure."

Jamie smiled at Dan, who looked stricken. "Diana isn't old enough to go out in cars," he said pointedly.

"Understandable," Jamie said, making sure she appeared to agree. "But does that apply to just accepting a ride home?" She turned to Paige. "Would your parents object?"

"Well, no. Dallas said if she couldn't get here by ten, it would be okay if we got a ride with Kevin, as long as we were all together."

By "all," Jamie assumed she meant the three at the corner table, too. She leaned against the counter. "Is that okay with you, Dan, since it's okay with Dallas?"

"I guess." It was Dan's turn to look trapped, and he was obviously none too happy about it. He turned to Kevin. "Straight to Paige's house, right?"

"Oh, yes, sir." Kevin nodded. "Thank you. I'm a good driver, Mr. Sinclair."

"I sure hope so." Dan started toward the door.

"Dan." Jamie waved a hand in front of his face. "You didn't place an order."

"Oh. Right." He turned back to the counter. "I'll have . . . whatever it is that Jamie is having."

"Two dishes of Peachy Mango Salsa coming up." Paige grinned.

Dan met Diana at the cash register and paid while Paige scooped their ice cream and handed over their orders.

"So, Diana," Jamie said, "I guess I'll see you in the morning."

"I'll be there." Diana's face said it all: Jamie had made a friend for life. She came out from behind the counter to hug her father. " 'Night, Daddy." She leaned close to his ear and whispered, "Thanks."

"Thank Jamie," he whispered back.

Diana turned to Jamie and mouthed the words *Thank you.*

Jamie winked, then steered Dan toward the door. Once outside, she fell in step with him. She knew he was annoyed at her, but she just couldn't keep her mouth shut when she saw the look on Diana's face that said, *You don't trust me to act responsibly because you think I am still six years old.*

Finally, when they got to the car, Jamie said, "I'm sorry if you're annoyed with me."

"I don't think you are," he replied.

"I didn't mean to embarrass you." She got into the car and snapped on her seat belt.

Dan slid behind the wheel and said, "You don't have the right to toss in your two cents. It's none of your business."

"You're right. It isn't."

They drove back to the inn in silence, but when he pulled up to the back door, he said, "I think you were right and I was wrong. I know I have to let her grow up a little, but I don't know how to do that. I don't *want* to do that. She's always been my little girl. This new person . . . I don't feel like I know her at all. And for the record, it sucks being a single parent. You have no idea . . ."

"You're right. I don't."

He stared straight ahead through the windshield. "When she was little, things were different. I was okay with her then. I was a good dad back then. I knew what to do with a toddler, with a small child. Even last year, things were different. But now . . . I don't know what's expected of me. I don't know what's what. I feel like the rules have changed, but no one's told me what they are."

"I think the rules are the same. I don't think they ever change. You love your kid and you try to do what's best for her."

"I don't know what's best anymore, that's the problem." He sighed. "How did you know what to do back there? How did you know what was going on?"

"I don't have a daughter, but I've been one. It was pretty clear that the other kids were waiting around for Paige and Diana to close up. When Diana came out of the back room, she looked positively mortified to see you."

"Mortified? Why?"

"Because she'd made plans she knew you wouldn't approve of. When you told her you'd wait for her, she looked like she was going to cry. For Diana's sake, I'm glad you didn't push it."

"When you were fifteen, sixteen, did your parents ever embarrass you?"

"Oh, dear God, yes." Jamie laughed. "But there were times when my dad, in particular, showed understanding I hadn't expected, so I guess it all balanced out."

"I hope Diana feels that way someday."

"She will."

"I still don't like the idea of her being in a car with a boy." He started the engine.

"Even if there are four other people in the car?"

It took him a moment to consider. "I guess that's okay."

"Get used to it, Pop," she said. "She's going to be a teenager for another four or five years."

Dan groaned and muttered something under his breath.

"Come on, let's go inside," she said.

They'd gone halfway across the lobby when someone called Dan's name. He turned and looked around. The only other person in the lobby was the woman at the reception desk.

"Mr. Sinclair," she called him again. "Could I see you for a minute?"

"I'll be right back," Dan said.

Jamie leaned against the newel post and waited for Dan to return. When he did, he appeared rushed.

"Something wrong?" she asked.

"We have three parties who haven't checked in yet. The good news is that they're still coming. The bad news is that Jenna can't stay to check them in. She has a babysitter who needs to leave by eleven."

Jamie looked at the clock that hung over one of the doors. "She's got twenty minutes. Does she live far?"

"Off River Road. Which means that I'm playing desk clerk until everyone checks in."

"Don't you have a backup? Someone who could step in for her?"

"You're looking at the backup. Come on, I'll walk you up to your room."

"You don't have to do that."

"I want to."

They walked up the steps side by side, not speaking. When they got to Jamie's door, Dan stood back while she unlocked it, then leaned forward to push it open for her. Once the door had closed behind them and they'd stepped inside, he pulled her to him. His mouth found hers and he kissed her, a good, long, kiss, a kiss that Jamie felt all the way to her toes.

"Thanks for, you know, the whole thing with Diana," he said when he let her go.

"Anytime. She's a good kid, Dan. I really like her."

"Yeah, well, you sure made points with her tonight." He reached for the door handle. "By the way, what was that between you and Curtis Enright?"

"What?" she said, taken off guard. She'd been hoping that he hadn't noticed after all.

"At the reception. What was that all about?"

"Oh. Well. He was asking me if I was related to Herb Valentine." The lie came easily. "He and my dad went to law school together. Small world, right?"

"And that's what you were discussing?"

"Yes."

Dan wasn't buying it. "That's not what it sounded like."

"Oh? What did it sound like?"

"Nothing like 'Your dad and I went to law school together,'" he said. "It sounded more like an argument. Like he was accusing you of something."

"I can't imagine what that could have been."

"Neither can I," he said before he opened the door, went through it, and closed it softly behind him.

Chapter 11

SUNDAY'S drizzle and humidity found many of the inn's guests opting for breakfast or lunch and shopping someplace other than the inn's dining room, so Jamie had her pick of the tables. She opted for her favorite, the window overlooking the bay, where she could watch the sky turn different shades of gray. It was still early when she finished—too early for Grace, she was sure, though she did check the office and found it locked. Back in her room, Jamie wrote and rewrote the opening chapter of her new book seven times. Finally, she gave up, turned off her computer, and turned on the TV, where she found a *Friends* marathon in progress. So much easier to watch others—even fictional others—bumble through their lives than it was to examine her own situation.

She alternated between deciding to forget that whole kissing-Dan thing from the night before, and reliving the moment and the warmth she'd felt when their lips first touched. *That was not in the plan,* she reminded herself. She'd just act as if it never happened, because it never should have happened. Friendship was the safest course for both of them.

Besides, it's ridiculous to make so much of one kiss. It's not like I haven't kissed a man before.

Of course, it had been a while . . .

The last time she'd been kissed, she hadn't enjoyed it nearly as much, and it had been . . . She was hard-pressed to remember just how long ago. It was before her mother's death, but that event and the aftermath had muddled time for Jamie. Things were *before* or they were *after*.

At a little after eight, Jamie went downstairs and found Grace happily at her desk, sorting through yesterday's findings.

"I can't remember when I had so much enthusiasm for a project," Grace told Jamie. "It's like seeing old friends again, or reliving past moments of my life. I can't thank you enough for spending your time working with me."

"Grace, I can honestly say that I've enjoyed every minute."

"Did you enjoy the exhibit last night?" Grace asked.

"I did. I really liked Shirley Wyler's work. She's so talented."

"I have to say I was surprised to see Dan at the reception desk when Ford brought me in last night."

"Why is that?" Jamie pretended not to know what Grace was getting at, though her intent was coming through loud and clear.

"Because the boy needs to get his priorities straight." Grace sipped her tea. "It was good to see him out and about, and it looked like the two of you were having a good time." She glanced at Jamie, apparently for confirmation that she and Dan did have a good time together, but Jamie kept her nose in the box marked 1955.

"He takes no time for himself, and when he does, it's as if he feels guilty about it." Grace was still muttering away. "Tethered to this place like his life depends on it."

"Why do you suppose that is?" Jamie put the stack of newspapers down on the table and took a seat.

"From the day his father got sick to this very day, he feels like the family fortunes are on his shoulders." Grace sighed. "Which, I suppose, they have been. And that's partially my fault. When my husband passed away, it was such a shock. Even knowing that his illness was terminal, when it finally happened, I had a very hard time accepting it. When Dan stepped in and took over everything, I let him, because for a long time, I wasn't capable. Habits were formed back then that, over the years, have proved very difficult to break."

Jamie thought it best not to comment. It was obvious that Dan was tied to his phone and that he believed every issue involving the inn, no matter how small, needed his personal attention or the roof would fall down around them.

"My Daniel was a wonderful man," Grace went on. "He was a terrific husband and a great father. But he was not a very good businessman. It was years before I found out that the inn was in terrible financial straits when Dan took over after his father's death. He worked tirelessly to get this place into the black and to build the business so his sister and brother could go to college and to ensure that the inn would remain in the family. I daresay he shouldered the weight of all of us and never complained, never let on the extent of the burden he carried alone." Grace stared at her hands for a long moment. "But it's time he realized that he doesn't have to do it all anymore. He needs to start living again." She looked at Jamie and added, "I was hoping that—"

Whatever it was Grace hoped for was lost as Diana breezed into the room.

"This is a nice surprise." Grace smiled and beckoned the girl to give her a hug.

"I told you I'd help." Diana blew her grandmother a kiss. "I'm all wet from the rain."

"Please tell me you did not walk from Paige's in this downpour." Grace looked over the top of her glasses.

"It's not so bad." Diana greeted Jamie with a "Hi."

"Hi, Diana." Jamie looked at the girl's clothing. "You really are wet, kid."

"Go on up and change your clothes," Grace told her. "And dry your hair while you're at it."

"I guess I am a little uncomfortable." Diana tugged at the front of her shirt. "But I'll come back."

Grace shook her head as her granddaughter left the office. "That child . . ."

". . . is a really good kid," Jamie finished the sentence for her.

"She is that. I adore her." Grace grinned. "But I suppose that's apparent."

"It's equally apparent that the feeling is mutual."

Jamie reached for a box. "What do you suppose we'll find today?"

She began to sort through the newspapers in front of her, checking the social pages for the photos Grace was looking for and any smidgen of information that she might find useful. The morning passed with little of interest other than photos of Curtis Enright and his wife.

"Oh, she was something, Rose Enright was," Grace said.

"She was very pretty." Jamie held up the page to get a better look.

"She was a beauty," Grace agreed. "One of the blossoms."

"The blossoms?"

"Rose Enright, Lilly Ryder, and Violet Finneran. Everyone in town knew them as the blossoms. Lilly was a bit older than the other two, but they were good friends. Violet and Rose were inseparable, the very best of friends. Violet worked for Curtis at the law firm for, well, forever. She still goes into the office a few days every week to make sure things are running smoothly." Grace took another sip of tea, then frowned. "I need a little hot water."

"Want me to—"

"No, it's fine. I should talk less and drink my tea and mind my own business."

What are the odds that's going to happen? Jamie thought.

"Anyway, Curtis had a health scare a year or so ago, and everyone thought his next move would be to a retirement home, one of those assisted-living places.

But didn't he surprise everyone by donating his house and property to St. Dennis and then moving into Violet's house with her."

"He's living with his secretary?"

"Oh, no, dear, not like *that*." Grace chuckled. "Curtis never in his life looked at another woman, even after Rose died. He's always maintained that she never left, you know."

"Wait. Let me guess. Her 'spirit' remains."

Grace ignored the sarcasm. "And what a strong spirit it is. Everyone in town has sensed her presence in the big house."

"What do you mean, sensed?"

"Curtis has always maintained that he could see her, speak with her."

"And people allowed him to handle their legal affairs?"

"Don't be so quick to judge things you don't understand, dear." For a moment, Jamie thought Grace was going to wag a finger at her. "And of course," Grace went on, "there are the gardenias."

"The gardenias."

"Rose's favorite flower. Though there hasn't been one in the house in the twenty years since she passed, the house still smells of gardenias." Grace looked up from her teacup. "That's how you know Rose is around."

"And you've experienced this?"

"Everyone who's been there since Rose died has experienced it."

"We were in the house last night. I didn't smell gardenias."

"Curtis doesn't live there anymore." Grace spoke as if instructing a child.

Jamie resisted the urge to roll her eyes. "So did Rose make the move with Curtis to Violet's house?"

"They both seem to think she did, dear." Grace set the cup aside and stared at the photo of Curtis and his wife, both of whom were dressed to kill, Curtis in a tux, Rose in a floor-length gown. "I remember this night as if it were yesterday. The last Harvest Ball at the old Grange Hall." She seemed to be lost in the past. "I wonder what happened to all the old negatives. The originals, I mean. I wonder if . . ." She tapped her fingers on the desk before picking up her phone. "Ford, would you give Ray a call and ask if he knows where the old negatives are? Yes, for the photos that ran in the paper over the years. Let me know if he finds anything." Grace hung up and told Jamie, "Ray's been with the paper for over forty years. If anyone can find things in that building, it will be Ray."

"That would be great. If he located the negatives, we could have them developed. Real photos would be so much more helpful than the faded pictures in the papers."

"Real photos definitely would be much more interesting," Grace agreed. "Displaying the real photos next to the articles would make a wonderful display. We could organize them chronologically. Just think, the evolution of the town in photographs, accompanied by the commentary of the day."

"It would make a fascinating time line," Jamie agreed. "A true social history of St. Dennis."

"Exactly." A few minutes later, Grace asked, "Have you come up with an idea for your next book yet?"

Jamie shook her head.

"I'm assuming you want to stay with the truth theme."

"I'm . . . not sure."

"You know, there are many angles to the truth. There's the flat-out, undisputed, no-question-about-it truth. 'The sun is shining' sort of truth. Then there's the truth as we see it. 'Shooting animals for sport is barbaric.' And there's the personal truth. 'My child is the smartest child in the world.'" Grace smiled at Jamie. "And then there's the opposite of truth. Have you thought about exploring the flip side of truth, Jamie? About the many reasons and excuses for why people don't tell the truth? Why we lie?"

"Write about lying?"

"Well, it is something we're all familiar with. We've all told lies at some point in life. I think there are probably as many kinds of lies as there are truths. White lies: 'Oh, no, that dress doesn't make you look fat.' There are lies of omission. There are the truths you never tell." Grace went back to the newspaper on the desk in front of her. "I would think you'd find plenty to write about. Of course, you're the writer. I'm sure you'll come up with exactly the right thing."

The truths you never tell. Well, that certainly hit close to home.

Jamie played with the phrase and its meaning, turning it over and over in her mind for the rest of the afternoon. Later, when she returned to her room, she turned on her laptop, and for the first time in months, she had something to write about. She wasn't sure what form it would take in the end, but she knew instinctively that Grace had hit on something worth thinking about. It no longer occurred to her to wonder how Grace knew.

DAN SAT IN his office, reading through the stack of messages that had come from the front desk. Every complaint, every compliment, was directed to him. He felt obligated to keep his finger on the pulse of everything that went on in the inn, good and bad. He'd worked his ass off for twenty-some years to earn that "Best of the Bay" rating the inn had held for the past five years, and he was determined to maintain it. He felt immense pride that the Inn at Sinclair's Point had been recognized as the top in its field. Getting and keeping that recognition of high standards had been more important to him than anything other than his family.

And yet for the last couple of days, it had seemed that his responsibilities were infringing more and more on something else that was beginning to matter to him.

He sighed and rested his arms on his desk. He was far from being a romantic. The day Doreen died, he'd stopped believing in living happily ever after. It had never occurred to him that something like that could happen. They were young and loved each other and assumed they'd grow old together. Well, up until the minute she told him she was leaving. After she died, his life had narrowed to raising his kids and turning the inn into something wonderful. He'd never expected to find love again, so he'd never made time for it. And yet here he sat, wondering what to call what he felt for Jamie Valentine.

Not that it would matter in the long run. He knew her time here was limited, that she'd booked the room for several weeks, and when those weeks came to an end, so would her stay in St. Dennis. She'd be gone, and that would be that.

Which was why, the night before, he was almost grateful to have an excuse to back away from her after one kiss. It had been a great kiss, as kisses went, but it was smart of him to stop at one, before something happened between them that would have made it even harder for him to say goodbye.

He wondered what her life was like back in Princeton. Who her friends were, how she spent her time. Was there someone waiting for her there? Someone she cared about? Someone she shared her time and her life with? Someone she went back to when the book tours and the TV appearances were over?

There were other things about her that he wanted to know.

Like what she was doing in St. Dennis and what did Curtis Enright know about her.

Like why she flat-out lied when he asked her about the conversation she'd had the night before with the elderly lawyer. Her explanation had been as big a lie as he'd ever heard.

The bits and pieces he'd overheard had been puzzling, to say the least.

I wish you'd leave this thing alone and go back where you came from, the lawyer had said. *No one is going to tell you what you want to know.*

And the most confusing part: *Your parents must be turning over in their graves. Poor Herb . . . if he were alive today . . .*

If he were alive today, this trip wouldn't have been necessary, Jamie had replied. Her voice had dropped then, and Dan had heard only her very last remark: *I will find out, Mr. Enright. I will.*

All of which proved that he'd been right about her: Jamie was hiding something, was searching for something that mattered very much to her. And whatever it was, Curtis Enright wanted just as much to keep it hidden.

Maybe it was time Dan called Jamie out on her lies and asked point-blank what she was doing in St. Dennis, what she was hoping to find. There was a good chance she'd tell him to mind his own business, or that she'd lie again. Then again, maybe if he told her what he'd overheard, she'd admit to the lies and tell him the truth.

Maybe, when it came to Jamie, the truth was the most he could hope for.

Chapter 12

⁓

J AMIE had played around with the idea for the book until way into the morning hours. She fell asleep around three but was up again at dawn. After a shower and breakfast, Jamie dressed and headed down to the lobby to meet Ford for the promised interview. She took a seat near the side window and watched new arrivals pull up near the lobby's back entry and pile out of their cars and excitedly come in through the double doors. A tall, handsome loner followed a family of five, and it took a moment for Jamie to realize it was Ford.

"Sorry I'm a little late," he told her as he approached.

"Not at all," Jamie assured him. "I was early and taking advantage of the time to people-watch."

"There's no shortage of people coming and going around here." He glanced around the lobby. "I think I heard something about there being a tennis tournament here this morning."

"That would account for all those white shorts and

T-shirts," Jamie noted. "Since you're in navy and tan, I'm going out on a limb to guess you're not playing."

"Tennis isn't my thing. I'd rather spend my free time on the water. Sailboats, canoes, kayaks . . . especially kayaks. I'm trying to get Carly into kayaking, but she's been tied up getting ready for last night's exhibit."

"It was great. There seems to be a lot of artistic talent in St. Dennis. There was some really fine work on display last night."

"They looked pretty good to me, but what do I know? Carly's the expert." He looked around the busy lobby. "Okay with you if we do this in Mom's office?"

"As long as Grace doesn't mind."

"Mom is at a meeting in the conference room. Something about the Fourth of July parade."

They went across the lobby to Grace's office, which was unlocked. Ford turned on the lights and offered Jamie the more comfortable of the chairs before seating himself.

"So how 'bout we start with a little bit about you, Jamie? Where you're from, your family, your background, that sort of thing."

Jamie filled him in on all the usual details, leaving out the part about having just found out she was adopted. Falling back on the official bio made her feel like an imposter. For a brief moment, she wished she could tell the truth—the whole truth—so that when he asked, "What brings you to St. Dennis?," instead of the generic "Working on my new book," she'd say, "Searching for my birth mother."

"So I understand you're working on a new book," Ford said. "Want to talk a little about that?"

"There's not much to talk about yet. I'm still working that out."

"Want to talk about your writing process?"

"Right now, it's hit or miss. One of the reasons I came to St. Dennis was to have a real vacation. I haven't had one in a long time, and yes, I am trying to work, but being away puts a different spin on it. I can work, and I can play, and I don't feel guilty, because I'm supposed to be on vacation."

She talked a little about having lost her mother recently and how being away was helping her to deal with the loss. It occurred to her then that Ford's mother was actually helping her to cope with the loss of her own. Not that Lainey and Grace had much in common—for one thing, Grace was a good ten or fifteen years older than Lainey—but Grace had something about her that was warm and gracious, like Lainey.

The interview took under an hour, with Grace joining them in the office for the last ten minutes. "I'll stop back," she offered when she realized they were still there.

"Don't be silly, Mom. We're almost finished, and maybe you'll think of something to ask Jamie that I've forgotten," Ford said.

"Your interview, your questions." Grace made the sign of zipping her mouth closed.

"Last question, then." Ford turned back to Jamie. "What do you think of St. Dennis, and will you be coming back to see us?"

"I love St. Dennis." Jamie was happy to have a question she could answer with total honesty. "I love the architecture, I love the inn, the shops, the restaurants, the ice cream at Scoop, and of course, the bay views. I would definitely come back."

"Great. Thanks." Ford closed the notebook he'd been scribbling in and turned off the recorder. "I'll have this typed up by tonight so I can get it into production by tomorrow afternoon. I'll email you the finished product first, if you'd like to take a look at it."

"That's not necessary," Jamie told him. "You have a deadline to meet, and I'm sure it will be fine."

"I appreciate your confidence in me." Ford rose and kissed his mother on the cheek. "See you at dinner tonight, Mom?"

"Of course," Grace assured him.

"Great. And thanks again, Jamie."

"Thank you."

"So, shall we get back to the task at hand?" Grace's eyes twinkled at the prospect. "You never know what we might find today."

"Let's hope it's something good."

"I have the feeling it might be."

The first indication that Grace might be right came about thirty minutes later, when Jamie came across a photo from 1975 that she found in the box marked 1957. Five smiling young girls in white dresses sat on a bench side by side, each holding a long-stemmed rose of indeterminable color. *High School Bound,* read the headline. *Five eighth-grade graduates from St. Dennis Elementary School smile for the cameras.*

If these girls were twelve or thirteen in 1975, they'd be the right age to have given birth to Jamie in October 1979. Had she caught her first break? Would one of these smiling girls—or one of their classmates—prove to be her mother?

Jamie held up the page to Grace. "Do any of these girls look familiar?"

Grace peered over the top of her glasses, then smiled. "Of course. All of them." She held a hand out for the paper, and Jamie brought it to her. With her index finger, Grace pointed to and named each. "Nita Etheridge—now Nita Perry. Eleanor Cash—she was Eleanor Borden back then—she owns the flower shop, you met her at Cuppachino."

Jamie nodded, studying the faces, looking for . . . something. "I remember."

"The next girl is Barbara Noonan."

"She never married?"

"No. Nor did Gail Hillyer, seated next to Barb." Grace looked up. "Gail is the principal at St. Dennis Academy now. The private school over on Cross Lane." She turned her attention back to the photo. "And this last girl is Heidi Richards. Heidi Clossin back then. She married a fireman from Baltimore and moved there right after graduating from high school."

"I don't know that I'd have recognized any of them from this photo," Jamie noted.

"It's the hairstyles, dear. They are so dated." Grace held the page up. "Let's keep this one aside. I think it would make a nice addition to our stash."

"Have you decided what you're going to do with

all those?" Jamie nodded in the direction of the pile of pages.

"I think an exhibit at the art center. I'm going to speak to Carly about it once she's finished with her current project. She's always looking out for St. Dennis–related photos and memorabilia to put on display. I'm sure there are more gems hiding in these old issues. Maybe once we have them all together, a theme will evolve on its own."

Jamie dove back into the boxes, hoping against hope that there'd be something else to point her in the right direction, but she spent the rest of the day without finding anything that could be construed as helpful.

At three, Dan came in to remind Grace that she had an appointment with her doctor and they'd better get moving if she expected to make it on time.

"I don't know why I have to be the one to hurry to get there on time when I know *he* won't be," Grace grumbled as she folded up the paper she'd been reading.

"Why don't you take a bunch of those with you to read in the waiting room?" Dan suggested.

"I'll take that new thriller that Barbara sent over last week. She said it was really good." Grace wheeled herself around from behind her desk. "Jamie, please feel free to stay and continue or to go. Absolutely up to you."

"I think I'll stay and go through these last few boxes."

"If you come across anything that looks interesting . . ."

"Of course. I'll put it aside for you."

"Thank you. All right, then, Dan, let's get this show on the road."

Jamie turned her attention back to the stacks of papers and, in Grace's absence, went through the issues much more quickly. She firmly believed that while she didn't know what she was looking for, she would know it when she saw it. She found some photos she thought Grace might enjoy seeing, and these she left on Grace's desk. But the subjects of those articles were all older than her birth mother would be.

She finished with the last box and closed up the office. She was dying to ask Dan to bring the boxes she needed, but then she'd have to have a good reason for wanting to see those particular issues. Better to wait until the right ones came to her than to rouse suspicions. Besides, experience had shown that the dates on the boxes and the dates of the newspapers in them didn't necessarily match.

She closed the door to Grace's office and retreated to her room, unable to decide how to spend the rest of her day. She sat at the desk and turned on her laptop and made a note about the photo she'd found that morning and the names of the girls in it. She wasn't sure why it felt significant, but it did, and that was good enough for her.

After yesterday's rain, the sunny afternoon beckoned Jamie outdoors. She walked down to the dock near the boathouse and admired the view across the bay. From there she went to the tennis courts, where she watched a couple of matches, then strolled the grounds and checked out the flower beds, overflowing with summer blooms. She sat in the gazebo for a while, then walked down to the marsh and sat near the pond.

"I thought that was you." Dan came up behind her, his footsteps so soft on the grass that she jumped. "Oh, sorry," he said when he realized he'd startled her. "Didn't mean to sneak up on you."

"How'd Grace make out at the doctor's?" she asked.

"Not as well as she'd hoped." Dan lowered himself to the ground to sit next to her. "I think she'd convinced herself that there was a chance the cast would be coming off today."

"Not happening?"

"Not a prayer. She needs at least another month before they'll even discuss the possibility. But all in all, the bone is knitting nicely, and she should be okay once the healing process is complete. Then she'll have physical therapy, when she'll make everyone crazy, but we'll get through it."

"I suppose that's good news, then."

"It's as good as it's going to get for a while."

"How's she taking it?"

"How do you think?"

She opened her mouth to comment, but he touched her arm and pointed. Across the pond, the flapping of enormous wings off to their left had drawn his attention. "Big Blue," Dan whispered, nodding in the direction of the bird that had just landed. "Sit really still and maybe he won't notice us."

Jamie turned her head slowly and watched the bird take a few steps into the water, his head moving in brief but sharp motions. "He's beautiful," she whispered.

"He's about as deadly a predator as we have around here." Dan's lips were so close to her ear that she could feel his breath on her neck. "He cleaned out the koi pond we used to have out by the gazebo. Ate every damn one of the fish before we realized what he was up to. It was all we could do to keep Mom from putting a bounty out on him."

As if aware that his reputation was being maligned, the bird swiveled his head smoothly from one side to the other. If he saw Jamie and Dan, he dismissed them as irrelevant and resumed the search for his dinner. After a while Jamie found herself leaning back against Dan, who didn't seem to mind. When his phone signaled an incoming text, his efforts to retrieve the phone from his pocket alerted the bird, which, after sending them the heron equivalent of a *Die, peasants* look, took off for quieter waters.

"Damn," Dan said as he opened his phone to check the text. "Show over. Sorry."

"I should probably be moving along anyway." Jamie sat up. It had been surprisingly nice to sit quietly for a few minutes, sharing the nature moment with Dan. Nice and oddly comforting.

"Are you headed back to the inn?" she asked after he'd finished reading the message and responded.

"Yes. Going my way?" He held out a hand to help her up. "Looks like one of our vendors failed to deliver on the goods for today, and the chef is having a fit because he won't be able to serve what he'd planned on cooking."

"Isn't that the chef's problem?" she asked.

"It's my problem."

"I take it you don't like to delegate."

"The bottom line is it's my responsibility."

"But you could pass that off, right? Let the chef decide for himself what he wants to cook?"

"I'll talk to him and see what else we have that we can substitute, and everyone goes on from there."

"The chef can't figure that out on his own?"

His glance told her that it had never occurred to him to have someone else make that call.

"Okay, then." She shrugged. "None of my business."

"But you can't seem to help yourself, can you." It wasn't a question, and he wasn't amused. At the service door, he said, "See you," and disappeared into the kitchen.

Well, damn. She blew out a long breath of air. Dan was right. She really couldn't seem to help herself. It seemed ridiculous to her that he couldn't seem to delegate even the smallest tasks. Talk about anal. She shook her head. But it really wasn't her problem, was it?

She went up to her room and sat on the balcony. It occurred to her that only three things had occupied her mind lately: the search for her birth mother; her next book; and Dan Sinclair. Right now she wanted to put two aside and think about Dan. The quest could be life-changing, and the book—if she could work out Grace's idea—might be a career changer as well. Dan . . . she wasn't sure why he should rank up there with the other two.

That mantle of responsibility was way too heavy on his shoulders. It was none of her business, but she hated to see a man as young as Dan so swamped that he couldn't sit for fifteen minutes and relax at the edge of the pond. More specifically, at the edge of the pond with her on a sweet summer afternoon. It was his fault. He could hire people and he could delegate. As particular as she suspected he was about whom he hired, he probably had people on his staff who could take over certain aspects of the business and give him a little downtime.

She knew he'd shouldered the burden of keeping his ancestral home in the family, and by all accounts, he'd done a remarkable job. Add the responsibilities of single parent to that plate, and it was a miracle his head hadn't exploded at some point.

But . . . right. It was none of her business. Forget the kiss, keep it friendly. Stop butting into his life. The last thing she needed was something that would complicate her stay in St. Dennis.

Was that all she wanted from Dan? Friendship? At this point, she didn't trust herself to know what she wanted. The last few months had been rough on her mind and on her soul, and she'd been swallowed up by emotions that had overwhelmed her. Grief over her mother's death. Shock over finding out she'd been adopted. Anger that she'd been lied to all her life. Guilt because she'd built a career on something that wasn't real, and guilt that had left her feeling that she'd been lying to her readers from the beginning. Indecision over whether to search for her birth mother. Fear that if her quest were successful, she'd be rejected all over again. Fear that if she came up dry, she'd spend the rest of her life searching and unsure of herself.

How could she possibly know what she wanted from Dan when she wasn't sure of who she was?

Jamie opened a new file on her laptop and typed up her notes on the findings from that day. Knowing how small details tended to get lost, she'd started a running journal about what might or might not be significant, referencing the date of the newspaper in which she'd found what could prove to be a clue, no matter how oblique. If it resonated with her some-how, she'd make a note of it. So far, she had only that one photo of the five eighth-grade graduates, but it was a starting place.

Tomorrow was her signing at Book 'Em, more opportunity to meet people, any one of whom might prove to be the one she sought. You never know. She'd make a point to remember names—maybe have a sign-up sheet for the newsletter her publicist talked about sending out. She could have people sign their name and address; then she'd make some sort of mark next to the names of women the right age who'd grown up in St. Dennis.

And how would she know? She'd ask.

Chapter 13

⁓

J AMIE'S name had been on the bike list for the past
several days, so she was excited when she got the
text assuring her that a bike would be waiting for her
on Tuesday morning. All she had to do was confirm
that she still wanted the bike and let the front desk
know what time she wanted it for. By return text she
reserved for six the next morning. Her book signing
was later in the day, so she thought a nice early-
morning ride would be just the thing after so seden-
tary a week. She left a note on Grace's office door that
she'd see her at Book 'Em.

So it's true what they say about riding a bike,
Jamie mused. After a bit of initial wobbling, she
was able to find and keep her balance, much to her
delight. She pedaled smoothly to the end of the long
winding driveway that led from the inn to Charles
Street, pausing only to choose a direction.

After a moment's deliberation, she turned right
onto the road's shoulder, the mixture of gravel and
ground oyster shells crunching under the wheels

before she eased onto the blacktopped road. She'd gotten accustomed to taking a left toward the center of town, but this morning she wanted to explore the other side of town. Yesterday she'd driven on every street in St. Dennis except the ones that lay between the Inn at Sinclair's Point and Cannonball Island. Today she'd leave all her doubts and questions behind for a while (*Will* she *come to my book signing? Will I know her? Will she know me?*), and she'd take a peaceful ride and relax her mind. Today she'd bike to the end of Charles Street and see what lay beyond the marsh.

She smelled it before she saw it, a pungent mix of decaying organic matter and salt water that made up the wetlands at the far end of the inn's property bordering the road. She passed a pond, the water alive with sparkly early light, and she rolled the bike to a slow stop to enjoy the view. A great blue heron, partially hidden by the reeds, paused in its pursuit of breakfast to consider whether the figure on the road represented danger. Could it be the same one she and Dan had seen yesterday at the inn? Apparently deciding that the spectator posed no threat, the bird continued its single-minded stare into the shallows. Like a shot, its beak plunged forward into the water and emerged with a hapless fish. With lethal elegance, it tossed its head back and swallowed its prey in one motion.

Jamie leaned forward on the handlebars, fascinated, preparing to watch as long as the bird dined, but this time her motion alarmed the heron, which unexpectedly took flight somewhat awkwardly before its wings reached their full and formidable span. It flew upward with a few powerful flaps, then settled into flight, soaring over Jamie's head.

Awesome. Jamie watched it disappear beyond the trees. *Just awesome.*

She got back on the bike seat and resumed pedaling toward the island, her spirit rising as the bird rose from the pond. Her grandmother Margaret had been fond of saying that starting a morning with a moment of wonder could carry your heart through the rest of the day, and Jamie thought it might be true.

She'd spent last night in her room, second-guessing her decision to come to St. Dennis and the direction she was taking. On her drive around the town yesterday afternoon and evening, she'd studied every house, as if seeking some connection. So many homes, and her birth mother could have lived—could now be living—in any one of them. The sheer number of possibilities boggled the mind.

She'd read somewhere that there was such a thing as genetic memory. If that were true, wouldn't she feel some sort of pull toward one place or another on the streets of St. Dennis? Though she'd looked at every house as if something in her DNA might recognize it, there'd been nothing.

But she'd been surprised when she awakened that morning feeling revived and invigorated and humming with positive energy, and was dressed and in the lobby at six sharp to pick up her bike. She'd politely declined the offer of a helmet and ignored the suggestion that a hat might be useful, inasmuch as the temperatures were expected to reach ninety degrees by noon. She'd wanted to feel the wind in her hair and on her face.

After a moment or two while she recalled how to balance, she'd taken off into the early morning mist. The sky was gloriously pink and coral over the trees where the sun rose, casting a glow on the town and on the bay off to her right. Jamie felt confident for the first time since she'd decided to take this journey into her unknown past. She was, she realized, as close to being content as she'd been in a long time. The feeling was unexpected, and while there was seemingly no explanation for the change in her mood, it felt so good that she refused to question it.

Accept each day as the gift that it is was another of her grandmother's favorite sayings. Today Jamie was in acceptance mode. She wondered what her grandmother would think of her quest. Remembering Grandma Marg, who was already old when Jamie was a child, brought a smile. She had been a feisty, tell-it-like-it-is woman. Jamie was sure she'd have told her only granddaughter to go for it.

Even the thought of facing so many people at the book signing that afternoon failed to shake her buoyant mood. Though she'd always loved interacting with her readers, the thought of talking about honest lives made her feel uncomfortable. But she promised herself that today she would trust her intuition and keep an open mind. Not that she expected anyone to tap her on the shoulder, throw her arms around her, and introduce herself as Jamie's long-lost birth mother— that was the stuff of made-for-TV movies—but maybe someone would remember who she reminded them of. If she came away from the day with nothing more than a name of a possible relative, she'd be well ahead of the game. It was, she knew, a total long shot, but stranger things had happened, right?

Stretching out ahead was the drawbridge to Cannonball Island, a low two-lane structure that had seen better days. Jamie paused at the side of the road to allow a SUV to pass, then followed it to the other side. She'd read that the road looping around Cannonball Island was eighteen miles long, and the island itself was sparsely populated due to the fact that its location made it a target for the worst storms year-round. Most of its residents were water men, engaged in fishing, crabbing or oyster farming, or a combination of the three. As she pedaled through the morning light, she passed few houses but several small coves where boats were moored at rickety-looking docks. Here and there, older boats on cinder blocks, their paint faded down to grayed wood, overlooked the bay as if nostalgically watching the newer vessels with envy and recalling the days when they, too, took to the seas and battled the storms and returned proudly with their hulls brimming with a catch.

The road wound past salt marshes on one side and the bay on the other. Jamie pedaled leisurely past a tiny chapel that had fallen into disrepair, its roof partially caved in, the adjacent churchyard fenced to enclose ancient graves. There were boarded-up houses, several of which were marked by similar white fences, the paint long gone, the wood grayed by age and weather. The closest thing she saw to an actual village was a grouping of ten or twelve houses built in the same general area. They were spaced fairly far apart, the front yard of each enclosed by the ubiquitous white picket fence. As she passed the closest house to the road, she noticed that grave markers lined one side of the yard, just as they had at the churchyard and the abandoned structures. A woman came out the back door, a laundry basket in her hand. She watched Jamie go by but did not return her wave.

Jamie rolled on into a morning that was growing increasingly warmer. Halfway around the island, she realized she'd downed the last of her water. She chastised herself for having been so foolish as to set out with no hat to shield her face from the sun and only one bottle of water.

Her pace slowed, the heat wearing her down. A thin bead of sweat slithered from the back of her neck right on down between her shoulder blades. She almost sang out loud when she spotted a weathered brown building with a sign that read GENERAL STORE over the front door. "Water," she murmured thirstily. "I bet they sell water."

She leaned the bike up against the front rail and went inside. There was no cheery bell over the door— though she'd expected one, for some reason—and the interior was dark, most of the light coming in through the open windows.

A wizened woman of indeterminate age sat in a chair near the side window, reading a newspaper. She turned to Jamie and asked, "Help you?"

"I was hoping to buy a bottle of water." Jamie reached into her pocket for the five-dollar bill she'd tucked there just in case. "Actually, two might be better."

"Water's in the case." The woman pointed to a cooler near the counter where an ancient cash register sat. Jamie grabbed two bottles and set them on the well-worn counter. "That'll be a dollar," said the woman, who left the paper on her chair and shuffled toward the counter on untied pristinely white tennis shoes.

"I have two bottles." Jamie held up both.

"Nothin' wrong with my eyesight," the woman replied. "Fifty cents a bottle."

"Wow, the price is higher in town." Jamie handed over her five.

"This all you got? Not much change yet this morning."

"It's all I brought with me."

The woman sorted through the drawers in the cash register, then went through a door into a back room. A minute later, she returned with four ones in her hand. She passed them to Jamie without a word.

"Thanks." Jamie stuck the bills into her pocket.

"That your bike out there?"

"I borrowed it from the inn."

"Gracie's inn?"

"Yes. The Inn at Sinclair's Point."

"Good people, Gracie is." She smiled at Jamie for the first time and added slyly, "She has the eye."

"The eye for what?"

The woman chuckled. "Ask her. She'll tell you, 'less she got shy about it. Which I doubt, since Gracie ain't likely to be shy about much of anything."

"I guess you know her pretty well, then."

"Since she was a girl. Came from a nice family. Married into a good one, too. Good man, her Daniel was. Them kids of hers were always polite when they were little ones. Ain't seen them in years." She paused. "They still around?"

"They're all there."

"Good. Gracie always liked to have her babies close. That young one of hers, he was always a daredevil, that one."

"You mean Ford?"

The woman nodded. "And that girl of hers, she was a pretty little thing. Married, I heard, to the Madison boy. Good boy, he was. I 'spect he's grown into a good man or Gracie wouldn't have had it."

"Grace has three kids. You're forgetting Dan," Jamie told her.

The woman laughed. "I'm not forgetting young Dan. Picture of his grandfather, that boy was. Smart, he was, but too serious for a young 'un."

"Hmph. Even when he was little?"

"Some folks just carry the weight, girl." The woman's eyes narrowed, and she stared at Jamie for a moment. "Up to some others to help with the load."

Jamie stared back. What was that supposed to mean?

"Well, then, you tell Gracie that Ruby Carter sends her best, you hear?"

The woman turned her back as if to signal the conversation was over, then she headed back to her chair and her newspaper.

"Thanks," Jamie said, then went outside and

opened the first bottle and sat on the edge of the store's front porch and drank until she started to feel revived. She had to remind herself to slow down, lest she make herself sick. Still contemplating the nature of Gracie's eye, Jamie tossed both bottles into the basket on the front of the bike and resumed her ride back to the inn.

She paused at the pond where she'd seen the heron, but the bird was gone and none had arrived to take its place. Ten minutes later, she was back at the inn and turning in her bike. She ran into Dan as she crossed the lobby.

He hesitated midstep to take in her appearance. "Early-morning . . . what?"

"Bike ride. All the way to Cannonball Island and back," she said with a touch of pride.

His eyes narrowed. "Are you the one who left without a helmet?"

"Yes, I didn't think I'd need . . ." Jamie frowned. "How do you know?"

"Jenny at the desk was concerned that a guest had taken off without one."

"I don't think it's that big a deal. I went to Cannonball Island, and that's only down the road."

"Two summers ago a guest borrowed a bike and went out for an early-morning ride. Thirty feet from the entrance, she was hit from behind by a couple of kids who thought it would be cool to scare the biker. She wasn't wearing a helmet because she didn't want to mess up her hair. Do I need to tell you what happened to her?" Dan sighed. "I'd hate to get the call and have to watch them scraping your brains off the side of the road like they did hers."

Jamie grimaced. "Nice image."

"Well, that's what happened."

"How did they know to call you?"

"Didn't you notice the little license plate on the back of your bike? 'Property of the Inn at Sinclair's Point.'"

"No, actually, I did not."

"All the helmets have the inn's logo on them. You would know that if you'd worn one."

"What's the inn's logo?"

"A great blue heron. Like the one on the sign for the inn down on Charles Street."

"I saw one this morning," she said, hoping to change the subject. "It was in a pond down the road where the marsh begins. I watched it fish for a minute or two. I think it might have been Big Blue."

"That's his 'hood. You'll find him there most mornings. He spends afternoons in the creek in the marsh down behind the inn's boathouse."

"How do you know it wasn't a different heron?"

"Blue is very territorial. He chases the competition away. He's been around for several years, so most of the other birds know to keep out in the mornings."

Jamie had started to move toward the steps. She was sweaty and hoped that neither Dan nor anyone else got close enough to figure that out.

"Anyway, next time take the helmet, okay?"

"Okay."

"Looking forward to your book signing this afternoon?"

"I am."

"Good luck. Looks like you're going to have a

good crowd. There are signs up around the inn, in case you hadn't noticed."

"Oh. No, I hadn't. That was nice of you."

"Nice of Mom. She likes to drum up interest in local happenings. Usually, she puts something in the newspaper, but there wasn't time. So she's making everyone promise to show up at Book 'Em today."

"That's really nice of her." Jamie's heart sank. The more people who showed up, the harder it would be for her to check out the locals.

"You know my mom."

"I'm beginning to." Jamie thought about what the old woman in the general store had said about Grace. She wondered if Dan knew the local gossip about his mother and her eye.

"Hey, did you wear sunscreen this morning?"

"No. Why?"

"You're going to have a nice burn on the back of your legs and across your neck, from the looks of things." His attention was diverted by a large group checking in, and he was off to the front desk.

Jamie frowned and looked over her shoulder at her calves, wondering how Dan could tell she was going to have a burn. On her way to her room, Jamie counted off all the blunders she'd made so far today: No *helmet*. No *water*. No *sunscreen*.

She unlocked the door to her room, almost wishing she could start the day over, wiser and better prepared for the outing she'd taken. Now she wanted a shower, breakfast, and a few hours to get her head together for the rest of the day.

• • •

DAN STOOD TO one side of the narrow room that served as the front section of Book 'Em and watched Jamie with both admiration and curiosity. She'd been signing books steadily for well over three hours, yet she'd remained totally engaged with every reader who thrust a book into her hands with a request that it be signed. He'd lost count of the number of times she'd been asked to write *Happy birthday!* Right at that moment, a woman stood in front of Jamie, dictating what she wanted the book to say: *To Norma: The truth shall set you free. Love, J.L.*

How does she keep that smile on her face? he wondered. His patience would have fled after the first "No, sign it *With love, J.L.,* like we're friends."

He watched the way she was with Diana, who'd appeared with several of her friends right before the signing began. Jamie had made Diana feel like a VIP by asking her to get the books to sign; she'd shown the girl what page to open to for the signature. Seeing the two of them together, watching them chat and laugh so easily, made Dan's heart hurt. When was the last time he and his daughter had shared such a moment? These days it seemed all he did was nag her and all she did was roll her eyes at him. It took a few minutes for him to realize that Jamie saw Diana as a person, an interesting young person, while he had continued to see her as his little girl.

Time to face up to it, bud. She isn't a little girl anymore. Maybe if he paid a little more attention, he'd find her as interesting a person as Jamie did.

As he continued to watch, something else occurred to Dan. There was something about the way

Jamie seemed to study the faces of everyone who approached her, as if searching for something. *So curious,* he thought. It only reinforced his feelings that she was up to something. But even considering everything that seemed off, it added up to nothing he could put a finger on.

Wasn't it enough that she was so genuinely nice to Diana? And that she'd been kind to Grace? Dan watched his mother holding court in one corner of the bookstore and smiled. Wheelchair-bound or not, Grace always seemed to draw a crowd. Even now, having staked out her turf, she was surrounded.

"Oh, yes, Dolores. We've all read J.L.'s books," he heard her tell one of those gathered around her. "They're just marvelous. I can't recommend them enough." And "She is staying at the inn. We've enjoyed getting to know her. If you haven't gotten your book signed yet, just go on up there and get in line."

No doubt about it. Grace would have been hell on wheels in marketing or public relations.

Dan took a few steps to one side to permit a shopper to pass, and in doing so, he was that much closer to the table where Jamie sat. After observing and listening for several moments, he began to see a pattern to her conversations.

"Are you from St. Dennis?" she asked everyone who approached her, almost by rote. "Is your family from here?"

Correction. She asked every woman. None of the men.

Was that just a coincidence? Dan wondered. Maybe the women readers were more chatty, more likely to enter into conversation. He folded his arms and leaned back against the wall for the rest of the afternoon. By the time the last patron left the store, Dan had heard the questions—*Are you from St. Dennis? Is your family from here?*—roughly thirty-four times, each time asked of a woman. He'd started counting as a means of amusing himself, figuring he'd prove his own theory wrong. But he never heard Jamie ask any of the men those same two questions.

Why would it matter to her where her readers were from? Was it merely a pleasantry, like "How are you today?" In that case, why wouldn't she have asked the guys as well?

"What are you hanging around for?" A poke in the back got Dan's attention. He turned to find Lucy clutching her newly signed copy of Jamie's newest book.

"I thought you already read that." Dan hoped to deflect the question. He wasn't really sure why he was still there.

"I did. This is for Clay's mom." Lucy slid the book under her arm, turning her wrist to look at her watch. "It's later than I thought it would be. Want to join us for dinner? Mom said the chef is doing some new shrimp dish tonight, and it sounded divine. Clay's going to meet us at the inn."

"Not sure what I'm going to do." He watched Jamie stand somewhat stiffly to chat with Barbara. "Would you mind taking Mom back to the inn with you? There's something I want to do."

"Sure. I'll round her up and pay for this on my way out. See you later." Lucy drifted to the cash register, where her mother was still chatting with her friends.

Dan waited until Barbara had herded the last of her customers to the front of the store before he approached Jamie. "So it looks like you had a successful afternoon," he said.

"Very much so. When Barbara says she can get books, Barbara gets *books*." Jamie laughed, then winced as she lifted her tote bag.

"You okay?" Dan asked.

"I'm a little stiff, I guess from sitting so long." She made a face. "Actually, more than just a little." She slung the tote over her shoulder, then winced again. "Ouch."

"What's wrong?"

"Sunburn." Jamie lifted her hair from her neck. "My neck and the backs of my legs are on fire. You were right about that." She took two steps forward and grimaced.

"How long a ride did you say you took this morning?" he asked.

"I don't know, to Cannonball Island and back."

"That's twenty-some miles."

"Give or take."

"When was the last time you rode a bike twenty miles?"

She paused, shuffling her pens and making a show of tucking them into her purse. "Maybe never," she mumbled.

"No wonder your legs are sore." Dan grabbed her tote and took her by the arm, his heart melting. She might be a busybody—okay, she was, that was an established fact—but she'd understood his daughter when he hadn't and had helped him to see Diana in a new light, and she was helping his mother with something important to her.

And if that wasn't enough, she was pretty hot.

"Come on, let's get you back to the inn, where we can do something about the sunburn and the stiffness."

They paused at the front of the store, where Jamie said goodbye to Barbara and thanked her for a great afternoon.

"Totally my pleasure," Barbara told her.

"Not to mention the pleasure of all those happy readers today." Nita from the antique store leaned on the counter. "I daresay there will be lights burning late all over town tonight as everyone digs into your books. 'The truth can be a shining beacon in your life, if you let that light in,'" Nita quoted from Jamie's epilogue. "Truer words, and all that."

Jamie smiled and left the store on Dan's arm, leaving behind some of the local ladies, who surely would be digesting this fact for the next hour or so. Dan knew his mother's friends liked nothing better than a good bit of gossip, and Dan Sinclair escorting J. L. Valentine from the store on Saturday—and seeming to be a bit smitten—would do nicely in the absence of anything better.

"How 'bout dinner?" Dan asked, slowing his pace to her snail-like crawl. "You have to be starving, and it's after five."

"I am, but I can barely move." She bit her bottom lip.

"We'll get some aloe on your burns, and you'll feel better," he assured her.

"I think it's going to take a little more than that," she muttered.

"Got any better ideas?" They approached the Jeep, and he unlocked the doors with the remote.

"Actually, I do not." Jamie tried to lift one leg to get into the car but was having a problem with that. Dan placed her tote on the floor, then helped her into the seat. "Sorry," she said, obviously embarrassed by her plight. "I can't believe how stupid I was this morning."

"Hey, it happens." He slammed the door and went around to the driver's side and slid behind the wheel. "You wouldn't have known how hot it gets here early. And if you don't bike a lot, you don't realize how sore your muscles can get when you overdo it the first time out."

"You're just being nice." She rested her head back against the seat. "And I really appreciate it."

He grinned and started the engine. "No point in beating yourself up. We'll do what we can to help you feel better tonight, then we'll get you a great dinner, and I guarantee you'll feel better by the time you turn in."

There was little conversation on the way back to the inn, and when they pulled up in front of the back entrance, Dan sat for a long moment. He'd planned on having dinner alone in the crow's nest, but hadn't he just promised her dinner? He never shared that space with anyone. It was his private sanctuary—the only place that was just his—and here he was, offering to share it. What was wrong with him?

He got out of the car, still wondering, when he re-membered that Jamie needed help walking. He didn't mind carrying her, but he wasn't sure he wanted to do that through the main lobby. "Not sure how this is going to work," he murmured. He thought for a moment longer, then got back into the car and put the Jeep into gear. "Got an idea." He drove around to the far back and parked near a metal door.

"What are we doing?" Jamie asked.

"Going in the least obtrusive way." He unhooked his seat belt, jumped out, and walked around the ve-hicle. "The kitchen staff uses this door." Dan opened the passenger door and helped Jamie out. When he saw she was having trouble walking, he lifted her.

"Is this a bit extreme?" she asked.

"You feel like walking?" He made his way back around the car and opened the metal door.

"I would if I could."

He swung her through the open door and let it slam behind them. A few of the prep cooks looked up, barely suppressing smiles at the sight of their boss carrying a woman across the room.

"Gentlemen. Ladies." Dan nodded as he passed the staff and went straight to the back wall.

"Where are we going?" Jamie asked.

"Freight elevator." He was getting out of breath. She weighed a little more than he'd figured. He hit the button for the elevator and waited for the doors to open. He stood Jamie up inside the cab and stepped in next to her. He hit the button for the third floor.

"I'm on two," Jamie reminded him.

"Yes, but we're going to three."

"Why?"

"You'll see."

The elevator ended its crawl and came to a stop, the doors opening slowly. Dan picked Jamie up again and carried her down the hall, stopping before French doors at the very end.

"Where are we?" Jamie shifted somewhat uneasily in his arms.

"The crow's nest." Dan opened the doors and carried her through. "On the roof." He lowered her to the floor in front of a cushioned wicker chair, one of four, that sat around a matching table. "Great view of the bay from here."

Jamie peered over the waist-high railing. "It's beautiful."

"I thought you'd like it." He watched her for a moment. She looked very beautiful and very vulnerable. "Make yourself comfortable, and I'll be back in a few with some aloe for your legs. If you don't mind sitting here for a little while, we'll get you set up."

"Set up for what?"

"That dinner I promised you."

Chapter 14

～

WITH one foot, Jamie dragged a nearby chair closer, then raised her right leg and rested it on the seat. Who knew that a few hours of bike riding could cause such pain in her thighs and her back? It had never occurred to her that a twenty-mile ride was something she'd have to work up to.

Add that to the pain across her shoulders from hours of signing books and the morning spent hunching over the bike—not to mention the sunburn—and she had an urge to dive headfirst into the bottle of wine that a smiling server had just retrieved from a cooler placed on the table.

"Mr. Sinclair said he'd be delayed a few minutes, but he thought you might enjoy a glass of something," the cheery young girl had chirped. "Would you like me to pour a glass for you? Or would you prefer beer?"

Jamie hesitated. "Which is coldest?"

"The beer. Definitely."

"I'll go with the beer."

"Great choice." The server opened the cooler, peered in, then asked, "Summer brew or regular?"

"What's the difference?"

"The summer is specially brewed and is only available for a limited time," she explained. "Made with scents and flavors of summer. This early one has hints of strawberry and rose hips."

"In a beer?"

The young woman nodded. "It's MadMac Brews' seasonal specialty." She held up a bottle with a pretty label that promised "the subtle taste of early summer." "MadMac is a local brewery."

"Lucy Sinclair's husband's company?" Jamie tried to recall what Dan had said.

"Right."

"I'll try that."

"I think you'll enjoy it." The server opened the bottle and poured into a frosted glass that had been inside the cooler, then handed the glass to Jamie. "Cheers."

"Thanks." Jamie took a first thirsty icy-cold sip. "Oh, it's . . . different. But good."

"Glad you like it." The server reached into the cooler and brought out a plate holding crackers, several different cheeses, and some fruit. She removed the plastic wrap that had been pulled tautly across the plate. "Mr. Sinclair said he might be a while, but he wanted you to be comfortable."

"Please tell Mr. Sinclair, if you see him, that I am." Jamie returned the smile. "And that I said thank you."

"Will do. Enjoy." The young woman returned the wine to the cooler, closed the top, and disappeared through the French doors.

Jamie sipped the cold beer and, within moments, felt the tension begin to leave her neck and shoulders. She sampled several of the cheeses and thought about the man who'd pulled this together for her on the spur of the moment. *I guess it's true what they say,* she mused. *It's good to be the boss.* The little bit of food went a long way to revive her. Even her sunburn didn't seem to hurt quite as much.

It had been such an odd day, she reflected. The morning's excursion aside, the book signing had made her head spin. She'd signed books for large numbers of readers in the past, but since this signing was in this place, at a time she was seeking, each face took on an air of possibility. She'd tried to weed out the locals from the tourists by asking where people were from, had even made check marks next to their names on the newsletter list, but it had done no good. There'd been no one who "felt" familiar, whose touch or voice reached something in her core. And much to her disappointment, no one had commented on her resemblance to anyone else, no "Hey, Annie, doesn't J.L. remind you of Cousin Lynne?" There'd been no tug of recognition, no instinctual bonding, no ping, no zing. So much for blood recognizing blood. If her birth mother, or someone related to her, had been in the room, Jamie's instincts had failed her miserably.

It had been nice of Grace to encourage the guests at the inn to attend and to talk Jamie up to all her friends, which, from their showing that afternoon, appeared to be legion. Jamie had heard snips of Grace's conversations throughout the day: Grace had sung the praises of Jamie's latest book and chatted about what a "lovely young woman" Jamie was, as if the success of the signing lay upon Grace's shoulders alone.

And there was that one conversation between Grace and a friend that Jamie had overheard and found encouraging.

"Hey, Gracie," her friend had called to her. "I ran into Ray at the drugstore yesterday, and he tells me you're trying to archive all the back issues of the *Gazette*."

"Ray's right. I am," Grace had replied.

"I told Ray, long as the *Gazette*'s been around, it's going to take you until judgment day to go through all that mess."

"You think so, do you, now?" Grace's back went ramrod-straight. "I admit I've had a setback, but I will get all those back issues organized if it's the last damned thing I do. You know that nothing has happened in St. Dennis in the past hundred years that wasn't reported in the *Gazette*."

"We always said if you didn't see it in the *St. Dennis Gazette,* it didn't happen. Who got married, who died, who was born," Nita said.

"Who went on vacation, who went to college, who joined the military," Eleanor from the flower shop had added in passing. "Nita's right. If it happened in St. Dennis, you read about it in the *Gazette*."

"Well, you wouldn't know that from the sorry state of affairs that office is in. I really wanted to go through the boxes and put every issue in order, going back to the very first."

Nita had nodded sympathetically. "You'll get it done, Gracie. We all know how you are when you get your mind set on something. And you know that any one of us would be happy to help."

"You all have your own things to do," Grace had said, "but I do appreciate the offer."

"I'm here if you need me," Nita had promised.

Hours later, the words still rang in Jamie's ears. *If it happened in St. Dennis, you read about it in the Gazette.*

That was exactly what Jamie had been counting on.

"So how are we doing?" Dan stepped onto the rooftop balcony.

"I feel so much better. Thank you so much for all this."

"Great. The chef was in a good mood, and it's early for the dinner crowd, so he had a little time to throw something together for us." He took the seat next to her. "I see you went for the beer."

"It's wonderful."

Dan reached into the cooler, pulled out a beer for himself, and popped the lid. He took a long sip, then set the bottle on the table. He looked at Jamie and said, "Why don't you stand up so I can put some of this aloe on the backs of your legs." He held up a bottle with a nozzle on top.

"It's a spray," she said.

"Of course it's a spray. Only a sadistic son of a gun would touch that burn."

Jamie stood and turned her back to him.

"Pull your skirt up just a bit so I don't get this stuff on your dress."

She did as she was told, then felt the cool, light touch of the gentle spray on the backs of her calves.

"How's that?" he asked.

"It feels really good. Thanks, Dan." She sighed with the relief of having the burn subside.

"If your legs aren't too sore from pedaling so that you can stand for a few minutes, it'll dry."

She felt his fingertips, like a soft breeze, on the back of her neck as he pushed her hair to one side. "Maybe a little bit on this strip of burn back here," he said.

The heat left her skin as the cooling spray went to work. "So much better," she told him.

"That's the idea. You really did a number on yourself today." He put the lid back on the spray bottle. "Now, while you're waiting for it to dry, take a look out over that way." He pointed off to the right where a group of sailboats gathered. "The race is about to start."

The small, colorful crafts maneuvered into place along a line Jamie could not see. A man in a bright yellow jacket stood on the bow of a larger boat off to one side. Moments later, he raised a red-and-white flag, then dropped it suddenly.

"And the forty-second St. Dennis Sunfish race— twelve-to-fifteen-year-olds—is on." Dan craned his neck to watch. He pointed to a yellow craft with a bright blue-and-white-striped sail. "That's my son, D.J."

"His first race?"

"No. He's been sailing since he was seven. He's really good, instinctual at the sail. Better than I was at that age. He's more like Ford when it comes to knowing the wind."

"I'm surprised you're not down there cheering him on."

"I can cheer him on just as well from here, maybe better, since this is a better vantage point. Besides, when you're out on the bay, you can't hear much from the shore. He knows I'm watching." Dan rested his forearms on the rail that surrounded the secluded balcony.

"How far is the race?" Jamie asked.

"Just out to the island off to the right there and once around, then back to the starting point." Dan pointed to a small outcropping that rose above the bay. "There, see? You've got three boats already on their way around the island. They'll come out the other side in a minute or two, then sail back to the starting line. If the wind holds, it should be over in less than five minutes."

"How's your son doing?" Jamie scanned the scene for a glimpse of the yellow boat.

"Respectably. This isn't a race he expected to win. He's just using it to gain experience for the longer races as the summer progresses. He said it's sort of like running surveillance against the competition. He'll sail in the end of the summer regatta with Ford, who is a beast on the water, and by then D.J. will have a book on everyone else."

"Clever boy."

"You betcha. I expect he and Ford will be pretty unbeatable. They make a good team."

"Does that bother you? That your son sails with your brother and not you?"

"Not a bit. That's Ford's thing. It was never mine. He always had more time to spend doing stuff like that."

"Stuff like sailing?"

"Competitively, yes. By the time he was old enough to get into it, I was already part-time with my dad, running the inn."

"Did you wish you could have done that, too?"

"Not really. Sailing was never my thing. It's cool that D.J. likes it, and Ford gets a kick out of racing with him. That's enough for me. I like to see my family happy." He took another sip of beer, then said, "That brings me to my daughter."

"Look, I'm sorry if I stepped on your toes. I appreciate that it's tough to be a single parent—"

He held up a hand to stop her. "I just wanted to tell you how much I appreciate the way you are with Diana. You treat her as if she's someone special, someone special to you."

"She is. I am very fond of her. She's smart, and she's funny, and she's great company."

"That's what I'm talking about. Of course I know all those things about her, but you've helped me see her in a different way. She always says that I treat her like a six-year-old, and she's right. Because in my mind, I wanted her to remain that little girl who depended on me for everything, the girl who thought I hung the moon."

"I think she still believes that. But she could use a little more space." Jamie paused. "If you don't mind my saying so."

"I don't mind." He took a deep breath. "Anyway, I just wanted to say thanks for helping me see her as you see her."

"You're welcome." Jamie had to remind herself

that her plan had been to remain friends with him, nothing more. She was wondering if her plan had been revised without her realizing it when his phone rang.

"Yes. Sure. Come on up." He ended the call and turned to Jamie. "Dinner is on the way."

"I thought that"—she pointed to the cheese and fruit piled high on the serving plate—"was dinner."

"That was just the warm-up. The chef got some rockfish in this morning that he promised would knock our socks off." He raised a hand to shield his eyes from the late-afternoon sun's glare and gazed out at the water. She could tell the second he spotted his son's boat. "You go, buddy," Dan said. "Fifth place is not too shabby, considering he's one of the youngest out there."

"How old is he?"

"He'll be thirteen in a few months."

Jamie watched the colorful boats gather loosely around the finish line, then moments later, start to drift apart. Soon the majority of them were headed to the dock.

A knock on the door announced dinner, and Dan turned to chat with the servers, who set the table for them, leaving covered dishes and plates.

"Thanks, guys," Dan said as the two young men left the balcony. He pulled out Jamie's chair and guided her to it. "Let's see what we have here." He uncovered Jamie's plate first, then his own. "Roasted fingerling potatoes, and looks like the carrots were roasted as well. Hope it's to your liking."

"Are you kidding?" Jamie's mouth was watering. "What's not to like?" She took a bite of the fish and grinned. "Perfection. It's delicious."

"A specialty of the Chesapeake," he told her. "Rockfish is the official state fish of Maryland."

"I don't think I've had it before."

"You did if you ever ate striped bass."

"It's delicious by any name," she said.

They ate for a few minutes before Dan's phone rang again.

"Excuse me," he said before getting up from the table and stepping to the side. "I did. Way to go, buddy. You did a great job. Fifth place against that field is a win . . . Sure. Go ahead. Just be back by ten. And congrats, D.J."

"Your son?" Jamie asked when Dan was reseated.

He nodded. "He wants to go into town for pizza with a few of his buddies—and probably a few of the young girls hanging around the dock."

"At twelve going on thirteen?"

"Earlier than that. Diana had boys calling her in fifth grade."

"Diana is an exceptionally pretty girl. Can you blame them?" Jamie polished off the last of the vegetables on her plate.

"Hell, yes. She's my daughter. I don't want guys noticing how pretty she is."

Jamie laughed. "Sorry, but I don't think you have any control over that."

"Sad but true. Fortunately, all the kids she's friendly with seem like good kids—I know peer pressure is probably the most influential factor in a kid's behavior, so I guess we're lucky there." He took a long swig of beer.

"Diana's not dating yet?"

"No. God, no." He ran a hand over his face.

Jamie laughed. "Dan, you know it's inevitable. A lot of girls are dating at her age."

"Sorry. Don't want to think about it."

"Avoidance on the part of the parent has never kept a kid from growing up. At least not as far as I know."

"It's happening too fast. I'm not ready to deal with boys and . . . and everything that goes along with that." He took another drink. "I never thought I'd have to deal with the whole boy/girl thing. I thought her mother . . ." His voice trailed away.

"How long has it been?"

"Eight years. Diana was just eight when Doreen died, D.J. was four. As hard as it was on me, it was ten times harder on them, losing her. My mom stepped in on a lot of levels, but of course . . ." He tapped the sides of his glass with his hands.

". . . it isn't the same." Jamie finished the sentence for him.

"No, it isn't the same. There's a lot to be said for single parents who can effectively play the role of both parents. I'm afraid I didn't make a very good mom." He smiled wryly. "As a dad, I'm pretty good, though."

"I'm sure you've done just fine."

"Anyway, I guess the bottom line is everyone's kids grow up and no one is ever completely ready for that to happen." He shrugged and speared a piece of fish with his fork. "But enough about me. What did you think of Cannonball Island?"

"A little peculiar, frankly. So close to St. Dennis, yet it seems so different. All the boarded-up buildings and the dilapidated boats just sitting around. Everything there looks like it hasn't been maintained. Like the houses all need a good paint job. As does just about everything else on the island."

"Cannonballers are a breed apart. Always have been. They've always been water men—good times and bad—and live essentially the same way their parents and grandparents lived. I think they don't bother with painting and that sort of thing because they see their homes as shelters, nothing more."

"Well, they're not very friendly to strangers." Jamie thought of the woman she'd waved to who'd ignored her.

"Not friendly at all," Dan agreed. "They're a tightly knit group, and they want to keep it that way. They don't like to consort with the town people because they don't want their kids to start thinking things might be better in St. Dennis. Their kids come here for school, but most of them don't participate in outside activities, sports and such. They keep to themselves, but there are fewer and fewer of them every year."

"Oh, I did speak with the woman in the general store when I stopped for water."

"Older woman? Like about a hundred years old? Face lined like a road map?" Dan finished his meal and placed his fork on the plate.

"Yes."

"Miz Carter. She is, by the way, one hundred years old."

"You're kidding." Jamie paused. "She looked old but not that old. And she had her wits about her, that's for sure."

"She doesn't miss a beat." Dan grinned. "Say, are you interested in dessert?"

"I could not eat another bite." Jamie pushed her chair back and turned it so she was facing him. "Miz Carter said something peculiar about your mother. She said, 'Gracie's got the eye.' What do you suppose she meant?"

"She meant that my mother has a reputation among the locals as having a sort of sixth sense about things." He shrugged. "The kids used to tease me about it a lot when we were in grade school, but I never really paid much attention to it."

"How do you suppose that got started?"

"I think it was probably because of Alice."

"Alice?" The name sounded familiar. Had Grace mentioned someone named Alice?

"There used to be a woman in town named Alice Ridgeway. She was a lot older than my mom, and she was said to be a . . . well, a witch. The rumor was that a lot of the younger girls went to her to learn how to do spells, that sort of thing. Most people didn't take it seriously."

"And your mother was supposedly one of the young girls."

He nodded. "Mom and a bunch of others. The rumor surfaces every ten or twenty years. I heard about it when I was a kid but not much since then. Alice lived in the house that Vanessa and her husband live in now. Grady—that's Ness's husband—said she found a lot of big musty journals when she moved into the house, and she gave them all to my mother."

"That's intriguing. Did you ever see them?"

"Alice's journals?" He shook his head. "If Mom has them, she's kept them out of sight."

"Did you ever ask her?"

"Did I ever ask my mother if she's a witch?"

"Well, not that, but if she has a sixth sense."

"I never had to ask her outright. She does." He sighed. "There are things that my mother knows that . . . I don't know how she knows them. She's been like that as long as I can remember."

"You mean she can see into the future? Predict things, like a psychic?"

"Not so much *see* the future as much as *know* things. It's like she can sense when something is going to happen, or she can know things about people. It's really hard to explain."

"Interesting." Jamie wondering what, if anything, Grace had sensed from her.

"It made for an interesting childhood."

"She knew what you were doing all the time?" Jamie teased.

"She always seemed to be able to read Lucy and me better than Ford, for some reason." He grew thoughtful.

"Did she pass this ability on to any of you?"

Dan shook his head. "No, but lately, I've seen little things in Diana that make me wonder if she inherited a touch of whatever it is her grandmother has."

"You said she went to this witch to learn how to do spells. Ever see any evidence of that?"

"No. I don't know. Maybe. My mother can be hard to read sometimes. It's tough to know what she's thinking."

"But you didn't inherit her sight or whatever it is?"

"Not a bit."

"So then you don't know what I'm thinking."

"Not a clue." He appeared amused.

Jamie leaned toward him and put her hand on the back of his neck, pulling him closer and, before she could talk herself out of it, kissing him full on the mouth. It was, she realized, something she'd been wanting to do all night. For just a second, Dan seemed too surprised to react. But he recovered nicely—and quickly. His hand held the side of her face gently, and when she thought to pull away, he eased her back into the kiss. Jamie felt it all slip away, the pain of finding out the truth of her birth, the conflict, the stress of the search. For a few seconds, she felt she was where she belonged. The thought startled her, making her pull away and open her eyes and look into the face of the man who unexpectedly had just shaken her world.

"I did not see that coming," he said. "Best surprise ever."

Jamie wanted to tell him that she wasn't sure what had prompted her to do that, she hadn't planned it, but his phone rang and she let it go. Maybe he'd misunderstand and think she was sorry, and sorry was the last thing she felt. A little confused, maybe, but not sorry.

"I forgot. Look, have their bags taken to their room and have Chris seat them in the dining room. Tell them I'll be right there. And send someone up to the crow's nest with a cart." Dan disconnected the call but kept the phone in his hand.

"Are you always on call?" she asked.

"Inevitable, I guess, when you live where you work."

"I take it you need to go."

Dan nodded. "We have guests checking in for their annual two weeks. They've been coming as a family for as long as I can remember. My dad always had them for dinner the first night, and I've continued the tradition."

"You're going to eat another dinner after that?" She nodded to their dinner plates.

"I'll just sit and chat for a while. They're really nice people and they've been loyal to the inn." He pushed his chair out from the table. "I'm sorry. I hate to bail on you."

"It's fine. I actually think I'd like to get to bed early. I'm really tired."

"Long, early bike ride, long afternoon. I expect you would be." He handed her the spray bottle of aloe. "You might need this later, and maybe again tomorrow."

"Thanks."

"I wasn't ready for the night to end," he confessed.

"It's okay. Go, be the innkeeper." Jamie smiled and stood.

"Thanks for understanding."

"Of course." She walked with him to the doorway, then paused to look over her shoulder at the comfy chairs and the remains of their delicious dinner. "So this is the crow's nest?"

Dan smiled. "That's what we used to call it when we were kids. The name stuck. It's about the only place in the inn that I keep private, just for me." He took her hand and led her into the hallway.

"Now I have to wonder how many ladies have shared that private table with you," Jamie teased.

Dan hit the down button on the freight elevator. "Actually," he told her, "you're the first."

Diary~

Life is so complicated sometimes, and for the life of me, I can't think of one good reason why it should be. Things have become so muddled, I hardly know what to think. For the record, let me say that it's extremely difficult for me to know things that I should not know. To see what I should not see. To pretend not to know.

The search is on, and Lord help me, I'm aiding and abetting. I know I should not deliberately turn the tide, so to speak—I know how far I can go. I just want to see this end, this heartache and uncertainty in those I care about. And make no mistake, I am starting to care for this lost child as I care for her mother. I hate being betwixt and between.

To complicate matters further, my boy is starting to care as well. No surprise there. I knew that Jamie was coming into our lives and would bring something important. I did not expect it to happen so soon, but if ever a man wore his heart on his sleeve, it's my Dan.

But, oh dear. It appears that I'm not the only one who noticed. At the reception, I had this pointed out to me by Curtis Enright, of all people—by way of a warning. Yes, indeed, Curtis warned me about letting Dan get too close to Jamie. "She isn't who she pretends to be," he confided. "Nothing good can come of her being in St. Dennis."

Well, little does he know that I know exactly why the girl has come here and what she's looking for. Apparently, he does, too. Funny how Curtis sees this as something to be avoided at all costs. I know in my heart that when the truth is revealed, it will bring great joy. But right now no one knows what lies ahead.

No one but me, of course. Oh, and Alice, who seems to know more about this entire matter than she should. Then again, that's always the way with Alice.

Grace

Chapter 15

Below Jamie's balcony, someone dragged a kayak from the water's edge to the boathouse, and even from this distance, Jamie could tell it was Ford. She thought about Dan's comment about having less time to spend on the bay than Ford—specifically, less time to sail—because he'd been busy helping his father at the inn. It was no secret that Dan had been forced to take over the day-to-day operations at a young age, and while he was clearly very good at it and obviously loved the place, Jamie couldn't help wondering if he would have done something else had he been given the choice.

What, she wondered, *might that choice have been?*

She pondered that while she took the steps—slowly—to the first floor, through the lobby, and to Grace's office door.

"Come in," Grace called when she saw Jamie in the doorway. "So how's the sunburn today?"

"Much better, thank you. Dan gave me some aloe spray, and that helped a lot."

"Good. And the sore muscles?"

"Much improved."

"Great."

"Grace, I wanted to thank you again for dragging everyone you knew to the signing yesterday."

"There was no dragging involved. Everyone was happy to come and happy to buy your book."

"I know you brought a lot of friends."

"It was an event, and everyone should have been there."

"I just wanted you to know how much I appreciate it."

"As I appreciate your help with my project." Grace wheeled back to her desk. "Speaking of which, let's get started. I can hardly wait to see what we find today."

"Me, too." Jamie removed the lid from a nearby box. "Where's Diana? Is she joining us today?"

"Lacrosse camp. First day. She couldn't miss it. I told her it was okay, I had you to help me, so I wasn't on my own." Grace smiled.

At that moment, Ford came into the room, knocking on the door as he opened it. "Today's issue of the *St. Dennis Gazette,* hot off the press for your reading pleasure." He passed a paper to Jamie on his way to his mother's desk.

"Oh, look, Jamie, you made the front page." Grace held up the paper.

"Must have been a very slow week in St. Dennis," Jamie said.

"Well, yeah, it was, but still, you're news. Everyone was talking about your book signing and how nice you are." Ford leaned a hip against his mother's desk. "My favorite comment overheard last night at the art center was 'She's just like a real person.'"

Jamie laughed. "Good to know."

"It's a very nice article, Ford." Grace appeared to be reading it. "Very nice."

Jamie opened the paper and scanned the story, smiling to herself when she saw that Ford had made her birth date prominent in the first paragraph. "'Born on October 12, 1979 . . .'" She'd repeated the date several times during the interview, hoping Ford would include it somewhere. Surely the date would get someone's attention. Surely someone would see it and wonder . . .

"I have to get moving." Ford got up and headed toward the door.

"Thanks, Ford." Jamie held up her copy.

"Thanks for a great interview. Mom, I'll see you later." He waved from the door before disappearing through it.

"I knew that boy would be a good newspaper-man," Grace said with no small amount of satisfaction. "He resisted, but I knew he'd give in, and I knew he'd do well. I always thought he was the one who should take over the paper."

"How did you know?" Jamie asked.

"Mother's intuition." Grace shrugged. "I wonder what we'll find today . . ."

Jamie began to thumb through the newspapers in the box she'd opened earlier. While there was nothing of particular interest to her—*Mrs. Ida Chambers hosted a tea on Tuesday afternoon at her home on*

River Road for the members of the newly formed ladies' card club . . . —Grace got a kick out of the photo.

Jamie was working on the third box when something caught her eye. She studied the photo carefully. Grace was on the phone, so Jamie put the photo aside. Two more boxes, another photo that drew Jamie's interest.

When Grace finally hung up from her call, Jamie showed Grace first the photo of Ida Chambers and the ladies' card club.

"Oh my, I do remember the card club. My mother was a member." She held up the photo that accompanied the article and grinned. "And there she is, third from the left. I remember the hat she was wearing." She shook her head. "My father hated that thing, with all its feathers."

Jamie leaned forward and studied the paper. Grace's mother was a tiny woman with white hair and a saucy smile. "You have her smile," she said.

"So people have told me." Grace nodded and folded the paper and put it to one side of her desk. "Let's see what else you've found for me." She skimmed through several papers. "Here's Nita's sister Nancy's wedding picture. Wasn't she a sight? All that lace covering her face." Grace shook her head. "One wonders what her mother was thinking." She turned the page around so Jamie could see the picture. "'Mr. and Mrs. Stephen Etheridge announce the marriage of their daughter, Miss Nancy Alder Etheridge, to Mr. Andrew Parker Noonan . . .'"

"Noonan? Isn't that Barbara's last name?"

"Yes. Andy is Barbara's older brother." She paused. "Older by, oh my, ten years or so, as I recall." She placed the paper on the *save* pile. "I do hope Ray can find the negatives to some of these old photos. The more I think about it, the more I think it would make a marvelous display. A sort of photographic time line."

Grace went through the remaining newspapers Jamie had saved for her. When she'd pulled out the ones she was most interested in, she told Jamie, "You've got an eye for this sort of thing. You must have grown up in a small town."

"I did. Caryville, PA. About as small a town as you can get and still have a post office."

Grace smiled. "St. Dennis used to be like that, and not so very long ago. Oh, we're still small-town, but we were a lot smaller ten, fifteen years ago. Once we were 'discovered,' well, people were coming into town looking for places to buy. Knocking on doors, asking residents if they wanted to sell, and at nice prices, too. Some folks sold and moved on, but for the most part, the newcomers either had to buy one of those new places out on the highway, or be content to spend a few weeks here at the inn or at one of the B and Bs that became so popular."

"Did anyone offer to buy the inn?"

"Oh my, yes. We turned down any number of folks."

"Not even tempted a little?" Jamie teased.

"Not for a second. First of all, for all his insistence that it was a family decision, it was really up to Dan, as far as the rest of us were concerned, because he was running the place. He had no interest in selling, though—for which the rest of us were grateful, since it's been Sinclair's since the day it was built."

"What if Dan had wanted to sell?"

"I'd have gone along with it. We all would have. Wouldn't have liked it very much, but it would have been fine. He's the one who had the burden. If he'd wanted to lay it down, I'd have agreed." Grace folded up the papers that hadn't interested her and gave them back to Jamie to put in order.

"Oh, I found two other photos," Jamie said, as if she'd just remembered and hadn't held them aside on purpose. She got up from her chair, the newspapers in hand, and placed the two issues in front of Grace. "Look at this one from 1976—and this one from 1977. The same five girls from the picture we looked at yesterday. First day of ninth grade, first day of tenth."

Grace adjusted her glasses and held the papers up. "So they are." She snapped her fingers. "Of course. I remember now. Eleanor's father did some of the photography for my dad from time to time. Looks like he found a way to get his little girl's picture in the paper as often as possible."

"That explains it, then." Jamie held out another issue, this one from 1978. "The junior prom. All five of the girls with their dates."

"Oh, would you look at that." Grace broke into a grin. "Nita and Howard—they were married after their freshman year in college. Divorced not too long after that." She slid her glasses higher on her nose. "Eleanor and . . . Oh, why didn't we include the boys' names? I can't think of his name. Gail's date was Jack Haslet—he was her first husband, died in a car accident shortly after they were married. She's been married four times and never changed her last name. Guess she knew what she was doing there. Think of all she saved on monograms."

She studied the photo a few seconds longer. "Barbara and her fellow, Captain Davis's boy. What was his first name? Carl, maybe? Nice boy. Very handsome, as you can see. Followed his father into the navy. Oh, and Heidi Richards with the Danvers boy. After high school, he went right to New York and did some work on one of those noontime soap operas. Always did have a flare for the dramatic, that one did."

Jamie stared at the page; she'd been hoping for something more. Something that would lead her to something else. While she still felt a pull toward these photos of the five girls, she wasn't sure why, and she wasn't sure which one was drawing her in. She couldn't help but feel, more than ever, that the answer to her search would be found in one of those boxes of old newspapers. She just wished she would hurry up and find the right one soon.

It haunted her the rest of the day. She called Sis to tell her she thought she was on the right trail, but she had to leave a voicemail. She wished she could tell her secret to Dan, or Grace, or someone who mattered to her. But the only person who knew—the only person who could know—was Sis.

Oh, and Curtis Enright, but he wasn't talking.

She hadn't wanted to admit it, but when she went down for dinner that evening, she was looking for

Dan. When she saw him across the lobby, she couldn't help but smile. He held a clipboard and was talking to a woman with short blond hair who was gazing up at him with stars in her eyes. Jamie saw him excuse himself and walk over to the stairwell, and to her.

"I was hoping to catch up with you," he told her. "We're interviewing for three positions, and I'm sitting in. Otherwise, I would have liked to have dinner with you. Or take a walk. Or . . . just about anything you felt like doing."

"Any of the above would be fine when you can fit me in."

"That's the thing, see. One of the jobs we're interviewing for is assistant manager. Trying to spread out the responsibilities a little. Give me a little more time to spend doing . . . whatever."

"You must be feverish. Here. Let me check." Jamie put her hand on his forehead, and he laughed.

"I don't know how long I'll be tied up tonight, but how about we do something special in the morning, you and me? We have a few more interviews scheduled for the afternoon, but the morning is free."

"Something special like . . . what?"

"You'll see." He leaned over and kissed the side of her mouth. "See you in the morning. Let's meet up at my mom's office around seven."

"Okay. See you then."

She watched him walk away before climbing the steps and going back to her room. She showered and put on a nightshirt and flopped onto the sofa to watch some mindless television. By the first commercial, she was sound asleep.

• • •

THE NEXT MORNING, Jamie stared at the boxes piled on the table in Grace's office and wished that, just for a day or two, she had Grace's eye. It would certainly save a lot of time.

At exactly seven, Dan poked his head in. "Hey, good morning," he said.

"Hi." She turned in her seat and smiled.

"Feel like taking a bike ride?" He held up two helmets. "It's a gorgeous morning. Cool, no humidity."

"Are you trying to kill me? I'm just getting my legs back from my last ride."

"Which is exactly why you should go out again today. Build some stamina so you can take those twenty or thirty mile rides and not suffer afterward." He tossed her one of the helmets. "Come on. Cannonball Island's waiting."

"No way I'm doing that ride again." She tossed the helmet back, and he caught it in one hand.

"Not the entire island. Today we're only going as far as the old chapel. That's about halfway." Dan tossed the helmet to her again. "Come on. It'll be fun."

"I doubt that. It wasn't so much fun the first time around." But she got up, helmet in hand, and glanced down at her attire. Short shorts. A tank top. Flip-flops. "Give me ten minutes to change."

He held the door for her just as his phone began to ring. "I'll meet you by the back door," he said before answering the call.

I must be nuts, Jamie mentally grumbled as she trudged up the steps in the lobby. *Nuts for even considering another bike ride on the very morning that my thighs have stopped screaming at me and I can walk without limping. How did he know?*

Then again, he was pretty hard to resist. Add nicely tanned—and buff—arms and legs to that boyish grin, and he didn't need to twist her arm very hard.

Back in her room, she changed quickly into cargo shorts, a short-sleeved T-shirt, and running shoes, not the optimum but steps up from flip-flops. She slipped her sunglasses onto the top of her head and her room key into a pocket along with her phone before heading out to meet Dan, the helmet in her hand.

"I think this is the right bike for you," Dan told her when she caught up with him outside. "Might even be the same one you had the other day."

"Well, it is red." She walked around to the back of the bike. "And it has that little dent in the back fender. It's the same one, all right." She made a cross with her index fingers, as if warding off evil. "Demon bike. Wasn't another one available? Perhaps one with a motor?"

Dan laughed. "Sorry, but no. Come on, Jamie. Show it who's boss."

"Does this helmet make my head look fat?" she asked as she strapped it on.

"Fat head is better than bloody head." He put on his own, got on his bike, and started to pedal toward the drive.

"Ah, again with the visual when a simple yes would have sufficed." She climbed onto the bike and followed him toward the road.

For the first ten minutes, he rode in front of her,

which she didn't mind. The view was pretty nice. They slowed at the pond, but Big Blue was nowhere to be seen. "Maybe on the way back," Dan said over his shoulder.

When they approached the drawbridge leading onto the island, Dan circled back around her. "No cars coming either way, so let's head across." He slowed to ride next to her. Once on the island's road, he asked, "How are you feeling? Legs okay?"

She nodded. "Fine. Good."

"We won't push it this time," he told her. "We'll go as far as the old chapel, then we'll stop at the store so I can drop off something to Miz Carter before we head back."

"Wait—the store is on the other side of the island. I thought you said we'd only go halfway."

"There's a shortcut that comes out right behind the store."

"Now you tell me. I could have used that the other day when I was gasping for water and dying in the heat."

"Next time you'll know."

"Next time I'll bring more water."

"There's a bottle in the cold pack in your basket if you need it."

Her hand reached into the basket and found the insulated pack. "Looks like you thought of everything."

"I live to serve." He took off ahead of her, hugging the left side of the road.

They passed the old abandoned boats that stood sentry along the narrow road.

"You'd think they'd sell those things," Jamie called to him, "or scrap them."

"Never know when you'll need a good boat," he replied, dropping back.

"None of them look all that good to me," she countered.

"I believe the thinking is that if some disaster strikes the boats that are used day to day, something can be salvaged from the old ones." He slowed to point out a derelict craft up ahead. "That old bowrider, for example. If worse came to worst, maybe some of the rotted hull boards could be replaced."

"I think rotting boards are the least of that boat's issues."

"If your life and livelihood depend on your ability to get out onto the bay, you do whatever you have to do. I'm not saying I'd trust a boat like that to get me out and back, but then again, I don't make my living on the water." He stopped in front of the boat under discussion. "I'm just saying that some might see these old workhorses as a sort of insurance."

"Do you ever wish you did?" she couldn't help but ask. He'd sounded almost wistful. "Make your living on the water?"

He hesitated. "Maybe when I was a kid, I thought it might be cool." He shrugged, but she could tell the pull was still there. "I'd watch the boats go out in the morning—I mean, really early, before dawn—and see them grow smaller and smaller until they disappeared. Then I'd watch for them to return, wonder what they'd caught, whether they'd had a good day. Whether the fish were running and the traps were full." He gazed off into the distance, as if still waiting for those ships to come back to port. "One of my mom's uncles was a water man, and his stories about his life on the bay always fascinated me. He had a skipjack that he and his brother built."

"What's a skipjack?"

"It's a wooden-hulled sailboat with a long boom, the bottom shaped like a V, no motor. In its day, it was *the* boat to dredge for oysters, because the law back then was that you couldn't dredge with a motorized boat. There aren't that many still working the bay, because that law changed back in the sixties to permit motorboats to dredge a couple of days a week. Down around Cambridge, they have a heritage skipjack race in late summer—the crafts that are still seaworthy, anyway. Last I heard, the number was down to about forty, and my uncle Clifford built more than a few of those. He had a place down by where the marina is now, where he built his boats. I used to think . . ."

"You used to think what?" she asked when his voice faded.

"I used to think that I'd take over that shop one day, build some boats of my own."

"That was your dream as a kid? To build sailboats?"

"To build skipjacks," he corrected her. "But yeah."

"Ever sorry you went into innkeeping instead?"

Dan shrugged. "It was always understood that I'd take over from my dad one day. I didn't think that day would happen as soon as it did, but that's the way it goes sometimes, right?"

"Any regrets?"

He leaned forward on the handlebars and appeared to be lost in thought. Finally, he said, "Not really. I love the inn, love that connection to my dad and my granddad and all the others who came before them. How many people can say they're carrying on a business that their family founded two hundred years ago?"

"So do you ever go to those races and look at the boats your uncle built and think about what might have been?"

"I go to the races and admire the crafts, not just the ones he built but the others. And then I come back to the inn and admire what was built there."

Jamie turned her attention to the landlocked boats on the dune. "They just all look so sad, abandoned out on the flats like that."

"They all belong to someone," he told her. "Someone's father or grandfather or great-grandfather fished from the bow or dropped his traps off the side of every one of them. Think of them as heirloom boats, and maybe you'll see the beauty in them."

Jamie pulled up behind him, her feet dropping to the pavement for balance as she stopped. "There is a sort of beauty there, I will admit that: standing out here alone on the grass, looking as if they're looking out to sea."

"When a boat is retired, they do place them so that they're facing the bay. Sort of a tradition here." He straddled the seat of his bike, signaling that he was ready to resume the ride.

"The other day, I noticed that almost all the

houses had fences around their front yards." Jamie, too, got back on her bike. "Another tradition?"

Dan nodded as he pulled away from the side of the road. "Most of the island families have been burying their dead on their properties for generations. The fences mark the makeshift cemeteries."

"I saw the white stones and wondered if they were grave markers." Jamie caught up with him. "Is that legal? To bury people in your front yard?"

"I guess it is, lacking a law against it. Cannonball Islanders make their own laws, more or less. They have for centuries. The people who settled here originally didn't choose to do so. They were St. Dennis townspeople who sided with the British during the revolution and were forced to leave by those who supported war against the crown. Since there were more rebels than Tories, the Brit sympathizers were the ones made to go. They were pushed across the sound to this island, which at that time was considered uninhabitable. Somehow those hardy souls managed to make a go of it, and their descendants are still here."

"Exiled," she said.

"Exactly."

"Which goes a long way to explain why the islanders don't like their kids to go to school in St. Dennis."

"Right." He pointed ahead and off to the left. "There's one of the abandoned chapels. Want to make a stop?"

"Only if you have a story to tell."

Dan laughed. "Of course. That's what Cannonball Island is all about."

A moment later, they were stopped in front of a

tiny chapel, the windows and door of which were boarded.

"There's another one like this about a mile from here," Jamie said. "I saw it the other day."

"Actually, there are three—this one and two others, all identical. This one was the first. The story goes that the minister, Reverend Jerimiah Sharpe, built this little church with his own funds. He was from Annapolis and had heard about the Tories being run out of St. Dennis. Thinking they needed some spiritual guidance, he moved his family out here and set up his church. Two of the more prominent members of the congregation had a falling-out, which resulted in one of the men leaving and building his own church. Since there was no preacher, he decided he'd do the preaching himself. That worked fine for a while, until—"

"Let me guess. He got into it with one of the members of the congregation, who decided to move on."

"You catch on fast. That's exactly what happened. So for a couple hundred years, there were three separate little congregations here. I'm not sure why, but about fifty years ago, the flocks began to diminish, until the chapels were boarded up due to lack of interest. I guess if any of the islanders feel the need for a sermon, they drive over the bridge to St. Dennis on Sunday morning."

"The more you tell me, the stranger I think the locals must be."

"They're a strange lot, that's for sure." He turned on his bike seat. "You had enough? I said we'd only go as far as the chapel, so I'm ready to turn back, if you are."

"I thought you wanted to go to the general store."

"I do." Dan turned his bike around to face her. "Let's head back toward the bridge."

"Ah, yes. The promised shortcut." Jamie's legs were beginning to tighten up slightly, so she was hoping the shortcut would be exactly that. She, too, turned around, and followed Dan the way they'd come.

They'd gone about five miles when Dan pulled off to the side of the road and got off his bike. "We can leave the bikes here," he told her.

She pulled up next to him. "And what, fly?"

"Walk." He pointed off to the left. "Over the dune."

"How far?" she asked suspiciously.

"Not far."

Jamie dismounted and left her bike next to Dan's on the sand. "Are you sure it's okay to leave these here? What if someone comes by and takes them?"

"Not likely. How many cars have passed since we arrived on the island?"

Jamie thought for a moment. "I don't remember seeing any."

"Right." He held out a hand to her. "Come on. There's a path."

"I thought I read somewhere that you're not supposed to walk on sand dunes because it kills the vegetation."

"I think the grass stopped growing here a long time ago. This path has been here as long as I can remember, and there's never been any grass or anything else growing on it."

The path was little more than a narrow trail, two persons wide, which they shared with a rabbit that darted in front of them, a few birds that rose from the ground to take flight as they passed, and a few curious gulls that circled overhead. Off the path, the grasses grew thick, and the early-morning breeze passed through with a *shhhhh*. Dan slowed his pace to match Jamie's, and their hips brushed briefly. Dan reached for her hand, entwined his fingers with hers, and pointed out an osprey overhead, on its way toward the bay.

Within minutes, the back of the general store came into view.

"I wish I'd known about this a few days ago. I was half dead by the time I'd ridden around the entire island," Jamie grumbled.

"Always good to know the terrain," he agreed.

They went around to the front of the building and up the two steps. Inside, the same old woman sat in the same chair, reading what Jamie suspected might be the same newspaper. The woman looked up when the door opened, and studied the duo as they came into the shop. After a moment, she stood, then walked toward them, her eyes narrowing. "You there," she said. "You look like one of the boys from the inn. One of Gracie's boys."

"That's right, Miz Carter."

"Which one of them boys are you?"

"I'm Dan."

"Hmmph. You be the oldest. Been a while since you came by."

"Been taking care of the inn," he told her.

She nodded. "You taking care of your mama, too? I hear she's been poorly."

"She's doing a lot better, Miz Carter. Broke her leg, but it's mending now."

The old woman nodded again. "Glad to hear it. You make sure to say I was asking for her."

"I will." Dan reached into his pocket and pulled out a fat envelope. "She asked me to give you this. Said she thought you might be running low."

The woman's gnarled fingers reached for the packet and opened it slowly, then she peered inside. A smile spread across her aged face. "You tell your mama that I much appreciate her thinking of me. Yessir, I much appreciate."

"Will do, Miz Carter. You take care of yourself."

"You do the same." The woman seemed to notice Jamie for the first time. "You there. Girl. You been here before."

"I was, yes. On Tuesday morning."

"Dragged in here like you was half dead, looking for water."

"That was me, all right."

She reached out and took Jamie's hand in her own. Her brows knit together, and she closed her eyes. When she opened them again, she told Jamie, "You're close to the end now. Mind the choices you make."

And with that, Ruby Carter turned her back and returned to her chair, shuffling her feet, her body bent.

Jamie's mouth dropped open, and for a long moment, she stared after the woman. "What do you mean, mind . . ."

"Mind the choices you make, girl," Ruby Carter repeated.

Dan tugged on Jamie's arm and whispered, "Come on. She's done." He practically dragged Jamie out to the front porch. Once outside, he pushed her onto the top step so she could sit, and he retrieved their water bottles from the bike baskets. "Here." Dan opened a bottle and handed it to her. "You look like you're about to pass out."

She reached up for the bottle and took a sip. "That might have been the spookiest moment of my life."

"What do you suppose she meant?" he asked. "About being close to the end."

Close to the end of my search, I hope. But how could she know?

To Dan, she said, "I have no idea." She took another sip.

"Really? You sure? 'Cause you turned fifteen shades of white in there." He was staring at her, and she knew the lie hadn't fooled him one bit.

"Well, it was disconcerting." She forced a laugh. "Having someone you don't know make a pronouncement like that. It sounded so . . . final. Like, you know, *The end is near.* It just startled me, that's all. I guess she likes to toss stuff like that out to shake people up. Maybe that's what she does for fun."

Dan said nothing. He was clearly not buying it, but he let it go. "Ready to head back to the inn?" he asked.

"Sure."

They crossed back over the dune, retrieved their bikes, then rode back in silence, Dan leading the way. Once at the inn, he held his hand out for the helmet.

"So how do you feel, having done a short ride?" he asked.

"My legs feel pretty good, thanks. You were right." She walked the bike next to his and put the kickstand up.

"Good. We'll do it again soon. Maybe next time we'll go as far as Reverend Moore's chapel."

"That would be congregation number two?"

He nodded.

"Sounds good." She stepped out of the way of the family exiting the inn. "Thanks again."

"See you later." He secured the bikes on the rack off to one side of the entrance.

Jamie had already passed through the double doors when it hit her. She turned and went back outside. "Dan, do you realize your phone didn't ring the entire time we were out? That has to be a record."

He reached into his pocket and took out his phone. "Turned it off," he told her.

For the second time that morning, Jamie's mouth fell open. There seemed to be no end to the surprises this day held. "You turned it off?" she repeated. "For a full . . ." She pulled her phone from her pocket and checked the time. "Almost two hours."

"Sounds about right."

"Are your hands shaking? Eyes twitching uncontrollably?"

Dan laughed. "Nope. All's well."

"How often do you do that?"

"Can't remember the last time." He stood with his thumbs hooked in his pockets, dark glasses covering his eyes. He turned the phone back on and scrolled for a few seconds before holding it up. "Nine missed calls."

"Why today?"

"Because I wanted to focus on you. Just you."

His words caught her off guard. "Well," she said, "what do you think? Was it worth it?"

"I could get used to it." He grinned. "Might even try it again tonight. Have dinner with me?"

"I'd love to."

"Seven in the dining room?"

"Perfect."

His phone began to ring.

"Your break's over," she told him.

"Apparently so. I'll see you tonight." He turned and answered the call. "Dan Sinclair . . ."

SHE WAS WORKING on the third box when something caught her eye. She studied the photo carefully, then set it aside. Two more boxes, another stack of newspapers for Grace, another photo that drew Jamie's interest.

Jamie stared at the page. She still felt a pull toward these photos of the five girls, though she wasn't sure why, and she wasn't sure which one of them was drawing her in. That changed forty minutes later when she opened an issue from August 1979 and saw the photo of four young girls about to begin their senior year.

Four, where there had been five.

Jamie searched the faces to find the one that was missing, and her heart skipped a beat. "Grace," she said, her voice barely discernible.

Grace looked up from her desk. "What is it, Jamie?"

Jamie brought the paper to Grace and opened it up in front of her. From the pile to Grace's right, Jamie pulled the previous photos of the same girls.

"Why isn't she in the senior-year photo?" Jamie put her finger on the girl who was missing from 1979. "She was in all the others. Why isn't she in this one?"

"Well, let me think." Grace pursed her lips. "That was the year her grandmother fell ill and she went to stay with her."

"She stayed with her sick grandmother for the entire school year?"

"She might have returned in the spring. Yes, I believe she may have come back to graduate with her class."

"Where did her grandmother live?" Jamie asked, although she knew what the answer would be.

"Somewhere in your home state, I believe." Grace appeared to think, then nodded. "Yes, I'm pretty certain her grandmother lived in Pennsylvania. Somewhere around Bethlehem, I think. This was her mother's mother—she was a literature professor at Lehigh University, if I recall correctly."

Jamie's heart began to pound. She'd met this woman and liked her. Her gut was telling her she was right. She looked up and met Grace's eyes, so full of understanding and sympathy.

"You know," Jamie whispered. "You *know*."

Grace nodded slowly. "Yes, dear, I know."

Chapter 16

～～～

H ow did you . . . how could you . . . ?" Jamie whispered.

"I've always known." Grace reached for Jamie's hand. "I knew the minute I saw you."

"How . . . ?"

"I can't explain it, Jamie. Sometimes I just know things, the way you know things about yourself. I knew who you were, and why you were here, the day you arrived at the inn. I saw you from the top of the steps, and I knew."

"Did you tell . . . her?"

"Of course not. It's not my place to interfere in such things." Grace shook her head. "I could not in good conscience influence the outcome in something as serious—as life-changing—as this."

"What do I do now?" Jamie's eyes brimmed with unshed tears.

"What do you want to do?" Grace's voice was so gentle, so filled with true concern, that Jamie's throat tightened.

"I don't know. I don't know what I should do. I think part of me didn't believe I'd ever find her, but at the same time, I felt I had to look. Now that I know . . . I don't know what to do about it."

"You might take some time to think over your next steps. Whatever you decide to do will have consequences in both your lives, you know."

"What if she doesn't want to know me? What if she doesn't want anything to do with me?"

"What if she does?"

Jamie fell silent, then gathered her bag and stood. "Thank you, Grace. For everything." She hugged her.

"Where will you go, dear?" Grace seemed to know instinctively that Jamie was leaving.

"I'm not sure. I guess to my house in Princeton." She leaned on the back of the chair she'd been sitting in and told Grace about her discovery of the adoption.

"Oh, dear Lord, what a terrible way to find out." Grace was clearly sympathetic. "Though surely your parents had their reasons—oh my, still, that must have been very difficult for you."

"My aunt—my mother's sister—thinks that my mother wanted to believe she was my only mother. My real mother."

"And so she was."

"I wish she'd given me the chance to tell her that. She's the only mother I ever knew. I wish she'd trusted me with the truth."

"Well, now you have the truth. Only you can decide what to do with it."

"I think about how my mom would feel about me

searching for my birth mother. Would she be angry? Would she be hurt? My father would be supportive, I think, but my mom . . ." Jamie shook her head. "I don't know how she'd deal with it."

"Speaking as a mother, I would say that you need to do whatever your heart tells you to do. I don't think your mother's opinion is the one that should count right now. Finding the woman who gave birth to you was important enough for you to put your career on hold and travel here. Only you can decide if you want to pursue this any further. Only you can know what it is you want from this woman."

"I never really thought about wanting anything. I just wanted to know who she was."

"Oh, my dear, I think you want much more than that. You have questions you want answers to. Answers you can only get from her. How badly do you want those answers?" Grace shrugged. "Only you can decide. If I were to give you any advice at all, it would be to follow your instincts. In the end, you will do the right thing. I think you just need some time to decide what that might be."

"Thank you, Grace."

Jamie hugged Grace again, then left the office and went straight to her room. She packed her belongings, then called down to the desk for a bellhop. She was half hoping, half fearing that Dan would show up at her door. What reason could she give him for leaving? He knew this woman—her birth mother. How could she tell him her story without giving away a secret that someone else had kept for thirty-six years? Better to just leave, so that no explanations were necessary.

She retrieved her car from the lot while the bellhop brought down her things. Parked outside the lobby doors, she eased her suitcase into the backseat, all the while looking over her shoulder for Dan. She knew he was interviewing prospective employees, but she didn't know how long he'd be tied up. She hated the feeling that she was running away, but at the same time, she could not fight the urge to flee.

She tore a page from her notebook, scribbled a short note, and ran back into the inn to slip it under his office door, then ran back to the car.

Behind the wheel, Jamie paused. She hadn't been ready to leave here, and a part of her wanted very badly to stay. But she needed neutral ground while she sorted through everything she knew, so she followed Charles Street through the center of town, past the shops she'd come to know. Jamie didn't dare so much as look at *her* place as she drove on. She was afraid she'd be tempted to stop, tempted to walk in, and, like the child who makes a loud and inappropriate announcement in a public place ("Mommy, when are you and Daddy going to get married?"), make an announcement that would change everything. Now that she knew, there were other decisions to be made, other people's lives to be considered. She needed to be alone, to give careful regard to her next move while she became accustomed to her newfound knowledge.

From the day Jamie arrived in St. Dennis, she had felt the air of history that surrounded the town. She'd wondered if part of her shared in that history, and now that she knew for certain it did, she wondered why she still felt rootless. She would have thought that the certainty of her lineage would have given her a sense of belonging, but now more than ever, her emotions made her feel that she had been set adrift, as if she belonged neither here nor in Caryville.

She followed the signs for Route 50 and, from there, the interstate that would take her over the bridge to New Jersey, to her house in Princeton. While it had never really felt like home to her, she had nowhere else to go.

"MOM." DAN APPROACHED the table where his mother was preparing to dig into a small steak.

"Hello, son. How did the interviews go?"

"Fine. They went fine." He glanced around the dining room. "Have you seen Jamie? She was supposed to meet me here at seven." He glanced at the phone he held in his left hand. "It's twenty after. She's not in her room. I even checked your office, but I can't find her."

"Oh." Grace placed her fork quietly on the side of her plate and looked up. "I'm afraid Jamie has left."

"Left?" He frowned. "Left the building? Did she go shopping? Did she say what time she'd be back?"

"No. She left the inn. She checked out this afternoon."

"What are you talking about? I was with her this morning, and we made plans for dinner." He stared at his mother for a moment. "Is something wrong? Is she sick? Is someone else sick?"

"Sit down, Dan," Grace said gently.

He looked as if he were about to protest, then he pulled out the chair next to hers and sat. "What's this all about, Mom?"

"Something came up that Jamie needs to deal with. Something very . . . complicated."

"If it's complicated, we can help her."

"No, son. It's something she has to work through on her own."

"What? What's so important that she had to leave without even telling me she was going?" He narrowed his eyes. "You know what it is, don't you."

"Yes, I do."

"And you're not going to tell me, are you."

"No, I am not. You will have to hear that from her. When she's ready to have that conversation with you, she will."

"This doesn't make any sense to me. She was fine this morning . . ."

"I'm sure she was. She just needs time, Dan, and we all have to give it to her. And while I know this is particularly difficult for you, you'll just have to be patient."

He frowned. If something was wrong with Jamie, why hadn't he sensed it? If he'd inherited his mother's eye, he would have known, wouldn't he?

"What, son?"

"I'm just wondering why I didn't know that something big was bothering her."

"Why would you have?"

"Sometimes I sense things. Sort of like . . . well, like you do." He lowered his voice and leaned in. "I think I have it. You know, the sixth sense that you have?"

His mother stared at him for what seemed to be a long time. Finally, she said, "No, son, you don't."

"Mom, sometimes I think I know what people are going to do—"

She gestured for him to stop with a wave of her hand. "That's called intuition. Lots of people have well-defined intuition."

"Isn't that what you have?"

She shook her head. "Not exactly."

"So you don't think I—"

"No." She patted him on the hand. "And don't look so disappointed, Daniel. It can be a great burden. Sometimes it's more of a curse than a gift."

"Like when?"

"Like when I know things about other people that I wish I didn't know."

He sighed. "So what do I do about Jamie?"

"Figure out what it is you feel for her, then tell her."

"I already know what I feel. I would tell her if she hadn't taken off."

"Just give her a little room right now when she needs it."

"Do you think she'll come back?"

"Oh, yes. She'll be back. As soon as she puts all the pieces together in the right order, she'll be back."

"Miz Carter said something to her this morning. Something like *The end is near*. It freaked Jamie out a little. She thought it sounded a bit ominous."

"Ruby was just seeing the journey Jamie's on. She saw the end of it, as I do."

Dan met his mother's gaze. "Can you at least give me a hint?"

She shook her head. "Sorry, dear. You'll just have to wait and hear it from Jamie when she's ready."

He nodded and got up from the table, his appetite gone, and headed toward his office. All those phone calls he was going to have his assistant manager handle so that he'd have a little more free time—he might as well deal with those himself. What good was free time if Jamie wasn't here to help him fill it?

He'd had a lot of time to think over the past few days. He and Jamie were on the road to something big, something good and important. He knew it, and he was certain she knew it, too. For all his mother's denial, he was pretty sure that this was one of those times when something stronger than intuition had been in play.

He'd planned on tonight being a night they'd both remember, a night that would mark a turning point in their relationship. Jamie was the reason he'd just hired an assistant, so that he wouldn't feel obligated to do every single damned job at the inn himself. Ironic that he'd seen the light on the very day Jamie chose to pick up and leave without a word to him. He'd thought they'd been well on their way to forming more of a bond than that. What had been so important that she couldn't have said goodbye?

Maybe he'd misread her all along. Maybe he had just been a way to pass some time while she was in St. Dennis. Maybe she really did have someone else back in Princeton or wherever. Maybe she missed him— this other nameless, faceless person—and couldn't wait to get back.

In about as foul a mood as he'd been in a very long time, Dan unlocked the door to his office and switched on the light. Stepping into the room, he almost missed the folded piece of paper on the floor. He bent down and picked it up, opening it while he walked to his desk.

> *Dan~*
> *Will be in touch~*
> *JLV*

He dropped the brief note on his desk at the same time he dropped into his chair, and wondered what was going on with this woman and how long he would have to wait to find out.

His gut told him that Jamie's sudden departure had something to do with the conversation he'd overheard between her and Curtis Enright.

I wish you'd leave this thing alone and go back where you came from, the lawyer had said. *No one is going to tell you what you want to know.*

Jamie's response had been an assured *I will find out.*

So had she found whatever it was she was looking for? Had someone told her what she wanted to know? And what, he wondered, had that been?

He could kick himself from here to Maine for not pressing her when he had the chance—when he'd known she was lying.

Women with secrets, he reminded himself. When would he learn?

His mother had told him that Jamie needed time to sort things out. Well, he'd give her time. He'd wait until he couldn't wait anymore, and then he'd do whatever it took to bring her back.

Chapter 17

~

JAMIE drove in a daze. She had no recollection of passing over the Delaware Memorial Bridge, nor of getting onto the New Jersey Turnpike. She'd gone several miles too far before realizing she'd missed her exit and had to take back roads to her lakeside home on a small side road off Route 27. She was surprised when she realized she was pulling into her own driveway. She turned off the engine and sat for a moment and stared at her house. Even this place, this place that was all hers and only hers, seemed foreign. Leaving her suitcase on the backseat, she got out of the car and walked to the red front door, unlocked it, and went inside. She gathered up the pile of mail that had come through the slot during the time she was gone and went through it quickly, searching for a letter from the adoption court telling her whether her birth mother would unseal her records, but there was nothing except bills, magazines, and the usual amount of junk mail.

She dumped it all on the console table in the foyer. Maybe tomorrow.

The three-hour drive from St. Dennis had left her exhausted and headachy, but she went into the kitchen and turned on the coffee machine, dropped in a pod, and waited for those three little words, *Ready to brew*. She took half-and-half from the fridge and gave it the sniff test before adding enough to the cup to turn the brew light golden brown. She opened the back door and stepped outside and took a deep breath of early-evening air, then walked toward the lake at the far end of her property.

Jamie had purchased the home not for its four bedrooms—though it had been nice to have a bedroom each for her mother and aunt when they both came to visit at the same time—but for the water view. It had been autumn when she first saw the house, and the blaze on the opposite side of Carnegie Lake had been breathtaking. The cobbled courtyard, accessed through French doors on three sides, and the remnants of an old stone wall, had sealed the deal for her—that and the large first-floor library overlooking the court-yard on one side and the water on the other; it made a perfect office. She rarely used the other rooms on the first floor, the formal living and dining rooms. She'd had to remodel the kitchen right after she moved in. When she was working, she drifted between the kitchen and her office, some nights falling asleep on the office sofa while she read through that day's work.

"It's an awful lot of money to pay for a house you're going to barely live in," her mother had told her.

"What do you mean, barely live in? I'm here almost all the time," Jamie had protested.

"You live in three rooms, am I right? You work, you cook, you eat, you sleep." Lainey had rolled her eyes. "Excuse me, you use the bathroom. Maybe two of them. Unless Sis and I are here, the rest of the house just sits. You could have gotten a condo for a lot less money and lived in the same amount of space."

Jamie had put her arm around her mother's shoulders and turned her toward the windows. "Ah, but then we wouldn't have that view." She'd pointed beyond the kitchen's French doors. "And you wouldn't have that garden you've grown so fond of."

"All that shade out there, you needed shade plants. Whoever planted that other stuff had no idea what they were doing."

"And now all is right in the plant world, and we can sit out in the courtyard and admire your handiwork." Jamie had kissed her mother on the cheek, and Lainey had grinned.

"Well, I did an exceptional job out there, if I do say so myself."

"Which of course you will," Sis had muttered, and Jamie had laughed at the look of indignation on her mother's face.

Times like those had made Jamie wish she'd had a sister. If not a sister, a cousin, someone who shared what Lainey and Sis shared.

And times like these, I wish I had someone who could tell me what to do.

She speed-dialed her aunt but had to leave a voicemail when Sis didn't pick up.

Just as well, Jamie thought. Sis wouldn't tell her what to do. Jamie could lay it all out for her, tell her what she'd learned, and Sis would say, "Follow your heart, sweetie."

If she'd followed her heart, she'd still be in St. Dennis.

Jamie sat on the old stone wall and sipped her coffee. She'd wanted to belong in St. Dennis, she really had. But not knowing how her birth mother would feel about her, not knowing if she'd want to keep their secret for the rest of their natural lives—who, Jamie asked herself, could take that kind of stress?

And then there was Dan.

Damn, but if he wasn't the icing on the St. Dennis cake.

She reminded herself that if she hadn't tucked tail and run, she would at this moment be sitting down to dinner with Dan. Afterward, they'd have . . . Maybe they'd have picked up where they were a few nights ago before he had to go, so his night clerk could leave on time. She had to grudgingly acknowledge that only a truly good man would be that concerned about his employee's obligations.

There was no denying that Dan Sinclair was a good man, one she cared about in spite of herself. She couldn't think of one thing about him that she did not like. Except, of course, the fact that he was tied to the inn and had a kind of tunnel vision where it was concerned. The inn was his anchor and always would be. And hers? Right now she had no anchor.

Though he had turned off his phone that morning so he could, in his words, focus on her. That was real progress, she thought. Maybe in time, he'd get rid of the damned thing altogether when he was with her.

Okay, maybe that isn't a realistic expectation, she told herself. After all, he did own the place. But letting someone else share some of the responsibilities once in a while—often enough to permit him to have a real life—that wouldn't kill him, would it?

In retrospect, she thought, she probably should have waited for him to get back from the interviews, but she'd been so overwhelmed with what she'd learned that all she could think of was escaping from St. Dennis and from the conflict and emotions that had arisen within her. Her quest had been to discover the identity of her birth mother, but she'd never stopped to think how she'd feel if she did find her. She'd been stunned when she figured it all out, and the reality had taken her breath away, and it had frightened her. How many times had she asked herself, *What if she doesn't want to know me?* Until today, the answer hadn't really mattered, because until today, she hadn't expected to find the truth.

Now that she knew, what was she going to do about it?

She finished her coffee and went back inside and made busy work for herself. She tossed out some items from the fridge that were past their prime. She emptied the dishwasher. She got her suitcase out of the car and put away her things, lingering on the white sundress with the red cherries that she'd bought at Bling. She remembered how Dan had tried not to look at her when she came out of the dressing room. His eyes had taken in every inch of her, and she'd known that even if she hadn't loved the dress the minute she saw it, she'd have bought it just because of the way he'd made her feel. Had anyone ever looked at her that way before?

Certainly not Thomas, the lawyer from Chicago who'd proposed to her with a ring the size of Lake Michigan and who'd charmed her mother. Lainey had been incredulous when Jamie told her she'd given the ring back when she discovered he'd do anything—anything at all, no limits—to win a case. Or Cal, who taught physics at the university and who, she'd found after one too many dates, lacked a true sense of humor. Peter—like Cal, a professor at Princeton—enjoyed accompanying her to book signings and had the annoying habit of introducing her to his friends as J.L. And then there was Jason, whom she almost married. Jason, who could never seem to let her work without interruption, even when she was closing in on a deadline or when she was so in the zone that she forgot to eat. His constant need for her attention drove her insane and interfered with her work, and that was the end of that.

If any of them had looked at her the way Dan had, or if one had his heart, she might not be here alone, in the house overlooking the lake, on a beautiful and peaceful summer evening.

But here she was, and here she would stay until she could find the way to answer her own question: Now that she knew her birth mother's identity, what was she going to do about it?

In the meantime, there was a book to be written, one that would be different from her past efforts. Exploring the nature of truth—and lies—had been Grace's idea, but it was Jamie's to run with. As a theme, it intrigued her, and she'd been playing around with different openings for the last couple of days.

AFTER FOUR DAYS of almost round-the-clock work—interrupted only to check the mail and talk to Sis on the phone—Jamie finally had a direction for her book and was in the middle of preparing a guide for moving forward. She'd made a cup of coffee that was now cold, and she was on her way into the kitchen to make another when the doorbell rang. Frowning at the intrusion and tempted not to answer, she peeked out a front window, and her heart all but stopped in her chest.

"It figures," she grumbled, looking down at the boxer shorts and T-shirt she'd slept in the night before and under which she wore nothing. "No time to change now." She opened the door, smiled a greeting, and tried to pretend she didn't look as if she'd just rolled out of bed.

"Are you going to invite me in?" Dan stood on the second step from the top, one hand on the porch rail.

She stood aside and gestured for him to enter. After she closed the door behind him, she said, "This is really a surprise. And wow, you're three hours from the inn. Have you suffered a head injury?"

"I thought about calling, but I was afraid you'd have an excuse for me not to come." He ignored the jab. "Like you were going out of town or had company or something."

"No company, no plans to leave home, but yes, I might have come up with something."

"I didn't want to take that chance." He sighed. "Jamie, we have to talk."

"Okay." She went into the kitchen and he followed. "Coffee? Iced tea? Beer?"

"Coffee is good. As you noted, it was a three-hour drive, and I left pretty early."

He sat at the table while she made coffee and small talk. She brought two mugs to the table and sat opposite him.

"So what did you drive all this way to talk about?" she asked. "You could have called."

"Some conversations need to be face-to-face."

"All right," she said warily. "We're face-to-face. You want to know why I left without telling you."

"That's part of it."

"What's the other part?"

"I just need you to listen and not talk, because I practiced this all the way from Maryland, and I don't want to mess up what I have to say."

"Okay."

Dan took a deep breath. "Maybe this is going to sound strange to you, but when I saw you walk into the lobby that first day, I knew you were going to be someone special to me. That you were going to matter to me. I'm not saying love at first sight—which I never believed in—but it was like a light went on inside me. I tried to pretend otherwise, but I knew. I didn't want it to be true, but I knew." Jamie opened her mouth to say something, but he held up a hand to stop her. "Save it till I'm finished, okay?"

She nodded.

"That first time we met, I knew I was going to care about you."

"Even after I mistook you for a bellhop and tipped you?"

Dan smiled and took his wallet from his pocket and pulled out a folded five-dollar bill. "I still have it."

That he'd saved that bill touched her, and she took a sip of coffee to have something to do with her mouth besides speak when he'd asked her to listen.

"Anyway," he continued, "I was really conflicted. I found myself wanting to spend more and more time with you. I wanted to see where this could go, you and I, even though it scared me to react so strongly to someone I didn't know. I wasn't looking for someone, you understand? I'd had someone, and that hadn't ended very well. I was okay thinking I'd spend the rest of my life alone. I didn't want to set myself up to feel that kind of loss ever again.

"Then you came along . . ." He'd taken her hand without her realizing that he held it. "After you left, I thought I'd be okay waiting till you came back, but I wasn't. I thought I could give you time to figure out whatever it was that had made you run, but after a couple of days, I couldn't.

"Here's the thing. I'm aware, maybe more than most people, that life doesn't come with guarantees. Things can happen that change everything in the blink of an eye. You always think there's plenty of time, but I know for a fact that there's never enough. I don't want to wait around to see if you'll come back to St. Dennis. I need to ask you to come back now, because what I feel for you is very real. I think you were starting to feel the same way about me."

Jamie nodded.

"I don't want to look back on this time and regret the things we didn't do. I want to look back and see the beginning of something that changed both our lives. I want to look back and see the beginning of something that lasts—and I don't want to waste any time we might have together, because there's no way of knowing how long that time might be."

His voice was so sincere, the look in his eyes so naked and honest, that Jamie tried to look away, but she could not break their gaze.

"All those little hints you dropped about me not being able to let someone else take responsibility for the inn—no matter how much I denied it, you were right. I have been hovering over that place like the parent of a newborn, and you'd think I would have learned my lesson."

"What do you mean?"

"The day she died, before she took the boat out, Doreen, my wife, told me that she was leaving us. All of us. Me, the kids . . ." He swallowed hard. "She said she just couldn't be an innkeeper's wife any longer. She'd grown up in California, and in her heart, she was still a California girl."

"Wait . . . she wasn't planning on taking the kids?"

Dan shook his head. "She said they could visit in the summer, but they loved everything about their lives—their school, their friends, the inn—and she wasn't going to uproot them."

"Surely you'd noticed something wasn't right between you before that."

"I'm embarrassed to say I did not. As a matter of fact, we were going to take the boat out so we could finish the conversation without the kids around, so they or anyone else couldn't overhear. But something came up at the inn, and she got tired of waiting for me. I don't remember now what the problem was, but at the time, it seemed so important. Too important to leave to someone else. She went out alone, and she didn't come back."

"You think if you'd gone with her, she wouldn't have drowned?"

He nodded.

"Was she experienced with the boat?"

"It was her boat."

"I thought you said a storm had come up out of nowhere."

"It did."

"So how do you think you could have made it to shore when she couldn't?"

"I should have been with her."

"So you could have died with her? You think your kids would have been okay with that? Think they would have been better off with no parents instead of one?" When he didn't respond, she said, "Look, I don't know why things happen the way they do any more than you do. I think when things like that happen, we have a tendency to look within ourselves to place blame because we can't blame anyone else. I understand why you feel responsible, but you aren't. I understand wanting to shoulder the blame, but don't. You weren't responsible for your wife's death, Dan. Maybe it's time to stop beating yourself up over something you couldn't control."

"For what it's worth, I've trying to delegate more at the inn. It might not happen overnight, but I do want more of a life. I don't want to make those mistakes again. I'd like you to be part of that life, so in the same way you've told me to let others share a little of the responsibilities for the inn, I'm telling you to let someone else share in whatever it is that's on your mind. Whatever is bothering you, whatever made you leave, I want to help you work it out."

"It's not that easy, Dan."

"Easy isn't an issue. You leaving St. Dennis, that's an issue."

She tried to find the words to tell him why she'd left, but she couldn't. He reached out to her, drew her to him, and pulled her onto his lap. "Come back with me. Whatever it is, we'll face it together."

She wanted to tell him that there was nothing he could do about her situation, but he kissed her, and what started as the softest, sweetest kiss ever deepened in a heartbeat to something much more. Her hands on either side of his face, she held on as if her life depended on it. A wave of heat flared up between them, and Jamie knew Dan was right. Whatever was between them could be life-changing. Was she willing to find out?

Her lips parted and his tongue teased the corners of her mouth, tentatively at first. His hands ran the length of her back once, twice, three times, each time adding a little more heat to the fire. Those knowing hands slid under her shirt, seeking her breasts, his touch light but sure, and she pressed against him, wanting more. She sat back and raised her arms to pull off her shirt, and his mouth was on her breast before she had her top over her head. A hot jolt went straight to her core, and a soft gasp escaped her lips. "Dan," she whispered.

He looked up at her through eyes that had glazed over with want, and he lifted her and himself from the chair in one motion. "Which way?" he asked.

Jamie pointed toward the foyer. "Upstairs. Second door on the right."

The shades were up, and sun poured in across the floor and the bed she'd neglected to make that morning. She shimmied out of her boxers and dropped them on the floor, watching Dan undress at what appeared to be the speed of light. He joined her on the bed and she wrapped her arms around his neck and closed her eyes, kissing him blindly, lost in a fog of want and need. His hands slid under her hips and raised them slightly as he entered her and began to move inside her, slowly at first, setting the tempo. She picked up the rhythm, instinct overriding everything else, while a soft sound emanated somewhere in the back of her throat, escaping her lips as the pace increased. She arched under him, crying out as the heat overtook them both and brought them to a pinnacle that slowly wound down, leaving them breathless.

"Holy crap," she whispered, unaware she'd spoken aloud, and Dan laughed.

"At the very least." He eased off her, resting on his side next to her, a hand on her hip.

"I guess you didn't mind that I hadn't made the bed this morning."

"Like I noticed." He looked beyond her, out the window. "Though I am noticing the view. It's beautiful."

"Not quite the view of the Chesapeake that you have from the inn, but for central New Jersey, it's pretty nice." Now slightly self-conscious, she pulled an end of the sheet over her torso.

"It's a great view. I can see why you love it. How did you end up here?" he asked. "Do you have family in the area?"

"No. Actually, I have very little family. Just my aunt Sis, and she lives in Pennsylvania."

"That's it? No siblings, no cousins, no grandparents?"

"None that I know of."

His brows knit together in concern. "That must be . . . That is, it's hard to imagine not having family."

"You were going to say lonely, right? Sometimes it was. I always wanted to be part of a big family. You know, the kind that got together for everyone's birthdays and all the holidays. When I was little, I made up a friend so I'd have someone to share things with. I used to set a place for her at the table, and I'd carry on conversations with her. At least I did until my parents made me stop. They were afraid I'd start to believe that she—Rosalia—was real."

"Did not talking to her make her less real?"

"Of course not."

"What happened to her?"

"She disappeared when I changed schools and

made real friends. I was thinking about her not too long ago, when I was cleaning out some papers at my parents' home. I drew pictures of her. It was funny to see how she changed when I did, clothes, hairstyles, that sort of thing. I remember when I was about thirteen, realizing I hadn't thought about her in a long time and feeling guilty about it."

"The same way as if you dropped a real friend?" His fingers tucked a strand of hair behind her ear. "Like the same way you left and didn't say goodbye?"

"I'm sorry. I am. I just . . ." Jamie sighed. "I just had to get away from St. Dennis."

"This all has something to do with the conversation you had with Curtis Enright, doesn't it." He wasn't asking.

Jamie nodded.

"I showed you mine," he said, "time to show me yours."

Jamie got out of bed, the sheet still wrapped around her. "Let's save that conversation for later. Right now I'm going to the shower. You can join me if you like." She glanced at him over her shoulder as she headed toward the bathroom door.

"If this is some cheap trick to seduce me into forgetting that it's your turn to spill . . ." Dan sat up and watched her disappear through the open door, then followed. "Okay, so I'm weak. I can be had. But remember, this is only a temporary reprieve."

"DO YOU SPEND a lot of time out here?" Dan sat at the round table in the courtyard and gazed out at the lake. Together they'd made lunch—rare roast beef sandwiches and potato salad Jamie had picked up at the local deli the day before—and carried it outside to enjoy the shaded patio.

"When I remember. Sometimes when I'm working, I forget to eat."

"I cannot imagine ever forgetting to eat."

"Our work is very different. You have certain things you need to do every day to keep your inn running smoothly, right?" When he nodded, she continued. "My work is concentrated in spurts. I can go for days writing notes to myself by hand or on the computer, but until it all starts to come together in my head, I don't work what most people would consider a full day. Once I have all the pieces lined up, I can start putting them together. Someone told me once that writing a novel was like that, too, but I've never tried to write fiction. I don't know if I could."

"Why not?"

"It's a very different discipline. I don't know that my mind works in what-ifs the way it has to in order to write a novel."

Dan pushed his plate back and rested his forearms on the table. "Fascinating," he said, "but I think you've procrastinated long enough."

Jamie sighed. She'd known this moment was coming, and Dan was absolutely right. She'd been procrastinating since he arrived. "Let's take our drinks down to the lake." She stood, her wineglass in her hand.

"Should I bring the bottle?" Dan asked.

"I might need it."

Dan carried the wine along with his beer and followed Jamie across the lawn to the water's edge, where two chairs sat looking out at the lake. Jamie sat in one and leaned back.

"So?" Dan sat in the other chair and waited.

"So I'm trying to figure out how to begin. I've only told one person about this, and she already knew most of it."

"Let me guess. My mother."

"How did you know? She didn't tell you . . ."

"Of course not. But not for lack of trying on my part. But come on. My mother knows everything about everyone, or so it seems." He took a swig of beer and nodded to her. "So start at the beginning."

She did. She told him about her childhood, and how great it had been growing up in Caryville as Herb and Lainey's daughter and only child. How her parents had always been there for her, had always made her feel loved and safe. How her father had died years ago and how close she and her mother had been. How she'd mourned the loss of her mother a few months ago, and how difficult it had been for her to clear out the house where she'd grown up.

And how shattering it had been to find the letter that had been hidden in the back of her father's desk drawer.

"Wait. You mean you didn't know?" Dan's eyes widened.

"No. There'd never been a hint."

"That must have been . . . I can't even think of a word. Earth-shattering."

"Try soul-shattering."

"Wow. That's huge." He fell quiet for a moment,

then asked, "So how does Curtis Enright fit into this story? He does somehow."

Jamie nodded. "Curtis and my dad went to law school together. He arranged for my parents to adopt me right after I was born."

Dan frowned, and she could tell he was trying to connect the dots.

She did it for him. "My birth mother was from St. Dennis. I learned that much when I called him after finding the letter, though he wouldn't tell me anything else. But he made a comment that made me believe she still lived there."

"So you decided to come to St. Dennis and look for her?"

"Yes."

"Without any clue as to who she was or what she looked like or her name?"

"Right."

"How did you plan on finding her? I mean, unless you asked around—and I'm assuming that didn't happen, since I didn't hear about it—did you really expect to locate her?"

"I don't know what I expected, but I did find her. At least I discovered who she is. I haven't contacted her yet, though, so in that respect, I really didn't 'find' her."

"You figured out . . . How in the name of God did you do that?"

She told him about finding the photos and asking questions of Grace.

"I knew she had to have a hand in this somehow."

"She knew all along, Dan. She said she knew

who I was the day I arrived in St. Dennis, and she knew why I was there. But she couldn't tell me what I wanted to know, she couldn't interfere."

"But in a way, she did." Dan sat back, a half smile on his face. "How did you know about her archiving project?"

"She mentioned it in passing."

"In passing? Like, casually dropped it into a conversation?"

Jamie thought it over, then shrugged. "More or less, yes. And with her knowing I was searching . . . Yes, I suppose she could have set it up so that I'd offer to help. But how could she have known what I'd find?"

"Are you kidding?" He snorted. "My mother knows everything that's happened in that town for the last half century. If she knew those photos were in the papers and knew you'd see them, she'd have been counting on you to ask the right questions. Which, apparently, you did."

"Huh." Jamie thought about it. "She did say she knew what I was looking for."

"Never underestimate Grace Sinclair." Dan grinned. "She is a wily old bird. But I still don't understand why you left St. Dennis the way you did, and why you felt you couldn't tell me."

"I came to find answers, but it never occurred to me how I'd feel if I actually found what I was looking for. Once I figured it out, I felt so overwhelmed, so unsure of what to do next. I didn't want to intrude on her life. I didn't want to upset her if she didn't want to know me. I mean, she does know me, but she doesn't know I'm her daughter."

"Wait a minute, you know her?"

Jamie nodded. "So do you. Which is why I didn't want to tell you. She had me when she was sixteen and handed me over to my parents right after I was born. I know you like her, and I didn't want you to think differently if you knew about her past."

"Why would I feel differently? It's her business, not mine."

"But it's my business now, and if you and I are to . . ." She left the rest unfinished.

"You and I *are* going to . . . whatever you were going to say. But I promise you, I would not think less of her. I think the thing you need to find out now is whether or not she wants to know you. I just don't know how you'll go about determining that."

"I sent a letter to the county court where I was born and asked them to contact her and ask if she would agree to release the information about her that was sealed when I was adopted."

"So if she says yes, that's like giving you the green light to go to her. Introduce yourself. So to speak."

"And if she refuses to sign the consent, then I'll know that she wants to keep me a secret, and I will have to respect that. Which will make it extremely difficult for me to be in St. Dennis, to know who she is and not be able to let her know that I know. I don't know that I would be able to go back, Dan."

"How long before you hear something?"

"I sent the request at the end of April. The state has something like a hundred and twenty days to contact her, then they have to contact me with her decision."

"So you should be hearing something soon, right? Assuming that whoever handled it for the court did the job."

"Right. It's just a matter of waiting."

"I can see it would have been hard for you to wait in St. Dennis, knowing what you know, but I wish you'd confided in me."

"I was so confused, I couldn't have discussed it rationally, Dan. I just wanted out of Dodge." She paused. "You realize you haven't asked me who she is."

"You'll tell me when you're ready. But now we wait. I guess you've been haunting the mailbox since you got home."

"I have." She paused. "Mail usually comes in the morning. I should go see what came today." She rose and went toward the house. Dan gathered the wine and beer bottles and followed her as far as the courtyard.

Within minutes, Jamie returned with a stack of mail. "Magazines—we can weed these out. Junk mail—why?" She rolled her eyes as she pulled the obvious offenders from the stack. "Bills. Bank statements." She set them on the nearest table. Her eyes fell upon the white envelope with the return address: County of Lehigh.

"Oh my God. Oh my God . . ." Jamie dropped the rest of the mail and ripped open the envelope with shaking hands, then skimmed the letter for the information.

"She did it. She consented to unseal the records and authorized the court to release her name." With tears in her eyes, she held up the letter. "She did it. She wants me to know. She wants me to find her."

She handed Dan the letter, and he read it through to the end. When he got to the name of her birth mother, he smiled.

"Somehow it's fitting, don't you think?" He put an arm around her. "That Barbara the bookseller would be the mother of Jamie the writer."

"I thought about that. Thought about how kind she'd been to me, setting up the book signing for me. She's such a nice woman, I didn't want to intrude into her life if she didn't want . . ." Jamie buried herself in Dan's chest, and the dam burst as the tears began to flow. "She wanted me to know it was her," she sobbed. "She's okay with letting me know."

"But she doesn't know it was you, Jamie Valentine, who was making the inquiry, does she?"

"I don't think so. I don't know how she would."

"So you have to tell her."

"I don't know what to say." Panic rose in Jamie's chest.

"Of course you do. You'll say, 'Barbara, I'm Jamie. I'm your daughter.' Everything else will fall into place after that." He reassured her with his smile and with his words. "Look, why don't you go throw some things in a bag, and we'll head back to St. Dennis, and you can—"

"I'm not ready. I need a little time. I need to think about what I'll say." She looked up into his eyes. "Will you stay with me tonight? We can go tomorrow, but tonight . . ."

"Sure. I'll stay." He kissed the side of her mouth. "Tomorrow's plenty soon enough."

Chapter 18

———

I 'LL drive my own car," Jamie told Dan as they prepared to make the trip to St. Dennis.

"Nope. You're too jumpy. You're going to sit back and relax, and I'll get you there in one piece."

"But then I won't have a car," she protested.

"If you need a car, you'll take mine. If you want to come back in a few days to get your car, I'll drive you back. But there's no way you're driving those three hours by yourself." He grabbed her suitcase and opened the front door. "Don't think I didn't notice how many times you got out of bed last night."

"I was rehearsing what I was going to say."

"We can do that all the way to Maryland. In my car. With me driving." He went out to his car and tossed her bag in the backseat, then returned to the house and asked, "You ready?"

"I just have to lock the back door." She went from room to room, checking the French doors and locking the one she'd used right before dawn to walk down to the lake.

"All set?" Dan stood in the doorway, watching her. "How much coffee have you had this morning?"

"Two cups. Why?"

"You're all over the place." He paused. "I know this is a big deal. I know you're nervous about what you're going to do. But I think you're scaring yourself." He lowered his voice. "Babe, it's going to be fine. I've known Barbara all my life. She's a good person, an honest person. She wouldn't have signed that consent if she didn't want you to know who she was. That paper is your invitation to knock on her door."

Jamie listened, then nodded. "Maybe you're right."

"I am right. She's just waiting for you. I think she's been waiting a long time."

Jamie forced a smile. "Then let's not keep her waiting any longer." She swung the strap of her bag over her shoulder and checked the tote to make sure she had everything she needed—her laptop, her notebooks— should she decide to work. One last glance around, and she closed the door and locked it. Dan had already started the car, so all they had to do was get in and go.

"Music?" Dan asked as he backed out of the driveway.

"Sure." Jamie strapped herself into her seat.

"What's your preference?"

"I like pretty much everything. My parents were children of the fifties and sixties, though, and musically never moved past that era, so I am a little partial to the old bands."

He opened the console and handed her a pack of CDs and said, "See if you can find something you like."

She glanced through the selection, which was heavy on British rock—the Who, Pink Floyd, the Beatles, Led Zeppelin, the Rolling Stones—but nothing appealed to her. She returned the CDs to the console. "Maybe the radio," she suggested.

He turned it on and let her scroll through the stations. Finally, she turned it off. "I guess I'm not in the mood for music after all," she told him. "Unless you—"

"No, I'm good."

Jamie sighed and leaned against the headrest.

"So tell me about your books," he said. "How'd you come to that whole 'honest life' thing?"

Jamie smiled. "One too many bad relationships. It seemed to me that no one in my life operated on a fully honest level. At the time I thought my parents were the exception, but we both know how that turned out."

"Everyone knows that people lie. They lie to hide things, and they lie to make themselves appear smarter. They lie about where they've been and what they've been doing. Why'd you decide to write about it?"

"The first book was supposed to be a sort of exposé on exactly that type of behavior. When I started it, it was mostly an exercise for myself, a way of blowing off steam after I found out that my boyfriend at the time was seeing someone else who also thought she had the exclusive. A friend of mine read it and asked if she could send it to her cousin who worked in publishing. The cousin—now my editor, RaeAnne—asked me if I'd write it in a more conversational form, but at the same time, treat the subject a little more seriously. I did what she asked, and the book was published, and somehow captured a lot of attention, and bam! Instant career." She paused to reflect. "I think it's what you pinpointed—the reasons why people lie—that resonated with a lot of people. Some people are afraid to tell the truth for different reasons; that's a different thing. The kid who goes to school with a black eye but lies to the teacher so that no one knows his father beats him. The woman who doesn't want anyone to know that her partner is rough with her because she knows he'll make things worse for her."

"Even when telling the truth might get them out of a bad situation?"

"When you're in a bad situation, you don't believe there's a safe way out."

"Voice of experience?"

"No. But I've spoken with a lot of women who were victims of abuse, and their stories all had a similar thread. That's an entirely different subject, though, one I'm not qualified to address. I wouldn't presume to write about domestic abuse." She thought for a moment. "And then there are people who just like to lie. Even when there's no reason for it. Everyone knows people who embellish every story they tell."

Dan grinned. "I know several people in St. Dennis like that. Even when they know that *you* know they're not telling the truth, they just keep right on going." He changed lanes to pass a slow-moving van. "What's the book you're working on now? Another variation on truth?"

"Same house, different room. I'm playing around

with the idea of truths we keep to ourselves, truths we don't share with others. Actually, I got the idea from a really wise woman." She smiled and looked at him across the console. "Your mother."

"My mother?"

Jamie nodded. "She even gave me the title. *The Truths We Never Tell.*"

"There will be no living with her now." Dan's phone rang, and he pulled it from his pocket to answer it. "Sorry," he told Jamie, "but after being AWOL for the past two days, I should probably take this."

"Take it," she agreed. "Go back to work." She reached for her notebook and began to jot down a few lines that had been swirling in her head for the past twenty-four hours. By the time they reached St. Dennis, she had an outline of a new chapter, and Dan had confirmed the hiring of a new assistant manager, told the chef to take over the interviewing of his new sous chef, ordered a new tennis net, and agreed to his contractor's price on renovations for the boathouse.

The inn was bustling, as usual, and Dan showed Jamie to the room he'd ordered prepared for her. "I'm sorry we couldn't get you back into your suite, but the minute you left, it was booked for the next two weeks," he said.

"No need to apologize." She looked around the room, which had a bed and a private bath, though no balcony. "This will be fine."

"And it's just down the hall from me." He pulled her close and kissed her.

"From you and your mother and your two kids," she reminded him.

"Well, yes."

"Where there's a will . . ."

"There is definitely a will," he assured her. "But right now I'm needed in a meeting downstairs." He took the Jeep keys from his pocket and handed them to her.

"I probably won't go until later, like tonight," she told him.

"Take them anyway. If you change your mind or feel like taking a drive, you have the car."

"Thank you."

"Sure thing. Just don't run off and forget to come back."

"That will never happen."

And it wouldn't, she thought after he left. *I am here, and I am going to do what I came to do.*

She freshened up from the drive and went downstairs, no destination in mind, but when she got to the lobby, it occurred to her that she didn't know where Barbara lived. She knocked on Grace's door.

"It's open," Grace called. She looked up and smiled when she saw Jamie. "Oh, you're back."

Jamie nodded.

"I assume you have a plan." Grace took off her glasses and placed them on top of the desk.

"I'm going to see Barbara tonight, I think. But I don't have her address."

"Oh, she's easy enough to find. She's four houses away from the Enright place, same side of the street. I don't recall the number, but it's a pale yellow clapboard house with blue shutters. You can't miss it."

"Oh, you pointed it out to me that morning we

went to Cuppachino and we took a drive after. I remember the house."

"So you decided to take a chance and talk to her?"

"She signed the consent form, so I'm assuming she's all right with being contacted."

"I'm happy to hear it. She's been grieving far too long."

"Grieving?" Jamie frowned. "I was under the impression that she never even talked about me."

"Which doesn't mean she hasn't thought about you, dear. You've always been in her heart, but I suppose that will mean much more coming from her." Grace leaned an elbow on the desk, chin in hand. "Just be yourself, Jamie. And whatever comes of this, know that you did the right thing by pursuing the truth."

Jamie nodded. "Thanks. Dan loaned his car to me, so I think I'm going to take a ride and clear my head."

"If you haven't had lunch yet, why not drive out to Blossoms for a change of pace?"

"I think I will. Thanks for the suggestion."

"And if I don't see you, remember that you have roots here." With both hands, Grace gestured for Jamie to come to her. From her chair, Grace reached up and hugged her, holding her for a very long moment.

"It's going to be fine," Grace whispered. "Believe it. Trust."

Jamie nodded and left the office, closing the door behind her. She found Dan's Jeep in the parking lot and drove into town. At Old St. Mary's Church Road, she made a right and drove slowly toward the end, where the Enright mansion stood. The yellow clapboard house with the blue shutters wasn't hard to spot. Jamie stopped in front of the house next door and put the Jeep in park.

Barbara Noonan's house had a wide front porch flanked by some large flowering shrubs and a bay window on each corner. There was a magnolia tree in the front yard, and a long driveway that led to a carriage house. The lot was deep, and the house, while not as large as some of its neighbors, appeared to be fairly sizable and well maintained.

Would I have grown up here if she had kept me?

After realizing that her presence had not gone unnoticed by one of the neighbors, Jamie waved to the woman who was watching her and drove off. Her stomach reminded her that she hadn't eaten since the early breakfast she and Dan had shared in her Princeton kitchen, so she headed for Blossoms.

Most of the lunch crowd had come and gone, so Jamie had her choice of tables. She sat near a side window and tried to concentrate on writing in her notebook, but her head was too full of Dan on the one hand and Barbara on the other to write anything that made sense.

The agony and the ecstasy, she reflected. The man who made her feel like a goddess and the woman who'd handed her off to strangers.

WHEN IT WAS time for Jamie to go, Dan held her and said, "No matter what happens, you need to know that you belong here."

"Grace said something like that earlier."

"Grace knows things," he reminded her with a smile. "Everyone knows she has the eye."

It was eight-thirty when Jamie parked directly in front of the yellow house and cut the engine. She checked to make sure there was a car in the driveway, then opened the door and got out. "Now or never," she murmured, "so it's gonna be now."

The walk to the front door seemed endless. Jamie's feet felt as if they were made of brick, her head was pounding along with her heart, and her palms were sweating, but she put one foot in front of the other and climbed the steps to the front porch. She rang the doorbell before she lost her nerve, then stepped back. She heard footsteps across a hardwood floor before the door opened.

"Oh. Jamie." The color drained from Barbara's face.

"If this is a bad time . . ." Jamie took a few steps back.

"Not at all. This is the very best time." Barbara's hand flew to her chest. "I'm sorry. I wasn't expecting you to . . . I mean, so soon after I . . ." She cleared her throat. "Please. Come in."

Later, Jamie would recall that the front hall had lovely Oriental rugs on the floor and some nice paintings, but when she entered the Noonan home, she blocked out everything.

"Oh, Jamie, you're shaking." Barbara reached for her hands and held them. "Come into the living room and sit down."

Jamie permitted herself to be led to a sofa. She sat and tried to remember the opening line she'd practiced over and over, but her mind had gone blank.

"So you received the notice from the court," Barbara was saying.

Jamie nodded. "I knew before then. I mean, I knew who you were."

Barbara frowned. "How could you have known?"

Jamie told her how she'd figured it out from the newspapers and the series of photos.

"Clever girl." Barbara smiled.

"But just now you didn't seem surprised. Did you know?"

"I had suspicions."

"How did you . . . ?"

"Little things. I saw the interview with Ford. There was your birthday. It just seemed like a sign, coming right on the heels of the letter from the court asking me to unseal your adoption records and your arrival in town. The only reason they'd ask is if someone is looking. Then there's the way you bite your lip when you're thinking—my sister, Angela, all over again. Your hairline—my mother. Little things." She laughed self-consciously. "The shape of your eyebrows." She lifted her bangs from her forehead. "Mine. But it isn't enough that you know who I am. You need to know the whole story."

"I know you were sixteen, and I know you went to live with your grandmother in Pennsylvania, where I was born."

Holding Jamie's hands, Barbara told her story, of how she and her boyfriend, a senior at Annapolis, had gotten carried away on prom night of her junior year. By the time she figured out she was pregnant, he'd graduated from the Naval Academy and shipped out for training. Her parents would not permit her to contact him, insisting that the only way out of the predicament was for her to disappear for a while, have the baby, and let some childless couple adopt it.

"I was sixteen and terrified, and my parents were very controlling. There was no defying them in anything, never had been. I hated what I did, Jamie, but I'd been given no choice."

"I'm not judging you. I'd never judge you. You did the only thing you could do." Jamie took a deep breath. "Did you ever tell him? Did he ever know about me?"

Barbara shook her head. "He never did. The few times he came back to St. Dennis, I was never around, by design. My parents' design, that is. I guess I could have managed to see him—he had relatives in town—but I couldn't face him knowing what I'd done. I don't doubt he'd have been relieved, frankly, had he known, but I couldn't bear to tell him. A few years later, I heard he'd gotten married and eventually settled in Boston, where he's from. There didn't seem to be any point in telling him. It was so long ago, and he had his own life. I saw one of his cousins about five years ago, and he told me that he—your father—had died in a skiing accident."

"What was his name?"

"Carl. Carl Davis." Tears filled Barbara's eyes and rolled down her cheeks. "I never stopped thinking about you and wondering how you were and if you were happy and if your parents were good to you and if your childhood . . ." She broke down and sobbed, her hands covering her face.

"I had a wonderful childhood and wonderful parents." Jamie rubbed Barbara's shoulders and her back while the woman cried her heart out. "The best."

"Thank God. I prayed every night. Curtis said they were fine people, that he'd known them for years . . ."

"My dad and Mr. Enright went to law school together." Jamie related what she knew about the circumstances surrounding her adoption and, finally, about finding the letter.

"You mean you just found out?" Barbara looked stunned.

"I did."

"That must have been terrible, especially coming right on the heels of your mother's death."

Jamie wasn't oblivious to the fact that Barbara referred to *your mother* and *your parents,* and she was grateful that Barbara respected the Valentines' place in Jamie's life. It somehow eased Jamie past the knowledge that this was a meeting Lainey had never wanted to take place.

"There's so much I want to know. What kind of kid you were and what books you read, what you liked and what you didn't like. Who your friends were and how you spent your time. What your favorite subjects were." Barbara rolled her eyes. "Overwhelming, I know. You don't have to talk about any of that."

"No, no, I'm fine with telling you. It's just an awful lot. And I have questions, too."

"Of course you do." Barbara shook her head. "You want to know about your family here. I have lots of photos . . ."

"I'd love to see them."

"Come into the kitchen and I'll make us some tea. I stopped at the bakery and picked up some cupcakes. I guess the universe was telling me to expect company."

Jamie followed Barbara into the kitchen, feeling that the meeting was somewhat surreal. They were chatting like old friends, not like mother and daughter who'd been separated for thirty-six years. *Everyone has their own ways of coping with awkward situations,* Jamie reminded herself.

"When I was little—seven or eight—I wanted to be a famous horse trainer," Jamie said as Barbara filled a kettle with water for tea.

Barbara put the kettle on the burner and turned to Jamie with tears on her cheeks and asked in a very quiet voice, "Would it be too much to ask if I could hug you?"

"It's not too much at all." Jamie rose and, for the first time in her life, hugged the woman who had given birth to her. It was a hug meant to mend the emptiness of the years and to soothe a soul that had been tortured for every one of those years. In it, Jamie felt Barbara's pain and the joy that their reunion brought.

Barbara broke away and pulled a tissue from a box on the counter and wiped her face. "I'm sorry, Jamie. This day has been a long time coming—frankly, I didn't believe it would ever come." She blew her nose. "It's just been so hard, waiting, wondering if you'd ever look for me, wondering what you'd think of me, worrying that you'd choose not to know me . . ."

"I had the same fears," Jamie told her. "I was afraid to come here tonight, even though I knew you'd signed the consent. I was afraid you'd wish I hadn't made that request to the court to unseal the records."

"I'm only sorry you didn't do it sooner," Barbara said.

"To tell you the truth, I don't know that I would have while my parents were alive," Jamie confessed. "Obviously, this meeting is something that my mother, in particular, would have been very upset about. I doubt I would have gone against her wishes." The kettle began to whistle, and Barbara turned to the burner.

"I understand." Barbara poured two cups of tea and handed one to Jamie, then placed a white bakery box with a pink label reading *Cupcake* on the lid on the table.

"Did you ever look for me?" Jamie heard herself ask.

"No. I never did." Barbara shook her head. "I didn't think I had that right. And I felt so guilty about everything. When I left the hospital after you were born, my mother kept telling me to forget what happened. *By the time you come back to St. Dennis and go back to school, you'll have forgotten that this ever happened.* And *By Christmas, this will all seem like a bad dream, and like a bad dream, you will forget about it.*" Barbara shook her head. "I never forgot, not for a moment."

They sat and talked until two in the morning, at which point Barbara insisted that Jamie spend the night in one of her spare bedrooms. It was too late to call Dan, and she wasn't sure if the inn's doors were all locked by then, so Jamie accepted the offer and dressed in a borrowed nightshirt, climbing into bed with so many emotions swirling around in her brain that she thought her head would crack open and everything she'd heard and said over the past evening would spill out.

She and Barbara continued their conversation over breakfast—so many questions to ask and so much to learn. They discovered that they took their coffee the same way (artificial sweetener and half-and-half) and liked their toast the same way (medium toasty brown, light on the butter). Neither had ever liked breakfast cereal, and their favorite sandwich was turkey, avocado, and bacon on a croissant.

Finally, reluctantly, Barbara had to leave to open her shop.

"I know you're going to want to keep this on the QT," Jamie said as she was leaving for the inn.

"I think that's something we'll need to talk about. For me, I don't care who knows. I've kept this secret for so long, and I'm tired of secrets. But you might want to consider yourself. You're well known, and you've built a career writing about how important it is to be truthful. How will your readers react if they think you've been less than honest with them? There are people who will accuse you of knowing all along that the life you talked about wasn't true, that you made up these fictional parents who inspired you to a truthful life, all to sell books."

"You let me worry about my readers. You need to think about St. Dennis and the people who have known you all your life, what they'll think and what they'll say."

Barbara waved a hand dismissively. "At my age, I couldn't care less. Besides, I am very proud of you. And I'd be just as proud if you were practicing law or training horses." She smiled and patted Jamie on the back. "But we can discuss the whens and the wheres of making our relationship known, as long as you're sure you want it known."

"I do want the truth known, but I want it done in such a way as to honor my parents," Jamie told her.

"I agree," Barbara told her. "And we'll work on the right way to do that. In the meantime"—she gave Jamie a quick hug goodbye—"I can't thank you enough for coming here and for being so understanding and nonjudgmental and just so . . . so *you*. Your parents must have been extraordinary people to have raised such a remarkable young woman. I wish I'd known them. I wish I'd had the chance to thank them."

Chapter 19

"How'd it go with Barbara last night?" was the first thing Dan asked after Jamie opened the door to her new room at the inn and they went inside. "I was starting to get a little worried when you didn't come back."

"No need to worry. It went well. Remarkably well. We started talking and talking, and one thing led to another, and the next thing I knew, it was two in the morning. Barbara suggested I stay in her guest room. Which made sense, since I didn't know if you locked the doors at night."

"We lock at midnight. You can get out, but you have to ring the doorbell to get in. You could have called me. I'd have met you at the door."

"I figured you needed to get some sleep. You were awake as much as I was the other night, if you remember."

"I do." He nodded. "Vividly. I am willing to pull all-nighters with you any time. Now would be good . . ."

"Don't you have to tuck your kids in?"

"They're teenagers. If they're home, they're in their rooms. Sometimes if I'm lucky, they'll poke out long enough to say good night, but that's a rare sighting these days."

"Still, shouldn't they know where you are in case they need you?"

"They have my cell number. They'll call." He lay back against the pillows on her bed. "In the meantime, I can tell you're all amped up. Want to talk about it?"

"It was surreal. Her talking about her family—my grandparents, my aunts and uncles and cousins I never knew I had. About my father and his family and why he never knew about me. About . . ." She sighed. "About the other part of my life that I never knew existed. It's overwhelming. I think I heard too much at once, like overeating at a buffet and then having to digest it all."

"So where do you go from here?"

"We agreed that the truth has to be put out there, but we're not sure of the best way to do that."

"That's a tough call. Barbara has a ton of family here in town—siblings and nieces and nephews. They'll all have to be told, and some of them, I can assure you, won't take the news kindly. Her father's side of the family is more likely to accept the news—and you—graciously, but I wouldn't expect the same from her mother's side."

"That's the impression I got from her. She said she's willing to face them and doesn't care what their reaction might be. I think there's a fair amount of risk there, but it's one she said she's more than willing to face. I suppose after having something like this buried inside you for so long, being able to bring it into the light must be a tremendous relief."

"And you? How are you going to handle it?"

"I guess I'll discuss it with my agent, get her advice on how to publicly deal with it. My books have all had references to my parents, so everyone who's read them knows how close I was to them. I don't want rumors to start floating around, so I'll have to address it head-on." She chewed on a fingernail. "A preface in the next book might be the way to go. I'll want to talk to Sis before I do anything, though."

"Your mother's sister."

Jamie nodded. "I think I'm going to rent a car and drive to Caryville tomorrow. I need to talk to her, let her know what's going on."

"How do you think she'll take it?"

"I think she'll be relieved for me, that my search was a success, but at the same time, I think she's going to feel protective of my mother's memory." Jamie lifted his arm and snuggled in next to him.

"When will you be back?" he asked, and in his voice, she heard a touch of fear that she wouldn't return at all.

"I don't know. I don't know what I'm going to do." She owed it to him to be as straightforward as she could. "As much as I appreciated Barbara's candor and her opening up to me and her offer to put our relationship out in the open, wanting a relationship with me, I haven't had time to reflect on it all. I think I need to take some time on my own and sort through it all."

"Can you do that in Caryville, in the house you grew up in?"

"My aunt is there, and she is all I have of my family. Of the family I grew up with. Besides, I promised I'd let her know what I found. I don't know how she's going to take the news. After that . . ."

"After that, what?"

She buried her face in his chest. "I guess maybe that's when I'll need to take some time to myself."

"I don't suppose that time would be spent here."

"St. Dennis isn't exactly neutral ground."

"Neither is Caryville."

"I didn't say I was going to stay in Caryville. I just need to be there right now. My aunt and my mother were very close. I want her to understand that my having a relationship with Barbara doesn't diminish the love I have for my mom and dad." She studied his face and the changing expression. Finally, she said, "Okay, spill. What's on your mind?"

"I was just wondering, now that you found what you were looking for here, whether you'd be back."

"Of course I'll be back." She couldn't believe he'd asked her that. "Why wouldn't I be?"

"It just seems like you have a lot of options besides St. Dennis. Caryville. Princeton. I'm just wondering where you're going to land when the dust settles." Dan's phone began to ring, and he cursed softly under his breath. "Dan Sinclair," he answered gruffly. "Okay. When? Can't Mr. Wyler pick you guys up and drive you home?" Dan sighed. "All right. Give me ten minutes." He slipped the phone back in his pocket. "Diana needs a ride home, and it's my night to pick them up at Scoop, which I completely forgot." He sat up, clearly unhappy with the way the evening was going.

"Go get her and come back." Jamie patted the space on the mattress next to her. "I'll save your spot."

ROAD CONSTRUCTION ON the interstate and a major accident meant Jamie's trip to Caryville took about ninety minutes longer than she'd anticipated. The added time behind the wheel of her rental car had given her more time to think, and by the time she reached her childhood home, she was pretty sure she knew how to handle things with Sis. She'd hated the look on Dan's face when she told him she needed some time to herself, but she'd been as honest as she could be. It had been difficult for him to understand that the space was about the changes in her life and how she would deal with them. She suspected that he equated time alone with needing a break from him, which was the last thing she wanted. He was just going to have to trust her.

Once the whole story was public, she could never go back to being who she once was, and she wasn't a hundred percent certain she was okay with that, despite her assurances to Barbara that she was okay with letting the world know the truth. She was starting to think of her life as having been split in two: before she found the letter in the desk drawer and after. What she needed was to reconcile the two, and she hadn't figured out how to do that.

She parked in the driveway of her childhood home and sat for a moment. The house looked abandoned, even though they'd hired someone to mow the grass. Sis came over several times a week to keep the flower beds watered and deadheaded, but it was obvious that the house had lost its soul. It saddened Jamie to see the house she'd grown up in—the house she loved—looking so desolate.

Inside, the silence pervaded every nook and cranny. Jamie's footsteps echoed as she crossed the hardwood floor to the kitchen. When she dropped her suitcase on the tiled floor, it sounded like a shot. That a home once so filled with love was now empty felt wrong. She walked from room to room, mourning the loss. She left by the front door and drove to Sis's, hoping she'd find her aunt at home.

Sis was in her living room, watching game shows and doing a crossword puzzle, when Jamie rang the doorbell.

"Oh my Lord, Jamie!" Sis threw her arms around her niece. "I am so happy to see you. Why didn't you call to let me know you were coming? Can you stay for dinner? Have you been by the house?"

"Can you take a breath?" Jamie laughed and hugged her aunt a second time.

"I guess things didn't go so well in St. Dennis, since I didn't hear from you." Sis folded the newspaper and tossed it and the pen she'd been using on the coffee table. "I figured if anything came of your trip, you'd have called."

"Actually, I found her. I found my birth mother."

"Wha . . . ? How? Did you meet her? What's she like? Is she a nice person? Or maybe you couldn't tell just by meeting her one time."

"Slow down and I'll tell you everything."

Jamie gave Sis the blow-by-blow, bringing her up-to-date through the night before, but leaving out the part about Dan spending most of the night in her bed instead of his own.

"Oh my Lord, Jamie," Sis interjected about five times as Jamie recited the story.

"She's a very nice person, Aunt Sis. I met her before I knew who she was, and I liked her right away."

"Somehow you must have known. Something in you recognized—"

"Uh-uh. I had no clue. But I liked her because she was warm and fun and had a sense of humor and loved books. I think you'd like her."

"Oh, I don't know about meeting her, Jamie. What would your mother think?"

"Mom's not here, and if Mom had been honest with me, I wouldn't have been looking for this woman now."

"It's hard to argue with facts." Sis got up and paced. "I have to tell you, Jamie, I feel like I'm betraying my sister, like she's watching and won't be happy about any of this. It's one thing for you to meet this woman but something else entirely for me."

"Try to look at it more as supporting me."

"Are you going to have some sort of relationship with her? Is she going to be part of your life?"

"Maybe. Probably. Right now I don't know how much a part, but yes, I think I will have a relationship with her."

"Then maybe I *should* meet her." Sis looked worried, and Jamie could tell she was uncertain.

"I would like that very much. I'm not suggesting that you become the best of friends, but it would mean a lot to me if you'd meet her. I think it would make me start to feel more whole."

"I don't know what that means, honey."

"It means that I feel like I've been torn in half. I need to reconcile the two pieces of my life so I can move beyond all this—this whole *Whose daughter am I, really?* Like it or not, part of me is Caryville, but part of me is St. Dennis as well. I need to know that part, and I need you to know that part of me, too."

"After all you've been through, there's no way I can say no. So one of these days, sure, I'll meet Barbara."

"How about tomorrow?"

"Tomorrow?" Sis made a face. "I don't think I can go tomorrow."

"If you're going to make an excuse, make it a good one. Not *I have to water the garden* or *I have books due at the library.*"

"Well, I do . . ."

"I'll pay the fine. Come on, Aunt Sis. You'll love St. Dennis. It's a pretty town, there's lots of history. And oh, some famous people live there. Dallas MacGregor. Beryl Townsend." Sis's eyes widened, and Jamie knew she'd used the right bait. Sis was a huge movie fan. "And I have it on good authority that when she's in St. Dennis, Delia Enright stays at the same inn we'll be staying in."

"She's my favorite author—after you, of course. I just finished her new book last week." Sis looked suitably starstruck.

Jamie moved in for the kill. "I heard that Dallas is

going to be shooting her first film in St. Dennis soon and will be looking for extras. Women of a certain age, so they say."

"I'll get my suitcase out of the guest room closet."

"I MADE A decision about the house," Jamie told Sis after they'd been on the road for a while. She wasn't sure how her aunt would take the news, but it had to be discussed. "For a while, I thought I'd keep it, you know, stay there whenever I came to Caryville. But being there yesterday and sleeping there last night made me realize it's not my house anymore. It needs a family to bring some life back to it. I almost felt that it had forgotten me. I know that sounds silly . . ."

"Not at all. I've noticed it, too. The air is dead there. Every time I go inside, I open the doors and all the windows to bring some fresh air in, but it doesn't seem to help. I think the old place has lost its heart, Jamie. So if you're thinking about selling it, I think that might be the right thing to do. I'm sure we can find a nice family to fill it." Sis turned in her seat to face Jamie. "As a matter of fact, I ran into Karen Williams at church last week. You remember her?"

Jamie nodded. "She was a year ahead of me in school."

"She said she was in your Brownie troop and remembered the picnics you used to have in the backyard."

"I'd forgotten about that. Mom was one of the troop leaders."

"Long story short, she said if you were going to sell, she and her husband were interested in buying."

"When you get back to Caryville, give your Realtor friend a call and tell him. I think maybe we should just let it go." Jamie turned the air-conditioning up a few degrees. The day had started off hot and gave every indication that it was going to get hotter. "I thought I'd feel Mom and Dad there, but I don't."

"I guess wherever they are, they're together and don't need to be tied to this world anymore." Sis added hastily, "Which isn't to say that your mother won't know what's going on with this Barbara woman or that she'll be okay with it."

"I'll take my chances," Jamie told her.

They passed a few miles in silence, then Sis said, "I hope that selling the house doesn't mean you're cutting your ties to Caryville."

"Of course not. You're still there. Mom and Dad are buried there. My roots are there. Well, some of them are." Jamie thought back to the one-sided conversation she'd had with her parents late yesterday afternoon when she visited the cemetery.

"You still have that lovely house in Princeton, so it's not as if you're going to be homeless."

"Actually, I'm thinking about selling that house, too."

"What? Why?"

"I'm thinking about buying a place in St. Dennis." Jamie held her breath.

"So soon? You're just going to pick up and move there so you can be close to your new family?"

"So I can be close to someone else who is very important to me."

"Let me guess. You've met a man."

Jamie nodded.

"Sweetie, do I need to remind you that you haven't exactly been lucky in love?" Sis said gently.

"This time is different."

"Oh, where have I heard that before?"

"No, really. You'll see."

"So I will be meeting him?"

Jamie nodded. "He owns the inn where we'll be staying."

"Does he know you're thinking about selling everything and moving to St. Dennis?"

Jamie smiled. "Not yet, but he will."

"YOU'RE LOOKING GLUM, my brother." Ford stood in the doorway of Dan's office and leaned against the jamb. "What's going on?"

"Nothing," Dan grumbled.

"This is your little bro you're talking to here, bro." Ford closed the door behind him and took a seat. "Talk to me."

"Go away. I'm busy." Dan shuffled some papers on his desk and picked up his phone, as if about to make a call.

Ford's eyes narrowed. "It's Jamie, isn't it? Mom said she left unexpectedly and then came back and left again. What's going on with her?"

"I really don't know."

"You're full of it." Ford leaned back and rested his feet on his brother's desk. "I'm not leaving until you tell me."

"Jamie came to St. Dennis to look for . . . for someone. She found what she was looking for, and now she doesn't have any reason to stay here. I'm sure she'll visit from time to time, but . . ." Dan sighed.

"But that's not enough."

"No. It isn't enough."

"Have you told her this?"

"Not in so many words."

"Then maybe you need to man up, tell her that occasional visits might not work for you."

"The truth is, if that's all I can have of her, I'll take it."

"You've got it bad."

Dan nodded. "Sad but true."

"Where is she now?"

"She went back to her hometown. She has an aunt there, her only family." Dan paused. "Oh, hell, you're going to find out anyway. Just act surprised when you hear it."

"Hear what?"

"Jamie was adopted as a newborn, but she didn't know it until after both her parents died."

"They never told her . . ." Ford shook his head. "That's messed up. How'd she find out?"

"She found a letter from the attorney who handled the adoption. Curtis Enright."

Ford digested the information. "So her birth mother is . . ."

". . . from St. Dennis. That's why she came here. That's what she was looking for. Now that Jamie's found her . . ."

"She found her? How?"

"Long story. But the point is, now that her search

is over, I don't know how much time she'll be spending here."

"Does she know how you feel?"

"I hope so."

"Which means you haven't told her, have you?"

"Not exactly."

"Take a little advice from your little brother. When you find someone who fills all the places in your heart, you hold on." He grinned. "And if you ever tell anyone I said that, I will kill you." He took a small box from his back pocket and tossed it to Dan. "I stopped at Harris's this morning and picked up this."

Dan opened the box, then whistled. "That's some rock, buddy." He looked up at Ford. "Does Carly know she's getting this?"

Ford shook his head. "I'm planning on giving it to her tonight."

"Well, I can't say I didn't see it coming. Congratulations, Ford. I know you and Carly will be very happy together. She's a great girl."

"She's the best, and yeah, we're really happy."

"If you're planning on getting married here at the inn, better talk to Lucy. We're booked into next fall already."

"We'll work something out." Ford stood and held his hand out for the box, and Dan tossed it back to him. "I need to get going. Delia Enright is here this weekend, and she's agreed to let me interview her, and I have about three minutes to get to her suite."

"Tell her I said hi."

"She's here over the weekend for the baby shower

for Brooke and Jesse's baby. All of Jesse's half sibs—Delia's kids—are here, so Delia came as well. I think she comes to hang out with Mom."

"Everyone likes to hang with Mom."

"True." Ford walked to the door. Before he opened it, he asked, "So Jamie's birth mother. Is it someone we know?"

Dan nodded. "Barbara Noonan."

Ford's eyes grew wide. "Barbara the bookseller?"

"Yes."

"Barbara the bookseller and Jamie the writer," Ford mused. "Somehow, that's very cool."

"Yeah, cool," Dan muttered to himself. He couldn't help but wish it had taken Jamie a little longer to figure it out. She'd have stayed in St. Dennis longer, spent more time with him, and maybe she'd have come to see that this was where she belonged. He knew it as surely as he knew he belonged here, too. But that was something Jamie would figure out on her own or not. It was the "not" that had Dan worried. What if she didn't feel the pull toward him as strongly as he was drawn to her? He hadn't heard from her since she'd left, and he was afraid that her connection to her home and hometown might be stronger than her connection to him. If she decided to stay there, what would that mean for them?

There wouldn't be a "them." There'd be Dan living his life in St. Dennis and Jamie doing her thing in Caryville. So much for his gut feeling that he'd found the one.

He left his office and went into the lobby, which was filling up with both arriving and departing guests.

The desk clerk was swamped and the line was growing. Dan stepped in to give her a hand. The computer screen had a list of registered guests as well as reservations. He glanced at the screen quickly, then looked back to make sure he hadn't misread the name. J. Valentine. Two guests. Arriving today.

Why hadn't she called him to let him know she was coming? Who was she bringing with her, and how long would she stay? His eyes kept returning to the door even as he greeted his guests and wished them a happy weekend in St. Dennis.

Finally, around four, Dan looked up and saw her coming through the double doors, and his heart stood still. He left his post at the registration desk and walked toward her. When she saw him, she smiled, and as always, that smile dazzled him.

"Hey," he said.

"Hey, you."

"I just saw your name on the register," he said. "Why didn't you call?"

"Because I wanted to surprise you."

"I missed you."

"I haven't been gone very long," she reminded him. "Still . . ."

"I missed you, too," she said softly.

Their gaze locked, and he held her by both shoulders to stop himself from pulling her into his arms and kissing her senseless in front of the entire inn.

"Dan, this is my aunt Sis. My mother's sister. I told you about her." Jamie stepped aside, and Dan saw a woman in her sixties with pale strawberry blond hair and an expression that bored right through him.

"I've heard a lot about you," he said, offering his hand.

"I've heard about you, too." She took his hand and shook it. "My niece tells me you're something special. I hope she's right."

Caught off guard, Dan nodded. "She's very special to me, too."

"Well, let's hope . . ." Sis paused, her attention drawn to something behind Dan.

"Dan." Grace was approaching in her wheelchair. "Son . . . Oh, hello, Jamie. That was a quick trip."

"It didn't take as long as I thought it would to do what I had to do," Jamie explained. "Grace, this is my aunt, Evelyn McCoy. Aunt Sis, meet Grace Sinclair, Dan's mother."

"How do you do?" Sis said somewhat stiffly.

"I'm doing well, thank you." Grace held her hand out as another woman approached them. "Delia, this is Jamie Valentine—you probably know her as J. L. Valentine."

"Of course." Delia Enright, stately and cordial as always, smiled at Jamie. "We share an agency, I believe."

"We do." Jamie returned the smile and took the arm of her speechless aunt. "Aunt Sis, Delia Enright."

"Oh my goodness, I'm such a fan," Sis blurted. "I just finished your new book."

"What did you think?" Delia asked. "Too gory?"

"Not at all. I thought that Aaron character deserved everything he got."

"So did I," Delia confided.

"Sis . . . may we call you Sis?" Grace asked, and

Sis nodded. "Delia and I were just about to go into the dining room and have tea. Perhaps you'd like to join us."

"Oh. Well, I . . . That is, yes, thank you." Sis's hand shot to her throat. "That is, if Jamie doesn't mind."

"Of course not. You go on. Enjoy yourself." Jamie patted Sis on the back.

"I hate to just dump you." Sis hesitated.

"Don't worry about me." Jamie smiled past Sis to Dan. "I think I can find something to do."

"Well, if you're sure."

"I'm positive. Have a good time." Jamie watched her aunt toddle off with Delia and Grace. She turned to Dan and said, "Sis is going to have a field day at her next book club meeting. I can hear her now. *Girls, you're not going to believe this—I had tea with Delia Enright. Yes, Delia Enright!* There will be no living with her now."

"I imagine they'll be awhile." Dan's fingers smoothed Jamie's hair back from her forehead. "Why don't I show you to your room?"

"Why, thank you." Jamie took his hand. "And on the way, I can tell you about some decisions I made while I was in Caryville."

"Do I want to hear them now or later?" They walked across the lobby, hand in hand.

"Please don't underestimate me. I can walk and talk at the same time."

"Okay. Talk."

"I'm selling the house in Princeton . . ."

"What?" To move to Caryville? He couldn't bring himself to ask.

"And the house in Caryville," she continued.

"Both places? Where are you planning on living?"

"Here. In St. Dennis." She paused on the bottom step. "I thought I'd buy a house here. What do you think?"

"I think . . . I think that's great. But why give up the other places that you love?"

"The Caryville house needs a new family, and I can visit my aunt any time I want, but I don't have to maintain a house there. The house in Princeton, while beautiful, never felt like it was really mine. Most of the things I want in my home are in storage because they just don't seem to fit that house. A decorator did that place," she admitted. She looked into his eyes. "I've been thinking about what you said, how life is short and there are no guarantees, and you're right. Things can change in a heartbeat. I realized that time I spent away from St. Dennis was time I spent away from you, and I don't want to waste any of the time we might have together."

Dan nodded. "I couldn't agree more."

"Then what are you waiting for, innkeeper?" She tugged his hand as she started up the steps. "Show me to my room."

"It would be my pleasure." He smiled and followed her up the steps, catching her on the landing and kissing her until her head was spinning. "You know we're very hands-on here at the inn . . ."

Diary~

As the bard said, all's well that ends well, but oh Lord, it did take time for things to work their way out. There's such a buzz in St. Dennis these days, one cannot walk—or, in my case, ride—more than five feet without hearing gossip of one sort or another. Once the truth about Jamie's birth was made known, the gossips had a field day! Once that whole nonsense died down, speculation began: Everyone joined in the "Who's her daddy?" game. I daresay there are only two people in St. Dennis who know for certain—that being Barbara, of course, and yours truly. Oh, some may think they know—and perhaps Barbara has confided to Jamie—but no one is confirming anything, so the sport goes on.

I am so pleased that Jamie decided to settle in St. Dennis. For one thing, the girl needs to know where her people came from and the part they played in building this town. Barbara has her child near for the first time—she is obviously delighted that Jamie has chosen to make her home here. And for purely selfish reasons, I, too, am delighted that Jamie is staying in St. Dennis, because my son has fallen in love with her, and is happy—really and truly happy—for the first time in eight years. I see Dan and Jamie together, and I know they will bring each other much joy in the years ahead. She is buying a house on Michaels Road, right around the corner from Dallas and Grant, and I sense the reason she bought such a large place was to eventually accommodate Dan and his children and whatever children they may have together. While I will miss them, frankly, it will be nice to have these rooms to myself for a change. Not that I would ever tell Dan, of course, but I'm older now and set in my ways, and I like a bit of quiet from time to time—hard to come by with two teenagers sharing your space.

And more happy news—Ford and Carly are being married next month here at the inn! The prime wedding times have all been booked forever, of course, so they opted for a Tuesday-night wedding. "We'll keep it small," they said.

"Ha!" I said. "Fat chance of that! This is St. Dennis." The list of invitees grows daily. Mother, of course, knows best.

And Mother knows other things as well. Like who will be the next to wed, whose first child will be born next summer (a boy, by the way), and who will soon be coming into our world and bringing another sort of drama. But as always, my lips are sealed.

Grace